ONE STEP FROM
GLORY

AMERICA IN WORLD WAR ONE

ONE STEP FROM
GLORY

AMERICA IN WORLD WAR ONE

Sidney P. Little

One Step From Glory: America In World War One

Printed in the United States of America
ISBN 978-1-64133-958-2 (hc)
ISBN 978-1-64133-959-9 (sc)
ISBN 978-1-64133-960-5 (e)

2024.12.04

This book is printed on acid-free paper.

The contents of this work, including, but not limited to, the accuracy of events, people, and places depicted; opinions expressed; permission to use previously published materials included; and any advice given or actions advocated are solely the responsibility of the author, who assumes all liability for said work and indemnifies the publisher against any claims stemming from publication of the work.

Blue Ink Media Solutions
1111B S Governors Ave
STE 7582 Dover,
DE 19904

www.blueinkmediasolutions.com

Table of Contents

PROLOGUE

Time - March 20,1917 at 0432 hours GMT.
Place - US Merchantman, *Vigilancia*.
Position - Mid North Atlantic - 38⁰ 09' West Longitude, 42⁰ 18' North Latitude. Just east of the Newfoundland Basin.

Wendell Sykes sat in the captain's chair during the third hour of his watch. How he loved the sea.

Ever since he was a boy he had envisioned himself as the Captain of his own ship. It was after he completed high school that this dream led him to sign on as a deckhand on a freighter, and he'd been at sea ever since.

Now his lifelong ambition was about to come true. Seven days ago, right before they set sail, he received word that he was to have his own command. He had waited a long time for this and had more than paid his dues through hard work and continuous study. His life, in a way, was just beginning, and he could not help smiling to himself as he thought of his future.

He sat in the sheltered comfort of the wheelhouse gazing out at the overcast sky filled with low scud and scattered rainsqualls. The only warmth he felt was the hot cup of coffee he held in both hands. The sea was persistently rolling with eight foot swells as the merchantman plowed slowly towards its destination, Dover, England.

As he was contemplating the future, the cry of the lookout high above the deck in the crows nest, brought him out of his reverie.

"Periscope off the starboard bow."

Wendell jumped to his feet and put the binoculars to his eyes and scanned the sea to the right of the ship. Seeing nothing, he shouted through the intercom for confirmation.

"Be specific man! I don't see it."

"Twenty degrees off starboard bow about 3000 yards, sir."

Wendell scanned the area again, and still saw nothing. But just in case, he yelled to the helmsman. "Turn to port 150 degrees and come to a heading of two, six, zero degrees, ahead full speed."

Wendell knew he could outrun a submerged submarine and by turning the stern to this predator of the sea, the ship would be a smaller target and soon out of range. He hoped he had acted soon enough.

Next he called down the intercom to the captain's cabin. "Sir, periscope sighted off starboard bow, we're turning tail and are running at full speed."

"Good, Wendell, I'll be right up."

The heavily loaded ship responded slowly to the rudder as it began its turn to the left. Wendell could feel the surge of power as the engines came to full thrust and the speed slowly increased. All the crew could do now was scan the water and pray that the sighting was false.

"Torpedo wake starboard bow, 300 yards."

Wendell gaped in amazement as he saw the torpedo close rapidly with the lumbering ship. He inadvertently pushed on the handhold in front of him as if he could push the merchantman faster in its turn.

The impact came just below the bridge, followed by a tremendous explosion. The last thing Wendell was conscious of was the huge loading boom crashing through the roof of the wheelhouse. He took one final gulp of earthly air, before all turned black and cold.

Captain Links, commander of the U-46, took another look through the periscope at the dying merchantman as it slipped quickly below the surface, bow first. This sight of a dying ship always stirred mixed emotions in his mind, excitement over the kill, but a feeling of despair for the loss. "Down periscope," he said, "take her down to 30 meters and come to a heading of one, two, two degrees."

"Aye-aye, sir."

"This has indeed been a successful voyage," he said to himself. "That makes our fourth victory in the last two weeks."

Time - March 23, 1917 at 0843 hours EST
Place - Oval Office, White House, Washington DC.

The slender, scholarly looking man looked up from his work into the eyes of the naval officer standing at attention on the other side of the desk.

"Proceed, Captain Dennison."

Captain Dennison, the president's naval attaché, then continued his report. "Mr. President, another merchantman, the Vigilancia, has been torpedoed and sunk. There was no warning nor did the U-boat surface to lend aid to survivors if in fact there were any."

"Are you saying all hands were lost?"

"That's correct, sir."

The president of the United States, Woodrow Wilson, thanked and then dismissed Captain Dennison and waited until the officer left the room before speaking to his chief of staff, who was seated in a large, comfortable chair off to the side in front of the desk.

"I have done all that I can do to appease the Germans, and they still continue to torpedo our merchant ships. The sinking of this ship and the loss of its crew is the last straw. Call for a meeting of the Cabinet for this afternoon."

The Calling of a Nation To War

The younger man jumped down from the wagon and ran to close the gate. After latching it securely he ran back, stopping on his way to scoop up the daily paper that had been carelessly thrown from the speeding rural delivery van. He then climbed in the seat next to the older man who, with a click of his tongue and a slap of the reins got the team moving.

"We need to get to town, load all of the supplies and return before noon. With your Pa down with the bad back we need to get your chores done at the farm and then git over to my place and finish those chores before dark."

The younger man nodded, unfolded the news, and began reading. The headline on the Daily Herald caught his eye immediately. "President Wilson calls for a special session of Congress for Monday night."

"Uncle Milo, did you see this? Does this mean we're going to be in this war now?"

After peering over Pat's shoulder to read the headline, Milo said, "I'd heard about it and talked to Clint Phelps a long time on the phone last night." He turned his attention to the horses. "Hey! Giddy-up thar! Stop your stalling." He turned back to Pat "You know Clint's the managing editor at the paper now. He feels that we'll have to enter the war as the Germans are sinking our ships without warning. The losses are mounting and Americans are dying. That in itself, I think, is almost enough to bring us in."

Both men fell silent. The only sounds were the steel-rimmed wheels grinding on the dirt road and the muffled pounding of the horses' hooves.

"C'mon, Moonbeam, pick it up!" Milo called out. When he spoke again, he gazed straight ahead. "I didn't say anything to your Ma 'n Pa, though, as I felt they had enough trouble just getting all you kids through college. I know that it will upset them, particularly if all three of you boys have to go to war."

Pat was silent but in his mind he was considering how these events were going to affect his life. It was Saturday morning and he had to be back on campus the next evening. He thought that at that time he could talk to his friends and see who would go with him to enlist in the army on Monday. There was definitely going to be conscription now and the smart thing would be to join before being drafted, that at least would give him some choices the draft wouldn't allow.

As they rode along in silence Pat thought back to just last year. It had been just after graduating from high school that he'd considered joining the army. He had felt for some time, ever since the sinking of the *Lusitania* in 1915 that the US was going to be drawn into this war. But it was at his mother's strenuous urging, he decided to wait and go to the University of Illinois instead. Now, he thought, the time had come to make his move and join up. "How exciting," Pat said to himself, "traveling to Europe and at the same time having a hand in winning the big war."

Milo was heavyset, medium height, and in his early forties. His appearance was that of a much older man for he was bald and his face was wrinkled as a result of working the fields for most of his life. Pat, on the other hand was smooth skinned and taller than Milo, slender in build with sandy hair and flashing brown eyes.

"We'll kick that old Kaiser's butt in no time," Pat finally said.

"Now hold on a minute, Pat," Uncle Milo responded. "War is no game, it's a dirty business and a lot of our boys are going to get killed. Remember, I served in Cuba and though that didn't last very long people still got shot. So don't go making this out as a grand and glorious thing."

"But Uncle Milo, just by sheer numbers we'll turn the tide in no time."

Uncle Milo frowned, "You tell me where all these well-trained troops are coming from. We're at peace and the regular army is small, probably not more than 100,000 men, and for that matter not well equipped, at least not the way those European armies are. You can't recruit a group of people into the army one day and send them off to war the next. Shucks, they'd all be dead in no time. We don't need to add American bodies to the countless number of French and British dead. Now you git this idea of being a soldier out of your head and git down to business and earn your degree."

Pat fell silent, but his mind wasn't on school. He was elsewhere, far away in eastern France.

Captain Dennison looked up from the papers spread across his desk when he heard the knock on his door and he called out, "Enter."

The door opened just enough for the aide to poke his head through the opening, "Sir, Captain Montgomery to see you."

"Send him in, Ensign," Capitan Dennison replied.

Captain Robert Montgomery, a short, plump naval officer, was the prime minister's naval attaché, or Dan Dennison's counterpart in England. Captain Montgomery was on a quick visit to the States working out details on improving the flow of materials from the US to

Europe. Though the US was neutral at the time, the Americans supplied a major amount of war materials to the Allies.

Captain Dennison and Captain Montgomery, though both in their late forties, were totally different in appearance and manner. Captain Dennison stood 6'2" and weighed 190 pounds, clean-shaven and in extremely good physical condition. He credited this in part to his daily tennis game and long morning runs with his Irish setter, Bridget. Captain Montgomery, on the other hand, stood only 5'10" and weighed around 200 pounds. He had a full, well-trimmed beard and was plagued by thinning hair. He abhorred athletics and preferred sitting back with a martini in one hand, a pipe in the other, surrounded by friends. Though they were quite different, they'd hit it off from the beginning and were quickly becoming close friends.

Dan got up from his desk to greet his visitor. After shaking hands and some small talk, Dan pulled up a chair, motioning to Robert to be seated, and then returned to his desk. Robert sat down and pulled out his pipe, struck a long wooden match and took several long draws, emitting great puffs of smoke.

"Bob, you look like death warmed over."

"Well, Dan, just before I left to come and visit you, I was handed the latest figures from the admiralty on the losses we have suffered to the U-boats." Captain Montgomery paused for a moment as he took the pipe from his mouth and exhaled a cloud of blue smoke. He shook the flame of the match out with his right hand, and then deposited it in an ashtray at the corner of the desk.

"If these sinkings don't slow down soon I may be just that, death warmed over, in a few short months. The Germans are sinking our merchant ships at an unprecedented level. In the last 11 days they have sunk 28 ships or, put another way, we've lost over 300 thousand tons of material to the Boche. We can't survive such great losses. Even though the shipyards are building 24 hours a day, we can't replace but about one half of those destroyed."

"Bob, now both of us know the best answer to that one," Dan said leaning back in his chair after putting the cap on his fountain pen that had laid open on his desk. "As we discussed the other evening, Admiral Simms has been working out the details on a convoy system for the merchant ships. This would be similar to what Admiral Nelson did at Trafalgar. The idea is to form the merchantmen and transports into one large formation and screen them on the parameters with destroyers and cruisers. If the subs dare to attack, we'll be able to concentrate our firepower on them. They won't have a chance—they can't outrun the destroyers."

"But Dan, we don't have enough warships to escort the convoys and send out the antisubmarine patrols too."

Dennison held up a finger. "That's just the point of Admiral Simms' plan; there will be no need for the patrols. When we stop sending out single ships and instead form them in convoys, we no longer need to patrol for U-boats. Case in point. Have you ever heard of a Battle group screened by destroyers and cruisers being attacked by the U-boats?"

"Well, no—but that's different."

"No it isn't, Bob. If the Germans could sink a battleship, wouldn't that be more of a prize for them than just a merchantman?" Before Montgomery could answer, Dennison answered his own question. "Of course it would, but they're not fools. They know that to attack a battle group would be suicide for a submarine and its crew. Well, the same principle applies to the convoy. The President is backing this plan of Admiral Simms. You must persuade Admiral Jellicoe to try this form of transport of material across the Atlantic. Without the convoy system in place we both know all is lost." Dennison leaned forward on his desk. "What do you think we need to do to get him to go for this plan?"

Montgomery shrugged. "Admiral Jellicoe has a huge responsibility and doesn't want to put the Empire in jeopardy. Remember what Churchill said, 'Jellicoe is the only man on either side who could lose the war in an afternoon.' In other words, if our navy lost so heavily as to lose its strategic superiority, our defeat would be certain.

"Besides, he really doesn't think that we have enough warships to escort the convoys, as I said, and I think he would feel that slowing down all ships to the speed of the slowest one in the convoy will make them all more vulnerable to attack." He sat back in his chair and took a long draw on the pipe before continuing. "However, I think if you could get the president to endorse it in writing and put pressure on the PM, that may turn the trick."

Dennison nodded. "I'll see that you get it in writing and I know Admiral Simms is anxious to set things in motion. You should also consider the strong probability that the US will be entering the war and therefore most of our warships based in the Atlantic will be available for escort duty."

"Yes, that's true, and it will be a tremendous boost." Montgomery said as he thoughtfully took another draw on his pipe. After he blew the smoke towards the ceiling he asked. "If the convoy system is approved, how soon could we start?"

"If approval comes within a week or two, we could assemble the first one for late May."

Montgomery looked at Dennison intently. "Dan, do you really believe this will work?"

"There are few other options open to us, it has to work!"

When the train started to slow for the station, Pat jumped to his feet, grabbed his satchel, and headed for the door. He wanted to be the first one off.

As soon as the conductor opened the coach door, Pat hit the ground running and he didn't stop until he got to the front porch of the fraternity house, some six blocks from the station. He was still buoyed by the possibility of a big change in his life.

He had given a lot of thought to joining up. He felt that given the issues, quite a few of his friends would probably go and join with him. He had not said anything to his folks while at home, as he knew it would lead to an argument, especially with his mother. They would find out soon enough, after he enlisted.

It had rained most of the weekend, but the temperature was unseasonably warm, and as Pat approached the porch he slowed to a walk and climbed the steps. There, on the porch swing he saw Isaac and in a nearby recliner was Jake each reading different sections of the Sunday paper. These upperclassmen weren't really the ones he wanted to talk to—they always raised his hackles by kidding him about his name, which was Elmer. This was a name he had never liked and one that both his father and older brother disliked as well and was thankfully changed before he could walk.

"Well if it isn't El-m-mer back from the plowing," Jake said. Jake stood a little taller than Pat, with broad shoulders, dark auburn hair and an air of command that normally made others stop and listen to what he had to say.

"At least, I'll know how to work when I get out of here," Pat replied. "Not just how to sit around and read the paper all day."

Jake grinned. "I think we've touched a raw nerve, Ike."

Without answering Pat went into the house and up to his room on the third floor.

"Jake, why do ya give him such a hard time?" Isaac said. "You know he doesn't like it and besides he isn't a pledge anymore, he's a full member just like you and me. I think if you really make him mad he could take you down. He's pretty wiry."

"Yeah you're probably right," Jake chuckled, "and I do like the kid. Maybe I should go up and make amends now. I'm not going to be around after I graduate next month."

As Pat finished putting his things away, he turned to leave and was startled to see Jake standing in the door. "Don't push me, Jake, I'm not going to take much more of your crap."

"Hold on a moment, Pat, I came up here to call a truce. Look, I just like giving all you pledges a hard time. But Ike reminded me you guys aren't pledges anymore so I need to go easy on you. Look, I'll be outta here in a month or so and, besides, you don't turn that beautiful shade of red anymore so what's the point. Shake?"

"That's fine with me, Jake."

They shook hands.

Pat hesitated a second and then asked. "You're in the ROTC program, aren't you?"

"You bet, I'll be a shavetail second lieutenant by June."

"Well, what do you think about the president's address to Congress tomorrow? I think we're going to declare war."

"Oh, don't kid yourself El – er, Pat. He's just going to back down again the way he did when the *Lusitania* was sunk. You think I'd still be in the ROTC if I felt we were going to war? Anyway, if we did declare war, the Huns would sue for peace before one doughboy set foot in France."

Pat shrugged. "Well, I hope you're right, but I still think he'll ask Congress to declare war."

After Jake left his room, Pat started going around to his other friends in the fraternity, talking about the war and joining the army. He was surprised that few saw the importance of what was happening in Europe. He couldn't stir up much excitement over enlisting in the military and few felt that conscription was coming. Most thought that if the draft were enacted, they would be exempt while still in school. To a man they felt the war would be over if the US were drawn in just because of the size of the US Army. But, Rob, Hank, and a few others were leaning his way.

He didn't want to sign up alone and he thought he should at least wait and see what the president had to say. Besides, as Frank pointed out, the semester would be over in just five short weeks. This made Pat remember that he'd have to help his dad complete the spring planting.

When Pat finally hit the sack a little after midnight, he was exhausted.

Pat was not a complex person, but there were two distinct sides to his character. On the one side he was extremely loyal to his friends and relatives. This meant there was a good chance that he could be swayed to join into what his friends were doing, even though he might not like it too well. On the other hand, he would not join in any activity that was counter to his beliefs or the law.

This did not necessarily keep him out of trouble. There were many activities that seemed to fall within a large gray area, and others at times could cajole him into participating.

As a young boy, for example, from his eighth year to his thirteenth, his cousin, Tom, would visit the farm for a month during the summer. Tom lived with his parents in Chicago and was a city boy.

From the time that Tom arrived at the farm for his summer visit, the two boys were constantly into some undertaking or cooking up one scheme after another to get out of work, sneaking off to go fishing when there were chores to be done or just being too rowdy. Tom usually initiated their antics. His standard phrase to Pat was, "It'll be fun, and there's nothing wrong with it."

They would sneak off to the chicken coop with their BB guns and pick off freshly laid eggs in order to improve their marksmanship, or they would shoot at the sparrows that lived in and flew around the silo, until someone caught them in their mischief.

The worst misadventure came in the summer of 1911 shortly after Pat's father, E.P., had bought his first tractor. E.P. had promised to teach Pat how to operate and drive it sometime before the summer was over, but before the lessons began, Tom arrived for his vacation.

Pat had bragged to Tom that he knew how to run the machine. Soon, convinced by Tom of his mastery over the tractor, Pat started it up one day when his folks had gone down the road to help Milo, and quickly he had it in gear and the boys were circling around the barnyard. After the joyride and as Pat was trying to carefully put the machine back in the exact location where he found it, next to the chicken house, he got a little flustered and was unable to get the brake in time. The tractor did stop, but not until it ran into the chicken house and knocked it off its foundation. What a commotion those chickens kicked up. Pat's parents returned home just then, and on hearing the ruckus out in the barnyard, Pat's mother, Matilda, rushed out to see what was happening.

Needless to say, harsh punishment was meted out and then all went on with their lives. Both boys were pretty well behaved during the remainder of Tom's visit. This, sadly, was the last summer that Pat spent with his cousin as Tom tragically succumbed to influenza during the following winter.

As Pat got older, he formed strong convictions based on his religious upbringing and a strong loyalty and love for his family and country.

In the days of his early youth, Pat never had a chance to travel. The rich black Illinois soil needed constant attention and his folks were busy raising a family of four children. The people in the community of Tolono and the surrounding area were not unusual. They were a supporting network of family and neighbors who worked the land and went to church. They developed pride and patriotism and a commitment to God and country. Their lives, on the whole, revolved around ethics and morality. Life was uncomplicated, but it required hard work to make a living off of the land.

During harvest season, all of the neighbors would help each other harvest the crops. The men would work the fields and the women would prepare the food. All worked equally hard. At mealtime the bell would ring to bring the field workers in. Washbasins were set up near the barn and if the weather permitted they would eat outside. The owner of the land would say grace before they ate and all would give thanks for their many blessings. They took great pride in the work that fostered fellowship and brotherly love.

This did not mean there were no disagreements, for there are always some arguments when two or more people gather. These matters were normally settled peacefully, with honor and dignity.

The End of Isolation

As the professor entered the lecture hall, there was a brief increase in the noise level created by shuffling papers and feet as students scurried to their seats. By the time Professor Werner Hinkle reached the podium, all was silent. Once there, the professor arranged some papers from his briefcase and began.

"Because of the impact of recent news, I've deemed it necessary to deviate from our schedule. So instead of discussing Gettysburg, we're jumping ahead in our American history to current times."

Professor Hinkle cleared his throat, scanned his audience, checked his notes and continued. "As you know, the war in Europe has been going on for approximately three years. Up to this time it has been an affair entirely devoid of US involvement. The events of these past few weeks may change that. Now it seems almost imperative that the United States enter this bloody affair. As it will most surely impact all of us in some way, I felt it necessary to spend this next hour discussing the events that have led us to these perilous times."

Professor Hinkle's booming voice easily filled the lecture hall, and probably for the first time since the semester started, he had the rapt attention of all the students.

"I don't want to sound too negative, but if the president asks Congress to declare war, then all of us in this room are going to be affected in some way or another. Don't kid yourselves, there's a life-and-death struggle going on in Europe at this very moment. I myself am not exempt. In my youthful and infinite wisdom, I joined the National

Guard some years ago. It seemed like a nice club to belong to with a real nice group of fellows. We've had some great times and frankly, we never gave a thought of going to war. That is, until a short time ago. Now, suddenly, we were all made aware of what we were all about—we are soldiers. Fortunately—unlike other guard units—we were not called up to go to Texas to look for the Mexican revolutionary Pancho Villa. Now things are different, as an officer of a trained military organization, I may find myself at the front before long."

Some of the students looked at one another in surprise.

"If this Congress calls for general mobilization, and I think they will, then all of you young men strong enough to carry a rifle are going to be called up." Professor Hinkle continued. "So I felt it wise to discuss how this European madness got started. What I'm going to discuss is based some on fact and some on supposition. Not having an inside track to the German or the Allied military planners' thinking, I've had to make some educated guesses as to what they intended this war to be."

Professor Hinkle paused a moment and wiped his glasses with a handkerchief he pulled from his lapel pocket. The professor was always immaculately dressed in three-piece suits, groomed to the point that it looked as if he were on his way to a cabinet meeting with the President.

Pat felt the tingle of excitement at what the professor said. He'd just told all of his fraternity brothers last night that he thought there was going to be war. Now the professor was confirming those convictions.

After returning the glasses to his nose and the handkerchief to his suit pocket, the professor continued with the lecture. "First let us start at the beginning. I think you could say that there were many causes to this war, but the roots go back to 1870 and the signing of the Treaty of Frankfurt. This treaty ended the Franco-Prussian War. Germany, being victorious, extracted many concessions from France; the most significant of these being that France cede the Alsace-Lorraine region to Germany. To the French this was like a knife in the back. It could be said that this one provision prevented peace. Though the warring stopped, the anger and resentment lived on. The French have been determined to regain this region and the Germans have been unwilling to give it up.

"There were numerous treaties negotiated and signed by various European governments during the latter part of the last century. Most involved either Germany or France with some other nations. Germany tried to maintain military superiority over France, while the French tried to maneuver into a position of strength against Germany. Eventually Germany signed a treaty with Austria-Hungary forming the foundation for the Central Powers. To counter this move and to increase their political and military muscle and maybe to outflank the Germans, the French signed a treaty with Russia, effectively placing adversaries on two sides of Germany. Then, in 1904, in an understanding called the Entente Cordiale, France and England resolved many of their differences and the British entered this group now called the Allies.

"Germany was later joined by Turkey and Bulgaria. As time went by the number of countries involved with each of the principals grew. With the alliances in place, the military strength of the belligerents remained somewhat equal. The Allies were stronger at sea while the Central Powers retained an edge on the ground. Now keep in mind that the treaties or alliances bound all members to come to the aid of any member attacked by an outsider. The agreements stipulated that if one nation was attacked, it was the same as if all members were attacked."

Professor Hinkle paused here for a moment to answer any questions that might come up. Seeing no hands raised, he continued. "The development of each new weapon by one side was countered with an equal or more powerful one by the other. A monumental arms race was underway. Armies, navies, weapons, and munitions were built in escalating numbers. War plans were developed, modified and revised over and over while the stalemate continued. The overall effect was contrary to what had initially been intended. Europe became a large weapons storehouse with two opposing sides, hating and distrusting each other. Little was needed to start the fires burning.

"On June 28, 1914, and most of you probably remember this, a Serbian terrorist, by the name of Gavrilo Princip, assassinated the Archduke Francis Ferdinand of Austria and his wife, Sophie, during a visit to Sarajevo, Bosnia. Though the archduke was not a significant player in Austria, he was still in line for succession to the throne. Few gave much thought to this incident and for a short while life in Europe went on as if nothing had happened. The Kaiser, on a cruise on one of his warships, remained at sea.

"The Austrians blamed Serbia, a close neighbor of Bosnia, for the murder of their heir to the Austrian throne. After much wrangling and inept handling of the situation, Austria launched a full-scale invasion in August. This attack set off the alliance agreements, dragging in all of the participants in a domino effect. Russia responded next by coming to the aid of her Serbian friends. They moved a large army to the Austrian border. The German Kaiser, Wilhelm II, stepped in and warned Russia not to invade or they would also have to fight Germany if they did. At this time, France was preparing to help her Russian ally.

"The actual fighting has turned out differently than anyone had originally supposed. All belligerents felt that even though the war would be fierce, it probably would be over by Christmas of 1914. As we know, this was not the case. All involved had planned and visualized a war that would move rapidly, being governed by offensive moves. Even though the weapons developed for this war were foreseen to be offensive in nature, they were in fact more effective in their defensive roles.

"Though the US will, in all probability, be involved on the Western front, this war is, in effect, a worldwide conflict with theaters of operation in Europe, Asia and Africa. Germany and Austria-Hungary are fighting the Russians in Eastern Europe, the French and British are engaged with Germany in France, and the English and Turks are embroiled in Asia. There are also some battles being fought in various colonies in Africa as well as in the Holy Land.

"Preparation for this war had been ongoing for a number of years. In the early 1890s, General Graf von Schlieffen developed a plan of attack in case Germany was to have a simultaneous war with France and Russia. His plan envisioned engaging and then defeating France while fighting a defensive action against Russia. After the defeat of France he would move his armies against Russia. This plan utilized a strike against France by a large wheel movement that would send his main strength through Belgium and the Low Countries to the coast and then south to Paris. General Schlieffen's plan placed a very heavy concentration of forces on the right wing of his army with the idea of pushing his adversaries south toward Paris. He believed that, with the capture of Paris, the French would capitulate, thus allowing the bulk of the German armies to move east against Russia.

"General Moltke, Schlieffen's successor and the one in control at the start of hostilities, did not understand the full impact of this plan and made changes that resulted in their inability to prevail. His most glaring error was the weakening of the right wing and moving some of these troops against the French in the Lorraine area, thus weakening his initial assault force. They were further hampered by inadequate communications.

"As far as we can tell, the German staff stayed a great distance behind the front, I believe in Spa, Belgium, and as a result they had an incomplete picture of the current developments. It seems that they did not lay phone lines fast enough to keep up with the armies and relied heavily on the wireless. Because the German command was forced to use wireless transmissions, the French and English were able to intercept their messages and, unknown to the Imperial Command, decipher the encryption. These developments allowed General Joffre, the Allied supreme commander, who was always a short distance from the front, to act quickly and decisively.

"We had in 1914 two sides that believed that their advanced weapons gave them an edge in battle. Therefore all plans and strategies were developed around offensive moves. The French had a strategy of their own—Plan 17—that relied solely on attack. They believed that with a powerful frontal attack in the Lorraine area, starting at the city of Metz, they could achieve a breakthrough and move into the interior of Germany, forcing their surrender. The French Plan 17 put too much emphasis on individual valor and courage of the French soldier, and this proved wrong and costly in both men and materials.

"In the northwest, as the German lines moved forward, they encountered abandoned battlefields potholed by previous battles. Their transportation system relied heavily on the railroad that was highly developed in Germany, but as they moved farther from the homeland the resupply of the right wing became nightmarish. Other problems developed, due to a lack of guidance from general headquarters. Local commanders made decisions that impaired the movement of troops or they lost focus on the overall goals. The First and Second Armies on the far right began to move from their original paths. For example, the Second Army embroiled on the Sambre asked for assistance from the First Army and both turned in a southeasterly direction. Moltke did not stop this error. The result was an inward turning of the wheel movement to the east of Paris, negating the effect of the wider sweep.

"This gave the British and French time to move their forces to the northwest to stop the German push and at the same time to try and outflank them. This ultimately resulted in what we now call the race to the sea. In other words, each side tried to outflank the other in the northwest and only was stopped when they reached the coast of the North Sea in Belgium. The final battle, during this race, at Ypres during October and November, culminated in stalemate clear across France. At this time both sides dug in and the war degenerated into the bloody trench warfare that exists now. The lines stretch for over 500 miles from the North Sea to Switzerland. Neither side has been able to overcome the defensive posture of the other. The power of modern defense has triumphed over attack."

The professor paused for a moment and took a drink from the glass of water he had earlier placed on a lower shelf of the lectern out of sight from the students. Hank glanced over at Pat and winked and gave a thumbs-up sign. Pat nodded and returned the gesture. After replacing the glass on the shelf, Professor Hinkle continued with the lecture.

"There have been events in the past that would seemingly propel us into this war, but President Wilson has endeavored to keep our country out. For example, on May 7, 1915, the English luxury liner, the *Lusitania*, was torpedoed and sunk by a German U-boat. Over 1200 lives were lost, 128 of them Americans. As you know, this sinking outraged the American people, but President Wilson did not declare war. To the contrary, Mr. Wilson did all he could to keep us out of it. In April of 1916, through diplomatic efforts, he was able to get the Germans to order their U-boats not to sink neutral merchantmen suspected of carrying supplies to the Allies without first warning them and then doing all within their power to aid and rescue crews and passengers. The American public was so supportive of these efforts on the part of President Wilson that they reelected him last November. His slogan, 'He kept us out of the war,' gained him a great deal of popularity and support.

"Because of their inability to attack suspect neutral ships without prior warning, the Germans sought other avenues of preventing war goods from being shipped to England and France. They have used spies and saboteurs sent to and recruited in this country to destroy and interrupt shipments of food and munitions. German agents have injected animals due for shipment to Europe with deadly viruses, so that when they arrived they would be unusable. Most of the sabotage has taken place on the docks. For example one ingenious saboteur devised a bomb that could be attached to the rudder of a ship. After a predetermined number of turns of the rudder the bomb would explode, leaving the ship rudderless at sea.

"One of the worst acts of sabotage occurred last July at Black Tom Island, a small man-made strip of land just behind the Statue of Liberty where most of the munitions for the Allies are loaded onto ships. As far as is known, several lives were lost in a tremendous explosion, heard up to 100 miles away; it has been determined that the blast was caused by a time bomb. Finally, late in January of this year, the Kaiser announced that beginning February 1, the Germans would begin unrestricted submarine warfare and a new and wider war zone would be established around England, France, Italy, and the eastern part of the Mediterranean.

"The Kaiser did say that the US could sail one ship a week to England if we adhered to certain rules, which of course were totally unacceptable to our government. There also is some credence being given to the idea that the Germans orchestrated Pancho Villa's raid on Columbus, New Mexico in order to distract the military and War Department.

"The actual attacks on American ships this last month by the German Imperial Navy, were the last straw. The deck gun of a U-boat shelled the *Algonquin*, and the *City of Memphis*, *Illinois*, and *Vigilancia* were deliberately torpedoed with some loss of life. That seemed to be as much as President Wilson could take and so he broke diplomatic relations with Germany and has called Congress into session so that he may address them tonight. I believe it is for the purpose of asking Congress to declare war on the Central powers."

Roy Littler, Pat's older brother, stood on the steps of the Capitol awaiting the arrival of the president.

This day had been a whirlwind of activity for him. It began at 6:00 a.m. with a loud knocking on his New York apartment door, rudely awakening him from a deep sleep of only four hours.

On opening the door, he was surprised to see Sam Goldstein standing there. Sam was one of the runners for the paper assigned to the political newsroom.

"Mr. Littler, Joe sent me to get you. He said to get your—pardon the expression—ass to the newsroom within the hour."

Joe Boswell was the senior editor and Roy's boss. Joe never minced words.

"What's up, Sam?"

"I don't know for sure, but I think he wants you to cover the President's speech in Washington tonight."

From that time on, there had been a flurry of activity. Joe was able, after superhuman effort, to get one pass to the gallery for the President's speech that night and he had selected Roy to cover it. This was a real forward step in his career and he jumped at the opportunity.

Although Roy had to stand all the way, he was able to get a ticket on a train that would get him to Washington in time to hear the speech. Joe had made arrangements whereby Roy could use a phone to file his report in time for the early morning edition, before grabbing a late train back to New York.

So here he stood on the steps of the Capitol, which were bathed in the luminescence of bright searchlights set up to help in the protection of the president. On close examination of the upper reaches of the building, Roy was able to discern machine gun nests manned by marines placed to protect the president and other important officials if an attempt was made on their lives. He overheard some nearby reporters saying that they had not seen the Capitol lit at night, one said, "It makes it stand out as the shinning symbol of our nation."

Soon Roy could see the president's limousine approaching down Pennsylvania Avenue. Mounted troopers whose dancing steeds' shod hooves could be heard above the din of traffic and the crowd that surrounded the car.

Roy had purposefully waited on the steps so he could see Mr. Wilson as he entered the capitol, then Roy would make his way to his own seat in the gallery. It appeared that he wasn't the only one with this idea. As the entourage approached, Roy could see people lined up 10 deep on either side of Pennsylvania Avenue. There were even some protesters in the crowd carrying signs denouncing American involvement in European affairs. The crowd on the steps made it difficult for Roy to see much of what was happening.

The limousine pulled up, stopped, and the President and Mrs. Wilson got out. The crowd was so thick, hemmed in by Secret Service agents surrounding the presidential couple, that Roy got only a glimpse of the president's head as he disappeared into the building.

Roy then fought his way through the crowd and found his seat just in time to hear the Speaker of the House Joe Cannon announce, "Ladies and gentlemen, the President of the United States."

The president took the rostrum amid loud cheers and applause. After a minute or so the large, crowded chamber was as quiet as if no one were there, all anticipating his words.

The president began in an offhand, conversational tone.

"I have called the Congress into extraordinary session because there are serious choices of policy to be made, and made immediately, which it is neither right nor constitutionally permissible for me to make."

The president then spelled out his message of war. He built his case against the Germans by detailing their actions against a free and neutral society. "Their ravage of the seas with their U-boats and their killing of innocent people is an outrage to all humanity.

"With a profound sense of the solemn and even tragic character of the step I am taking and of the grave responsibilities which it involves, but in unhesitating obedience to what I deem my constitutional duty, I advise that the Congress declare the recent course of the imperial German government to be in fact nothing less than war against the government and the people of the United States that it formally accept the status of belligerent which has thus been thrust upon it and that it take immediate steps not only to put the country in a more thorough state of defense but also to exert all its power and employ all its resources to bring the government of the German Empire to terms and end the war."

As the president ended his sentence, there was a loud rebel yell that came from none other than the 72-year-old chief justice of the Supreme Court who had fought for the south during the Civil War. The chief justice then threw his hat into the air and jumped to his feet, clapping his hands, and all rose as one, cheering and applauding the president.

When the applause died down, the president concluded his speech.

"The American people must take up arms and fight for the ultimate peace of the world and the liberation of all people. The world must be made safe for democracy..."

Roy hastily scribbled in his notebook as the president continued:

"But the right is more precious than peace, and we shall fight for the things that we have always carried nearest our hearts—for democracy, for the right of those who submit to authority to have a voice in their own governments, for the rights and liberties of small nations... and make the world itself at last free. To such a task we can dedicate our lives and fortunes, everything that we are and everything that we have, with the pride of those who know that the day has come when America is privileged to spend her blood and her might for the principles that gave her birth and happiness and the peace she has treasured. God helping her, she can do no other."

With this the crowded chamber burst into a frenzy of emotion. Roy, overcome by the moment, cheered and screamed with all who were there. It was a moment no one there would ever forget.

The phone was for Pat. He ran down the stairs taking two or three steps at a time, and answered into the box on the wall.

"Hello, Pat, this is Clint Phelps."

"Hi, Mr. Phelps, I haven't seen or heard from you in a long time."

Clint Phelps' father had been a longtime friend of Pat's grandfather, such a good friend in fact that both Pat and his father bore the family name "Phelps" as a middle name.

"Well, Pat, I have intended to give you a call ever since you started at the university last fall. So how are you liking school?"

"I like it fine, though some of the math courses are tough. But I'm passing everything and I should come out with a B average."

"Well, you should be finished up for the summer in about a month, right?"

"Mr. Phelps, I know Uncle Milo put you up to this call, didn't he? I know he's concerned that I'll join the army."

"I guess you caught me. But I did want to urge you to at least complete the current semester."

"Have you heard what the president said tonight in his speech to Congress?"

"Yes, I did. It just came over the wire a short time ago. We're going to war. But I hope you will stay out as long as possible."

"Is there going to be a draft?"

"Yes, I'm sure there will."

"Then how can I stay out of it even if I wanted to?"

"I can't answer that one, Pat. But at least finish up this semester. The draft won't get you before then."

"Well, to be honest, I was tempted to go down today and sign up, but the same thought crossed my mind. I do plan to sign up before I get drafted, but I figured I needed to finish this semester first. I would appreciate your not passing this on to the family. I would prefer telling them myself."

"I'll keep your confidence, and if you need anything, just call." Clint said. "It was nice talking to you again."

"It was nice talking to you, and thanks for calling."

Clint Phelps had been a newsman for 20 years. He had worked for a couple of New York papers and for the *Chicago Globe* before taking over the managing editor's job at the *Champaign Daily Herald* just last year.

After Pat hung up the phone, he slowly climbed the stairs to his room and once there found his roommate Hank sitting on his bed reading.

Hank Seiler was Pat's best friend, though they had not met until this last year when the fraternity pledged them both. Through the pledging period of the first semester and the adversities of initiation, they became very close friends. Now they shared a room on the third floor. Hank was just a little under six feet tall and had a trim build, brown eyes, and thick black hair.

"Hank, I just heard that the president asked Congress to declare war. That means there will be conscription. Did you know there's a field artillery unit that's part of the National Guard here on campus? I'm going to look into it tomorrow, are you with me?"

"You know I am. Why don't we go see Professor Hinkle? Maybe he knows about it or can give us some other ideas."

Secretary Tumulty found the president sitting at a large table in the dimly lit conference room late at night long after the dinner guests had left. He was sitting and staring blankly down the long table in the semi-darkness.

"Mr. President, is there anything I can do for you, sir?"

"They applauded and cheered at what I said. Did they not know I signed the death warrant for many of the flowering youth of this great land?"

With that President Wilson cradled his head in his arms and wept.

The Call To Arms

The next five weeks seemed to fly by. Course work had to be completed and then there was the preparation for final exams. For Pat it meant getting all of his studying done during the week in order for him to be able to go home on the weekend and help with the chores. The family farm was located near the small town of Tolono about 15 miles south of Champaign. Late every Friday afternoon he would rush to the station to catch the 5:45 for the twenty-minute ride south. Either his Uncle Milo or his dad, Egbert, would meet him at the train and drive him the remaining three miles to the farm.

The last weekend before finals, May eighth and ninth, rolled around all too quickly. Pat feeling somewhat unprepared loaded all of his books and notes in his suitcase so he could do his last minute review while he was home. As he sat back in the coach seat he thought of his dad. He couldn't recall a time anyone other than his mother ever called him Egbert. Woe to the poor person that made that mistake as his father abhorred his given name and he had been called E.P. by all that knew him for as far back as anyone could remember. Pat chuckled to himself as this thought crossed his mind, as he too, detested his given name Elmer, which his mother had conferred upon him.

His next thought was about his father's improving health. His back seemed to be getting better, giving him greater mobility with each passing week. Still E.P. stayed away from heavy lifting and let Pat handle that for him on the weekends. The other thought continually on Pat's mind was the difficulty of running a 300-acre farm; no easy project for just one man. He then thought of Roger, his older brother a lawyer in Champaign who never seemed to have time for the farm. Then there was the middle brother, Roy just a few years older than Pat, who worked as a newsman in New York and seldom had the time or opportunity to come home. Finally there was his sister Ethel, who was in her second year of medical school in Chicago, which took all of her time. This left a heavy burden on his dad, and was the reason Pat traveled to the farm most weekends.

This particular weekend was even more difficult for Pat, as he had decided that this was the time he would tell his parents that he and Hank had enlisted in a National Guard unit in Champaign. He was excited about his decision, and knew it wouldn't be long before the Guard would be activated. Still, he worried about how his folks would handle all of the farm-work. There had always been someone around to help with the chores and the last few years he had been that one. Now for the first time, he thought, his dad was going to have to handle it alone. "I only hope that Uncle Milo will be able to help," he said to himself as the train began to slow for the Tolono station.

Milo Lewis, Pat's mother's brother, had been a widower for 20 years following the untimely death of his wife and young baby in a train accident. Milo's 200-acre farm was just down the road from the Littler spread, and Pat's hope was that Milo would have the time to help. Milo was an important member of the family and was always at the Sunday dinner table.

After church on the ninth of May Pat and his dad completed the planting in the early afternoon. They were late this year, as the spring had been particularly wet and the fields too muddy to work. It was going to be tough getting the famous Illinois corn "knee high by the fourth of July".

After they finished their work in the fields and slopped the hogs, they washed up for dinner. Pat's mother served a large, and succulent roast chicken with all of the trimmings. E.P. blessed the food and the four of them quietly enjoyed the meal. Milo sat in his usual place. The conversation was primarily about the crops and prices on the markets. Pat ate lightly and didn't enter the conversation, being too concerned about how he was going to break the news to his folks.

Finally as they were finishing the meal, Pat blurted out, "I can't go on without telling you that,—well—I enlisted in the U of I National Guard unit two weeks ago."

The news brought all activity to a standstill. Matilda held the bowl of mashed potatoes in midair for what seemed like forever and E.P.'s chin dropped. Milo sat quietly, staring at Pat, and slowly nodded his head.

"Mom, Dad, you know the draft has been enacted. By enlisting now I can select the type of duty I want. If I wait I'll have no choice in the matter."

Matilda continued holding the bowl of potatoes and was still unable to find her voice.

"Son, I knew this day was coming," his father finally said. "I've thought a lot about it ever since last year when you were determined to enlist after high school. I guess that if I were your age I'd do the same. I just hope and pray that this war will end before any of you boys head for France. I think Roger is too old for the draft, but Roy will probably be called."

By this time Matilda had found her voice and set the potatoes down with a bang. "You are too young to go into the army, I won't have it."

"Mom you know that's an unreasonable statement, I'm fair game. They're going to call all young men from 18 to 26, and I'm at the head of the list."

"Now, Matty, we'll discuss this later, but Pat's right and you are going to have to accept it. There's little we can do."

By presidential proclamation, the First Illinois Field Artillery was called to active duty on June 30, 1917.

This artillery regiment consisted of six mobile batteries. Battery A was from Danville, Batteries B, C, D and E were from the Chicago area, and Battery F was from the University of Illinois at Champaign.

Each battery was built around four mobile artillery pieces. The First Illinois would use French-designed 75-millimeter cannon mounted on two wheels, pulled by a team of four horses. Until the regiment moved to France, they would be using old and outdated American made three-inch field pieces.

Besides the four cannon each battery had other horse drawn, rolling equipment, including ammunition caissons and a field kitchen.

In addition to the six batteries that made up the fighting arm of the regiment, there was a headquarters company, a supply company, and a medical service unit. All of these units were ordered to report to their respective armories to await transportation to Fort Sheridan where the final stage of the mobilization was to take place.

The various units of the First Illinois had anticipated the call to duty and they were actively recruiting men in order to bring their manpower requirements up to wartime strength. The personnel of the Champaign Battery were made up of local or town boys as well as students attending the university. In order for Battery F to bring their staffing up to the mandated level, there was a small contingent of new Chicago recruits joining the battery on July 1. On July 2, the battery consisted of 146 men and 7 officers.

He felt overdressed wearing a suit, tie, and straw hat, but he didn't want to upset his mother who had insisted that he wear his good clothes. After all, both of his parents were up early and dressed in their Sunday best to take him to the train. The send-off was a somber and tearful experience for Matilda and E.P. It wasn't every day parents saw their youngest son off to war. "Now you be sure to eat, you're skinny enough as it is." Matilda admonished. "Don't forget to write us every day, we want to know what's happening," E.P. added.

"I don't know anything about the food but I heard that it wasn't too good," Pat said. "And I'll write as often as I can but I doubt if I'll have the time for a letter every day."

As the train arrived, it pushed a big gust of wind in front of its wake that nearly lifted Pat's hat from his head. He quickly clamped it to his head with his left hand as he stooped to get his satchel. Matilda grabbed her hat with her right hand and held a handkerchief over her face with the other. Not many more words were said as Pat stooped to kiss his mother who flung her arms around his neck and held tight for at least a minute. "Mom, I have to go," he choked out tearfully. When she released her grip he turned to his father and took his hand. "I love you both," he said, before turning to climb the stairs to the coach.

"Write as soon as you get settled," his dad called after him before he disappeared into the coach.

Before he could find a seat the train lurched forward, nearly sending him into the lap of an elderly lady, sitting near the aisle. After regaining his balance, he sat down in a nearby empty seat.

Nearly 20 minutes later, he stood in line waiting to get off the train in Champaign. He thought that this scene—parents saying their good-byes to their children—was being played out all around the country and it would continue for a long time to come.

When the coach stopped and the conductor opened the door at the Champaign station, the passengers started to file out. Pat picked up his satchel and stepped onto the platform. There were a fair number of passengers waiting to board, and not many getting off. But it was only 7:30 in the morning and the town was not yet up and about.

Pat had elected to take the 7:10 out of Tolono in order to ensure his arrival at the Guard armory well before the 10:00 a.m. deadline. He had about a mile and a half to walk and would arrive in plenty of time.

He set his satchel down and dug into his pockets looking for his orders to report. When he didn't find them in the first two pockets, he began to panic. "What if I lost them?" he muttered to himself. He started to feel flushed and a cold sweat formed on his brow. Then he remembered that his mother had put them in the bag. He breathed a sigh of relief, picked up his things, and headed for the stairs that would take him to the street. Once there, he got his bearings and started off in the direction of the armory.

Beyond the halfway point of his walk, he found the little restaurant he had frequented several times during his last semester. His mother had fixed him a small breakfast earlier, but he was still hungry and there was still some time to kill, so he went in.

There were only two other patrons and he plopped down at the first table he came to and sat with his back to the door. He ordered bacon, eggs and coffee. The waitress bought his coffee and he sipped it as he waited for his food, daydreaming about his future. He heard the door open but didn't look at the new customer. This person sat at a table facing Pat and when he did glance up he recognized the man as Jack

Bayless, an older member of the battery who had befriended Pat and Hank during the first meeting they had attended with the Guard unit.

Jack also recognized Pat and got up to come over and join him, juggling his cup of coffee on its saucer with one hand and his suitcase with the other.

Jack was about Pat's size and maybe a year or two older. He worked for the Champaign Post Office as a rural mail carrier. He had said that he was bored with the work and joined the battery in order to find some excitement. He'd been in for over a year and was still waiting for something exciting to happen.

"I see you got an early start, too," Jack said. "I couldn't sleep very well last night so I got up early to come here for some breakfast before I went to report in."

"Well, I sort of did the same thing. I caught the early train out of Tolono. I thought if I waited for the next one I may get here after ten."

Jack was dressed primarily in a uniform. He had a campaign hat, the winter blouse, and britches, but his shoes and socks were non-issue.

"I see you don't have a uniform yet, Pat. I have most of a winter one but I sure don't have everything. I don't know whether the army will ever get it right. Only those who went to Mexico last year have a complete outfit. Oh well, they told me to wear what I had."

"I don't have anything yet. My mother insisted that I dress up for the first day, but I have some older clothes in my bag."

"You'll need them."

They continued talking as they ate, mainly speculating about training and eventually about the war. Before they knew it, it was nine o'clock.

Jack was the first to stand as he dug in his pocket for change to pay for his meal. After they were on the street, they set a fast pace and started for the armory. Neither said much during their walk.

Most of the men were there by the 10:00 a.m. deadline, but Hank overslept. He straggled in at 10:25.

After he arrived, all were accounted for. Hank had to spend five extra minutes doing 25 push-ups for the group under First Sergeant Heath's supervision, to demonstrate to the group that orders were to be followed.

The battery commander, Captain Arnold, presented the initial greeting.

"Gentlemen, as you know, the First Illinois Artillery has been officially activated. We will remain in Champaign for no more than a week. At that time we will move to Fort Sheridan, north of Chicago, to join the rest of the regiment and await orders for our deployment to France."

With this there was a buzz of excitement from the men.

One of the other officers shouted, "Attention!" and the talking stopped.

Captain Arnold continued. "For those of you who live nearby, you may stay the nights at home until we leave for Fort Sheridan. The rest of you will stay in the tents you will set up today. I want all of the officers to meet in my office right now. Sergeant Heath, get the men to work on the encampment."

At this point the men were issued squad tents that were to be erected about one half mile from the armory near a swamp. While waiting in line with Hank, Pat asked that he hold his place. He then dashed into the locker room and changed into his older clothes. He rejoined Hank just as he was receiving the tent from the supply sergeant.

As they carried the tent out to the campsite, Hank said to Pat, "Come on home with me, you can stay at my place until we go to Chicago."

"I won't argue with you, if you think it'll be all right with your parents."

"Naw, they'd love to have you. So it's set. When we're through here we'll go to my place. It's about three and a half miles. Tomorrow my dad will drive us over or let me have the car."

Most of the men in the battery were new to army life, though there were some "older" members who had been called to duty at an earlier date and ultimately sent to Texas in the vain search for the Mexican revolutionary, Poncho Villa. These men quickly became known as the "border veterans." The neophytes of the battery, including Pat and Hank, were immediately introduced to drill and military discipline.

On the morning of July first, Pat and Hank were up at 5:30 a.m. so they could be at the campsite in time for 6:30 reveille. This was followed by calisthenics. The first sergeant seemed to think that the unit needed to be put into competitive physical condition before breakfast. The moaning and groaning grew louder with each new exercise. If one of the men tried to stop for a quick breather, one of the junior officers, all of who were stationed in the rear, would come forward and goad the slacker on.

After calisthenics, the troops were marched to a local restaurant for a breakfast of powdered eggs, fried bread, and coffee. The stay in Champaign was to be a short one and therefore the field kitchen was not set up.

The meals fed to the troops were of poor quality, lacking in taste, and worst of all in sufficient quantities to allow them to maintain their strength. It didn't take long before they were spending their own money at other local eateries to supplement the inadequate diet. Of course the town boys had at least one regular meal at home. They were much envied by the others, even though the local men would bring cookies and other goodies to share with their out-of-town brethren.

Foot drill for the rookies occupied the rest of the day.

At noon the new Chicago recruits arrived on the train. Their trip down was supervised under the watchful eye of a Lieutenant Allen.

Lieutenant Howard W. Allen had spent all of his adult life in the regular army starting at the rank of private and working his way up to sergeant. At the declaration of war he was immediately promoted to second lieutenant. It did not take long for him to show his disdain for the National Guard, officers and men alike. In loud and disrespectful language, he found fault in everyone. Many of the enlisted men felt that he was trying to impress all within hearing range of his superior wisdom and significance. These frequent outbursts were soon interpreted as nothing but bravado and in fact, it was soon discerned that he was not really the heartless rogue many at first perceived him to be. In truth he wanted the battery to be the best in the regiment, for soon he was as quick to praise, as he was to criticize. One of the border veterans had sarcastically referred to him as "Pappy," a moniker that stuck throughout the war.

Calisthenics and foot drill continued, interrupted only by observance of the Fourth of July holiday. In keeping with the blue laws in effect at the time, the pool halls and movie theaters were closed, leaving the nonresident members of the battery with little to do.

Dan Dennison left the front door of the house open, so guests could just walk in. His wife, Doris, was in the kitchen, making final preparations for their annual Fourth of July party. With the nation on a war footing, most of their military friends would soon be reassigned. Some had already left for new duty stations, either at sea or in Europe.

Dan had requested sea duty and been assigned to command a destroyer, the *Hampton*. This was a brand new ship heavily armed and outfitted for escorting convoys. She was equipped with the new electronic hydrophone, a system designed to locate submarines by the sound the U-boats produce while submerged. Time was short for Doris and Dan, as many of their friends would be gone next year.

Captain Montgomery was coming to the party, even though he was scheduled to sail back to England the following Wednesday. His short stay in America had been extended several times because of the declaration of war on Germany by the United States, but now his work in Washington was finished and it was time for him to get back to the war.

Dan went into the kitchen at the back of the house and sat down at the table while Doris finished with the tray of hors d'oeuvre.

"You know, Doris, this may be the last party we'll have for awhile. Quite a few of our old friends have been reassigned, and I think most will be leaving Washington before the summer is over."

Doris and Dan had been married upon his graduation from college. They had always been of like mind and seem to know each other's thoughts. She had pretty auburn hair just beginning to show highlights of gray, stood just three inches shorter than Dan, and had a striking figure.

"Well, with you going to sea again, I'm glad we decided to keep the house here. On top of all this turmoil with the war, it would be difficult to move to a new place. With you and Ike both facing duty overseas, I'm going to be awfully lonely. At least Sarah Baker and Susan Miller are staying here so I'll have somebody to talk to."

"I know it's tough being a Navy wife. I want to go to sea but I don't want to leave you alone. I guess there's no answer short of the war ending."

Doris continued working with the tray, lost in her thoughts.

"Well, I sure hope Ike gets some leave before I have to go to sea," he said. "I miss not having him home this summer."

"Well, at least I should be able to see him if he has to go to France. I would think he could stop here before he ships out." Doris sat down at the table across from Dan, and took his hand in hers. "This stupid war! I just wish they'd leave us alone."

"We've had a good life, and a little rain must fall sometime. I think this is our sometime. Things will get better, so let's enjoy this day." Dan squeezed Doris's hand and then stood up. "I'd better mix some martinis."

"Yes, and I need to finish with the condiments before the guests arrive."

After he mixed the drinks, Dan went to the front door as a taxi pulled up in front. Out jumped Captain Montgomery.

"Our first guest has arrived!"

"Oh dear, I'm not ready yet."

"It's Bob Montgomery. I'll entertain him till you're ready."

"Oh, I'll come out right now. I want to wish him a bon voyage before the others get here."

As Bob came up the walk, Dan went out on the porch to greet him. "Bob, welcome. We're glad you could come."

"I wouldn't miss this for anything. I thought it would be a great show to see how you colonists would celebrate your Independence Day."

"Oh, we do it up big. Are you ready to head home?"

"Yes, sir, I am. I will miss the American hospitality, but it's time for me to be off."

"Well, we'll miss you. May I get you a martini?"

"Yes, thank you. Say, I understand you have a new command? A destroyer, a four-piper, I believe."

"Your sources are good. She's the USS Hampton. Just commissioned and I'll be on a shakedown cruise within a month. As a matter of fact, our first duty will be escorting a convoy in November."

"You know, you were right about those convoys," Montgomery said. "They seem to work. The Jerries are finding it harder to attack the merchantmen. The amount of tonnage getting to both England and France is saving the day. Thanks for your assistance. By the way did I tell you that I, too, put in for sea duty?"

"No, you didn't. Has your request been acted upon?"

Montgomery shook his head. "Not yet, but I expect to have the reassignment orders when I get home. I've requested command on a Q-Ship. I have a score to settle with the Jerries. I'd like to sink some of those subs."

"Best of luck to you and write me the details, I want to keep track of you."

"I sure will, Dan. By the way, how about your son Isaac? Is he going to be here today? I would like to meet him."

"No, Ike is still at the University of Illinois. He graduated in May and he's been commissioned in the army as a second lieutenant. We expected him home for a short leave, but he stayed at the university to take his ground school in preparation for becoming a pilot. I hear Doris coming down the hall and our other guests will be arriving soon, so prepare yourself for a great celebration, we're going to have a good old-fashioned barbecue before the fireworks."

Pat and Hank slept late into the morning of July fourth and enjoyed a huge breakfast prepared by Hank's mother. Before noon, the two young men, using Hank's father's sedan, paid a visit to Betsy, Hank's girlfriend. The three of them took a short ride out of town to a small park near the Sangamon River, where they rented a boat and just drifted on the river for a time, talking and relaxing.

In the late afternoon they joined the other members of the battery at the Community Park, located in downtown Champaign. The picnic was followed by a fireworks display, all sponsored by the local chamber of commerce.

The next day, calisthenics and foot drill continued. In the afternoon the rookies started their equitation, or horse drill. Many of the recruits, especially those from Chicago, had never been on a horse before, let alone bareback. The ability to sit astride a mount is difficult, to say the least. These rookies were unfamiliar with horses and found it almost impossible to mount them in two counts, even after a demonstration and long explanation by Lt. Coffey. After what seemed like forever, the last student was astride and the group began circling the field, encouraged loudly by the border veterans with shouts of "Ride 'em, cowboy."

This part of the drill went well as long as the horses were at a walk but when the lieutenant ordered them to trot, chaos reigned. As the horses picked up the pace, the recruits grasped at anything, manes, reins or whatever was at hand to stay aboard. As they bounced on their steeds each seemed to land on a different spot on the animals' posterior. In his attempt not to be thrown Paul Driscol leaned forward to put his arms around the nag's neck but failed in the attempt and did a somersault over its head when it bucked. Only Lieutenant Coffey's roar, "Who the hell told you, you could get down?" prevented the other recruits from trying this ploy in order to end their pain and suffering.

Both Pat and Hank had been reared on farms and were familiar with horses and even riding bareback. The antics of the other recruits made it possible for them to join in with the border veterans for a good laugh.

After the riding drill the recruits were introduced to the currycomb and brush. Many found out, through painful experience, that while working in a corral of horses, one must keep his feet active or be stepped on. This experience soon led many of the recruits to scheme all sorts of plans in order to become the cannoneers of the battery and leave horse tending to more experienced hands. Neither Pat nor Hank wanted to spend the war caring for the animals, so they were careful not to show their talents too openly.

That night quite a few of the rookies were in great pain. Tom Brooks, one of the principle sufferers, was unable to find rest in any position. He was reduced to some choice words of profanity in vehemently expressing his feelings about the war, the army, and particularly horses. "What exasperates me the most is that I volunteered for this punishment," he whined as he rubbed his backsides with both hands.

For the recruits the days that followed were filled with drill and hard work, calisthenics before breakfast followed by marching. The break at mid-morning involved learning how to salute and show respect for the superiors, corporals on up. When this drill was completed, the men worked on the grounds around the tents, trenching, digging latrines, and lining the walkways with rocks. This was followed by standing gun drill in which all of the men joined in, including the border veterans. Standing gun drill was essentially a simulation of loading and firing the cannon.

In the afternoon, they would start with the equitation drill, then tend to the animals and finally, clean the equipment.

On Sunday, July 8, after standing gun drill, the battery supply sergeant issued the troops mess kits, saddlebags, haversacks, pup tents, and other personal items. After receiving the equipment Hank whispered to Pat. "This stuff seems to be left over from the Civil War, I think it would be more useful in a museum." Pat laughed out loud and was quickly shushed by one of the junior officers. The men were then carefully measured for uniforms that were to be issued at Fort Sheridan. This turned out to be no less than a practical joke by the War Department, for when the uniforms were issued they were just handed to the men without regard to size or fit.

At evening retreat a detail lowered the flag to the bugler's off-tune rendition of "To the Colors". From all appearances, the ceremony went well. As Pat stood at attention during the observance, he saw that Lt. Allen was red in the face and appeared livid over something.

When the ceremony was over, the men found out what had gone wrong. Corporal Bayless had allowed the flag to touch the ground. Lt. Allen sprang into action with a tongue-lashing none would soon forget. "You inept clod-hopper! The American flag is never to touch the ground under any circumstance. Even in your final act of life itself you are to see that the flag is protected. You got that?" His voice was undoubtedly heard throughout the county as he made the entire battery feel a grievous crime had been committed. This was not a lesson in showing respect to the flag, but a clear warning that this National Guard unit was not going to be haphazard in any aspect of its performance. They were going to look and act like the regular army.

The next day the battery began moving all men and equipment so they could join the rest of the regiment at Fort Sheridan. This post was located on the north side of Chicago along the shore of Lake Michigan.

A detail was assigned the laborious task of loading the horses, rolling equipment, and miscellaneous supplies at the depot. The rest of the men dismantled the camp, taking down the tents, packing those items that needed to go with the battery, and storing away those items that weren't being moved.

The local citizens had planned a picnic dinner at a community park near the train station for the men before they left.

It was truly a sight to behold as the battery personnel marched to the festivities. Each individual had a blanket roll slung over one shoulder and many carried saddlebags on the other. Most were without complete uniforms and many of those were dressed totally in civilian garb. From their colorful oxford shoes to their straw hats they presented quite a sight to the citizens of Champaign. Each man had been issued an ammunition belt that was buckled around the waist. From this hung an ancient haversack that swung as the men marched hitting them in the buttocks, adding impetus to each step.

After the meal, a local band played several selections by Sousa. This was followed by speeches by the mayor and a judge from Chicago who was in town visiting a son who was enrolled in the aviation school at the university.

According to these men, the war would end suddenly as the enemy became aware that such a magnificent military organization as Battery F was being placed on the line, opposite them.

Call to National Service

Pat sat back in his seat, finally able to relax, at least during the trip to Fort Sheridan. He thought back over the last labor intensive hours spent just getting the battery moved and loaded on the train. "Is it going to be this tough every time we have to move?" He said to himself. "If so we'll never get to France."

He thought back to the wonderful send-off party of the night before and how afterward they'd spread their blankets on the ground to get some shut-eye at around eleven. He and Hank had talked for half an hour or so until finally drifting off into a deep sleep. Then at 2:45 a.m. they were rudely awakened and marched to the train. Here, instead of getting onto the coaches, they had to finish loading the remaining equipment on the flat cars and then their personal effects in the baggage car.

Many of the local folks, particularly family members, were up early and came to the station to wish them luck and to say goodbye. A nearby restaurant had made sandwiches for their noon meal and after they collected their box lunches they boarded the passenger cars where the guardsmen fought over the seats, each wanting to sit by the window. Pat and Hank found two seats together at about the middle of their car and were able at last to settle down. Soon after they heard the engine's whistle, followed by a mighty surge and the train was underway. Though the local members of the battery were sad about leaving, the new Chicago recruits' attitude was best summed up in Paul Driscol's statement, "In just a week, I spent a whole year in Champaign."

All of the men were anxious about what lay ahead as each man anticipated the biggest adventure of his life.

To Pat it seemed as if they had been traveling forever, though he was not complaining. The trip was not fast, as the train had to pull to a siding every time another train was encountered. All of the men were tired and many were dozing. Some of the young men were talking, some were reading, and others were playing cards.

They had been in the coach for over four hours before the train finally reached the outskirts of Chicago. Hank had fallen asleep, his head against Pat's shoulder. As Pat was contemplating a way to move and stretch without disturbing Hank, the train came to a rather jerky and abrupt stop, tossing some of the unprepared to the floor. One of the new members, Philip Norwood, a Chicago recruit and an old railroad hand, said they were in the process of switching to the Belt Railroad track that would take the battery north to the gates of Ft. Sheridan.

Hank was wide-awake now and all the men were looking or leaning out the windows, which had been opened earlier in an attempt to cool the men from the stifling heat. As they passed through the city, many local citizens came out to wave at the troop train. At one point in their travels, they observed patrons standing out in front of a saloon, holding up their beer mugs in salute to the troops.

Finally, at 2:30 p.m. the train came to a stop near the main gate of their destination.

The regimental commander, a Colonel Henry J. Reilly, had anticipated the battery's arrival. He and his staff, along with the regimental band, were at the siding to greet the troops as they stepped from the train. After off-loading and a short greeting ceremony, the battery formed in squads and marched through the gate and to their new home, a site on the north side of the reservation abutting Highwood. This whole area had been set aside for the regiment and named Camp Geismar in honor of a little known French hero. This area was not much more than a stump filled swamp that had been partially cleared. It was here that Battery F set up their tents and prepared to stay. It was here, also, that the new recruits met the new first sergeant.

Just prior to leaving Champaign-Urbana, First Sergeant Kenneth Heath transferred to the Air Service and stayed in Champaign so he could complete the ground school at the university. As a result the battery was without a first sergeant during the trip. However as the battery traveled north, regimental headquarters appointed a Sergeant Baker to that position.

Sergeant Marion Baker was one of many regular army NCOs that had been assigned to work with and train the Guard units that were being mobilized. Prior to coming to Fort Sheridan, Sergeant Baker had been with the troops under General Pershing's command, trying to chase down Pancho Villa. In the years before going to Mexico, he had served at numerous posts around the country and around the world. Shortly after he enlisted, in 1898, he had fought in the Philippines during the Spanish-American War. He stood an even six feet, he had a back as straight as a ramrod. When topped off with a campaign hat, he gave the appearance, at least to the recruits, of a man ten feet tall.

The military life was all he knew and it was up to him to turn these green young men into the best artillery battery on the face of the earth.

Camp Geismar was to be their new home for the next six weeks. Here the rookies would learn to become soldiers and the older members would have some of those old civilian habits trained out of them. Camp Geismar was an area that covered the north end of the Fort Sheridan reservation. The land stretched from the shoreline of Lake Michigan to the bedroom community of Highwood. The ground on which the regiment was to set up camp was swampy with numerous stumps of old trees scattered throughout. The area had been partially cleared by a previous tenant but it needed a great deal of work before it would be livable.

When the battery arrived at their site, Sergeant Baker was there, waiting for them. He had the men separate into two groups—recruits and those with experience.

It had been cloudy all day and the smell of rain was in the air. As the men began setting up camp, the sky opened up and rain came down in torrents. It wasn't long before they all were soaked to the skin. It was impossible to stay dry. The tents were without flooring and worst of all, they hadn't been trenched properly. The water was soon flowing over the ground and puddling in the low spots. Pat's shoes and feet were soaked.

Once the tents were erected along what became known as "recruit row," the men huddled under the awnings of their tents. While they were contemplating what to do next, they heard a loud commotion and banging at the north end of the row. It was none other than Sergeant Baker running a baton around the inside of an empty metal oil drum. "Out of the tents, form up in ranks. It's time we do a little work around here."

"But sarge, it's raining," came a meek voice from behind Hank.

"Well, if ya don't like the rain it's time ya learned to. You! Get down in the mud and give me 25 push-ups, that oughta make ya learn to love this hallowed ground that's gonna be your new home. The rest of you men form a line, taller ones on the left. This is the US of A Army and you are going to learn to be soldiers. So don't any of ya say nothing. You cain't go home to mama, it's too late fur that. You're here for the duration. So the sooner you get used to it the better it's gonna be fur the both of us. My name is Sergeant Baker and my job is to keep y'all among the living. When you address me you *will* say Sergeant Baker or *sir*. Y'all got that? Now count off."

So this was the beginning of a new phase in Pat's life. Everything was new, and so far not so grand and glorious. He had high ideals and a strong sense of right and wrong, and early on he'd made up his mind that the Germans were wrong in their fight with the Allied armies in France. It felt right to enter this war.

Sergeant Baker had the men break out picks and shovels and start the trenching work around the tents. Next came the folding canvas cots. Their labors were eased when the rain let up and then eventually stopped.

The regimental commander, Colonel Reilly, was a man of superior intelligence and had a thorough military background. He was a graduate of West Point and had truly earned the right to command, unlike many other Guard commanders who had been appointed to their position through a political patronage system. His job was monumental, for he had to mold a fighting team out of a collection of men with greatly varied backgrounds, from tradesmen to professionals and from farmers to teachers.

Soon after the outbreak of war, in 1914, Colonel Reilly was on the Western Front as a news correspondent and as a military observer. It was during this time spent in France that he became a student of modern warfare. He was able to study and analyze the strategies of both the Allies and the Central powers. The colonel was a stickler for discipline. He knew that an organization lacking in strict control was its own worst enemy.

The men of the First Illinois Artillery were proud to be under his leadership and their affection and admiration intensified as they benefited from his superior judgment during their service. The regiment became known as "Reilly's Bucks," a name of which each man was proud.

The first notes of the bugle sounded at 5:30 a.m. Before the last note there was a loud commotion at the far end of recruit row as Sergeant Baker marched down the walkway.

"Get off your backs and on your feet. It's reveille and time to get moving. You have a big day ahead of yous."

Pat tried to shake the sleep from his head and get up. This turned out to be a little more difficult than he thought it would be. The long hours spent in setting up camp didn't allow them to get to bed until after 11:30 p.m. In addition to the late hour, they had to sleep in their wet clothes on the canvas-slung cots. He seemed to ache all over.

"Now listen to me, you recruits. You're in the army now and everything you do will be regulated by me." Sergeant Baker shouted from the north end of recruit row. "Before this day is over you will begin to act and look like soldiers. First you will police this area so that it will be spic and span. There will be no trash of any kind inside this area. You got that?"

Silence followed and a few nodded their heads.

"You men aren't with me," roared Sergeant Baker. "When I ask you a question I expect each man to be standing in front of his tent at attention and to respond at the top of his voice, 'Yes, Sir!' You got that?"

This was followed by brief scurrying to the front of the tents and a loud, resounding, though dissonant "Yes, sir!"

All of the young men began to clean their respective areas, gathering items strewn about since their arrival the day before. Before the bugle sounded again for breakfast, Sergeant Baker had all of the enlisted men in the battery doing calisthenics. It was disorganized and out of sync, but it was a beginning. Then the bugle sounded and they marched to breakfast.

The "old-timers" hadn't been idle since their arrival in camp, and had spent most of the time cleaning up the area and helping set up the field kitchen.

After eating, the recruits stopped by the barber, where everyone had their hair cut to the scalp.

Next stop was the quartermaster, where they were issued some of their uniforms and other necessities. Clothing was handed out with no or little regard for size or fit. There were numerous shortages and few of the men received complete uniforms.

Each man received shoes, which seemed to come in sizes either too large or too small. Next came the dress uniforms. The pants were riding breeches, large in the seat and thighs, and then tapered to the knee. Next came the wool coat with a high collar that had a nasty habit of rubbing the neck raw. This was all topped off with a broad brimmed campaign hat. Lastly came the leg wraps, strips of cloth six foot long and about three and a half inches wide, that were to be wound around the legs from the knees to the foot. These had to be put on with care—if too loose, they would fall, and if too tight, they cut off circulation.

After returning to their tents, the recruits went through a lesson on bed making and the arrangement of personal items in a military manner.

The object was to get every item in the tent as uniform as possible.

Next came the lesson in saluting.

"Men, you will salute anything that moves," Sergeant Baker said, "other than another lowly recruit such as yourselves. Your personal area around your bunk will be spotless and uncluttered at all times. You got that?"

"Yes, sir."

The sergeant's face turned dark as he barked out his instructions. He clenched both fists and placed them on his hips and bent slightly forward from the waist. "Failure to follow rules will result in some extra duty. Extra duty means KP duty, policing the parade ground or the area around these here tents. If you all don't perform the way I like, we could go fur an extra walk. That would mean about 20 miles with full field pack. So y'all better plan on some work. Before we are through with training you will be able to cover long distances on foot and you are going to outfight the Huns in hand-to-hand combat. Any questions?" All voices remained silent.

Once the housekeeping chores were completed and the recruits changed into the uniform of the day, they headed for the practice field and began in earnest to learn military discipline. Standing at attention, at ease, marching in step, and all the elements that go into the making of a soldier.

At one point, while standing at ease, Pat leaned over and said to Hank, "I'll sure be glad when dinnertime comes, I'm ready to hit the sack. This seems like it's been going on forever."

"Pat, don't you know it's only 10:30 in the morning? This day has just begun."

Pat looked at him in disbelief. "You're kidding me. I thought it had to be at least 5 p.m. I was ready to call it a day. This has to be the longest day of my life. I hope we make it."

"Yeah, I know what you mean. Here comes Baker, so be ready to do it again. I don't think that we'll ever be able to please that one."

When they were finished with their foot drill, the recruits went back to work on the battery's encampment until the midday meal.

The afternoon was spent with the rest of the battery in equitation drill, horse breaking, cleaning harness, and equipment, and making improvements to the site. The battery streets needed to be leveled and trenched, brush and stumps had to be removed, and the area around the tents needed attention.

During their third day at Fort Sheridan, the men of the battery formed up and marched to the infirmary, where they were given their physical exams, performed by the regular army doctors.

Upon arrival all were told to strip and form a line. This indignity that of walking around while being poked, probed, and prodded lasted all too long. Five of the men failed to pass, due to one physical limitation or another, the primary culprit being high blood pressure. These men were subsequently discharged and sent home.

At an assembly after the physicals, the men agreed that each would contribute fifty cents per man per month toward the salary of a good cook, provided they could find one and induce him to enlist. The food had been terrible. The appointed cooks, Girard and Goode, had a penchant for burning everything, including the oatmeal. When they received a quarter of beef they tried their best to find a way to turn good beef into leather. Their worst fault was that they would flavor coffee with an ample dose of salt.

On the first Saturday at Fort Sheridan, Colonel Reilly inspected the camp. Everyone was nervous about what he would think of the job they were doing. Lieutenant "Pappy" Allen and Sergeant Baker were everywhere urging the battery to do a better job and clean everything to perfection. This paid off, for Colonel Reilly soon announced his satisfaction with the way the battery was progressing. Passes were even issued to those who were not on duty Sunday and for those who were in possession of a complete uniform.

On Monday, work on the encampment continued, as well as the drill work. In the afternoon all of the men were, again, marched to the infirmary and given the first para-typhoid inoculation. Hank was amazed that some of the fellows fainted. Claude Bedowski, one of the better physical specimens of the battery, quivered like jelly and fell off in a dead faint when the needle penetrated his skin. The razzing that followed was merciless.

When the showers were finally erected on July 17, Pat said to Hank, "I think some of the fellows are getting ripe. Even me!"

"But you know," Hank replied, "it's hard to get clean in the allotted five minutes with cold water and that stuff they call soap."

Another meeting of the battery was called for that afternoon and Captain Arnold addressed the men. Captain Arnold was the battery commander and knew little of the military and less about command. He was an assistant professor of biology and looked the part. He was a small man with thick glasses and thinning hair and looked as if he should have been in a library doing research instead of leading an artillery battery. He had been a member of the battery since coming to the University of Illinois eight years before. Fortunately his junior officers were able to keep the command under control, and it was through the efforts of these men that Battery F maintained such a high efficiency rating.

"We are to be part of the second battalion," Captain Arnold said. "Our new battalion commander is Captain Noble, who is replacing Major Donaldson who has failed to pass his physical. The first Battalion will be under the command of Major Green. The preparation of the camp is about finished and I've directed the sergeants, working with Sergeant Baker, to select men for the gun crews. All men, including recruits, will be considered. These selections are not set in stone and there will be changes. I've further directed that a carpentry crew be assembled in order to erect a screened-in area for the kitchen."

From an indiscernible source, a voice said, "That may keep the flies out of the food, but it sure won't keep the cooks away."

Snickering from the ranks followed this declaration.

Captain Arnold was somewhat taken aback by this outburst, but chose to ignore it and continued. "As you know, the camp has more than the First Illinois Field Artillery stationed here. So we are going to share some of our equipment. Case in point, the artillery officers in training will use our horses and guns in the mornings and we'll have them in the afternoons. For those of you not assigned to gun squads, you will work at the corral in order to break in the new horses. Finally and most importantly, the entire regiment will be mustered into federal service tomorrow."

The days that followed became monotonous for the new recruits. The bugle now regulated their lives—from revelry to lights-out they were constantly training. They barely realized that they were getting stronger and physically fit; nor did they realize that they were beginning to look and act like soldiers.

The food did not improve, and the battery, so far, had not been able to entice an experienced cook to enlist. This proved to be a financial gold mine for Milly's Delicatessen located just outside the campgrounds in Highwood, adjacent to the battery. Their specialty was sandwiches, along with soft drinks and pie a-la-mode. Before mealtime, the self-proclaimed epicureans of the battery would file by the field kitchen to take a sniff of the air, check the menu, and if it did not meet their standards, which was the usual case, off they would go to Milly's.

After three weeks the recruits were no longer separated from the rest of the battery for morning drill in military discipline. Sergeant Baker and the other NCOs had done their best in bringing the recruits along and had more pressing duties in preparing the battery for war.

Near the end of July, Pat and Hank were selected to train as mechanics. They, along with Tom Wagner and Paul Driscol would work under Head Mechanic Martyn and keep the four cannons in "perfect" working order. Pat was disappointed that he wasn't selected as a cannoneer as he had dreams of firing the shells into the enemy lines. "At least," he said to Hank after their selection as mechanics, "we'll be with the guns during the fighting rather than in the rear echelon with the animals."

Hank nodded his agreement, but added, dolefully, "It would have been better firing and loading the guns."

On July 26, an exhibition battery was formed from the various batteries of the regiment. Their express purpose was to present a mounted artillery exercise for the benefit of the many visitors who were coming to the camp. This included the many dignitaries as well as the ordinary folk who came to Fort Sheridan on the weekends to visit the family members who belonged to the First Illinois Artillery.

On that same day, an order was issued for wooden floors to be placed in all tents. Up to this time the weather had been relatively dry, but when it did rain, life in the tents became unbearable. Even a moderate shower would quickly overflow the perimeter trenching and come rushing through. The addition of the flooring would improve the lot of the cannoneers.

Even though an order had been issued for flooring, there was precious little wood planking to be had. On the night of July 30, Pat was abruptly shaken from his sleep. Opening his eyes, he saw a large form standing over him. Before he could say a thing, the man put his finger to his lips and whispered, "Shh, it's me, Bayless."

"What's up, Jack?" Pat asked somewhat groggily.

"Sergeant Martyn has located a truck-load of wood, so we're going to get it."

"At midnight?"

"Yeah, so get dressed and meet me out in front in five minutes."

Pat and Hank and the other two men in their tent dressed in silence, shivering a little in the cold night air, and rushed out to join the other six men for the operation.

Sergeant Martyn had located a truckload of lumber, destined for Battery D, and parked about one hundred yards from Battery F's field kitchen. The men assembled in the pitch darkness and lined up in front of Sergeant Martyn. He was a big man with dark hair, broad shoulders and strength unmatched by few other men in the battery. He, in a harsh whisper, quickly filled them in on the plan.

"We'll go to the truck and when I get behind the wheel and release the brake, you guys push it. We'll take it to the other side of our camp. There we'll unload it and then push it back to where it was originally parked. Now be quiet. The two guards closest to the truck are our men, Bedowski and Jordan, and they're in on the plan. They won't even know you're there. But the others are from Battery D, so keep quiet."

Off they went into the dark. When they got to the truck, Sergeant Martyn climbed up and into the cab and released the brake with a loud thud that reverberated throughout the camp. All of the men froze in their places, holding their breaths. After about 20 seconds of silence, Sergeant Martyn leaned out of the cab and said in a loud whisper, "What the hell you waiting for, daylight? Get to your pushing."

The men let out their collective breaths and put their shoulders into their labors. Soon they had the truck rolling. Hank stumbled over a rock and went sprawling facedown in the dirt. Pat couldn't contain himself and started snickering, and soon they were all laughing so hard they could hardly push the truck.

Sergeant Martyn leaned out of the driver's seat again. "What in tarnation is going on? You boys'll wake the whole camp. Now shut up."

When they finally got to the other end of the encampment, they started to unload their treasure.

Pat and Hank were on either end of a load of boards they'd just taken off of the truck and Pat, in the lead, was backing into an empty tent in which they were hiding the planks until they could be assembled into the floors. As he was backing into the tent, he ran into someone and said "Hey, look where…" Then he suddenly realized he had bumped into Lt. Allen and almost lost his grip, nearly dropping the load. "Oh, sorry, sir. I."

"Don't worry about it, soldier. Just don't make so much noise."

It turned out that the whole plan had been Pappy's idea.

After the wood was unloaded, the men pushed the truck back to its original position and headed back to their tents and bed. The whole operation had taken a mere two hours.

After he was in bed again, Pat said to his tent mates, "I was never so scared as when I bumped into Pappy. I thought we'd bought the farm and would end up in the brig, and here it was his idea all along."

The mystery of the missing wood went unsolved by the men of Battery D.

The Saturday routine consisted of an early morning inspection, followed by the issuance of passes to those who had a complete uniform. Those who were on duty or under some sort of disciplinary action were not eligible to leave the post.

There was a great deal of swapping of apparel items among the men in order to get a complete uniform together for those individuals who wanted a pass, usually for some of the Chicago boys who wanted to go home for the day.

On special visitors' days, usually on Sundays, the exhibition battery would display their skills by galloping onto the parade ground, setting up the cannon, and firing a few blank rounds. They would then reattach the field piece to the hitch and gallop off into the smoke. Visitors were always favorably impressed.

Those individuals who did not want—or those who were not eligible—to leave the post on Sundays normally stayed around and created their own entertainment. Pat and Hank fell into this category.

They took part in singing, short skits, and even movies provided by the YMCA. There was usually a keen boxing competition pitting the battery's pugilists against the fighters of rival units. Each battery fielded its own baseball team and the one from Battery F was unbeatable. Many of these men had played university ball and offered great talent. Paul Stuart, the player manager, was a standout pitcher on the U of I team and therefore carried the battery through many no-hitters.

On their time off, some of the men of the regiment took to swimming in Lake Michigan. The local residents of the exclusive North Shore took this as a personal affront, as few of the men had suits and entered the water naked. Those North Shore residents who used their yachts to run up and down the coast were the first to launch a complaint. Finally a formal protest was filed with the Fort Sheridan command and an order was issued for the arrest of any man found swimming in the lake without proper attire.

One Sunday, no less than fifty men were put under arrest and paraded to the brig. As there was not enough room for them, they were released to their company commanders with a severe reprimand. The local commanders thought it to be somewhat humorous and let the men off the hook with light punishment.

During the battery's stay in Chicago, the food did not improve. In fact it deteriorated to the point that it was almost inedible. Things came to a head one Monday morning when Lieutenant Allen, after a weekend of imbibing too heavily, demanded a cup of coffee to help clear out the cobwebs. This was one of those mornings when the inept cooks had heavily sweetened the coffee with salt.

Pappy, after taking one large swallow, bellowed so loudly that he awakened the whole camp. He announced in rather profane language that the men deserved better than this and that something had to be done immediately to procure for the battery, the services of an experienced cook.

A young second lieutenant just assigned to the battery, by the name of Robert Wynland, was ordered to find a cook within a week. Bewildered as to what to do about this request, he called the newspapers, local restaurants and other agencies in his search. One of these agencies suggested that he call the Culinary Association of Chicago. This he did, and after much discussion with various staff members, he hit upon a likely prospect, Henry Pontious. Henry, who had been looking for a way to return to his treasured Greece, saw this as an opportunity to get him there. The added incentive of the 50 cents per man per month was enough to get him to agree to enlist.

On August 1, Henry showed up in camp at ten in the morning with an apple pie in his hand and presented himself to Captain Arnold and Lieutenants Allen and Wynland. After a brief tasting session, the contract was signed and the kitchen fell under the supervision of a real cook. Other than his love for sharp spices and, in particular, ginger for flavoring stew, the food improved beyond expectations.

Shortly after the first of August, the regiment received the new khaki uniforms. For the first time since they had entered the National Guard, Pat and Hank were able to dress completely in government-issued clothing. With the advent of uniforms for everybody, demand for passes increased. Those who were now eligible to meet the dress code could leave the camp on a pass. Those lacking funds to go into Chicago had to find their entertainment in the neighboring suburbs. The men that liked—or at least could tolerate opera—would go to Ravinia Park, find a dark corner and climb over the fence, unseen by the park's security. Once on the grounds they could pretend that they were regular visitors and mingle with the young local society debutantes, particularly those who were accompanied by men without uniforms.

August also brought an increase in the tempo of drill. The men all knew they were not going to be at Fort Sheridan forever. Calisthenics, foot drill, gun drill, and horse breaking became the order of the day every day. Sergeant Baker was everywhere whipping the battery into combat readiness. When they weren't drilling, the mechanics were learning to tear the guns down and then put them back together. There was also guard duty, which seemed to come around all too often.

Sunday was the only day the men could kick back and relax, provided they weren't scheduled for guard duty or some other sort of commitment.

It was on the 12th of August that the country learned of the creation of a new division, henceforth, to be called, the Rainbow Division. From that day forward, the First Illinois Artillery was to be known as the 149th US Field Artillery. It was also at this time that the regimental command redoubled their efforts to bring the manpower up to wartime requirements. When the regiment was recruited to strength, they would join the other elements of the division at a staging area on the East Coast and then embark for France.

Towards the middle of the month Captain Arnold made several changes in the enlisted ranks that ultimately resulted in a promotion for Pat. He was now a corporal. This was not a promotion he expected and soon after he became aware that many of his buddies held the rank in contempt. It took some time before he felt accepted by those who, heretofore, had been his friends, Hank being the only exception.

It seemed like years since Ike had decided to enter the flying service. Actually, it had been just three months. Now here he sat in the back seat of the OX-5 powered Jenny, ready for his first solo flight.

The Curtiss JN-4D, or Jenny, was the first aircraft of its type built in the United States. It was a tractor-style biplane with the engine mounted on the front of the enclosed fuselage with a pull-type propeller. This type was being used almost exclusively in the European conflict. Prior to this, all American aircraft were based on the Wright Brothers, open-to-the-wind design with pusher-type engine/propeller combinations. Though the Jenny was not comparable in performance to the fighter aircraft currently being used in the war, it was a great plane for training pilots.

The plane was made primarily from wood and covered with fabric stretched taut with dope. The engine, the 90-horsepower OX-5, was also designed and built by Glenn Curtiss and was a heavy, underpowered, water-cooled engine, best described as a failure just looking for a place to happen. Because of the great weight and low energy output of the engine, the Jenny's wings were particularly large. The struts and bracing wire held the plane together in flight and the wires were well known for the harmonic cords that resulted from their vibrations in different flight attitudes. In spite of its many shortcomings, the airplane was docile and easy to fly.

During training flights, the instructor sat in the front cockpit and the student in the rear, and each had an individual set of controls. A solo pilot flew the plane from the rear cockpit in order to maintain proper weight and balance.

The plane had a conventional landing gear. Better stated, it was a tail dragger. The main landing gear struts were mounted on the fuselage at the leading edge of the lower wing and a wooden skid mounted under the tail. The front wheels were close together, giving the plane a strong propensity to ground loop. To minimize wing tip damage in such occurrences, the lower wing tips were provided with curved wooden skids.

Flying had seemed pretty simple to Ike, with his instructor in the front seat grabbing the joystick or kicking the rudder pedals whenever he made a mistake, but now he was to be on his own. His instructor, Bill Bullock, had put him through everything, straight and level flight, turns, stalls and spins. They even had done some low-level flying at about three to four hundred feet.

Bill Bullock, a man of thirty-eight years, was considered too old to fly as a combat pilot in the war. He, therefore, volunteered as a flight instructor to the Aviation Service as his contribution to the war effort. He was a short man with a thick shock of graying black hair that stood nearly straight out from his head. He was a tough taskmaster, and he drove his students hard, but the men thought the world of him.

As Bill was climbing out of the front seat, Ike swallowed hard and concentrated on what his flight instructor was saying.

"Now, Ike, I'll start the engine and pull the chocks from the wheels. I want you to taxi out using the S-turns, as we've done during training, to allow you to see what's in front. Okay?

Ike nodded.

"Taxi to the end of the runway and take off. Don't bother with an engine run-up, it's still warm. Stay in the pattern and land. Taxi back towards the takeoff end of the runway and I'll meet you right over there. Got that?" Bill said, pointing to an area off to their left.

Ike nodded again.

"Good luck. You won't have any problems."

Ike nodded again. His mouth was extremely dry, making it difficult to talk.

Bill stepped down from the wing and walked to the front of the plane. "Switch off, throttle closed?" he shouted. "Switch off, throttle closed." Ike repeated.

Bill pulled the prop through once and then positioned it for starting. "Switch on, throttle cracked."

"Switch on, throttle cracked."

With a strong downward pull on the propeller with both hands, while at the same time swinging his body away from the plane, Bill tried to start the engine. It sputtered and completed three or four revolutions and died.

"Switch off, close throttle."

"Switch off, throttle closed."

Bill positioned the propeller in order to pull it through again and yelled, "Switch on."

Ike responded. Bill pulled it through again and this time the engine started, somewhat rough at first, and continued at a very low rpm.

Bill stepped away from in front of the plane to where Ike could see him and pumped his left hand forward and back from his waist to indicate to Ike to advance the throttle.

As soon as Ike pushed the throttle forward about one half of an inch, the engine came to life at normal idle.

Ike glanced around and saw Bill as he emerged from under the wing with the wooden chocks under his left arm. Bill then stepped out of the way of the plane and saluted. Ike waved back with his right hand as he advanced the throttle further with his left.

The engine's roar increased as it strained to pull the plane forward. It started to move slowly, and Ike increased the throttle some more and the plane gathered speed. As she came to a speed equal to a brisk walk, Ike retarded the throttle a little in order to maintain this speed. As he taxied, he used the rudder to S-turn the plane, first to the right and then to the left, as he had been trained. As Ike drew near the approach end of the runway he checked for traffic around the field. He saw only one other plane and it presented no problem for his takeoff. He pushed full left rudder so that the plane turned into the wind facing the takeoff runway. At the same time, he pushed the throttle full forward. This movement was too fast and the engine coughed and stopped firing. Realizing his predicament, he closed the throttle while the propeller was windmilling and it coughed again and started running normally.

"Whew, that was close." Ike muttered.

"I let that thing stop running right here and there's hell to pay, plus some extra duty."

This time he started easing the throttle open slowly, until it was wide open. The engine rpm came up smoothly to full power and the plane picked up speed as she moved down the grass landing strip.

As the speed continued to increase, he eased some forward pressure on the joystick and the tailskid came up off the ground. When the tail came up, the plane had a tendency to turn slightly to the left. He countered this with right rudder in order to keep the plane moving straight ahead.

As the airspeed increased past 40 mph, he began to add a little backpressure and the plane seemingly jumped into the air. It surprised Ike that the plane came up so fast, but then it came to him—no instructor. The plane was at least 180 pounds lighter. What a difference this made in overall performance. He let the plane climb to 500 feet and began a left turn onto the crosswind leg of the traffic pattern.

He continued to climb till he was about a half mile from the runway, and turned left again using coordinated movements on the controls. He continued to climb on the downwind leg until he was 800 feet above the ground, at which point he set up a straight and level cruise and reduced power to about 70 percent of that available. When he was opposite the spot on the runway where he wanted to touchdown, he reduced power to idle and set up his best glide angle. He then performed his pre-landing check and soon turned left onto his base leg of the pattern. While on the base leg he looked for other traffic in the pattern. Seeing none, he began his last left turn onto final approach. Here he added a little power to clear the engine and insure that it was still running and to clear any ice buildup that may have developed in the carburetor. Everything checked out fine.

The glide continued as he approached the touchdown point. He'd misjudged his rate of descent a little and added some power in order to make the field. When he was sure that he could make the threshold of the runway, he reduced power back to an idle again.

As his altitude reached 10 to 15 feet above the grass landing strip, he started adding backpressure to the control stick in order to slow the plane down and to break the glide. As he got closer to the ground, he gradually pulled the stick back further and further until it was completely in his lap when the wheels touched the ground. A perfect full stall landing.

Ike felt pleased with his performance. It was the best landing he'd ever made.

"Wow."

He took his feet off of the rudders and let go of the joystick. "This is easy."

The plane then took an immediate right turn and headed off at right angles to the runway.

"Oh my God! I ground looped."

Ike looked over his shoulder and sure enough, there was Bill Bullock at a full run.

When Bill reached the plane, he was out of breath and it took a few seconds before he could speak. "You okay?"

Ike nodded. He was really going to get it now.

"Well, that sure was a honey of a landing. Next time don't let go of everything until the plane stops rolling. Fortunately you didn't drag that wing tip and break something. Now I want you to taxi back to the runway and take her around three more times. Make them full stop landings and when you're through, take her to parking and tie her down. Then meet me in operations. Don't forget, keep your hands and feet on the controls until you are stopped."

Ike couldn't believe his ears. He was being commended and allowed to fly some more. "Yes, sir!" Ike said, grinning.

This time, he would keep control of the plane after touchdown.

The next solo landings were all right but not as good as the first one, with the exception that he maintained control once he was on the ground.

When he completed the third landing he taxied to parking, shut down the engine, and tied the plane down. He then walked towards the operations shack for debriefing with a feeling of exhilaration.

"If I have to go to war, this was surely the way to go," he mused to himself.

After Pat had been made a corporal, one of the men in the squad, Claude Bedowski, took particular pleasure in giving him a hard time. After an order was given Claude would refuse to do it, saying he was just too tired, or mimic Pat's voice, or animate his response to such an extreme that it would get a big laugh from the others. This was an unbearable situation for Pat and soon others in the squad started giving him a hard time, too.

It reached a boiling point one night when a book came flying through the air and hit Pat on the side of the head.

"Gee, I'm sorry, I was aiming at the Kaiser," Bedowski said, followed by a roar of laughter from the others.

"That's it, Bedowski. You and me out behind the latrine."

This is just what Claude wanted to hear, and the whole squad plus some others who were nearby went up for grabs and soon all the money was on Claude.

Pat stood an even 5' 11" and weighed in at 175 pounds, soaking wet. Claude, on the other hand, stood 6'2" and weighed 200 pounds; he had very broad shoulders, a muscular build, and prided himself on his physical strength. He had thick blond hair, but when cut close to the scalp, as it was, he appeared bald, that combined with the steely blue eyes gave the appearance of a fierce gladiator. He had been an amateur fighter before enlisting in the army. There was little doubt about the outcome of the fight, before it even got started.

Pat knew he had to do something to earn the respect of his squad, but after he reached the area behind the latrine, he felt that maybe this had gone a little too far.

It was a dark, cloudy night, with the roll of thunder off in the distance. The lightning lit the sky occasionally, giving a surreal appearance to the scene. As the storm approached, the wind picked up and Pat could feel a few drops of rain on his face.

Many from the battery were out watching the spectacle as the fighters started to dance around. Pat held his fists up to protect himself, just like the pictures he had seen of prizefighters in the newspapers. He landed the first blow, a shot off the side of Claude's head. Then out of nowhere Claude hit him with an uppercut that sent Pat to the ground with a bloody chin. He got up, resumed his stance, and started moving around again. Claude moved lightly for a big man and danced quickly on the balls of his feet. He was too fast for Pat and stayed out of range whenever Pat would swing. As soon as Pat would approach, Claude would land a few punches. Another round house swing by Claude sent Pat to the ground again.

Four more times he was put down by one of Claude's blows. He landed a couple of shots but nothing the ex-boxer couldn't handle. After the seventh time down, it was too hard to get up. He just sat there blurry eyed with a bruised ego, a bloody chin and a very sore jaw.

Claude came over and lifted him to his feet and helped him walk back to the tent.

"Anyone whose got the guts to fight me the way Littler here did can be my squad leader anytime. And, if'n any of you wants to argue the point, well, he can meet me behind the latrine."

There were no takers and from that time forward, the squad was Pat's. He was unable to give any useful commands for the next day or so because his jaw hurt whenever he tried to speak, but these were given for him by his new friend, Claude.

Coming to Wartime Strength

As the time for the regiment to move to the East Coast drew ever closer, Colonel Reilly's concern over his manpower requirements grew. There were still many openings in the ranks that needed to be filled before they reached combat readiness. He therefore ordered the formation of a recruiting detail that would establish a headquarters in the heart of Chicago's Loop. The Conway Building was selected as its base of operation and command was established in some unused space on the first floor that had been donated to the regiment. Men were selected from each battery to participate in this effort and those fortunate enough to be selected would earn a five-day pass for their efforts. For reasons Pat was unable to explain but to his great joy, he and Hank had been chosen for the detail. So on Monday, the 13th of August the members of the detail along with some men from the Regimental Band boarded a special train at ten in the morning and by early afternoon they were marching in the first of many parades through the loop carrying banners that read "Berlin or Bust." With the band in the lead playing spirited marching music, all commerce came to a stop as Chicagoans paused to applaud the efforts of the recruiting detail. Every man of serviceable age was asked to enlist and if he refused he was asked to show his registration card or else explain his position to a nearby policeman. The majority of those confronted had their papers in order but preferred to wait until the draft caught up with them.

The recruiters worked hard for twelve to fifteen hours a day and were somewhat successful in their endeavors. By the end of the fourth day, Thursday, they had enlisted more than 100 men, thirty of whom were eventually assigned to Battery F. Later that same evening, the detail was relieved by a new group of men from the regiment and shortly after their return to Fort Sheridan; every man in the first detail received his five-day pass.

He hadn't been able to sleep well and was up and dressed before 4:30 doing what he could to get the slumbering Hank up and to the five a.m. train that would take them from Fort Sheridan to Chicago. There, they had a three-hour layover until they caught the Illinois Central southbound headed for New Orleans. Hank would get off at Champaign and Pat would travel on to Tolono.

After clambering aboard the coach, Pat collapsed into a window seat with Hank next to him on the aisle. His thoughts were on the grueling 10 weeks of training they'd just completed and he felt very weary. Finally there was this break, a pass, almost a week. When word came down that they would receive a five-day leave, Pat had sent a telegram to his folks telling them that he was coming home on Friday, and Friday had finally arrived.

Hank broke a long silence as the train sped through the southern suburbs of Chicago. "I sure hope Betsy comes with my folks to meet the train. Not that I won't enjoy seeing my parents, but that's nothing like seeing my girl. I really missed her."

"Well, you sure wrote her enough. I guess you're lucky to have a girl to come home to. I'll probably spend most of the time on the farm, catching up on some much needed rest and some good home-cooked meals."

They both fell silent again, and Pat sat back watching the Illinois countryside fly by as he listened to the steady click, click, click of the coach wheels as they crossed the rail sections. In a short while he spoke, almost as if to himself. "We'll be leaving for the East Coast in two or three weeks. We may not get to see home again."

"Oh, don't be such a killjoy. We'll be back, and as heroes. Ya know this thing will be over before we even get to fire a field piece. Just think, we're going to France, maybe even to Paris!"

"Yeah, it'll be great. I guess I'm getting a little nostalgic." Again they fell silent, lost in their own thoughts.

Soon the conductor called out, "Champaign. Next Stop."

"Well, I guess this is where I leave you Pat. Are we still going to meet at the frat house next Tuesday morning?" Hank asked.

"Sure thing."

Hank stood up to gather his duffle bag from the overhead rack. After he placed his bag on the seat, he bent down and whispered to Pat, "We look pretty snazzy in our uniforms, don't we?"

"We sure do, I've noticed a lot of the passengers glancing at us. It's a great feeling. Well, I'll see you in four days. Call if anything changes."

"Will do." Hank answered and headed down the aisle.

Pat was on the wrong side of the car to see the platform so he just sat back and closed his eyes.

The next thing he was conscious of was his shoulder being shaken and the conductor standing over him. "Corporal, Tolono's the next stop, about two minutes."

"Oh, thanks." Pat replied as he struggled to get up to retrieve his belongings from overhead. He put on his campaign hat and threw the duffle bag over his left shoulder, picked up his books and newspaper with the other hand, and started up the aisle.

The homecoming was more than he could have wished for. As soon as Pat stepped from the train his mom, dad, and sister, Ethel, and even his uncle, Milo, rushed to greet him. He was showered with hugs, kisses, pats on the back and handshakes. Everyone was talking at once, asking about the training, the trip home, and how he felt, and exclamations as to how good he looked, though Matilda thought him to be too thin. Before he knew it, he was in the old sedan with his dad behind the wheel, his mother in the right front seat and, he, Ethel, and Uncle Milo jammed into the rear seat.

Ethel was Pat's older and only sister who just completed her second year at the University of Illinois Medical School in Chicago. Ethel was of average height, slender, with short brown hair, and she wore glasses giving her a somewhat scholarly look.

"What are you doing home?" Pat exclaimed, when they got underway.

"I just finished up my summer classes and I came home for two weeks, before the fall semester starts." Ethel answered.

"Roy is coming home this weekend too," Matilda chimed in. "And Roger and family will be down for the day on Sunday."

"What's Roy doing?" Pat asked.

"He's now working as a correspondent for the Stars and Stripes, you know the Army's newspaper," his dad answered.

"You mean the whole family will be together this weekend?" Pat asked. "That's great!" he said before anyone could answer.

When they were about a mile from the farm, Pat and Ethel began reminiscing about the countryside. "Do you remember when I fell off the horse over there?" Pat asked Ethel. "Oh, I'll never forget that, and I remember how you got your foot caught in the stirrup and Chico dragged you along as he tried to walk back to the barn."

"I was laughing so hard that I couldn't reach up and free my foot as the dogs were walking along beside me and licking my face," Pat added. "I wasn't free until my shoe finally came off and then old Chico took off like a shot for the barn."

"I never heard about that," Matilda chuckled. "We didn't tell you as we didn't want you to worry," Ethel said.

Pat leaned back in his seat and said, "At last I'm home, after a ten-week absence. The longest time I've ever been away. It sure feels good to see all these familiar surroundings." In earlier days he had covered every square inch of the ground they were now traveling, either by foot, car or on horseback. "I remember when Roy and I would crawl through the tall grass on our stomachs, right over there by the trees, playing cowboy and Indian. Or that path over there, we used to walk, on our way to school. Boy, things have sure changed."

As they turned off the road and up the long driveway to the house, the family's two English setters, Duke and Sophie greeted them. The dogs ran up to the car, then turned on their heels and raced the vehicle back to the house.

As soon as Pat stepped out the dogs went wild, jumping up and all around. Sophie, who from her days as a pup had claimed Pat to be her very own, wagged her tail and hindquarters so hard that the tip hit her ears as it whipped from right to left.

The weekend was magnificent. They all laughed and talked of times gone by and of the great fun they all had growing up. They also spoke of the not-so-happy times, also gone by. Few words were said about the future. It was in the good Lord's hands and there was nothing they could do about it.

On Sunday when Roy arrived and Roger and his family were there, many of the same things were said and enjoyed again.

Instead of enlisting or being drafted Roy had enlisted as a correspondent for the Stars and Stripes. He, too, would soon be heading for France. This family gathering had become a very special event indeed.

Late Sunday evening after dinner and after Roger and his family had left, Ethel, Roy and Pat sat out on the porch. The late night was beautiful. The stars stood out as bright little diamonds and gems in the western sky. The harvest moon just broke above the horizon in the east and was so large that it appeared you could just reach out and pluck it from the sky. The ground fell away from the porch to the south and they could see a light mist hovering over the freshly mown hay. A few fireflies still flickered around the bushes near the house and occasionally brought small dots of light to the shadowy blackness.

There were a few gnats and mosquitoes flying around and the stillness was occasionally interrupted by the slap of a hand on the skin. The only other sound was the squeak of the porch swing as Ethel swayed slowly back and forth. The sweet perfume of the cut hay filled the air.

Pat sat on the top step of the porch with his back against the railing post and Sophie lay next to him with her head on his knee. Duke was stretched out on his side in front of the porch door. Whenever anyone would move you could hear his tail thump on the wooden floor as he tried to wag it from his prone position, maybe in the hope that someone would go out and play with him.

Roy broke the long silence. "Pat, I read a dispatch the other day that they are forming another division made up of different guard units from around the country. Does that affect you?"

"Yes, I think it does. We're going to become the 149th Field Artillery attached to the 42nd Division. We're headed for someplace near New York City before going to Europe. They told us to be ready to go in two or three weeks. I suppose we'll be packing everything after I get back next week."

"Well, if you're anywhere near the city, I'll try and come out and see you. Maybe if you can get a day off I'll show you around. I'll probably be in New York for another few months before I go to France."

"That would be great. I'll need to see a friendly face before we ship out."

They continued to enjoy the late summer evening in silence and one by one they got up, entered the house, and climbed the stairs each to their own room and sleep.

On Monday evening after dinner the family was sitting around the dinning room table talking and trying to piece together a jigsaw puzzle. The telephone rang that special code to let them know it was for them. All of the Tolono area was on a big party line and each family that had a telephone had their own special ring. Pat's mother answered and then called to Pat, "It's long distance for you, Elmer." Matilda still called her youngest son by his given name.

Pat got up to answer and said as he reached for the earpiece "It must be Hank with some change for tomorrow." He answered into the mouthpiece that hung on the wall.

"Pat, this is Hank, guess what?"

"I take it you're not meeting me tomorrow."

"You got it, old chum, but I have more exciting news for you than that."

"What's that?"

"Betsy and I got married yesterday."

"You got what?" Pat blurted out.

"Yeah, we didn't want to wait till I get back. We're on our honeymoon here in Champaign at the hotel. It's really great."

"I guess congratulations are in order. Tell Betsy I'm real happy for her. Did you two elope?"

"Nope, just a small family wedding at Betsy's house. Just the families, otherwise I'd have had you come up."

"Well, thanks for calling to tell me. I sure can't match your good news, but my leave has been great, too. My older brother Roy is here so we're having a good old-fashioned family reunion."

"That sounds great Pat, but I gotta go. We're meeting my parents for dinner in a few minutes but I just had to tell you. I'll see you on the train Wednesday."

"Yeah, I'll talk to you then. Thanks for calling."

On Tuesday, the day before Pat had to get ready to go back to Camp Geismar, Roy, Pat and their dad had gone pheasant hunting. Around noon after trudging through the fields, they were sitting on a log near a small stream about two miles from the house eating a lunch Matilda had packed for them. The day was crystal clear and the bright warm Illinois sun beat down on them. It was just a great day to be alive. Duke and Sophie were out chasing a squirrel near the stream and both were soaking wet, but the water only added to their enjoyment.

After finishing his sandwich, E.P. said, "Boys, I've got something I need to tell you before you're off. You remember that bad back I had in the spring?"

"Sure do, Dad, remember you made me do all of the heavy lifting," Pat said.

"Well, it wasn't a bad back. I went to the doctor and was told that my heart wasn't in very good shape. He told me to cut back on the work or the physical exertion would kill me."

"Dad!" Roy exclaimed. "What do we do, how can we help? You know if you told me I would have come home and helped."

"I know you would have Roy, and I didn't want to spoil your newspaper career just as I didn't want Pat dropping out of school. Milo helped me out. Your mother, brother and sister know, and we've come up with a plan. Milo will farm about 200 acres and Clint Phelps' bother, John, will handle the rest, you know the south field that adjoins his place. Then Roger got us a house in Champaign on Chalmers Street, about three doors down from his. So I guess it means I go into retirement. Now don't worry about me because I'm in the Lord's hands, just as you two are. You're both facing some pretty terrible things in Europe and I wanted you both to know that all is all right with me, and that I will be obeying the doctor's orders."

Pat and Hank arrived at Fort Sheridan late Wednesday night, the 22nd, shortly before taps. They soon learned that the regiment had been ordered to New York and would leave Labor Day, September 3. The three-inch field pieces and other equipment not going to France had been returned to the government.

On August 27 the packing of gear and equipment took up most of the time. It was also learned that, though the recruiting drive had some success, the regiment was still short of men. As a result, 69 men from the 122nd Field Artillery were transferred to the 149th. Of this number, 12 were assigned to Battery F.

On Tuesday the packing continued and the men received their second para-typhoid inoculation. Wednesday, the horses were loaded into cattle cars and started their journey to France after a stopover in Newport News. Presumably they would arrive before the regiment and rejoin the 149th in France. A detail of experienced handlers, nine men in all, went with the animals under the command of Lt. Coffey. The remainder of the week was spent in packing the rest of the gear. On Saturday, the cots were packed and the men slept on the ground for the next two nights.

Sunday, there was a great influx of visitors to the camp, most coming to say their goodbyes and wish the troops well.

On Monday, Labor Day, the regiment completed the packing and the cleanup of the camp. Packs were strapped into position and the troops marched to the loading platform with Colonel Reilly and the band leading the way.

The process of loading the first section went swiftly and by 9:30 the locomotive roared to life and chugged out of the station.

As the train rolled by, people along the right-of-way brought out American flags to wave at the train as they cheered for the troops. Workers in the nearby factories thronged to the windows to see their hometown boys off to war.

Former professor, and now Major, Werner W. Hinkle had been activated on August 1 and sent to Camp Albert L. Mills on Long Island, New York. This was a great-tent covered plain adjoining the Minneola Aviation Field. Camp Mills had last been used after the Spanish-American War as a mustering-out depot for the men who fought in Cuba. It was now being pressed into service once again as a staging area for the troops as they prepared to sail to the continent.

Thirty-eight-year-old Werner Hinkle stood just less than six feet and had a trim build. His dark brown hair was parted in the middle and he wore a rectangular mustache under a somewhat flattened nose. When he donned his spectacles, he bore a striking resemblance to a young Teddy Roosevelt.

Major Hinkle had been charged with an enormous task, that of bringing all elements of the Rainbow Division together. Just a few weeks prior, he had been preparing to get back to the University of Illinois and start the new term that would usher in a new gathering of students. But the war had interrupted his plans. The Illinois National Guard had since been activated and his old unit would become part of the 42nd Division. Supposedly, because of his organizational skills, he was promptly moved up to divisional level and was named the assistant chief of staff, G-1.

The Rainbow had been officially formed on August 5, 1918, and just nine days later the news was leaked to the press. This was the first non-regular division to be readied for overseas duty. The majority of the men in the Rainbow worked at civilian jobs and lived in the neighborhoods of America, but on occasion trained as soldiers. Only one other division had been deployed to France, and it consisted of regular Army personnel. Most civilians thought of the regulars as being different, adventurous individuals who lived apart from the regular citizen. But the men in the Guard, they were friends, neighbors and relatives.

Prior to Major Hinkle's arrival, orders had been processed and issued to those units that would make up the Rainbow, but there were terrible hang-ups in getting all these individual elements from 23 states together at Camp Mills by the middle of September.

Major Hinkle had been legendary in the Illinois guard units because of his organizational skills, but these skills had been used primarily for organizing social events, parades, and other special occasions. Now, at Camp Mills, he was being put to the supreme test. Twenty-seven thousand men had to be transported, along with their equipment, from almost every nook and cranny in the continental US to Long Island. The logistics of the move seemed insurmountable.

As methodical men do, Major Hinkle broke the job down to the smallest tasks and put his staff to work. The military had broad powers to requisition things that they needed. The biggest needs were the railroads, and they were very willing to work with the army and in particular with the staff of the Rainbow.

The 42ⁿᵈ had been named the Rainbow Division to express and recognize the diversity of men and equipment of which it was comprised. For instance, there was the old New York 69ᵗʰ Infantry regiment, renamed the 165ᵗʰ Infantry, and the old Fourth Alabama Infantry, renamed the 167ᵗʰ Infantry—these two units had opposed each other during the Civil War. Some National Guard infantrymen were to be the machine gunners and they were to come from three different parts of the country. Four companies of the Fourth Pennsylvania regiment were to make up the 149ᵗʰ machine gun battalion, three companies of the Second Wisconsin were to become the 150ᵗʰ battalion, and three companies of the Second Georgia were to become the 151st battalion. The three field artillery regiments were to come from Illinois, Indiana and Minnesota. The Engineers were to come from North Carolina and California. The ammunition train was to come from Kansas, the supply train was to come out of Texas, and the signal corps was coming from Missouri. The military police were to be brought in from Virginia and the trench mortar battery was coming out of Maryland. Men from New Jersey, Tennessee, Oklahoma and Michigan were to drive the Rainbow's ambulances. And finally, men from the District of Columbia, Nebraska, Oregon and Colorado were to run the field hospitals. The Rainbow's headquarters troop was made up of Louisiana Cavalry.

Amidst much blood, sweat, tears and cheers, all of the individual units that made up the Rainbow Division assembled for the first time in one place on September 13, 1917, that place being Camp Mills on Long Island.

The Gathering

The train came to a stop in Garden City, New York, and the men of Battery F of the 149th Field Artillery prepared to disembark. Once they detrained and gathered their duffle bags, Sergeant Baker had the men line up in marching order for the final push into Camp Mills, just a short distance from the station.

Everyone was bone tired, as the trip had taken the better part of three days for what normally should have taken one to one and a half days. But for some reason the troop train had to pull off to a siding every time another train was encountered.

"I think we spent more time waiting than we did moving," Jack Bayles conjectured, after stepping down from the coach. "If that's the last time I ride on a train, I sure won't miss it. Next time I think I'll walk."

Captain Arnold had the battery brought to attention and he gave them their orders. "You are to collect your belongings and prepare to march into camp. We will be watched by members of the regular army, so be sharp and show them how good we really are."

In silence the men hoisted their gear to their shoulders and on command from the First Sergeant did a smart right face and began marching in two columns towards the camp's main entrance. With the band in the lead they marched through the gate directly to the regimental campsite. Once all of the equipment was unloaded, the men erected the tents in one long line and began unpacking their personal things with the hope of being able to lounge around for the rest of the day; but this was not to be for the order came for them to form up out in front of the tents.

Training had not been left behind in Illinois. Soon they were out on the parade field drilling, marching, and going through more training. Those who thought they would be able to kick back soon found that this was not the case. For six days a week they would work and drill.

Camp Mills was the first of many great camps set up specifically for the gathering of troops waiting to board the ships that would take them across the "big pond" to France.

All of the men here at this time were volunteers, many being rookies. There had been some hasty recruiting for most of the units in order for them to meet their manpower requirements before coming to Camp Mills. The order of the day was drill, drill and drill, all day, every day. Even though they were the pick of the nation's National Guard units, the grizzled regular Army drill sergeants harried them in an unmerciful manner. The large drill field was a sweating, cursing little world of men preparing for war.

Sergeant Baker discovered that many of the regulars were old friends he had served with at different duty posts in years past. These men seemed to delight in giving their all to see who could be the hardest on the troops during the training. Though it was difficult for the men they were, indeed, becoming good soldiers used to following orders rapidly and accurately.

Sundays were different. This was a day of leave taking and merrymaking. Officers in particular were invited to parties at many of the nearby homes. Some enlisted men were invited also, but they normally left to go sightseeing or to round up a good time.

The next two days were spent making the camp habitable. First the outdoor showers were walled with diaphanous burlap, which gave the appearance of semi-privacy, though there was no overhead covering. The carpenters of the battery next constructed mess tables. Meanwhile, all of the tents were trenched properly and a general cleanup of the area was continued.

Once the camp was established each regiment tried to outdo its neighbors in beautifying their site. Walkways were bordered with whitewashed rocks and stones and soon the camp took on a respectable veneer.

On September 8, Colonel Reilly and his staff completed their first inspection of the 149th. Prior to their reaching Battery F, Lieutenant Allen and Sergeant Baker were everywhere seeing to it that the battery would pass with flying colors. The inspection went well, so well in fact that some lucky individuals received passes that were good until reveille. Others received passes that were good until 10 o'clock in the evening.

As the time passed, many of the communities that bordered Camp Mills were crowded with soldiers from the 42nd Division. Many of these men had passes, but the majority did not. The enterprising citizens soon offered all types of entertainment to the men of the division. These activities ranged from the very depths of depravity to the heights of noble goodness. Rackets of every conceivable type existed, even down to the bootlegging of liquor. The local bus operators created devious routes, in order to convey those without passes, to and from the camp without detection by the military police.

With each passing day a new unit or two would arrive at the camp. For example, on September 8, the Minnesota artillery regiment arrived and on the ninth the Indiana heavy artillery entered camp.

As the time for the division to depart for the continent drew near, brigade headquarters devised a more rigorous training that went into effect on Monday, September 10. The regiment began the morning with calisthenics. After breakfast, the men engaged in foot drill. Next, those who were involved with communications went to wireless and telephone school. The mechanics and cannoneers were in school learning about the 75mm guns the battery would be using. The remainder of the men in the battery varied their foot drill by simulating mounted drill in which men acted as horses, or carriages. This routine continued for the remainder of the week.

On their second Sunday at Camp Mills, the first divisional review was held. No less than General Mann, the division's commander, and General Hoyle, the commander of the US Army's Eastern Department, observed this maneuver.

After the ceremony, Pat and others in the squad were gathered in his tent discussing what they were going to do with the rest of the day.

Some were ready to catch the train and head into the city while a couple wanted to just rest in camp. A few others headed for Garden City. Pat and Hank were trying to make up their minds when no other than Roy barged in.

Pat was flabbergasted and could hardly speak when he saw his brother. After introducing Roy to the others, Roy sat on the bunk next to Pat.

"I sure had a hell of a time finding you. It took the better part of an hour."

"How did you know I was here?"

"I kept watch in the newsroom. If you're not aware, you guys are big news around the country. I was in Washington last Sunday, so I couldn't come out then, but this Sunday I'm free. Did ya know you're the first all-volunteer division being readied to ship out? The only other divisions in France or getting ready to go are regular army. But that's not what I'm here for. I borrowed a friend's car and I thought we would go sightseeing. Ya wanta go?"

"Anything to get me out of here for a little while. Can anyone else go with us?"

"Well, only three can fit in the seat and it'll be tight in the old roadster, but sure."

"Great, I'd like to ask Hank. He's been pretty lonely since we left Illinois."

"Oh, is he the one that got married when you were on leave? Bring him along."

So, off they went, amid cheers and jeers of the friends they left behind.

Pat had become used to Chicago when they were stationed at Fort Sheridan, but New York was different. They drove and walked around, gawking at all of the sights. Both he and Hank loved the Statue of Liberty and Roy was at his best showing off his adopted home.

They stopped for dinner at one of the fancy restaurants and snacked and ate foods they'd never seen or heard of before. Hank had forgotten his loneliness for a while, but it came back at dinner. The three of them were talking about it when Roy came up with an idea.

"Look, Hank, on the way back to Camp Mills, why don't we stop at the newsroom of my old paper and you can call Betsy from there, they owe me a favor. Then I think you should ask her to get on a train and come out here to spend a Sunday or two with you."

"Can he do that?" Pat asked.

"Yes, I don't see a problem with it. Didn't you see all of the visitors in camp today?"

"Sure would be great," Hank responded. "I'd be indebted to you for the rest of my life."

Roy smiled. "You get her out to New York, and I'll meet her and set her up in a place to stay and you can see her, at least on Sundays. By the way, do you guys have any idea when you're shipping out?"

"As far as we can tell, sometime during the latter part of October, but that could change," replied Pat.

"Okay, you get her to come out before next Sunday the 26th and if she can stay a week she can go back on a late train the 3rd of October. I'll work on getting her in a good boarding house near the camp."

Betsy was anxious to come, but all sorts of obstacles seemed to stand in the way. Through three days of telephone calls, Roy was able to get Betsy into New York on a late afternoon train on Saturday. Roy met her and drove her out to the boarding house, and because of his status as a *Stars and Stripes* correspondent, he was able to enter Camp Mills and meet Hank and Pat just before taps with the news.

Hank was exhausted and the night of September 22 could not pass fast enough for him. After the normal day of training, Sergeant Baker felt that the men were getting soft and therefore led them on a nine mile hike before dinner, with full packs. Even though he was totally worn out, he was not able to sleep well. All that he thought of was Betsy, who was less than a mile away. When reveille finally sounded, Hank was up in a flash.

Hank knew the morning would drag on endlessly, as the division had to pass in review for Secretary of War, Newton D. Baker.

The secretary was seated in his automobile, and the units of the division marched by his vehicle in platoon formation. The 149th Regiment had to wait its turn, so it all took several hours. To add to the delay, the camp of the 149th was chosen for the inspection by Secretary

Baker, and this took an additional hour. When the men were finally dismissed, it was well past noon.

Hank would, at long last, get to see and be with his beloved wife.

As Pat and Hank were in the tent getting ready to leave, Pat said, "Well, does the time seem to just drag along for ya, Hank?" Pat asked, followed by a chuckle. "I guess I don't blame you for being anxious. As a matter of fact I'll be glad to see Betsy too, but that won't take too much time. Soon after we drop you off, Roy and I are going to go on another tour. I know you'll be well cared for."

"Pat, I got to tell you, I wasn't even this excited for our wedding. I think I must have counted over a million sheep just trying to sleep. No good, I was wide awake all night."

"Oh, I think you'll get some sleep today! Now you remember to be back at camp by 10:30 sharp. You don't want to spoil this by not making roll call. Remember you have another Sunday to go."

Hank smiled. "Yes, yes, I know. You treat me like a little kid. Oh well, I guess you're just looking out for me."

"Well, ya finally got something right!" Pat said with a broad grin.

Roy had been at the camp since 10:00 a.m. and hadn't realized that all of the morning's activities would last so long. It wasn't until shortly after noon that the three of them piled in the borrowed roadster and were on their way. The boarding house was just a little more than a mile from the encampment and they were there in no time.

As Roy drove, he said to Hank, "Now the old couple that runs this place knows you're married and I don't think they'll bother you. They're exceptionally nice people and understand your situation. I'll just warn you that the walls are thin and sound travels easily to adjoining rooms. So the rest is up to you."

As they turned into the driveway they saw Betsy waiting on the porch with a glowing smile. She was of medium height and wore a full-length white dress that did not hide her girlish figure. Her long black hair hung nearly to her waist and was tied back with a red ribbon. Hank, who was riding next to the passenger door, had it open and was running up the steps before Roy could come to a complete stop.

"Roy, I need to say hello for a minute," Pat said, "and then we can be off." They both then stepped from the car and waited at the bottom of the six steps that led up to the porch of the old frame two-story house.

When the moment was right Pat started to climb the steps "Betsy, you sure look great, it's nice seeing you again."

She released herself from Hank and came over and gave him a big hug and kissed him on the cheek. Pat pulled back, a little embarrassed, and turned a bright red.

"Without you this would never have come about," she said.

"Well, it was Roy's doing," Pat stammered. "He was the real catalyst and did all the work."

"Just a huge thanks to both of you," she smiled, and went to Roy and kissed him on the cheek.

"All in a day's work," Roy said.

After several minutes of small talk about the trip, the two brothers excused themselves and headed for the car.

"Don't worry, Pat, I'll be back by 10:30 and I'll walk," Hank said. "See you later and thanks again, Roy." With that, Betsy and Hank disappeared into the house.

All the next day, Hank seemed to be walking on air. As far as anyone could tell, he was in some sort of a trance.

The training schedule became more rigorous as the days slid by. Calisthenics followed by march and drill, then more calisthenics, rigorous schooling; on and on it went. By taps, the men were worn out.

By Wednesday, Hank was anxious for Sunday. Time went so slowly. He and Pat were talking during a break on Thursday when Hank brought up his idea.

"Now, Pat, I know this sounds a little risky, but Friday night after taps I'm going to sneak out of camp. I've got it all worked out. I talked to the company clerk and he confirmed that there'd not be a divisional review on Sunday. As a matter of fact, I bribed him into getting me a weekend pass; don't ask me what I gotta do. There's a place I can go directly to the road and not be seen. We haven't had a bed check since we've been here and with the pass I don't have to worry about roll call on Saturday. Can you just keep quiet about it till we all come back on Sunday evening?"

"Are you sure you want to try this? If so, don't worry about me talking."

"Thanks, I won't forget it. Now don't pay any attention to me Friday night. I'll be gone like the wind."

Hank was true to his word. On Friday after taps, Pat listened for Hank's departure. At eleven, he glanced over at Hank's bunk and to his surprise it looked as if he was still there. Pat then promptly fell asleep and didn't stir until revelry. He woke up and still saw Hank's form under the covers. Pat picked up his shoe and threw it, hitting the lump in the back, and discovered the form was Hank's pillow and some clothes. Pat got up, mumbling under his breath, "That dirty dog did it and I didn't even know he was gone."

Pat quickly made up Hank's bed and headed off to breakfast.

As Roy had some other things to do that Sunday, he didn't show up at camp until around three in the afternoon. The plan had been for Roy to pick up Betsy at four and drive her to the station, and Pat was going to walk back with Hank to the camp. At exactly four o'clock, Roy turned into the driveway to the boarding house. Hank and Betsy were sitting in the front porch swing, holding hands.

After a very touching goodbye, Pat opened the car door for Betsy, and she came over and gave him a hug and got in the car. Pat closed the door and she grabbed his hand.

"Pat, don't let anything happen to him. Take care of him and bring him back for me," she said with tears in her eyes.

"Don't worry, Betsy, I will. You know this will all be over before we get into it." Pat didn't really believe what he said, but he thought it would make her feel better.

They all said their good-byes and the roadster drove off, leaving Pat and Hank standing in the drive.

"That was a great week, but now it's gone," Hank said.

They started walking back to camp. Pat asked, "Did you have any trouble getting over here Friday night? I didn't see or hear you go."

"It was easy. I was here with Betsy by 11:30. As a matter of fact I spent every night with her. What a great week."

"You did what?"

From there they walked in silence back to the camp.

After his graduation and commissioning exercises, Second Lieutenant Daniel G. Jacobson – or Jake as he was called—went to infantry school at Camp McCord in Georgia. Jake, who stood about six feet, was more powerfully built now and had sandy brown hair and deep blue eyes. He was an apt student and learned well the lessons of fighting a war, for he knew these lessons could mean the difference between life and death. The rigorous 10 weeks of training had developed strength and stamina he didn't even know he had.

On completion of his training sometime around the end of July, he was assigned to an Alabama National Guard infantry regiment that had been mobilized and was awaiting orders. This was the Old Fourth Alabama Infantry.

On August 26th they received their orders to move to Camp Albert Mills on Long Island and, at the same time, the unit was renamed the 167th Infantry regiment attached to the 42nd Division.

On the day after Labor Day, Jake's regiment boarded the trains that would take them to Garden City, New York.

The trip to New York was a nightmare for Jake and the other junior officers of the regiment, for it fell upon them to keep track of the men. As long as the troop train kept moving his job was uncomplicated. However, when the train stopped it became difficult if not impossible to keep track of the men in the platoon. They were using the rest rooms, buying souvenirs, or out looking for a good time. Like all troop trains, theirs had to pull off to a siding whenever another train came by. All sorts of delays were encountered on the trip and when they finally pulled into Garden City, the officers breathed a sigh of relief, thinking the worst was over.

At Camp Mills, though, things did not improve. The 167th encamped next to the 165th infantry regiment, or the old 69th New York Infantry. Normally this would not be a problem except these two units had fought each other during the Civil War. Immediately fistfights broke out. At times, Jake wondered if the War Between the States had ever ended. There was constant fighting going on, at least a couple of times a day, and on some occasions it seemed as if there was one every hour. With the rigorous training schedule and the refighting of the Civil War there was little time for rest.

Sundays offered welcomed relief for the junior officers of the 167th as well as for the officers of the 165th, for the men of both regiments seemed to take time off from their reenactment of the Civil War.

To help relieve the rigors of camp life, local citizens from the surrounding area held numerous parties for the officers and men. These were usually held on Sundays. In addition, visitors from all over the country came by car and train to visit friends and relatives of the men in the Rainbow Division. These Sunday social gatherings did much to relieve the rigors and demands of camp life that overwhelmed the men during the week.

Jake and his fellow officers were always able to locate a party, and of course the women who attended them. Jake was a charmer with the gift of gab and he soon became a favorite of the garden party set.

This usually meant free meals and booze whenever he was off duty, something that did not get by his fellow officers. They would hang onto his shirttails and go with him into the houses of the local "upper crust." Whoever went with Jake would end up with the free food and drinks. But, Monday would come around all to suddenly and back to training they would go, many with a terrible weekend hangover.

The young second lieutenant sat in the officer's club slowly sipping his drink with one hand and holding a cigarette in the other. He sat looking blankly out the window as the sun began to sink into the western horizon. It had rained earlier in the day and the sky was beginning to clear. The colors were magnificent—orange, gold, blue and mauve with blinding streaks piercing into and through the clouds, almost like the brilliant spokes of a giant wheel with the sun on the horizon as its hub.

He didn't hear the words at first—it was like someone far off speaking to him.

"It's a beautiful sight, isn't it, Lieutenant? Lieutenant?"

The young man shook his head as if to wake from his trancelike state. "Excuse me."

"I'm sorry to bother you, Lieutenant, but all of the other tables are taken. Would it be all right if I sat here for a short while?"

The young man quickly sized up the middle-aged civilian. He was a tall man in his late 40s or early 50s solidly built, with salt-and-pepper colored hair. He had a friendly face and a pleasant demeanor.

"Yes, sir, go ahead and sit down. I was just daydreaming and admiring the sunset."

"Thank you," the older man said. "My name is Clint Phelps. I'm with the *Champaign Daily Herald*. I just finished an interview with your post commander and thought I'd have a drink before I head back to town. I didn't realize the club would be so crowded."

"I'm glad to meet you, Mr. Phelps, my name is Dennison, Ike Dennison."

"The pleasure is mine, Lieutenant, and I thank you for the place to sit."

"Call me Ike, I have trouble with this military lingo."

"Well, Ike, I see that you've earned your wings."

"Yes, sir, just last week. It seems to take forever. Not enough aircraft for the number of trainees coming here to Chanute. But I was finally able to complete the primary course. I'll probably be heading out for advanced training soon."

"And where would that be, Ike?"

"I'm not sure as I haven't received my orders yet. But I'm pretty certain we will be heading for France, probably in November."

"That's just next month. Are you from around here?"

"Yes and no. My father is career navy and currently stationed in Washington. But I just spent the last four years at the University of Illinois and graduated in May. I guess you would say I lived there longer than any other place."

"Well, that's interesting. I have a nephew – well, not a nephew—but the son of a great family friend going there. Maybe you know him. Pat Littler?"

"You're kidding? He's a fraternity brother of mine. As a matter of fact I helped pledge him last year. How is he?"

"Oh he's fine, he enlisted in a National Guard artillery unit that has since been activated and he will be finishing up basic training soon. They are part of the 149th Field Artillery and I believe they will be shipping out soon, too. Small world, isn't it?"

"Sure is. If you see him, tell him I'm doing fine and send my best to him."

They fell silent for a time, slowly sipping their drinks. The sun had slipped below the horizon and the colors intensified. Finally, Ike broke the silence.

"Mr. Phelps, I sure envy you living here in Illinois, but it looks as if I won't be seeing this part of the country for a long time."

"Well, confidentially, I won't either. This is my last week with the *Herald*. I'm going to Europe, too, as a correspondent for the *Chicago Globe*. I felt that with all you young men going off to war I'd better be going, too. People here at home will want to know what's going on."

They watched the beautiful prairie sunset for a few more moments; then Mr. Phelps drained his glass. "Well, Ike, best of luck to you. I must get back to Champaign and file my story. I hope that we meet again."

"Thanks, Mr. Phelps. It's been a real lift talking to you."

As Mr. Phelps walked away, Ike shivered a little, even though it was warm in the club. For the first time in a long time he felt a little homesick. In his short time as a pilot he had already seen some of his friends die, either through pilot error or through aircraft failures. He wished he could see his family again before going overseas. Mr. Phelps had reminded him of his father.

The week after Betsy left, Hank was depressed and anxious. Pat and others in the squad tried to cheer him up, but their efforts were futile. Fortunately, the waking hours were filled with assigned duties and training. Only during the fleeting night hours following taps did Hank find time to reflect, and found little respite from the aching loneliness.

On Wednesday, Pat, sensing that Hank's state of mind was not improving, suggested that he go to the chaplain for some counseling.

The Reverend James proved to be a great help and was able to help him put things in their proper perspective. On Friday, Hank was feeling better and confided that the chaplain had helped him. "The Reverend got down on his knees and prayed for me and with me," he told Pat. "It was a prayer about my faith and me. It's been a long time since I thought much about God, but it sure helped me to view things differently. I even slept well last night, the first real sleep I've had since Betsy left on Sunday."

"Well, it sure makes me feel good to see you come out of this," Pat replied. "I was almost afraid you'd hit the road and go AWOL."

"Pat I may be a little crazy, but I hope I'm not that far off the wall."

"That's the old Hank talkin'. That'll make the good news I have to tell you all the better. I saw Roy last Sunday and he will be here this coming Sunday morning at ten or so to take us out for some more sightseeing. In fact, we're even going to one of those big society parties here on the Island. He wrangled an invitation for all of us, including that family friend I've told you about, Clint Phelps."

"What's he doing here? I thought he worked for the *Herald* in Champaign?"

"Well, he did, but he wrote Roy a couple of weeks ago and said that he was leaving the *Herald* and going back to the *Chicago Globe* as a war correspondent. He felt he needed to go to France and report on the progress of the war to the folks back home. His first assignment was to come here and write about the Rainbow Division. But, back to the subject, these parties are usually reserved for the brass and other high ranking muckity-mucks, but we're going to be there too."

"Hey, I'm ready for anything and that sounds like fun, much better than all this training."

The high society bashes were held primarily for the officers of the 42nd Division and for an enlisted man to be able to attend was a distinct honor. Pat and Hank received a lot of rough but good-natured ribbing from the others in the squad, who were more envious than anything else over this invitation.

Finally, Sunday arrived. Both Hank and Pat got up early in order to get all spruced up in their dress uniforms. After the 8:30 church services, they got back to the tent and found Roy waiting for them.

The day was enjoyable for all three men. Roy showed them places and things they hadn't seen before, from Wall Street to the wharf. After lunch they headed back to Garden City.

The party was large, noisy, and extravagant. Neither Pat nor Hank had ever seen anything like it before. These people even had a swimming pool and tennis court on their estate. Pat couldn't remember the name of the family that owned this extraordinary estate, but he did hear that they owned a munitions factory over in New Jersey. This type of wealth was not what he aspired to in life, but he felt delighted to be able to take advantage of it.

Hank was awestruck. "This is the way Betsy and I are going to live after I finish school," he said, giving the others a good laugh.

It was at this point that Roy spotted Clint Phelps coming through the door out to the patio. "Pat, there's Clint."

"I don't see him. How can you tell with such a large crowd of people?"

"Don't worry, you guys stay here and I'll go get him," Roy said, and disappeared into the crowd.

Pat turned to Hank. "Well, the cat got your tongue?"

"I just didn't believe people lived in such opulence. This is incredible," Hank said looking around. "My parents' home would fit in the living room of this place."

Pat laughed. "Well, that's a bit of an overstatement, but I know what you mean. I told you this party was going to be something."

"Never in my wildest imagination did I think it would be like this. Did you get a look at all the officers around here? I think I saw a general over there. Are we supposed to salute all of them in here?"

"Naw, don't worry about it, though I sure wish I'd see another enlisted man."

Just then, Roy returned with Clint in tow. Clint immediately threw his arms around Pat and gave him a big bear hug.

"Great to see you, Pat. It's been so long since I've laid eyes on you. You were in high school, I think. The uniform looks great and I know it'll be served with honor and courage."

"Thanks, Mr. Phelps, I've looked forward to seeing you ever since Roy told me you were going to be here. I have a lot of questions to ask you. But, first, I want you to meet my best friend, Hank Seiler."

"Hank, call me Clint, and that goes for you too Pat. Great meeting you. They tell me you're the one that just got married, right?"

Hank smiled as his face reddened. "Yes that's right. I guess Pat had to tell the whole world."

"Well, congratulations. Never tried it myself but they tell me it's a great institution."

"It sure is, sir."

Roy pointed out a table in the yard that was empty, and the four of them walked down the steps onto the grass and sat down. They spent time talking about home and the happenings since they were last together. Hank was able to join the conversation, as Clint had known Hank's father for a number of years. They had been fraternity brothers in college.

After a short while, Pat got up to get some drinks for himself and Roy. After the bartender filled the glasses, he picked them up, turned, and nearly ran into the man standing in line behind him. The man was a major and Pat nearly spilled his drinks on his uniform.

"Excuse me, sir, I'm very sorry," Pat stammered. "I...professor Hinkle," he blurted out. The major eyed him with a quizzical look. "Do I know you?"

"Sir, my name is Pat Littler. I was in your history class last semester, at Illinois."

"Well yes, I remember you now. Of course, you sat in the row next to the window and it was you and your friend who sought my advice on joining the army."

"That's correct, sir. I did. But I'm terribly sorry to have almost knocked you over."

"With this crowd here, I'm surprised everyone isn't wearing a drink of one sort or another. What I need to do is find a place to sit so I can be safe."

"Sir, you're welcome to join me and my friends. You remember Hank Seiler from class, and my brother, Roy, who's a correspondent for *Stars and Stripes* and my uncle, Clint Phelps, who also is a correspondent."

"Clint Phelps? Isn't he from the *Champaign Daily Herald*?"

"Yes, sir. Or at least he was, but now he's with the *Chicago Globe*."

"Well, I'd like very much to meet your friends, and it'll give me an opportunity to get away from an extremely overbearing and boorish woman who's been following me around. So, please lead the way."

Pat weaved his way back to the table with Major Hinkle following close behind. As they approached their destination, Pat held both glasses in one hand and grabbed an unoccupied chair, setting it down when they reached the table. "I have another friend here who will be joining us. I'd like for you all to meet Major Hinkle, Professor Hinkle from the University Of Illinois. Professor, this is my brother, Roy, you know Hank, and this is my pseudo uncle, Clint Phelps."

"I'm so very glad to meet you all, it's like being home. And please, Hank, don't stand at attention, we'll consider this more like a history class than the military. Please sit down. Mr. Phelps, I've read many of your editorials and I like your thoughts. I would think Champaign is missing out on some good writing."

They all began to converse about various topics. The major quizzed Hank and Pat about their enlistment, basic training, and which unit they were serving in. This was also of interest to Clint and Roy, who delved into questions about the Rainbow Division and various aspects of its future, a subject close to the major's heart.

Pat and Roy were leaning forward in their chairs to better hear the conversation when Pat heard a familiar loud voice behind him.

"Well, if ain't Elmer back from the plowin'."

At the sound of his name, he swiveled around in his chair, and standing there behind him was none other than his old fraternity brother, Second Lieutenant Jake Jacobson.

Pat stood and awkwardly offered his hand, which Jake grabbed and shook vigorously. He then recognized Hank and shook his hand also. Pat quickly introduced him to the others.

Jake said, "Major, I know your name, but I never was in any of your classes sir!"

"Well, another U of I boy. We decided before you joined us to call this a history class, so don't worry about the saluting or sir stuff, at least for now."

"Thank you, ah, Professor. Is this like home or what?"

"It's somewhat of a coincidence," Clint said, adding. "We're glad you can join us. I take it you're in the 42nd Division also?"

"Yes, sir, I got my commission after graduation in May, trained in Georgia, and have been assigned to the 167th Infantry Regiment out of Alabama."

"We sure had a heck of a time getting you fellows up here by mid-September. All sorts of delays," Major Hinkle added.

"I know, sir, we sat on a siding for about eight hours one day. But we're here and ready to go."

Major Hinkle asked Jake about the trouble between the 167th and the 165th infantry regiments.

"I feel they're both just anxious to get into the war," Jake said. "I believe it'll settle down once we get to France. Just don't put both units on the same boat or we will fight the Civil War again and probably sink the ship in the process."

They all laughed heartily, then Major Hinkle asked Roy and Clint not to focus too much on the disputes, since they could be blown way out of proportion. Both Roy and Clint agreed.

Clint turned to face Major Hinkle: "Professor, how do you, as a historian, view the war now? It's hard to determine when this stalemate will end. Will our troops be able to turn the tide soon?"

"You ask a very difficult question, Mr. Phelps. Though the stalemate continues, change is in the wind. The US will make a difference, but not right away. As I see it, we are not ready to enter the front lines yet, at least in the active sectors. There is more training before we can do that and it won't be before late spring or early summer of '18 before we can take our full share of responsibility. The British and French are rapidly running out of manpower and can't continue a war of attrition forever. The Germans are getting tired, too, but the fearful thing from that viewpoint is the revolution in Russia. If the new Russian government signs a separate peace treaty with the Central Powers, and I'm sure they will, the Germans are going to be able to move a large number of combat-ready divisions from the Eastern front to the west. As you can see, timing becomes all-important."

Clint nodded.

"I expect to see the Germans launching a great offensive before America is ready to enter the war as an equal power with the other Allies," Major Hinkle continued. "So to answer your question, the Allies need time and they need the strength and fortitude to stand up to German power for another six to eight months. If they can hold out that long, the US should be able to put about two million men into the line and thus turn the tide."

"Does that mean we're going to be going over right away?" Hank asked.

"I can't tell you when, but it will be soon, probably before November. But that's only a guess from a history professor."

The group smiled at his modesty.

"The American divisional makeup is different from that of the continental armies," Major Hinkle explained. "An American division such as the 42nd has approximately 26 to 27,000 men, whereas the British, French and German divisions have 8 to 9,000. Therefore, don't be fooled when you hear that a large number of divisions – German, for example—have moved into the line. If we move one division, the Germans will have to move approximately three to equal our manpower."

The others mulled that fact over silently.

"So that's my view of things to date. Well, look at the time. I must be getting back to camp as I have a big week ahead of me, so I will bid you all adieu. It's been fun talking with you," Major Hinkle said, and turned to Pat and Hank. "Great seeing both of you, I wish you the best. And don't worry; you won't be seeing much action for a while. I'm afraid you'll be training very hard, and that goes for you too Jake. And Mr. Phelps, why don't you come to the camp at 9 a.m. on Tuesday. My aide will meet you at the gate and bring you to my office. I'll give you a tour and perhaps I can coerce the division commander, General Mann, to meet with you. If not, I'll get you an interview with Colonel Doug MacArthur, our chief of staff."

"Well, thank you, Major, I'd appreciate that very much, it makes my job easier. Well, good night and I'll look forward to seeing you Tuesday."

They all said good night and the major disappeared into the crowd.

"Well," Clint said after a pause, "I think the professor has done his homework and he's given me some new insights. Thanks for bringing him over, Pat. You boys have a lot ahead of you. Roy, you and I will have a lot of writing to do. Oh, by the way Pat, Roy, I talked to Uncle Milo before I left on Friday. He said to tell you that your folks are moving into Champaign the first of November and that they both were in high spirits about the move. And, of course, he sends his regards and love to the two of you. Now I must be off. Wait, I'm forgetting something. I ran into a fraternity brother of yours a little over a week ago and he sent his best to you. An Ike Dennison, I believe."

"Ike? He was my best friend all through college," Jake said. "What's he doing?"

"He just earned his wings at Chanute Field in Rantoul and thinks he'll be shipping out to France in November."

"I'll be damned," Jake said, shaking his head and smiling. "I always told him I thought he was for the birds. Well, good for him."

"Now I must be going," Clint said as he stood and shook hands all around.

It was getting late and they all began offering their good-byes. A new bond had formed among Pat, Hank and Jake. There was no longer a distinction between upper and lower classmen, but instead a true friendship developed based on mutual respect, as the party drew to a close.

After the others left, Jake thought back on his school years and the great times he had had. "Now here we are, all ready to go to war. Instead of enjoying the future, we're dreading it and wondering what it will bring. Oh, Lord bless us all and grant each of us a safe journey," Jake said under his breath as he began searching for his ride back to camp.

Crossing 'The Big Pond'

Monday, the eighth of October, the day following the big party, the combat training intensified yet again. Orders were issued that guests would no longer be allowed to enter the camp. The garden parties and dances were now a thing of the past.

This added some credence to the rumor that the division was shipping out soon, and everyone's apprehension was evident. On Tuesday, General Summerall led the entire brigade on an eight-mile hike. The men were required to carry a full backpack, weighing in excess of fifty pounds. Following this exercise, Captain Arnold called the battery together and gave a short lecture on the temptations that would confront the men once they landed in France.

"As you men may not know, there will be many new and tempting sights for you after we land in France. It is my duty to inform you that sexually transmitted diseases are very prevalent among the women in the seaport towns." He cleared his throat. "This can prove to be fatal to you if you contract, ah, syphilis, for example. There is nothing modern science can do to guarantee a cure for you if you are so unfortunate as to contract it. Therefore a word to the wise – control yourselves. Now to another subject concerning an article you would be wise to take with you, toilet paper. It seems that French customs differ from ours and there is little commercial value in trying to sell this product there. Consequently, it is difficult if not impossible to obtain it. As a matter of fact, out in the boondocks you may be considered less than civilized if you suggest its use."

It was apparent to the men that the prudish captain had a great deal of difficulty speaking on these and other personal subjects, and once he finished, he quickly disappeared.

Many of the men took the subject on toilet paper to heart and there was a run on the product at local stores. When the regiment finally boarded the ships their backpacks swelled with this essential tissue.

On Saturday, all married men were urged to secure an allotment of their pay to go to their wives. Government insurance was made available to all of the men of the battery. Jack Bayless, who was company clerk at this time, busied himself for the remainder of the Division's stay at Camp Mills preparing the necessary paperwork.

In an unusual action, the units were ordered to start their packing on Friday the twelfth and told that Sunday was no longer to be a day off. Through all of the rigors of training and even the fighting between the various units, the division was developing an *esprit de corps* that was not unlike the spirit of young college students for their alma mater.

Meanwhile, the quartermaster corps was desperately trying to equip all of the men properly. This responsibility rested squarely on Major Hinkle's shoulders, at the same time he and his staff were struggling to coordinate transportation for the 27,000 men of the division from Camp Mills to the ships that were to take the Rainbow to France.

Finally, on Tuesday, word came down that the Division would begin moving the next day.

At two a.m. on Wednesday the eighteenth, with few lights and little sound, the 117th Trench Mortar Battery out of Maryland and the 2nd Battalion of the 166th Infantry out of Ohio marched to a waiting train in Garden City.

Pat had been restless for most of the night and finally he heard the 166th Infantry Regiment march out of camp. With all sorts of thoughts and visions dancing through his mind he had little or no sleep. It came as a welcomed relief when the movement of these troops around the area fully awakened him. He dressed quickly and got the rest of the squad up just as the bugler was playing reveille. Once dressed, they headed over to the field kitchen for a meager breakfast of coffee, bread, and syrup. Few words were spoken, as the men were lost in their own thoughts and anxious about the future. Those who did talk spoke in hushed tones.

They returned to their tents after breakfast and completed the packing, policed the grounds, and tossed all of the trash in a nearby incinerator. By 4:30, Battery F had completed the preparations and the men sat on their bags and luggage as they awaited orders to move to the train.

Pat paced slowly back and forth in front of his luggage lost in thought. He stopped and turned toward Hank and said, "This is what we've been waiting for, but now that the moment has arrived I'm not sure I'm ready."

Hank, who was lying on the ground with his head propped up against his bag and his campaign hat pulled down over his eyes, lifted the rim of the hat with his right hand and looked at Pat and said, "I'm as excited as hell. I can't wait to get to the ships and then to France."

"I was too," Pat replied. "But now I'm having doubts."

"Oh, you get too emotionally tied up over these things. Look at the positive side. The war will be over by the time we get to the line, so let's go and enjoy the sightseeing." Hank then let go of the rim of his hat and closed his eyes.

"I guess you're right," Pat said as he turned to watch an orange glow on the eastern horizon, as the sun struggled to rise. "Besides there isn't a damned thing I can do to stop the process."

The battery started moving around 5:00 a.m., the only significant light was provided by the burning of the trash in the incinerators, strategically placed around Camp Mills and the ever-increasing glow of early dawn.

They marched the short distance to the waiting train at Garden City and climbed aboard. From there they were taken to the ferry at Long Island City that took them to Hoboken. The battery eventually arrived at the docks at 1:00 p.m.; there they waited until it was their turn to board the *President Lincoln*.

Jack who was sitting on his duffle bag near Pat and Hank looked up at the great ship that towered high above their position on the dock said, "Well it should be a lot roomier than the train, it might even be luxurious."

"Don't count on it," came the voice of Sergeant Martyn, standing a short distance away. "I've heard we'll be jammed in there tighter than sardines in a can."

"Just our luck." Jack replied, under his breath.

This ship, at one time, had been a luxurious ocean liner before she was converted to a troop ship. Indeed, all of these beautiful vessels were no longer opulent ships of beauty and grace. They had been painted with zigzag stripes of black, gray, and white, making them less conspicuous when viewed through a periscope of a moving submarine.

The creature comforts that had at one time pampered the transoceanic passengers had been ripped out. The stately ballrooms and dining areas were no longer discernible. They had been replaced with dormitories that stacked bunks four high. The men of the Rainbow were literally crammed into the ships, just as Sergeant Martyn had surmised. Some of these ocean liners held as many as seven to eight thousand men where normally, in peacetime, they would carry only one or two thousand passengers.

The quarters set aside for Battery F were situated amidships, four decks down. They shared this space with the supply company. Their bunks were nothing but canvas stretched between iron pipes and stacked four tiers high. There was barely enough room between the rows of bunks for a person to pass. If two men encountered one another going in opposite directions, one would have to either sit in a bunk or back up to let the other pass. The only light for the entire area was provided by two light bulbs that had been painted green. All portholes were painted over and sealed shut, not allowing any light to enter or escape. As this was normally the hold of the ship, there was just one hatchway overhead that provided the only entrance and exit to the dormitory.

The remaining units that made up the Rainbow, followed close on the heels of Battery F. By six p.m. the convoy of ships, the *President Lincoln*, the *Covington*, the *President Grant*, *Tenadores*, *Pastores* and *Mallory* weighed anchor and started down the Hudson River, out of the harbor through the narrows and out to open sea. There they would be joined with other merchant ships and their naval escort made up of warships of all kinds.

They formed groups of five or six ships, one behind the other, in long parallel lines with the warships patrolling the perimeter.

By daylight of the 19th, land was no longer in sight.

The first day aboard was a new experience for most of the men. Though they were told to stay in their assigned place, most found a way to go exploring. From stem to stern and from top to bottom, men of the Rainbow could be found. It didn't take long for orders to come down that men found outside their designated area would be severely reprimanded.

The ship was crowded and the men were restricted to the general area of their assigned dormitory. They were allowed up on deck only couple of times a day, in shifts.

After this initial exploration by most of the men, followed by the fear of repercussions if found outside their assigned boundary, they quickly settled down to a monotonous routine. The obligatory games of chance soon popped up throughout the ship, poker, craps and blackjack being the most popular. Pat and Hank did not join in.

"I have one philosophy when it comes to gambling," Pat said, "I lose!" That stated it succinctly for many of the non-participants. They ended up playing long games of hearts and bridge. Once started, these games seemed to never end, for when one participant grew weary of playing, there was a new player ready to take his hand.

By the end of the first 24 hours, many of the men were beginning to suffer their first bouts with seasickness. At the end of the second day, the head was full of soldiers emptying their stomachs of their contents. Few men were able to meet the call for guard duty.

Pat and Hank missed the evening meal at the end of the second day, as both were unable to get out of their bunks. By the third morning, Hank was up and feeling a little more like his old self but he ate lightly, just in case. In the late afternoon of that day, Pat was getting his sea legs and able to eat some. The food, though, was nothing to write home about, and on top of that the mess sergeant, a navy man, doled out such small portions that the men who were able to eat walked from the table still hungry.

Their quarters housed many men and quickly developed an unforgettable odor, which made the trips to the deck and the fresh air like a reprieve from the death sentence.

Because enemy submarines still patrolled the seas in great numbers, the ironclad rule governing the integrity of the convoy prevailed for the entire voyage – a strict lights-out policy at dusk and no smoking after dark, for even the glow of a cigarette could be seen for miles in the pitch black environs of the ocean. Even garbage had to be weighted down before being thrown overboard. Floating garbage and trash would leave a trail for a good submariner to follow and eventually locate and destroy his prey.

The men went through daily lifeboat drill and often slept in their life jackets.

On the fourth morning the *President Grant*, carrying the 168th Infantry Regiment, was no longer to be seen in the convoy, which led to the rumor that she had been torpedoed. This scuttlebutt sent chills up and down the spine of each man. Coincidentally with the ship's disappearance lifeboat drills were intensified that very day reinforcing these rumors. It turned out that the ship had developed engine trouble and had returned to port.

Because space was so limited on board the *President Lincoln*, the men were required to do physical drills and calisthenics. These exercise periods would last 15 to 20 minutes, and only those on sick call were excused. Other than their short tour on deck several times a day, the men were pretty well confined to quarters. This led to a great number of arguments, which occasionally broke out into fistfights. The NCOs, such as Sergeant Baker and the junior officers, were kept busy trying to keep a lid on these disturbances.

Ike Dennison had never wanted to be like his father. A career in the Navy was not his calling. As a matter of fact, he didn't want to have anything to do with the military at all. That was one of the reasons he had gone to the University of Illinois and majored in agriculture, to get as far away from the sea as possible.

Ike's father, through his position with the Navy in Washington, had been convinced for some time that war in Europe was inevitable, and that in some way the war would involve the United States and eventually draw her military into the conflict. Therefore, Dan insisted that Ike take reserve officer training as an elective course during his freshman year at the university. Ike, not too happy with the situation, purposefully joined the army ROTC instead of the naval training unit. He felt that this little gesture would eventually appease Dan while at the same time getting in a little dig at his father's career. Ike reasoned that he could drop these military courses prior to his senior year and thereby avoid a commitment to military duty following his graduation.

Ike started at Illinois in the fall of 1913 with the full intention of dropping out of the ROTC program in his sophomore or junior year. However, in August of 1914, shortly before he went through registration for his second year, the European conflict started. With this added impetus, he decided to stay in the program at least for another year.

At the start of both his junior and senior years, the world was still embroiled in war and he felt that maybe his dad was right after all, he might have to serve in the military, so maybe it would be better to serve as an officer.

Ike was a gentle person and pretty much of a loner. Those who did not know him well frequently misunderstood his innate shyness. His aloof, standoffish manner frequently led others to misidentify him as a snob. It was further believed that his close association with Jake, his only true friend, implicated him with the hazing of the freshmen. These rituals began shortly after a freshman pledged himself to the fraternity during the early part of the first semester and carried on into the early part of the second one, through Hell Week, which usually took place during the first week of the second semester. After this, the neophytes were finally brought into full membership in the fraternity. Little did the pledges realize that Ike was the one who empathized with them the most and was actually the one who kept the hazing from getting out of hand.

Ike liked the others in the fraternity and socialized with them frequently, but he found it difficult to get close to them, except for Jake. Though Ike and Jake were opposites in many ways, they—despite these differences—had become close friends from the beginning.

One of his reasons for not wanting to be in the military was that Ike didn't like directing the activities of others. On the flip side of that coin, he resented others telling him what to do. If he was out with some friends and they were engaged in an activity he was disinterested in, he'd just walk away and do his own thing. He never felt compelled to join the crowd. This is one of the qualities Jake admired in Ike, for Jake could not control him like he could others.

Ike's introvert nature was the principle trait that led him to join the flying service, for here he could act alone and make decisions that didn't affect others. Of equal or perhaps even greater importance was his fascination with flight. Ever since Ike had seen his first airplane in 1912, he'd dreamed about flying. He had fantasized about being able to cast aside the bonds of the earth and soar as a free spirit above the clouds.

Now here he was, a bonafide pilot, maybe not as free as he'd dreamed of being, but at least when he was alone in a plane he felt detached from the struggling, earthbound masses below. Ike's flying skills developed quickly and after his first solo flight he'd taken to the air aggressively and graduated from basic training at the top of his class with just less than 40 hours of flying time. Now, he was not only a pilot, but also a fighter pilot on his way to war.

With silver wings attached to his uniform, he headed for New York to board a ship bound for France. He and his fellow pilots had two weeks to get to the big city, so Ike made a brief stop in Washington to visit his folks one last time before sailing for Europe.

His stay in Washington had been relaxing. This was the first time he had been home since the previous Christmas, a little over 10 months ago. His mother, Doris, outdid herself in fixing whatever Ike desired. He'd arrived on October 23, with nine days of leave before he had to report to New York and eventually ship out to France.

Ike and his mother had a great time during his short stay. They reviewed the old family album, did some sightseeing, and took a short car trip across the border into Virginia to visit his mother's sister.

His father had been at sea on a shakedown cruise since early September and was due home on leave on the twenty-seventh. Ike looked forward to visiting with his dad—he felt they had much to talk about. Ike had come to realize that the military life was not as bad as he had once thought, but still he didn't want to make the military a career.

However, in the past few months, he had developed greater admiration for his dad and his accomplishments with the Navy.

The night was dark as pitch, and the overcast sky made it even darker. It was just a little after midnight as Captain Links stood on the Conning Tower Bridge scanning the French coast. With the aid of binoculars and the pattern of city lights along the shore, he was able to determine the mouth of the river near the port of St. Nazare located just off Belle Isle. The U-boat was about five miles offshore. The sea was calm and there was no wind. The only sound came from the low rumble of the boat's diesel engines as they gurgled away, recharging the massive batteries. The executive officer, Lieutenant Jensen, stood at his captain's side.

"How much longer for the batteries to be fully charged, Hans?"

"About thirty to forty minutes, sir."

"Let me know as soon as they're ready, we need to start moving soon. We must enter the river at about two a.m. We will submerge about two miles from the mouth and navigate using the periscope. Its use must be minimized or else someone may see it. The report said that the troop convoy would be entering the port around ten in the morning. We need to be about two miles up stream in order to launch the torpedoes without being seen. If this works, we can get more than one of the American troop ships and give those Yanks something to think about."

"Aye, Captain."

Hans Jensen had been sailing with Captain Links for nearly two years now and had become accustomed to his reckless manner. He didn't have the nerve to ask him how they were going to get out of the river after torpedoing the troop ships. He didn't want to be submitted to that terrible temper Links was famous for. But the captain was well known for taking chances and always seemed to come through without a scratch. After all, he was one of the most decorated submariners in the Imperial Navy.

When the batteries were charged, the U-boat got underway and started for the mouth of the river. Two miles out the boat submerged to periscope depth, and continued upriver. They proceeded slowly. The charts revealed sufficient water depth but their mission was made hazardous by the presence of the unpredictable, ever shifting sandbars. To run aground here would mean certain capture.

Once in position, the sub was brought to the surface to take on enough air so that at daybreak, it could settle on the bottom and wait for their prey to arrive. It was still dark and the lookouts were instructed not to speak or show any light unless there was an emergency. They were within 200 meters of the shore and could hear the sounds of a town that was waking after a night of slumber.

When Captain Links could see the eastern sky glow with the light of a soon-to-rise sun, he motioned the lookouts down and went below, ordering the sub to submerge.

Nineteen-year-old Agnes Bovay, was anxious to get to school. She had run down to the boat ten minutes ago thinking her father was right behind. Finally, he came out of the house and meandered down to the dock. It seemed to take him forever to load his fishing gear, climb aboard, and start the motor.

When the weather permitted he would take Agnes to school in the boat before he would leave the harbor for a hard day of fishing in the Atlantic.

Once they were underway, Agnes sat up in the prow of the boat with her elbows on the gunnels and gazed at the water while the wind blew through her hair, daydreaming about her future and the traveling she so desperately wanted to do.

The clouds were beginning to clear and she could see the reflection of blue sky off the surface of the water. There was a chill in the air but it felt good as she breathed in its' freshness.

As she was daydreaming, she saw a large semi-submerged log ahead and motioned to her father to turn out away from the shore. Agnes had always liked sitting in the bow of the boat and looking for the hazards that might be in their way. It gave her time to be alone and think about most anything without being interrupted.

The trip down the river from Agnes's home to the point where her father would drop her off for school took about twenty minutes. A little beyond the halfway point, Agnes saw another object in the water, dead ahead. She motioned to her father to steer a little more to the north.

He acknowledged with a wave and turned the boat a few degrees to the right.

Agnes looked again at the object to be sure they wouldn't hit it. It was then that she saw that it was a metal object, not wood. It was vertical and painted black. It seemed to be a strange place for a metal pipe to be sticking out of the water, for she knew it was very deep here.

Suddenly the object swiveled and caught the sun with a blinding reflection. Instantly, she knew it was a periscope.

It was eight a.m. and Captain Links ordered the boat to come to periscope depth. He peered into it and scanned the western horizon directly west of the harbor. He could make out the smoke from the convoy and the tiny specks that were the ships. They should be nearing the harbor in about one hour. He asked Hans if he wanted to take a look. Hans immediately bent to peer through the eyepiece.

"That's our target, Hans. Just like ducks on a pond."

Hans agreed and stepped away to let the captain take a last look.

Before lowering the scope, Captain Links started turning it in a circle to get a view of his total environment. Just as he was looking toward the stern, he saw it, a boat, almost on top of him.

When Agnes realized what the object was, she screamed and frantically waved both hands at her father. Upon hearing his daughter's screams, he reduced the motor to idle and stood to peer over the bow of the boat. Agnes's words were clear and loud.

"Periscope, periscope, a German submarine."

He quickly pulled his rifle from under the seat, found the target, and fired two rounds at it before it disappeared below the surface. He worked his way forward to Agnes and they both peered over the side into the murky water. They saw nothing.

Her father started back towards the stern and said, "We must get to shore and report to the authorities and tell them what we have seen."

With that, he reached the tiller, pushed the throttle full forward, and turned towards shore as the boat picked up speed.

Captain Links saw the figures in the boat and saw the man lift a rifle, "Down periscope, full speed ahead," he yelled. "Come to a heading of 285 degrees and take her down to 30 meters."

Slowly, the U-boat started to move and begin its dive. Captain Links looked at his executive officer. "We've been discovered. A fisherman in a boat almost ran us down. He fired his rifle at the periscope. We must leave the harbor at once, before word gets to the patrol boats. In five minutes take her to periscope depth, get your bearings, and then take her down. We can't afford to surface again till we're well out at sea. I estimate that the fisherman will not be able to notify the authorities for about ten minutes."

"Aye-aye, sir."

Early in the morning of October 31, 1917, the shouts that land had been sighted brought all of the men on the President Lincoln to the deck. Though they had been at sea for only thirteen days, the men reacted as if they'd never seen land before.

When the French pilot was brought on board, he was cheered as a conquering hero. Every person seen, mainly fishermen in their little boats heading out for a day's work, got a robust shout of joy from the men of the Rainbow.

The men were having a great time and didn't give a thought to the war, but the celebrating ceased when it was announced that they were to return to their quarters immediately. German U-boats had been sighted. As the men went below, the ships began a turn away from the harbor. The last thing Pat saw as he went down the ladder were three sub chasers from their escort speeding into the harbor.

Pat, Hank, and two men from the supply company sat on the bottom bunks talking to one another across the aisle and playing a spirited game of bridge. After going below, the men tightened the straps on their life jackets and sat waiting for news. As nothing seemed to be happening, they started the card game. Joe Hensley, one of the men from supply, said, "I sure don't want to start using this thing now," pointing to his life jacket. The others nodded.

"So near, yet so far," Hank said, then added, "Three spades" in response to his partner's bid.

The card games and conversation continued interrupted only by occasional reports that filtered down from topside—"We're going around in large circles" or "We're headed north." But nothing about the threat of the U-boats. The men didn't appear worried. They were confident the Navy could handle the threat.

Late in the afternoon, Captain Arnold made the long climb down the hatchway ladder and gave the men the official word.

"Men, the Navy has swept the harbor clean and there is no longer a threat from the subs. We are at this very moment entering the harbor, and will be dropping anchor around dusk. Once that is accomplished the portholes will be opened."

There were some loud cheers and applause from the men.

"But," Captain Arnold continued, "you will have to stay here until mealtime. It will still be a few more days before we disembark."

With that comment there were a few boos and other expressions of unhappiness.

"Any questions? Good, carry on." With that said, Captain Arnold turned and started up the ladder.

After anchoring, the portholes were opened and the fresh air rushed in, each man breathing it in with great delight. Those who were lucky enough to be close to the portholes reported events on the outside to their shipmates in the interior portions of the ship.

The 42nd Division was officially acknowledged as being the fourth American division to arrive in France. The 1st and 26th Divisions and the vanguard of the 2nd Division were the only other American units to precede the 42nd Division to France. In total, after the arrival of the Rainbow, there were fewer than 100,000 American troops in France.

To Coetquidan

Prior to his return to England in July, Captain Montgomery had felt compelled by events, to put in for sea duty. He was terribly concerned over the great success the German U-boats were having in their campaign to strangle the sea-lanes into England.

The convoy system was beginning to make significant strides in preventing losses, but there was still more work to be done in thwarting the U-boat menace.

Captain Montgomery had spent many years at sea. His last command was in late May, 1916, as the commander of the destroyer, *Christopher*, attached to the Third Battle Cruiser Squadron under the flag of Horace Hood on the *HMS Invincible*.

After coming under attack from the German Second Scouting Group of light cruisers, Admiral Hood, late in the evening of May 31, 1916, ordered the destroyer flotilla to proceed with a mass torpedo counterattack. It was during this fray that the *Christopher* was hit by two salvos from a German cruiser's 12-inch guns. Captain Montgomery and what remained of his crew soon found themselves swimming frantically for their lives, in order to put as much distance between themselves and the fighting that was raging around them. This, the Battle of Jutland, in the North Sea was the one great sea battle of the war between the British Grand Fleet and the German High Seas Naval Command.

This great battle ended in somewhat of a draw. Though the German fleet inflicted greater numerical losses on their enemy than they suffered at the hands of the British, the High Seas Fleet withdrew under the cover of darkness and returned to homeport, never to venture out again.

After being fished out of the water and a short recuperation period in the hospital, Robert Montgomery was reassigned to work with the admiralty as a naval attaché.

He liked the work but he always had a longing to return to the sea. It was when his friend, Captain Dennison of the US Navy, told him that he had requested sea duty and then was given command of a new destroyer that Captain Montgomery's longing to return to shipboard duty intensified.

Before returning to England, Robert Montgomery put in his request for reassignment, and was granted a new command shortly after returning home. He finished his duties with the Admiralty in September and early in October he took command of a newly outfitted Q-ship.

The Q-ship was a naval warfare concept developed, in the early stages of the war, as a means of confronting and destroying the German submarine menace.

Late in 1914, Captain Montgomery had been a member of the committee that developed this weapon that came to fruition late in November of 1915, with the launching of the first ship of its kind, the *Baralong*.

These ships soon became England's primary weapon employed by the Admiralty against the U-boat. The Q-ship, from outward appearances, was a merchantman, fishing trawler, tramp steamer or yacht that plied the coastal waters around the Channel and the western approaches to England.

In reality, a Q-ship was a ship of war that was in disguise. The vast majority of these ships were old freighters, outfitted with five or six heavy guns, maybe some deck-mounted torpedoes, and some even were equipped with depth charges. All of the tools of war were mounted in concealed locations around the ship's main deck. The weapons were normally hidden in fake deck cargo or cabins whose walls could be quickly pushed out and down in order for them to come into play against the enemy. These ships would appear as harmless tramp steamers delivering goods to English ports.

The ships had the necessary equipment on board to change their appearance overnight. Under the cover of darkness, they would be repainted and false masts, funnels, cabins and deck cargo would be put into place, for if a U-boat observed the same ship sailing up and down the coast, they may become suspicious of its presence and not attack, or worse, attack with torpedoes.

As the German U-boats had limited storage space for torpedoes, it was not uncommon for them to surface and sink the single, unescorted merchant ships with their deck guns, especially when the weather and the condition of the seas permitted. This practice allowed them to remain at sea, on station for longer periods of time, without having to return home to take on more of their deadly missiles.

It followed that the Q ships patrolling in the same waters, needed to change their overall appearance frequently so they would appear as a merchant on their way to or from an allied port.

The ruse went beyond just the outward appearances. There were even extra crewmen who would abandon ship when they came under attack from a U-boat's deck gun. The crewmen dressed the part of common seamen and the ships flew flags of different nations, until they were ready to fire on the enemy. At that time, the foreign flag was hauled down and the white ensign was raised.

The purpose of the supplementary crew was to present to the U-boat a picture of men in panic, men that were running in fear of their lives, leaving the appearance that the ship had been left derelict in the sea. In the meantime, the other members of the crew, unseen by the enemy, stayed at their battle stations.

This act had a purpose—to draw the submarine in close enough to the Q-ship in order for the gunners to bring their guns to bear and inflict serious damage prior to the U-boat's attempt to submerge and thus escape. The whole purpose behind the concept of the Q-ship was to entice U-boats into this kind of surface fight.

Early in November 1917, with Captain Montgomery in command, the 3300-ton collier, the *Londondary*, set sail to ply the waters along the western coast of England.

For the first time since boarding the *President Lincoln*, the men of Battery F slept well. The ship was anchored, stationary and secure, in the harbor of St. Nazaire. The portholes were at last opened, allowing the fresh air to circulate throughout the hold. The men were able to sleep with the fresh, sweet-smelling sea air.

Early in the morning of their first full day in France, little boats loaded with merchandise and fruit made their way from the docks of St. Nazaire to the ships. The local merchants of the chamber of commerce and other business associations rowed and sailed to the troop ships, offering their goods to the new arrivals. Soon, men who were still confined to their quarters below deck were lowering their campaign hats from the portholes on long thin ropes in order to purchase the wares the peddlers had to offer. This eventually led to some misunderstandings and hard feelings due to language problems and the fact that the French business people had no intention of learning the American monetary system and frequently would not return change for goods purchased.

Tom Brooks and Paul Driscol, who felt they were shortchanged, teamed up to extract their retribution. Tom dangled his campaign hat out of the porthole, just aft of the head discharge pipe, giving the appearance that he wanted to make a purchase from the merchants in the small boats below. As always, when a campaign hat was lowered, the French businessmen made a mad dash for it, in order to be the first to get the Yanks' dollars. When one of the boats came too close to the ship just under the pipe, Paul, at Tom's signal, would open the valve and drench the boat and its passengers with its contents. These two were not the only ones to indulge in this game, and it didn't do well in creating good relations between the Allies.

The enlisted personnel had been confined to their quarters since midmorning of October 31, and had been in the hold from then through the third of November. Their only activity was helping to unload the ship. Some were allowed to work on the docks handling the equipment and supplies off-loaded, while the remainder spent the time filling the loading nets, dropped into the hold from the large cranes. With the heavy work and confinement, the men were getting restless and bored. Tempers were short and the confinement only added to the problem. As a result, when the supplies were all on the dock, the decision was made to issue passes on November 4 to those who were not on kitchen or guard duty.

Pat, Hank, Paul, Tom and Jack joined up shortly after hitting the dock. This was their first opportunity to see France firsthand. They started at the small cafés along the harbor and gradually made their way into town. They stopped and sampled all kinds of foods, mainly pastries and candies, everything being new and different to these Midwesterners.

"Our thoughts seem to be of food above all else," Jack said, who seemed always to be hungry and, he was the only one of the group that didn't need to eat all of the time. Jack wasn't fat but for his 5'10" height his 200 pounds placed him on the portly side.

"Yeah, I could eat everything in sight. Those little pastries are something else," Paul responded. "It's all particularly good after that tasteless garbage they give us on the ship."

The five young men continued to make the rounds of the town and stayed away from the local streetwalkers, particularly, after viewing the movie put on by the YMCA the night before which graphically depicted the results of contracting venereal disease.

During the late afternoon as their tour was coming to a close, Pat said, "Do ya notice anything strange about this place?"

"Other than we're in France and everything is completely different?" said Paul with a laugh.

Pat ignored Paul's sarcasm. "There are no young men. I guess it's the result of the war we're here to fight! And did ya notice all of the women in black?"

This first leave was all too short and they were soon back at the ship. The men had many things to discuss and to write home about, the most sobering subject being the missing young men and the women in black. It was a silent testimonial to the suffering most French citizens had been through either directly or indirectly because of the war.

The next day, passes again were distributed but soon withdrawn, as orders were issued instructing the troops to prepare to leave the ship and head for a temporary camp outside St. Nazaire.

After close to three weeks aboard the *President Lincoln* the men of Battery F were permitted to become landlubbers again.

During the afternoon of November 5, in full marching gear, the regiment assembled on deck and proceeded down the gangway. On the dock they formed up in columns and marched through town on their way to Rest Camp No. 1.

Curious crowds lined the sidewalks to watch the Yanks. There was a polite applause but the citizens were wondering and questioning whether these youthful soldiers from across the Atlantic were good enough to change the fortunes of war. The men, who had spent eighteen days on board ship, were too involved in keeping up with Colonel Reilly, who had set a rigid and rapid pace, to worry about the reception the locals were giving them. Every muscle in the men's bodies ached under the load of their packs, and before long they were gasping for air. It would take some time to recondition the body to the rigors of a soldier's life on land.

It was a four-kilometer march from the city to the camp, and this new location presented the regiment with another little surprise from the War Department. From the tight, dry confines of the ship, the men found the camp awash in ankle-deep mud. There were no floors in their portable barracks, and the men spent the nights on the ground. Comfort was out of the question.

It rained continuously. The men had only blankets between them and the ooze the first night on land.

The next day a load of straw was dumped in the area between the barracks of Battery F and Battery D. During the following melee, all friendships were cast aside as the troops fought over the straw that could be put under the blankets to help keep out the damp and cold.

The Rainbow Division took seven days to disembark and settle in at the camp. During that time, they received word of the Italian reverses at the hands of the Austrians at Capretto. Worst of all was the news of the collapse of the Russian government and their intention of signing a separate peace treaty with the Germans. Home was thousands of miles away and it appeared that the war would last well into its fourth year. In addition to the news and the living conditions, most local stores and cafes charged exorbitant prices. All added to the heavy gloom that hung over the men during their first days in France.

After establishing their office in the camp, Major Hinkle and his staff began ironing out the details of locating the various units in their training areas. The Artillery Brigade, which consisted of the Illinois,

Indiana and Minnesota Regiments, was to go to Camp Coetquidan in Brittany. The Trench Mortar Battery was headed for Langres, and the divisional headquarters and the infantry regiments were off to the Vaucoulers area.

The railroads were no less crucial to the movement of troops than they were in the United States. Major Hinkle's fluency with the language permitted him to conduct the negotiations for the needed transport. The division was to be moved, in most part, on what the men fondly called 40 and 8s, as each of the side loading doors were marked: "HOMMES 40, et CHEAVAUX 8". These were rail freight cars that could accommodate either 40 men or 8 horses.

As the trains became available, the divisional units gradually began leaving St. Nazaire for their advanced training areas.

Early in the morning of the eleventh, the men of the Second Battalion of the 149th Field Artillery were awakened and ordered to prepare their equipment and themselves for the trip to Brittany.

After a breakfast of bread and syrup, the men marched to the station and boarded the 40 and 8 cars that would take them to Camp Coetquidan. There they would prepare the area for the arrival of the rest of the regiment, scheduled to arrive in the next two days.

As the troop train rambled through the countryside, the men fortunate enough to be located near the loading doors or windows reported to the others that the landscape was hilly and rolling, marked with various-colored fields and small towns. They even passed an occasional chateau or castle that would bring the others to the doors to see. This led to a constant maneuvering in the freight cars as the men fought over the choice seats by the doors. Every man wanted an opportunity to see the countryside.

After a very long ride, the train pulled into the village of Guier, where the standard gauge rails ended. There, in the late afternoon, the troops left the train and boarded trucks that transported the battalion the remaining distance to their destination.

Once the troops arrived in camp they were pleasantly surprised to find their barracks had wooden floors and steel-framed beds with real mattresses and pillows. To add to their wonder, mail forwarded from Camp Mills was distributed. As soon as it had been handed out, the barracks fell silent as each man read his letters from home. The quiet was punctuated with occasional brief and subdued exclamations, as someone would relate bits of news to friends nearby.

Hank let out a moan of desperation as he opened a package from Betsy only to discover she had sent him a baked ham in hopes he would receive it at Camp Mills. Instead it had been buried away in some old tattered mailbag for over five weeks. It was putrid and emitted an offensive odor.

"That's disgusting," was Pat's only comment as he looked up from his own mail.

After finishing reading his letter from home, Pat shared some of the chocolate chip cookies and brownies his mother had baked and sent to him. The baked goods were dry and rock hard, but it was great eating some "home-cooked" food.

Betsy's letter to Hank was filled with excitement as she had heard, from reliable sources, that "the Rainbow Division would spend the winter at Camp Mills before leaving for the continent." She looked forward to seeing him soon. Hank could do nothing but heave a deep sigh, as tears came to his eyes over this bit of misinformation.

The next day the battery prepared to take over the barracks that, up to this time, had been occupied by German prisoners. With the large influx of troops into Camp Coetquidan for the purposes of training, the prisoners were being moved. The 149th would occupy nearly 25 barracks to accommodate the six batteries. Battery F alone would occupy four buildings, three for housing the troops, about sixty men each, and one to serve as the mess hall.

This was the first up close look the Americans had of the enemy. They had seen some earlier, from a distance, on the docks at St. Nazaire. These prisoners appeared old, dirty, and unshaven. Their uniforms were in tatters and they didn't appear very formidable.

Some of the men started trading articles with these poor wretches, generally cigarettes for watches, metals, or other trinkets still in their possession. This seemingly harmless barter was soon put to a stop by the French commandant, who did not want the prisoners to enjoy the luxury of a good cigarette or any other "fraternization with the enemy."

After the German prisoners departed from their barracks, crews moved in and tore down the perimeter wire, removed all furnishings, and with shovels and picks in hand they tediously dug out the top six inches of soil from the hard clay floors. A second detail, clad only in blue denims, entered the buildings with a generous mixture of creosote and whitewash and cleaned the walls and ceilings.

These extra-ordinary measures were taken to clean the barracks and in particular rid the dwellings of the cooties that had infested the previous occupants. "Cooties" were little parasitic bugs that would bore their way into and under the skin, resulting in extreme discomfort and itching. All of the men in the cleaning detail had their hair cropped close to their head to lessen the chance of the little critters finding a hiding place there. Prior to rejoining their comrades in the battery, the detail was required to strip and bathe in their own cleaning preparation.

This process of preparing quarters for the regiment took two days, and by the end of November 14, metal cots, mattresses, and pillows were placed in the barracks. The camp was ready for the arrival of the rest of the regiment.

The First Battalion's job had been to load all of the equipment and rolling stock on the trains for transport to Coetquidan.

The camp at Coetquidan had been established by Napoleon as a holding place for his political prisoners. Its isolation and the year-round inclement weather made it a very inhospitable place. In recent years it had been converted to an artillery training camp. At that time, modern barracks with a sanitary system, running water and electricity had been built, but not for the use of the 149th Field Artillery. With the advent of German prisoners two years earlier, utilitarian barracks had been erected. These were simple wood frame structures covered with tarpaper and oilpaper windows for light. Ventilation was not a problem, for the structures were little more than a windbreak, and forestalled only the lightest of sprinkles from dribbling through.

These austere surroundings were to house Battery F for the next ten weeks.

The first Saturday after settling into the encampment, weekend passes were issued to 10 percent of the regiment. The passes were dispersed equally among all units attached to the 149th. At three in the afternoon, there was a mad rush for the little narrow-gauge train that would carry the leave takers into Rennes.

Hank and Pat, not being one of the 10 percent crowd, remained in camp. But all was not lost. The little villages located near the camp and within walking distance offered the enticement of hard liquor, wine, beer and sour cider.

In the evening the little cafés were filled with American and French artillerymen, sampling the offerings. The French Poilus, an endearing term used by the French when referring to their fighting men, sipped cider, all they could afford on their meager pay, while the Americans sampled vin rouge, vin blanc, brandy, and even champagne. Though unable to understand each other's language, the American and French got along famously.

Pat, Hank, and a large number of others from the battery were crowded around a group of little tables sipping wine and talking in loud voices in order to be heard. While talking to Hank, Pat stopped in mid sentence when a large group of Poilus started singing the "Marseilles." When finished, Jack Bayless, who was three sheets to the wind, shouted over to a barmaid and ordered a bottle of wine for the "frogs," whose appreciation was expressed in yet another song, "Madeline," but at a much higher volume.

This rendition, when finished, brought Hank to his feet, and in a beautiful tenor voice, he started singing "The Battle Hymn of the Republic." Soon every other Yank in the bar joined him. This selection was followed by a rendition of "Dixie," sung in honor of the southern Illinois contingent of the battery. The trading of songs between the Allies went well into the night.

Not since before the beginning of the war had the barmaids, who lived in the vicinity of Coetquidan, had so much attention as they now received from the Yanks. The war years had taken its toll on these women who served in the little bars and cafes. Their appearance and personal hygiene had slipped into disrepair. New and stylish clothes, including those foundation garments that kept the girlish shapes, were no longer available. If they existed at all, they were certainly out of reach of a barmaid's wages. The three years of war in France had brought about shortages of civilian goods and spiraling inflation. Many of the foods rich in the nutrients needed for healthy teeth and bones were scarce, and medical and dental care were just not available.

No matter their appearance, the young American soldiers treated them as debutantes and they warmed to the attention. Fun and romance had once again returned to their dull, drab lives.

By the time they all had to head back to camp, Jack was under the table. Pat and Hank, feeling no pain themselves, lifted him to his feet and walked him back to the barracks. He promptly deposited his supper on the floor by his cot and fell back on the bed, dead to the world.

"That takes care of Jack. I don't know about you, Hank," Pat said, "but I'm off to bed myself. He can clean up his own mess in the morning." With that, both men headed for their bunks Sunday, the men had most of the day to themselves—after the necessary cleanup chores and recovery from the previous night's hangover.

"I'm not going to repeat last night, ever again," Jack mumbled as he sat on his cot rubbing his temples. "Just cleaning the mess up was bad enough, but this hangover is terrible."

In the early afternoon, four French vehicles pulled up next to the mess hall and placed four 75mm guns between it and the street. These were the weapons Battery F was to use in the coming months. It was a solemn reminder that war was just around the corner. Captain Arnold had ordered the weapons upon their arrival in France.

Early on Monday morning, November 20, training began in earnest. Artillery specialists of all kinds descended on the 149th Field Artillery. These were primarily French soldiers who had years of battle experience, particularly in the use of the 75s.

The specialists for Battery F went through a lengthy discussion on the canon, naming its parts as they field stripped the gun and pointed out the item's function. When they completed tearing the gun down, they reassembled it in what to Pat seemed like mere seconds. They talked about handling ammunition, loading, aiming and firing the weapon.

When the day drew to a close, Paul Driscol leaned across to Pat and said, "Did ya get all of that?"

"Yeah, in one ear and out the other."

Just then the French gunnery sergeant said in his perfect English, "This is just an overview of the 75. Don't expect it all to stick with you now. This has been just a beginning and it will all fit together in time."

The French team then demonstrated loading and firing a blank cartridge. After a loud report, the instructors demonstrated cleaning the weapon and dismissed the men as the day was drawing to a close.

The remainder of the week involved schools and drill. Telephone men learned to lay the wire, the mechanics learned more about the internal workings of the guns as well as necessary maintenance. Engineers worked on digging trenches, emplacements, and roads. All of the men were schooled on signaling using both mechanical and visual means. They also went through standing gun drill learning the art of the cannoneers, aiming, loading and firing. They were also subjected to gas drill, unregistered firing problems, terrain exercises, moving the guns, disciplinary drill, marches with full packs, and on and on.

On Friday afternoon, the entire regiment attended a funeral for a Corporal Johnson from Battery A, who succumbed to pneumonia on Thursday evening. This was the regiment's first Casualty, and it weighed heavy upon the men.

Preceded by the band playing Chopin's funeral march, all of the troops marched to the little cemetery, across the road from the main entrance, for the interment. General Summerall, Colonel Reilly, and the French commandant led the parade. After some words by Reverend James and a salute by the firing squad, the bugler played taps and the men returned to camp to a Sousa march.

On the second day at Camp Coetquidan, another regular Army artillery officer, First Lieutenant Case, was assigned as second in command to the battery, and was immediately put in charge of training.

Infantry at Vaucouleurs

Soon after the 167th Infantry Regiment boarded the 40 and 8 freight cars, the train started moving and they were on their way to the Vaucouleurs area. Originally the infantry and the Headquarters Company of the 42nd Division were to go to Rolampont, but because that area wasn't ready to receive an American-sized division, the infantry was temporarily diverted to Vaucouleurs. The desperate need to train the Americans and move them into the line required adjustment to the training programs.

Vaucouleurs was located near the city of Toul in the province of Lorraine. It was from Toul that Joan of Arc started her great crusade in 1429. This historical fact did not impress the doughboys as much as the large and pungent manure piles that were located in every front yard of the local citizens. These piles were to be found throughout the region and, according to custom, were a means of showing off one's worldly wealth.

The trip on the train had been long and excruciatingly slow. The enlisted men suffered the discomfort more than the officers, who rode in regular, though old, passenger cars.

Jake spent most of his time playing poker, reading or sleeping. The train stopped innumerable times and always with a series of jerks. This made sleeping difficult, if not impossible. When Jake would finally get to sleep, the train would grind to a halt, and he was wide-awake again.

If nothing else, his pockets were full of cash. His father, a professional gambler, had taught Jake all of the intricacies of poker before he had deserted the family some ten years ago. It was his father's guilty conscience that had put Jake through the university.

It seems that his dad hit it big in a game of chance about two years after leaving the family, and he sent a large sum to Jake's mother. She invested the money wisely and it eventually put Jake through college with the aid of a scholarship he had earned in high school. His mother died the year he entered the tenth grade, ostensibly of heart failure, but more likely of a broken heart.

Jake was sent to live with his loving maternal aunt, who helped the troubled lad turn his life around. It was she that eventually brought Jake to the Lord, though his actions at times belied his beliefs.

Jake had only heard about his father once since the money arrived, and that from an unreliable source. Apparently he'd been shot and killed in a poker game in New Orleans. Jake didn't care that much, as he had little feeling for his father, particularly after what he had done to his mother.

At 3:00 p.m. on November 20, 1917, the train ground to its final stop; they finally arrived just outside Vaucouleurs.

It took several days for the regiment to establish their semi-permanent living area. This gave Jake and his fellow officers some time to reconnoiter the area. They found many places to buy food and wine and after hours they would create their own parties.

All too soon they were back to their intensive training regimen. Jake found himself back in the so-called classroom, where experienced officers and enlisted men from the other allied armies brought the Americans up to date on modern warfare.

It didn't take long for the hospitals at Camp Coetquidan to start filling up as many men fell victim to influenza and pneumonia. The marches to the little cemetery across the road were not that infrequent.

For those who maintained their health, the intensive training continued. It was on the third weekend in Coetquidan that another 10 percent of the regiment received passes. The mechanics of Battery F were included in the group this time and Pat, Hank, Tom and Paul were soon on their way to Rennes. Early Saturday afternoon, they joined the rush for the little narrow-gauge train that would take them into the city.

After arriving in Rennes, the enlisted men literally ran to the best hotels and normally ended up in the best rooms. The officers, on the other hand, felt it was below their dignity to run and they ended up with the lesser quality rooms that were left.

No matter how events turned out, all had a great time. Pat and Hank did their Christmas shopping while there, as did many of the others. It was necessary to get the packages off to the states before the end of November if their loved ones were to receive their gifts by Christmas day. The weekend flew by and late Sunday night the train, loaded way beyond capacity, chugged its way back to camp.

Before they knew it, Monday morning was upon them once again, and the men were back at the routine of intensive daily drill. The training and selection of cannon and other important crews was progressing rapidly, however little was being done in determining who would be picked to be drivers for the battery. The horses and mules sent to Newport News were still in the states and the regimental harness had been aboard the *President Grant*, the ship that had been forced to return to New York because of engine trouble. It would be a couple of weeks before the all-important harnesses would begin to show up in camp.

On November 25, Captain Arnold was sent to staff school at Langres. The men from his hometown, Champaign-Urbana, did not lament his departure. The good captain had the best interests of the battery at heart, but he was not the man destined to lead the battery into battle. Command fell upon the shoulders of the newly assigned executive officer, First Lieutenant Case.

Lieutenant Samuel Case was regular Army, a graduate of The Citadel who had spent ten years in the service. He was an expert in artillery logistics and movement. He had also developed a true skill in dealing with people and was soon highly respected by the entire battery, including the hard-to-please Lt. Allen who was also promoted, to the position of executive officer of Battery F.

Time passed quickly, and soon Thanksgiving was upon them. This festive day fell on Thursday, November 29, and was declared a holiday, much to the delight of the men. Many of the troops spent the morning in the little cafes around the camp, whetting their appetites for the afternoon feast. In the early afternoon there was a football game between the men of the First and Second Battalions.

Finally at 4:30, dinner was served. The traditional holiday feast consisted of turkey and dressing, potatoes, cranberries, apple pie, donuts, hot chocolate, and rolls. A big party followed the meal, in the mess hall. Wine flowed, and though it wasn't of quality, there definitely was a lot of it.

Training returned to normal the next day and the men endured the schools and drill in spite of their hangovers.

The daily training continued until December 5, when the guns were finally hauled out to the firing range for the first time. The men had looked forward to this day for a long time, the first real test of their ability to fire live ammunition.

Lt. Case was in overall command of the drill and stood in the observation tower, leaving Lt. Allen in charge of the guns and their crews. Pappy ordered the number one gun crew to fire their weapon without going into "abatage." This simply was the process of firing the piece without lowering the brakes that normally prevent the gun from rolling backward from the recoil at the moment the projectile leaves the barrel. The force of this recoil nearly knocked the gunner and number one cannoneer from their seats, which were mounted to the frame of the cannon.

With each shot Lt. Allen would shout, "Ride that gun." And ride it they did. Then each of the other three guns fired four or five rounds without going into abatage. The cannoneer on gun three was thrown from his seat on the first round and then held on tenaciously for the other rounds. Once Pappy was satisfied that the men could handle the recoil, he ordered the guns to be put into abatage.

As the firing continued, the men gained confidence and started tossing the shells around with reckless abandon. When Jess Terry dropped a shell, Pappy came unglued. "Do ya want to kill us all, every soul in the battery? You better start handling those shells with tender loving care."

Next, at gun position two, a shell failed to fire and the loader, Tom Driscol, pulled the missile from the breech and cradled it in his arms. He thought that he heard it hiss and ran around in circles for he was sure it would blow at any second. Pappy grabbed him by the shoulders and headed him off to a point in front of the gun and told him to take it out 25 yards or so and set it down carefully and then hightail it back, which he did.

The shell didn't explode, but most of the men, particularly Tom, breathed a sigh of relief when he got back. It turned out that much of the ammunition was defective and frequently exploded prematurely, or not at all.

As school continued, more and more time was spent on the range. After daytime training there was always guard duty, a task no man liked.

In the evenings or when the guns weren't in use, eight men were detailed to the firing range to guard the cannons. This was the only guard duty the men could describe as being pleasant. The Officer of the Day rarely took time to go out to the range and the men soon stopped walking posts. One man would take over the duty for a few hours before trading off with another. His job was to gather firewood and keep a lookout for any officer who would "dare" to venture out to the range.

The other men would set up shelter halves and wrap themselves in blankets and keep warm by sitting around the fire. Any food they could steal from the kitchen would be cooked over the open fire. This usually consisted of bacon, bread and coffee. Day and night the air was filled with the aroma of frying bacon and freshly brewed coffee. This was the only agreeable guard duty the men could find.

Shortly after the regiment arrived at Coetquidan, a couple of enterprising Parisian businessmen built two little cafes just outside the main gate of the encampment and they had little difficulty finding patrons from the camp. Off-duty hours were frequently spent at these and other nearby establishments.

After Thanksgiving the weather turned cold and it rained more frequently. On December 8, the first contingent of horses arrived. These still were not the original nags from Newport News, but rather some local underfed, unshod, and scraggly-looking animals the army purchased from some neighboring farmers. As the battery's handlers were still en route, the handling of these horses fell on the shoulders of two Chicago boys who had difficulty telling one end of a horse from the other. It soon became apparent that the job was too big for them. It, consequently, was placed in the hands of some German prisoners who were familiar with horses.

The ensuing days were filled with monotonous drudgery; schools and drills during long, cold, rainy days. The men spent more time out on the firing range where high explosive shells were now in use, almost exclusively, and the cannoneers' accuracy was improving with each passing day. The new ammunition was more reliable and there were fewer misfires.

In an effort to head off further respiratory infections such as head colds and flu, the regimental command, in its infinite wisdom, erected showers for the men of each battery and supplied them with plenty of hot water. However, the showers were outside, and once out from under the warm stream of water, the cold was almost unbearable, and many of the men soon found an assortment of excuses for omitting the weekly bath. This action was not well received by anyone who came into contact with the non-bathers.

As a result, Pappy devised a shower log system in order to try and force all of the members of the battery to bathe at least once a week. Some found a way around the regimen but the plan, on the whole, did work.

Christmas

Christmas was fast in coming, and in order to relieve their cramped space, the post office released packages to the men on the Sunday before that eventful day.

Pat and Hank, both in pensive moods, sat in the little cafe outside the gates of Coetquidan late Sunday evening, sipping glasses of red wine. They reminisced about all that had happened over the past year.

"Can you believe Christmas is just two days away?" Hank said.

"Quite frankly, no!" Pat retorted. "Just a year ago I was home on the farm worrying about final exams that would start right after the Christmas holidays. As I remember, I was also apprehensive about the fraternity's Hell Week that was to start with the beginning of the second semester. The last thought in my mind was being here in France, or in the army for that matter. Things sure have changed for us."

"Yeah, I know, I never for a moment thought I'd be here, and a married man at that."

"It's going to be hard being so far away from home at Christmas. But what the hell, we've got to make the best of it. The guys in the battery are sure a great bunch."

"They're a good group, all right, and at the very least, we're not alone," Hank said.

"That Paul Driscol is really a character. One of the funniest guys I've come across.

"Ya know when they released the packages this morning, he tore into 'em just like a little kid, and all he got was canned beans and corned Willie. Why, he was fit to be tied."

Pat laughed. "Well, wouldn't you be mad, too? That's been our main diet for over the past month and a half, and here his parents send him another month's supply. Boy, did they miss the boat on that present."

"When are you opening your packages? I'm waiting till Tuesday," Hank asked.

"Yeah, Christmas Day for me too. That's always been the family tradition. Then there's that big barracks party tomorrow night, and I'm afraid it'll last well into Christmas morning."

They fell quiet for a while until Pat spoke again. "When do ya think we'll be moving out and into the line?"

"I really don't know, but latrine talk says it'll be late January or early February."

"I wonder what it'll be like."

Hank shrugged. "The only thing I know for sure is that we're in the artillery and not the infantry."

"You bet, and we're damned lucky."

Jake sat at the table in the little cafe in Toul, enjoying conversation with a few other officers. With him were Tom Sands and John O'Doule, both platoon leaders like Jake, and their company commander Captain, Joshua Hammonds.

"Well, at least we have Christmas Eve off!" said Lt. O'Doule, "though there isn't a damned thing to do but sit here and drink."

"Well, things could be worse. Besides, I understand we're having a feast tomorrow, turkey and all of the trimmings," replied Lt. Sands.

"I have it on good authority that we'll be staying here until spring," Hammonds said, "so settle down and enjoy. The duty could be worse."

Jake tuned out the conversation. The other three, their heads together, were whispering about the new barmaid that had been waiting on them, a very pretty young thing. The last discussion Jake was conscious of was about who would win her over first. From that point on, Jake was lost in thought over a variety of different things. He hadn't heard from his aunt in a while and he was genuinely concerned about her. He felt a light squeeze on his shoulder and heard a familiar voice behind him.

"Lt. Jacobson, I presume."

Jake turned and looked up, but couldn't make out the face with the bright overhead light shining in his eyes. When he saw the field grade rank of the soldier, he jumped to his feet at attention, at which point he recognized the man, "Major Hinkle, sir!"

The professor stuck out his hand. "Good to see you again, Jake. It seems like years ago that we were at Camp Mills. How are things going for you?"

Jake's three companions, realizing that a senior officer was in their midst, snapped to attention. After introducing everyone, Jake asked the major to join them.

"Relax, gentlemen, no reason for formality here. I'm in a bit of a rush, but I will sit for a minute or two."

As they sat down, Jake explained to his companions how he knew the major, and spoke of their casual meeting at the Camp Mills party.

"How are things going for you boys?"

"Fine, fine," replied Captain Hammonds. "The training has been intensive, but the men are coming along and anxious to get into the fight. The only complaint is with the supplies, sir; clothes, shoes, winter coats, and so on. You know some of my men have shoes that were issued eight to ten months ago, and the leather is getting awfully thin. In addition, very few have winter uniforms and it's been downright cold lately."

Hinkle added. "I know that's a serious problem. We have the apparel en route but it's still a few weeks away. I just hope the weather doesn't get worse."

"When are we moving out, Major? Jake asked. "We've had a little bet as to whether we stay here or go to Rolampont, which is my guess, as originally planned. Are you able to shed any light on that?"

"I think I can, if you keep this under your caps for a day."

"Sure will, sir," replied Hammonds.

"Well, I have orders being typed up at this very moment ordering our departure for Rolampont. We will leave early the day after Christmas, on Wednesday."

"How far is it, Major?" Lt. Sands asked.

"About 100 kilometers."

"I guess that can't be too bad, just a couple of days walk." Lieutenant O'Doule said.

"It'll take longer than a couple of days, and pray that the weather holds. If we have snow and rain, things could get sticky."

"When will we all be brought together again," Jake said. "I mean the artillery and so on? When will we move into the line as a division?"

"Well, only a guess," Major Hinkle said. "But that would be between 30 and 60 days. The Germans are moving men and equipment from the Eastern Front, and I feel that they will probably hit north of here and try to drive a wedge between the English and French with the hopes of breaking through to the coast. We have to be ready to fill in at the quiet sectors, so the French and British armies can be mobile enough to move quickly to meet the assault head-on.

Jake nodded.

"Of course, the French, and the English for that matter, want to absorb us into the line piecemeal, so that we, in essence, become part of their armies." Hinkle continued, "You know, an infantry regiment reinforcing one of their divisions here and an artillery battalion there, reinforcing another division or army. Old Blackjack Pershing will have nothing to do with that. He's insisting that we become an equal partner in this war and fight as an American army. So the sooner we can move as an independent army, the better off we are. That boils down to 60 or 90 days. The Germans, in my opinion, are going to attack before we get to that point. So there you are, draw your own conclusions as I have drawn mine."

"So that means stepped-up training in order for us to reach a parity with the French and English, if we are to stay together?" Captain Hammonds said.

"That's it in a nutshell, gentlemen." He stood up. "It's been a pleasure chatting with you men. I hope we run into each other again, and I'd like to wish all of you a Merry Christmas."

"Merry Christmas," they repeated, almost in unison.

They all stood up, shook hands, and the major left.

After they were reseated at the table, Captain Hammonds was the first to speak. "Well, Jake, friends in high places? It never hurts to have them. I guess you were right and I was wrong. Rolampont, look out, here comes the Rainbow."

The restaurant was crowded and noisy. The three young airmen sat at a table near the middle of the room. Each had a glass of wine and the waiter, who had just taken their dinner order, was wending his way back to the kitchen.

"I never thought we'd make it to France," Ike said, nearly shouting in order to be heard.

His two friends, Lieutenants Jon Nelson and Frank Linki, nodded their agreement as they sipped their wine. Frank and Jon were of slight build and both were just six feet tall. Frank had red hair with deep brown eyes while Jon was blond with hazel eyes.

"Didn't I tell you this was the place to come?" Frank shouted back. "They say all of the pilots and newsmen come here when they're in Paris. The Chatham Bar is world famous."

"Yeah, did you notice all of the different uniforms? I've seen Canadian, British, and of course, French," added Lt. Nelson.

"Well, it's a great place to have dinner, but remember we have to be at the station early in the morning to get the Issoudun train," Ike yelled back. "I need to get some shut-eye."

"Yeah, yeah, don't bore me with details," Frank replied.

"Ike do you want another glass of wine? I think I'll go to the bar and get it, instead of waiting for the waiter, which as we know, could take forever."

"Sure thing, Frank."

"Wait, Frank, I'll go with you. I've gotta hit the head. Ike, you hold down the fort," Jon said, rising to follow Frank through the crowd.

Ike settled back in his chair and stretched his legs out under the table. His thoughts went back to the ocean crossing that had brought them to La Harve early that morning and the mad scramble to get the train that got them into Paris late that afternoon.

It had seemed to Ike that he'd never make it to France. His ship originally left with a convoy that sailed on November 25, but had to turn back on the 27th, due to mechanical difficulties. They were in port for three days and set sail a second time on December 2.

The ship, the *Leviathan*, was once a German passenger ship, truly a queen of the seas. She had been impounded in New York Harbor by the United States government at the outbreak of hostilities and then converted for use as a troop ship. A strange twist of fate indeed, for she became a means of transporting Germany's new enemy, the AEF, to France.

When she left port on December 2, the ship sailed alone, unescorted. She was one of the fastest ships on the high seas and her captain, as well as the US Navy, did not fear the U-boat menace. They felt she could outrun and outmaneuver any submarine on or under the surface.

With her sailing a straight course, she had made the crossing in close to record time and landed in La Harve on December 12. Normally, most ships and convoys sailed a zigzag pattern during their time at sea to avoid any lurking U-boats. This frequent changing of course was used to avoid detection and to avoid any torpedoes that might be sent their way. For a slow, unarmed ship, it would be suicidal to sail a straight, unescorted path across the Atlantic. But it was felt that the swift ships would be safe.

Soon Ike's two friends arrived back at the table, just in time for the appetizer that the waiter brought from the other direction.

"Ike, Frank and I met this lovely American nurse at the bar. She's waiting to be joined by two of her friends for dinner. I invited them over to join us, any objections?" Jon said with a sly laugh.

Before Ike could even respond, Frank added. "Since there are no objections, our night is taken care of, and Ike, with your pigeon French, see if you can get the waiter to hold off on the main courses until our guests arrive."

As they were finishing their appetizers, the three young nurses approached the table. The men stood and started scooting around to make room for their guests. Ike spotted a couple of empty chairs nearby and brought them to the table. When he returned, and as Frank was greeting Lisa, the tallest of the three, Jon nudged Ike with his elbow and whispered, "See, what did I tell you. Isn't she a dish?"

All three were beautiful. The two Americans were tall, slender, and had short hair, one was blonde and the other was auburn. The third nurse, was French, and was about an inch shorter than her companions. She had pitch-black hair that hung down over her shoulders. Her skin was an alabaster white, and her dark eyes sparkled under long black lashes. Ike found that he couldn't take his eyes off of her.

"Ladies, I'm so glad you could join us," Frank said. "I would like to introduce you to my friends. This is Lieutenant Jon Nelson and Lieutenant Ike Dennison, and I am Frank Linki. "Gentlemen, this is Lisa Wagner. Lisa, you'll have to introduce the others."

Lisa turned a light shade of red and said, "These are my friends, Beth Stern and Agnes Bovay. Beth and I are from the states, but Agnes just finished her training in St. Nazaire and joined our surgical nursing team about two weeks ago. Her English is a little rough, so do any of you speak French?"

"I do, well a little," Ike blurted out before the others could respond. "I took three years in high school and a year in college."

"Well, that settles the seating arrangement," Frank said smiling. They all sat down and the conversation came somewhat easily.

"This is our first night out since Agnes joined our group," Lisa explained. "Beth and I have talked of coming here ever since we arrived in France, but for one reason or another we just haven't come, until tonight."

"Our work has kept us close to the hospital," Beth continued. "So tonight we decided it was time for a break and Agnes was anxious to come too, and here we are."

"I had heard of the Chatham ever since the war started," Agnes said in her accented English. "My older brother was in the French flying service, before he was killed last year. He had talked fondly of this place and I wanted to see it. I never dreamed it would be so crowded."

"We knew that lots of Americans came here, and that gives us a chance to catch up on the news from home," Lisa said. "We never would have found a place to sit if you hadn't of asked us to join you. Thank you very much."

"It's our pleasure," Frank replied. "Ike talked to the waiter and their holding off our dinner until you place your order."

"And I will go to the bar and get you something to drink," Jon said as he stood. "What is your pleasure?"

After Jon took the drink order and headed for the bar, Ike turned to Agnes and asked, "You have such a pretty name, Añ-ñes, how do you spell it?"

"A-g-n-e-s," she replied.

"That's Agnes, at least in the English context. I like the sound of Añ-ñes, much better."

Jon soon returned to the table, and the six of them sat and talked late into the night. The American girls had come from the states in the late spring of 1917 to help in the hospitals in caring for the wounded. With the involvement of the US in the war, they transferred to the American hospital in Paris. Agnes, who had completed her surgical training in St. Nazaire in November, had been assigned to work at the same hospital, where she met Lisa and Beth and they had quickly become friends.

Around 12:30 in the morning, Ike excused Agnes and himself and said he was going to take Agnes back to the hospital. They said their good-byes and left the Chatham.

After they stepped outside of the restaurant, they found there wasn't a taxi in sight. "It looks like I'll walk with you to the hospital," Ike said. "How far is it?"

"About two kilometers," Agnes replied.

"I don't want you out alone, so let's start walking, it shouldn't take too long."

As they walked they talked, using both French and English. Both had a little difficulty expressing themselves in the other's language.

The more that Ike used the French the more he remembered words that had long ago slipped from his vocabulary. Their conversation sometimes brought on fits of laughter as they realized they said things that they didn't mean at all.

As they walked by a small park near the hospital, Ike grabbed Agnes's hand and pulled her to a nearby bench under a street light. "Don't go in just yet," Ike said. "Let's talk some more."

Agnes willingly sat with him and they talked for hours. Even though the weather was nippy, neither noticed the cold.

Early in the morning of December 13, Frank and Jon stood in the station waiting to board the train that would take them the 200 kilometers south to Issoudun.

"I wonder where Ike is?" Frank said to Jon. "He was the one who wanted to sleep and be here early to catch the train."

"I know" Jon said. "He didn't even make it back to the room."

"He really seemed smitten by that little French girl. You think he got lucky?"

Just then Frank caught sight of Ike and yelled and waved his arms. Jon, not seeing him, waved and yelled also, in hopes of being heard over the noise of the station. He put his fingers to his mouth and whistled as loud as could, and that did the trick. Ike saw the two of them and started to head their way.

He caught up with them as they were boarding the coach and raced with them to grab three seats together.

"Where the hell you been, Ike?" Jon asked. "You spend the night with that pretty little Frenchy?"

"As a matter of fact, I did. We walked around Paris for a while and then sat on a park bench and just talked. It wasn't till the sun started to come up that we realized how late it really was. She had to rush to get to work and I took a taxi to catch the train. What a great girl!"

"And you're expecting us to believe all of that?" Frank said.

"You believe what you want to believe," Ike said as the train started to move out of the station.

The Issoudun training center was the largest of 22 different centers being set up in France for the express purpose of training the American pilots. When Ike and his friends arrived, its collection of eight airfields and attendant buildings were still under construction. German prisoners of war and special laborers brought in from French Indochina were doing most of this construction. The work moved rapidly forward under the close supervision of the French engineers responsible for the overall project.

The pilot trainees were immediately put into makeshift classrooms and briefed by French officers and airmen seasoned in the art of aerial combat, who taught survival techniques. When they weren't in class, they were pitching in on the construction work.

The winter of 1917-18 was one of the worst ever recorded in France. It was exceptionally cold and wet, the ground alternating between frozen mud and oozing clay. Ike and all the other trainees were kept extremely busy, for when they weren't in class they were helping to complete the training center. They spent their first two weeks slipping and sliding around Issoundun, and there was no escaping the cold, damp winter weather.

Ike appreciated the work. He had developed strong feelings for Agnes and needed to keep busy so he wouldn't think of her so often. He started writing to her on a regular basis once he arrived at Issoundun, and was a little surprised when she answered his letters.

Soon after Ike and the others arrived at Issoundun, the United States medical personnel stationed at the training center decided that the manure piles in the yards of the surrounding farms were hazardous to the health of the men and ordered their removal. It fell upon the American airmen to do the job, since German prisoners were not allowed to work near the French civilians. As the Americans went about this unpleasant task, the French peasants, who had lived in and around the piles for generations and wondered why they should suddenly be a hazard to one's health, watched them closely.

This process of completing the construction of the training center and the removal of the manure piles took approximately two weeks. If the French citizens were confused, the American would-be pilots were dismayed. They were now somewhat less than impressed with the French countryside, for they had come here to fly, and to rid the country from the ravages of war, not to perform this particular type of manual labor.

Finally, shortly after Christmas, Issoudun was ready to take on the job it was set up to do, that of training pilots. This training was uniquely French. Even though Ike and others had earned their wings in the states, they were required to take lessons from the French instructors.

Soon these fledgling airmen were introduced to the Rouleur. The Rouleur was a single seat biplane built with a tractor-style airframe, fitted with the conventional landing gear and a tailskid. This aircraft was similar to the Curtis Jenny and normal in every way except for the wings.

The wings were peculiar in that they had been clipped and were no more than ten feet in span. The training Rouleur, not unlike birds whose wings have been clipped, was unable to fly. The trainees would spend hours gunning the rotary-engined machines around on the ground, ostensibly adjusting to its peculiar idiosyncrasies. Once the instructor was satisfied with his student's proficiency, he was given an unclipped version and simply told to fly it.

Two days after Christmas, Ike was sitting alone in his room studying some information the French had given the students concerning the Rouleur. He was having a little difficulty concentrating on the material when Jon and Frank both came barging into the room.

"Ike, did you hear the news?" Jon asked.

"News? What news?"

"We just heard from command that the *Leviathan* has been sunk. She was going at full speed on her way back to New York when she was struck by a torpedo."

"You're kidding," Ike gasped, dumbfounded.

"Honest gospel truth," Frank said. "Somebody's got to be scratching his head over that one. The captain kept telling us on a daily basis that it was impossible for a U-boat to sink her."

"Well, I'm sure glad it didn't happen on the way over," Ike said, shaking his head. "I'll write my dad and ask him what the deal was. He may know what happened. It really makes you stop and think, doesn't it?"

Dan Dennison just made it home in time for Christmas. The *Hampton* arrived in port on Saturday, but it had taken some time to get the crew off and on leave, then turn the ship over to the port authorities for cleanup, rearming and refueling. There was also a serious problem with the number four boiler—it just wasn't developing the power it should. Dan's chief engineer felt the problem could be catastrophic if not looked into immediately. They had spent the last three days at sea on just the three remaining boilers.

On Monday, after going over the problem with the port engineer and his workmen, Dan caught the train that would take him to Washington and home. He had two weeks leave and then he'd be off again for more convoy work.

To date, the convoy duty had been uneventful. Dan was beginning to think that this was the way it was going to be. They hadn't seen hide nor hair of a U-boat in two months of sea duty.

As the train pulled into the station, Dan stood with the other passengers waiting for the doors to be opened. While they were slowing to a stop, Dan bent down to look out the window and saw Doris waiting for him. As the car slowly drifted by he tried to wave, but she didn't see him. He became anxious to get off and run back to where she was. It took forever for the conductor to get the door open and then for the other passengers in front of him to file off.

Doris was still waiting in the same spot he had seen her when the train pulled in.

Dan yelled to her and started quickly back to where she was, standing on tiptoe, trying to see over the crowd in order to get a good look at the disembarking passengers. Doris caught sight of him when he was a mere ten feet away and ran to him and they embraced, and kissed for an extended time.

Coming home to her had always been a thrill for Dan. Even though they had been married for twenty-five years, the homecomings had always been special. Their usual routine was in place. Doris would meet Dan at the station and they would drive to their favorite restaurant.

They jumped into the old family Ford and headed off for Sylvianos. Doris had made all of the arrangements. Philip Sylviano greeted them at the door and after the usual cordial greeting; he took them to their table and seated them personally.

"Captain and Mrs. Dennison, I have outdone myself again. I have fixed your favorite, veal scaloppini, with a new sauce that is out of this world." Phil had a propensity to speak with his hands, and he put his fingertips of his left hand to his lips, kissed them, and raised his hand to the ceiling. "It is based on the usual recipe, but I have added a secret ingredient that makes it the best you'll ever taste, so sit back and enjoy. Roland will serve you your Caesar salads after you have your martinis, and then I will personally bring out your meal, fit for a king."

"Thank you, dear friend," Dan said. "After so many weeks at sea you could serve me the scraps from your kitchen and they would be delicious after so many months of sea rations, but to have all of this, is more than I could hope for. Thank you."

Philip grinned and they both watched him move off to the front of the restaurant.

"He sure loves the old flattery treatment, doesn't he?" Doris asked.

"He sure does. Some things thank the Lord, do not change." Dan looked Doris in the eye and said, "It's so good to see you, how are you doing? You look radiant, so you must be well?"

"You know how I miss you, but I've kept busy working with the European Relief Foundation, and so I haven't had time to get too lonely. It's been hard having you at sea again. I was getting used to having you around, after your five years in Washington and your being home most of the time. I've had to readjust to the old ways, but I'm managing all right."

"Well, we have two weeks to do whatever you want to do. So let's enjoy our time together. This could be my last tour at sea. In another year I could put in for retirement."

"Do you really mean that, Dan? It would mean so much to me."

"We'll talk about it later, but yes I do. Now you said in the car you'd heard from Ike. Tell me all of the news."

Doris continued to recount the adventures Ike had related in his letters—the trip over on the *Leviathan*, the stopover in Paris, and the work at Issoudun.

"He's getting tired of the manual labor and he is anxious to fly. He said that the enlisted men refer to the pilots as the Million-Dollar Army that's because they are paid as officers and draw their flight pay as well, and all they do is remove the manure piles and help with the construction. He sounds a lot like you Dan. You know how you couldn't wait to get to sea? Well, he can't wait till he gets in the air. Oh, it scares me, but it seems to be his first love."

"It sounds familiar. I guess I was absorbed with sea duty in the early days," Dan replied. "I sure wish I could see Ike. But we no sooner hit France and we turn around and come back to pick up another convoy. I hope I can get some time to spend with him."

Doris and Dan enjoyed their meal and talked for what seemed like hours. When they were through, they drove home to relax and enjoy one another before going to midnight Christmas service.

On Christmas morning, they exchanged gifts and both felt lonely for Ike. This was the first Christmas since Ike was born that they had spent without him.

"It's sort of like those Christmases before we had Ike," Dan observed.

"Not quite. We were much younger then, Dan."

The gift Doris gave Dan was an envelope containing a copy of the reservations she had made for a week's stay at the hotel they had gone to on their honeymoon. He was thrilled.

"What a great present. You know how much I love the place. You're the greatest! The best part, we'll be there tomorrow."

Though Dan gave her a beautiful ring in honor of their twenty-fifth anniversary, her greatest gift was the thought of his retirement. He'd never wanted to talk about it in the past, but now here it was. She treasured the thought.

In the afternoon they went to Doris's sister's home for a grand Christmas meal.

The next day, December 26, they took the afternoon train to Virginia Beach for their weeklong getaway.

All too soon their time ran out, and Dan was on the train back to the *Hampton*, which was scheduled to sail January 15.

In the late afternoon on Christmas Eve, a detail of eight men was sent to guard the cannon, which were located on the range near the small village of Beignon.

On Christmas Day, most of the men in the regiment slept late and performed the minimum of duties at a leisurely pace. In the spirit of the day, Sergeant Baker approached some men in the battery and asked them to help him carry some food and coffee out to those who had to work the guard detail the night before. At mid morning, they walked the six kilometers to take some stew, coffee and Christmas cheer to the poor hardworking guards.

They were shocked by what they found. The security of the guard post had been left to one man, Jason Newcum, a known teetotaler, while the remainder of the men had gone into Beignon on a toot.

They had eaten of the best foods and drunk their fill. It was cold when they returned and they slept close to the fire, so close that some of the blankets had holes burned in them, and some of their overcoats had been scorched. The ground was littered with empty wine bottles.

When the rescue party of Hank, Pat, Jack, Paul and Sergeant Baker arrived, the "guards" were standing around the fire trying to shake off the effects of the night before.

Sergeant Baker and his small crew were made to feel unwelcome, and the stew was received less than enthusiastically, eventually ending up in some nearby bushes.

Sergeant Baker was not pleased. He maintained the spirit of the day and said little to the eight men on duty, but his actions in subsequent days towards the seven who went into Beignon left little doubt that he hadn't forgotten the incident. Jason escaped the sergeant's wrath, as he had dutifully stood guard throughout the night.

When the rescue party returned from the range, Pat, Hank and Jack went directly to the barracks to open their packages and celebrate the holiday.

The biggest surprise came for Hank,—a note in his package from Betsy brought some unexpected news. She was expecting his child, which was due around the eleventh of July.

Pat was looking at Hank while he read his letter in silence. When he looked up after reading the note, Pat asked, "What's going on, Hank? I saw about ten different emotions cross your face in the last minute. Good news or bad?"

"I, ah, I'm going to, ah, well, I… I'm going to be a father."

"You're kidding, that's great. Hey, everyone, Hank's going to be a papa."

Hank shook his head in disbelief. "I'm amazed, I don't know what to say. How did this happen?"

"If you can't figure that one out, Hank, I think you better go back to school," Jack said, followed by a loud guffaw.

Soon the shock of the news wore off, and Hank was walking on air. As they were readying themselves for dinner, he kept repeating all kinds of names and asking others what they thought of them.

The remainder of the day was festive and the holiday feast was soon served. Again the men were treated to turkey and dressing, accompanied with baked potatoes, cranberries, celery, apple turnovers, blackberry pies, doughnuts, and hot chocolate. Every man ate his fill and there were seconds for those who wanted them.

In the evening, many stayed in the mess hall talking, gaming, drinking, and enjoying the spirit of the season. But soon it was over and the men were back to work.

The next two days followed the same old pattern, gun drill, schools and stables.

Finalizing For War

On Thursday, the battery had another turn at the practice range. They arrived at 5:00 a.m. and fired until noon. That afternoon, Lieutenant Case made an important announcement to the men of the battery. "Gentlemen, the regimental horses have finally arrived at St. Nazaire. Colonel Reilly has personally selected the men of Battery F as the ones that will go and get them. This is indeed an honor for our unit, and it is my pleasure to ask for one hundred of you to volunteer for this adventurous undertaking. Those of you who wish to take part in this endeavor will leave at noon tomorrow and go by train to St. Nazaire and then proceed to the remount center and bring the herd back to Coetquidan."

It seemed every man was eager to have a part in this diversion from the routine. The selection process was quick and the first to be accepted were those with the most experience with handling horses.

At noon on Friday, December 28, Pat, Hank and 98 other men set out under the command of Sergeant Baker. Loaded down with harness, saddles and packs, they boarded trucks that took them to the village of Guer. There, with their gear in tow, they boarded 40 and 8's for the ride to St. Nazaire.

At dusk the men arrived at the remount station and were greeted by Lieutenant Allen, who had arrived the day before.

"All right, you men," Pappy began, "we have a hot meal for you down at the remount center, mess hall. You will then be billeted here in the barn. We will begin at first light. Each of you will saddle up one animal on which to ride and then harness three others to take in tow. We will be underway shortly after breakfast."

Soon after eating, the men made their way to the barn to pick out a place where they would sleep for the night.

The following day dawned clear and beautiful, though it was still cold. Pat, Hank, and Paul were sleeping in the loft of the barn and each had burrowed deep into the hay for warmth. The other mechanic of the battery, Tom, had stayed up late talking to the regular Army men working at the remount center. As the barn was dark as pitch when he finally went to bed, he lay down in the first space he could find that was unoccupied. This proved to be a feeding trough. When he awoke he found that the horses had eaten off all the hay he had covered himself with before falling asleep so that he would remain warm throughout the night.

"No wonder I was so cold last night," he said to Paul and the others as they headed off to breakfast.

While they were waiting in line for their bacon, fried bread, syrup, and coffee, Hank said to the other mechanics, "I looked over this herd pretty close last night and they seem highly spirited. Now, Tom and Paul, you two follow Pat's and my lead. As soon as we're through eating we'll get down to the corral and pick out the gentlest of the bunch. Believe me, leading three horses while riding another ain't no easy task, especially when the nags are not used to the halter. So eat up and let me and Pat choose for you."

"You're the boss," Paul replied.

When they'd finished eating, the four of them headed for the corral. As they approached the gate, Tom said, "I think only a few other of the boys have beat us here, and so get the easy goin' ones for us. The closer we get to actually playing cowboy has me worried."

Pat and Hank immediately went to work cutting out twelve animals. They took their time in order to get the least skittish of the group. When they corralled one they would put the halter on and then turn it over to Tom or Paul to hold.

Tom and Paul were both from Chicago and confirmed city boys and felt more comfortable leaving the selection process to old farmhands like Pat and Hank. When all twelve animals were captured and harnessed, they moved outside the corral and each man then saddled his riding pony and took hold of the lead rope of each of the horses that would be in tow.

When about fifty men and 200 horses were ready to move, Sergeant Baker sent them on their way. "Now take it slow and move out to the edge of town and wait for us there," he instructed them. "And keep control of those animals."

The start was a little shaky, as some of the horses weren't about to be led where they didn't want to go. However, this first half of the troop was made up of the more experienced handlers when it came to horses. They were able to get to the edge of St. Nazaire without too many complications.

The second half of the troop encountered difficulties. Not only had the tamer animals been cut from the herd, but also those that remained had more space in which to run. Pappy and Sergeant Baker were in the middle of these events, losing patience as the numbers thinned. The profanity began to flow, and both men were sweating profusely even though the temperature still hovered in the low thirties.

The men, trying to chase down horses, had to frequently duck the kicking of those still left in the corral. The army regulars who worked at the corral were having the best time, with repeated shouts of "Ride 'em, Cowboy," as they sat complacently on the sideline fence.

Finally the capture process was complete, and all of the men were mounted with their ponies in tow. With Lieutenant Allen in the lead and Sergeant Baker in the rear, the column started moving through the streets of St. Nazaire.

This second section of the troop did not fare as well as the first. These horses were definitely not going to be led anywhere. It started in the rear of the troop, when the horses in tow behind Jason Newcum broke free of his grasp and charged up through the column. Other men then lost the grip on their charges and/or were thrown from their mounts. A stampede was underway. The air became filled with loud shouts of profanity and prayers.

The frightened horses charged up and down the streets, overturning carts and even some pedestrians who had the misfortune of being in the way. It took several hours to regain control, and Pappy, who seemed to be everywhere, was fit to be tied. Finally, with the help of some MPs, the column was reformed with everyone and all of the horses accounted for. Fortunately for the citizens of St. Nazaire, there were no serious injuries.

Once out of town, the situation did not settle down. Tom's horse had a knack for unseating its handler and heading out for the pastures. Many of the animals being led would find mysterious ways to get wrapped around telegraph and fence poles. The horses would rub up against a wall, fence or one another bringing cries of pain from the riders, whose legs were clamped as if in a vise.

Pat, Hank, Sergeant Baker, and other experienced riders were in great demand all through the day to chase down strays.

By nightfall, they arrived at their first destination, the sleepy little village of Saint Gilds de Bois. Amazingly enough, all horses and men were accounted for. The morale, though, had been shot to hell.

The men were billeted in local stables and when Sergeant Baker asked for guards, he was shouted down with such vehemence that he thought he better do it himself if he expected to continue the trip in one piece. Soon all of the weary travelers were sound asleep.

The second day, December 30, proved to be a little easier than the previous one. All, including the horses, were a little more in tune with the regimen. The men were awakened at 5:30 a.m. and served a breakfast of bread, syrup, and coffee. After gathering the animals, the parade started north on the road to Coetquidan. The sky had turned cloudy over night and before the day was over they ran into some light rain showers. The horses were better behaved and the parade proceeded without any significant incidents.

Around noon, the detail passed through Redon, a large town on the route. Many of the local citizens came out to watch the "Yanks" parade through. This gave the men some time to flirt with the young, pretty girls. It was also an opportunity for the men to take their minds off of the pain they were enduring.

The large number of troops they saw impressed them. There were, of course, French soldiers, but there was also an abundance of Japanese troops as well.

In the late afternoon, they arrived in the little town of La Gacilly, their second and last stop before reaching Coetquidan. Here the men bedded down the horses before breaking up in small groups to hunt out food and maybe some drink. The four mechanics found a quiet little restaurant off the main drag and anxiously sat down to enjoy their evening meal.

"I don't know whether I'll ever be able to sit comfortably again," Paul said.

"My butt is so sore I can't get comfortable in any position, and that includes standing," Tom added.

"You'll survive and even get used to it," Pat added, secretly wondering if he'd ever feel right again himself. He didn't want to admit that he was suffering as bad as the others.

The troop of men spent the night in a local schoolhouse, and in the morning when everyone arose, the place was truly a mess, with empty wine bottles scattered far and wide. After eating, the men went back to collect their packs and were met by Sergeant Baker, who stood in the doorway.

"This here place looks like a hellhole, and if'n you men care about your lives, it better be cleaned up in the next ten minutes or all of yous will be pullin' guard duty and KP for the remainder of your natural born days. You got that?"

He continued reading the riot act until everyone was mounted and underway. Many references were made to the ancestry of all in general and to many in particular.

As they rode, Pat said to Hank, "He used words I'd never heard before, but I know they weren't complimentary."

Hank just laughed, "You got that right."

When the troop was mounted and finally underway, there was a collective sigh of relief as Sergeant Baker took up position at the end of the column, out of hearing range of the others.

On this, the final day of their march, the weather had turned cold and they encountered numerous snow showers along the way. Just after noon, the troop finally arrived at Coetquidan. The men and animals were all weary after their three-day trek. The horses were turned over to handlers from the various batteries. All of the black horses went to Battery F, as that was their designated color.

The men were so tired that most who were on the detail hit the sack early after dinner. The fact that it was New Year's Eve didn't concern them.

The day after Christmas, the infantry regiments of the 42nd Division were up at 5:00 a.m. After breakfast, they completed their packing and with full packs prepared to start the long trek towards Rolampont.

The weather had been cloudy and the temperature was in the mid-thirties. Jake thought it might rain, so he had the boys in his platoon break out whatever rain gear they had, just in case.

Prior to leaving, the company commander, Captain Hammonds, called his platoon leaders together and related the details of the upcoming march.

"We will be two days en route to LaFoche. There we will stay about three days and then march another three days in order to reach Rolampont by January 2. Watch your men closely, as the equipment situation is not good. Shoes are my main concern—we don't want anybody going barefoot in this cold weather." There was a smattering of chuckles from the platoon leaders and the captain dismissed the gathering.

Actual departure did not get underway until late in the morning, due in part to the delays in preparing all of the rolling stock. This included the field kitchens and supply wagons.

The first day proved to be uneventful. Most of the men complained about the walk in good humor. The weather held and the ground underfoot was firm, even though it was a dirt road. They encountered few vehicles and fewer local farmers.

The first night they stayed in a little village that was little more than a wide spot in the road. Jake couldn't pronounce the name and was so tired he didn't even try. He and the other platoon leaders were too busy to participate in much chatter and soon after a meal of cold corned Willie and beans all turned in for the night.

The second day saw a light rainfall in the afternoon, and by the time they reached La Foche, the road was getting slippery. La Foche allowed time for the stragglers to catch up and gave the men some time to rest before they continued with the second and longer part of their journey.

The stay in the small town was not uncomfortable. The platoon leaders and many of the men slept in local barns and buildings provided by the citizens. A few field grade officers stayed in a nearby hotel.

Lieutenant O'Doule and Jake were in the barn the night before they left for Rolampont cleaning equipment and preparing to leave early in the morning.

"Jake, you know that rain the other day sure played havoc with the leather on my shoes. They were thin to begin with and now that they're dry, they're cracked, I sure hope they hold out."

"Yeah, I know what you mean, the soles of mine are looking pretty thin. But what's got me worried is how cold it's getting. Oh well, as long as it doesn't snow."

During the late hours before they were to leave, a cold front moved through and the temperature dipped down into the low twenties. By the time the division was moving out, a wind-driven snow started to fall.

As Jake marched beside the ranks of his platoon, he drew the muffler tight around his neck and the loose end over his mouth. He was thankful that he had heard from his aunt at Christmas, and particularly thankful she had had the foresight to knit him the Khaki muffler and gloves.

The thousands of tramping feet soon turned the semi frozen dirt road into a wet soggy, slippery clay. Jake's right boot soon developed a small hole in the sole and his sock was wet and his foot was cold. One man in the platoon had the stitching on the sole of his right shoe break from the toes back to the arch. Jake tore a strip of cloth from an old shirt and wrapped it around the shoe in order to stop the leather from flapping.

All of the men were cold. Few of them had full winter gear. Most of these men of the 167th were reared in the south and many had never seen snow before. The novelty of the white stuff quickly wore off as they became numb with the cold. As they walked further into the wind and snow their faces became caked with ice. The further they proceeded the heavier the snow fell.

The first night found them in a little farming community that opened its doors to the weary, half frozen travelers. After eating the evening meal, they stood and stomped around the numerous fires that had been lit upon their arrival, but this barely sufficed in keeping them warm. Soon the troops went to bed. Most found room in barns and a few lucky ones in homes or buildings of the small village. The remainder set up small tents and bundled up against the cold as best they could.

The medics and doctors of the medical unit were up most of the night tending to sickness and frostbite.

Some of the men had their shoes fall apart during the day and had to wrap their feet in rags. Many, such as Jake, found old papers to stuff in the shoe in an attempt to keep dry. One man in the platoon put his feet in cold water in an effort to draw the frost out.

It continued to snow all night. In the morning the temperature started to fall as the snow began to let up. The wind was still blowing hard and it penetrated to the very core of each man.

Captain Hammons talked to his platoon leaders once again before they started out.

"Things are getting worse. B Company has had an outbreak of the mumps. There are rumors that some men are down with influenza. Keep up to date with what's happening to your men. Our ambulance service is slow, but no matter what, keep your men moving. We will begin to march at 0700 hours. We have some limited supplies and can help a little. There are some extra blankets, so bundle them up as best you can. This is beginning to look like Valley Forge all over again."

The second day of the march was worse than the first. Men dropped out as they became ill with mumps and pneumonia. The cold was nearly unbearable. Jake saw many bloody foot tracks in the snow. There were few horses and mules at the time and fewer automobiles, but the divisions kept moving on sheer grit alone. Late in the evening the 42nd reached their second rest stop. The snow had stopped but in places it had drifted three to four feet deep that made forward movement difficult. During the second night the temperature fell to zero.

The third and last day of the march saw more and more men succumb to the elements and fall along the wayside. Many field grade officers were on mules, but not a small number gave up their mounts to help men in trouble. One regiment alone had five hundred men drop out. The medics were constantly in demand and the ambulances were loaded with victims of the hike. These vehicles were not only loaded down with those who were ill, but were constantly getting hung up in snow drifts and had to be pushed, and were forever slipping and sliding off of the road.

Finally, late into the night of January 2, the truly bedraggled bunch of men that comprised the Rainbow Division infantry arrived at their destination, Rolampont. The doors of every warm building were thrown open. The men of the division huddled around fireplaces and stoves trying to bring warmth back to frozen bodies.

After Jake got what was left of his platoon bedded down, he went to the officers' quarters and stood with his back to the wood-burning stove, swaying from side to side as he tried to warm his whole body.

Tom Sands came through the door and stood next to him. "I've never been so cold in all my life," he said. "There was a time this afternoon I was ready to lie down and die."

Jake nodded. "You made it. It's amazing what the human body is capable of when the going gets tough. I kept wondering what would have happened if the Germans had hit us. You know they could've wiped us out in the blink of an eye."

"I never thought about it," Tom said. "I guess I'm glad I didn't. Did you hear how many men didn't make it all of the way?"

"All I heard was that everyone lived, but as to how many are in hospitals, I have no idea. We probably won't know for a few days. It's going to take some doing to get back into fightin' trim."

The days of January were cold and wet. Frequently the temperature would fall well below freezing and stay there for days at a time. However, when the temperature went above freezing, the ground would thaw and all was awash with mud. Frequent rains only added to their misery. The roofs in the barracks leaked profusely, requiring many to set up shelter halves on their beds in order to remain dry.

No matter the weather, the training continued day after day. The mechanics were constantly tending to the guns as they were fired more and more frequently. Equitation drill was a daily exercise, as the horses needed training and adjustment to harnesses. Now that the remainder of the regiment's horses had arrived from St. Nazaire, the 149th was up to full combat readiness.

During this period, rumors abounded. There was talk of revolution in Germany, or that a cease-fire was about to be signed. The men placed bets as to whether they would get into battle or not. No matter what the rumor mill ground out, the training continued at an ever-faster rate.

Phone lines were laid and taken up again. New bunkers were dug and old ones filled in at numerous positions around the various ranges of the camp. The horses were harnessed and hitched to the gun carriages and marched throughout the area, then unhitched and bedded down again. There were days that the horses couldn't make it to the firing range, as the roads were frozen and slippery. The unshod animals ended up falling and had to be unharnessed and helped to their feet only to fall again. The mud around the stables and watering troughs was so deep that at times it literally sucked the shoes or boots off of the men. More than one went barefoot to the barracks at day's end.

When it was impossible to make it to the firing range, the troops would occupy their time by cleaning and repairing the harnesses and other equipment.

On January 19, the drivers were up at three in the morning to harness and hitch the guns. At 6:30 the entire regiment was out on the range putting the guns into position for the first try at working as a unified whole. By nine, the firing began. The communication system was in disarray and the cannoneers were dissatisfied with their targeting as they were unable to fire at the normal rate. Unit four had mis-positioned their aiming stake and hit wide of the target all morning.

On their return to camp, late in the evening, the men were discouraged and angrily discussed the failures of the day. "I heard that if we don't make the grade as artillery men they'll transfer the whole goddamned regiment into the Military Police." said George Dungan, cannoneer of unit three.

This sent the chills down Pat's spine. "I sure as hell didn't come here to be no damned policeman," he said, knowing that what George had said could happen.

A heavy gloom hung over the batteries as each man silently contemplated this thought.

Later in the evening, Colonel Reilly addressed the men of each battery. He was dressed in his best uniform that was spotless and without a wrinkle. His leather boots and Sam Brown belt shined and glowed from the polish. He was a striking figure, tall, slender, and his booming voice was full of confidence.

"Today is a turning point in the 149th's history. Since our coming together in July, we this day are crossing the dividing line between our organization, initial training, and our period of real service to the AEF. Behind us is the struggle to become part of the Rainbow Division. Also behind us is our training and transit to France. Still before us is the war. This regiment will be called upon to participate in the greatest battles ever fought since the beginning of time. So don't pay attention to the stories and rumors you hear about the war ending soon or that the regiment will not participate. We all will be confronted with fighting soon enough. When we enter this conflict, and all indications are that this will be soon, we must be prepared. We will be prepared to meet the enemy head on and defeat him."

After the colonel finished addressing the men, Pat felt relieved and confident that they wouldn't be transferred to the military police. "I sure was worried that we wouldn't ever see the fighting," he confided to Hank. "I was afraid that after today's performance on the range, our days in the artillery were at an end. But the colonel put my mind at ease."

Hank nodded in agreement, "I was beginning to feel the same, particularly after what George had to say this afternoon."

The day following the colonel's address to his command, the target practice at the range saw a marked improvement in efficiency and accuracy, as the men felt motivated and enthused, now that they knew they were going into battle with the enemy.

On January 24, a gun belonging to Battery F of the 151st Regiment exploded during their turn on the Beignon Range. This tragedy killed the crew outright except for the chief of section and the loader, who both were seriously wounded.

Early the next day, as the battery passed by the sight to take up position on the range, they marched in silence past the scene of the previous days mishap. The position was a shambles. The wheel spokes were shot out, the gun barrel was shredded, and whatever was left was blackened from the blast.

"I ain't ever seen anything like that," Tom whispered to Pat. "I didn't even know such a thing could happen to these guns."

"Not only will the Germans be shooting at us, our own cannon may do us in," Pat whispered back.

"I wouldn't give a plug nickel for our chances of living through this war," Hank said. "Our odds at survival seem slim."

Drill and marches continued unabated as rumors continued to circulate that peace would soon be declared. Jason Newcum, the battery statistician, held large bundles of money as the bets continued to build as to whether the regiment would enter the conflict.

On the first of February, the rumor mill ground out the news that the regiments at Coetquidan would soon be leaving to join the rest of the division in the east.

A Draw at Sea

The merchantman was making its way through a moderate sea. The day was bright with a fast-moving, high thin overcast, propelled by a 20-knot breeze out of the northwest.

Captain Montgomery stood on the bridge scanning the water to the east. His uniform was disheveled and even threadbare in places, and long curls of hair cascaded down to his shoulders from under a hat that had seen better years. He was looking for submarines. He had received a wireless report earlier in the morning that one had been sighted in these waters just twelve hours ago.

He had, as of this day, been in command of the *Londondary* for exactly three months, and they had yet to come upon an enemy. Life on the Q-ship was not dull, though, as there was always something that had to be done. The crew rehearsed their duties endlessly, and had repainted the ship just the night before. As part of that exercise, they had set up the fake second funnel. They were now flying a South African flag and the ship appeared to have her hold full of cargo, as she sailed low in the water.

Indeed a juicy target for a Boche submariner.

The part of this duty that Robert Montgomery disliked the most was the costumes he had to wear. The worn, old-looking clothes were bad enough, but the wig and long hair disgusted him more than the shabby clothing. "Oh well, it's just part of the act, for king and country," he muttered as he continued to scan the sea.

One basic assumption made by the crews of Q-ships was that they were under constant surveillance by an unseen periscope. The crew's appearance and actions were considered vital in carrying out the deception. This ruse was even continued at the homeport in case there were enemy spies lurking about. Once below decks and out of sight of prying eyes, standard naval chain of command courtesies prevailed.

Late in the morning on January 21, 1918, the lookout's cry from the crow's nest, located high above the deck on the main mast, got Robert's quick attention.

"Smoke, fifty degrees to the starboard bow, about ten miles, sir!"

The captain turned to his right and focused his glasses to the southeast. Sure enough, there was another merchantman and it appeared to be burning; the smoke was not entirely from its funnel.

"Come to a heading of one five zero degrees, ahead full speed," he yelled to the helmsman.

"Aye-aye, sir, turn to one five zero degrees and ahead full speed."

"Mr. Rogers, come to the bridge," the captain yelled down the intercom.

"On my way, sir," the first mate replied from somewhere below decks.

The *Londondary* was deceptively fast for a freighter and she was soon heading southeast at twenty-six knots. This Q-ship had been built specifically for her task as a submarine hunter. Her haul was of shallow draft and lightweight. Most importantly, her power plant was large, giving her the high speed she needed for her work. To a casual observer she appeared to be an old, fully loaded merchantman.

As the *Londondary* approached the floundering ship, the distinct sound of cannon fire was heard by all of the crew. As soon as Mr. Rogers reached the bridge, Captain Montgomery ordered him to sound battle stations. Large secondary explosions were occurring from the interior of the stricken ship.

Robert felt the adrenaline flow through his whole being. At last he was going to enter battle, once again, against the dreaded Hun.

Captain Links had surfaced in order to attack the lone merchant ship with his deck gun. He wanted to conserve his torpedoes in order to stay at sea for a longer cruise. He felt little or no remorse for the crew of this Canadian ship, and as soon as the U-boat surfaced, the gunners were on deck preparing the canon to fire.

The crew of the stricken ship was manning the lifeboats when the first round smashed into the bridge with a thunderous explosion. The second round ripped into the forward starboard lifeboat, dumping and throwing its occupants into the cold sea. The U-boat's cannon continued firing rounds into the helpless merchantman, and soon all of the foredeck and bow were ablaze.

One round hit amidships setting off explosives in the main hold, and a tremendous fireworks display engulfed the ship and soared high above. The crew of U-46 was mesmerized by the display, including Captain Links.

Finally, the captain said to his executive officer, "Hans, which of the lifeboats has the captain and the ship's papers?"

"That one, sir, off to the stern, the one trying to get around to the other side of the ship," Hans said as he pointed to the lifeboat just rounding the stern of the sinking ship.

"Let's get after them, I want those papers to confirm our kill."

"Aye-aye, sir."

The U-boat turned and started for the other side of the disabled merchantman.

The Londondary was closing fast on the distressed vessel.

"Captain, I see the bow of the U-boat coming around the stern," Mr. Rogers yelled above the sound of the wind and exploding munitions.

"All engines stop! Turn the bow to the sub; act as if their presence is a surprise. We'll sit here and see what she does. When they fire on us, start the abandon ship procedure, at my command."

"Aye-aye."

The U-46 rounded the end of the stricken vessel, and upon seeing the *Londondary* laying about three miles off the port side of the Canadian ship, started towards her. The gun crew quickly changed their sights of the deck gun to the *Londondary*. The first shot splashed twenty yards to the port side. The next shot splashed ten yards to starboard.

Captain Montgomery ordered the ship to half speed forward, and the secondary crew to start the "panic to abandon ship" procedure.

The third shot hit the *Londondary* amidships on the port side, doing little damage. The next shot fell harmlessly in the water behind her.

The normal ship's company for the *Londondary* was twenty-eight men. However in addition to these men was the crew that handled the weaponry of the Q-ship, an additional thirty men.

The panic party was well rehearsed. When the alarm bell began to signal the "abandon ship" drill, the mock boiler room crew rushed up from below in dirty, greasy clothes, hatless and in panic, crawling over each other, fighting their way to the lifeboats. Other crewmembers appeared from different parts of the ship, scrambling to the lifeboats.

Here the panic was acted out even more realistically for the U-boat's benefit. One lifeboat was lowered in a clumsy fashion, one end dropped at such a steep angle that it appeared the boat would hit the water in almost vertical fashion. Crewmen at the boats would suddenly disappear into the ship and quickly reappear with a seemingly prized possession.

Captain Montgomery then went into the wheelhouse, where another man dressed identically to him dashed out with what appeared to be the ship's papers and logs and ran to the last lifeboat being lowered into the water. After the last lifeboat was away, the ship appeared to be abandoned and adrift in the sea. Captain Montgomery remained in the wheelhouse and in command of the hidden crew.

The U-46 approached cautiously, not getting any closer than two miles. At this point she began to circle the *Londondary*, firing her cannon with less frequency, scoring some hits on the superstructure.

Captain Montgomery soon realized he was faced with a dilemma. If he uncovered his guns and returned fire from this range, he might not be able to score enough hits to prevent the U-boat from submerging, and thus make his ship a torpedo target. On the other hand, if he let the U-boat continue raking the ship with its deck gun, they might sink him without his ship ever having fired a shot.

By prearranged plan, the lifeboat with the captain and ship's papers moved to a position where they hoped to entice the U-boat back closer to the *Londondary*. The *Londondary* carried six concealed guns—two were located in dummy deck cargo, two in deck cabins, one of the other two was located on the poop deck, and the sixth in one of the main deck structures. There were two deck-mounted torpedoes, an armored bridge used for fire control, and an arrangement of pipes through which clouds of steam could be vented to give the appearance of further damage than had actually been inflicted.

After a second shell hit amidships, Captain Montgomery ordered that the steam be released, giving the indication that the engine room had been hit. He then ordered all engines stopped. They soon sat dead in the water.

Captain Montgomery watched from the wheelhouse as the U-boat circled his ship for another ten minutes, before submerging. At periscope depth the submarine continued to circle and slowly approached to within one mile of the *Londonary*. By this time, the Canadian ship was disappearing below the waves of the sea.

The cat and mouse continued for another thirty minutes. Robert was receiving reports that the sub was still circling his ship at a distance of one mile. He ordered the crew to stay hidden and not make any moves that could be seen.

Finally the U-boat surfaced again, directly astern and within a mile. As soon as the U-46's gun was above the surface they started firing on the *Londondary*, wreaking tremendous damage around the poop deck and killing and wounding some of the crew.

Montgomery continued to hold his fire.

The U-boat made a dash towards the *Londondary*, turning to her starboard side and paralleling its course, and drew up to within 400 yards to execute the coup de grace.

Captain Montgomery saw this move coming and breathed a sigh of relief—now he could uncover his guns. He ordered the South African flag to be lowered and the white ensign to be raised. Next, he ordered the crew to drop the covers on the cannons and commence firing.

As the U-46 drew alongside with its deck gun blazing at about five rounds per minute, the crew of the *Londondary* dropped the sides of all of the false enclosures and opened up with a withering fire. Within the first five minutes four rounds from the *Londondary's* twelve-pound cannons struck home, hitting the deck and conning tower of the sub.

The crew on the U-boat's deck dove for the hatches as the sub began its decent. Just as it was disappearing from view, a final shell took out the secondary periscope and damaged the mechanism for raising the primary. Below the surface, the U-boat was taking on seawater at a horrendous rate and was forced to resurface. Within twenty minutes of the initial exchange of fire with the *Londondary*, the U-46 was back on the top of the ocean.

As the sub broke the surface with its back towards the *Londondary*, it fired two torpedoes from the stern tubes. The *Londondary* continued firing her deck guns, scoring a few hits on the deck and conning tower.

As soon as the U-boat had surfaced, Captain Montgomery ordered the *Londondary* underway and turned toward the sub. At that moment, one of the torpedoes struck the middle of the ship with a glancing blow. The second passed behind the *Londondary* and continued into an empty ocean. The explosion was loud and the ship shuddered throughout, but the damage didn't stop her. She continued towards the submarine.

With superior speed, Captain Montgomery continued his attack on the U-boat and ordered the ship to pull along a parallel path on the port side of the U-46. As the *Londondary* stood about 400 yards off the port side of the sub, she was hit low in the stern by the German's cannon, disabling her rudder and screw shaft, rendering her unable to move. This also added to the tremendous fire on the poop deck just above the ship's magazine.

The U-boat fired five or six more rounds into the *Londondary* as they sailed away. One round hit directly on the wheelhouse, blowing it and its occupants to smithereens.

Transition to the Air War

Finally, at the end of January, Ike was finishing up with the Rouleur and would soon graduate to the Nieuport. There wasn't anything wrong with the Moraine-built Rouleur. In fact, the French had used it in combat during the first two years of the war. It was sturdily made with a parasol upper wing and a very short-spanned lower wing, but it was not a pursuit aircraft.

Times had changed since the war began, and so had the state of the art in fighter or pursuit aircraft design. Now the Nieuport 27 was the next airplane the Americans were to receive. Ike was anxious to get his hands on one.

On the first day Ike was to fly the Nieuport, he and the four other trainees gathered around their instructor, Captain DeNard, on the aircraft line. The captain stood by one of the Nieuport's at the trailing edge of the lower left wing where it joined the fuselage.

Captain DeNard had at one time been a French ace of aces with over 15 kills to his credit. His combat flying ended in the spring of 1917 when he had been shot down, and in the process lost his right leg at the knee and the use of his left arm. His job now was to pass his combat knowledge on to the fledgling American airmen.

"Remember, the Le Rhone engine is much more powerful than what you were used to in the Rouleur," Captain DeNard began in his heavily accented English. "The gyroscopic effect of this engine requires that you be vigilant on takeoff. As soon as you get the tail off of the ground you will need to apply a generous amount of right rudder to keep it straight down the runway. The undercarriage is narrower than on the Rouleur and the tendency to overcontrol could result in a ground loop. Once airborne you'll find the plane responds rapidly to control pressures. You'll love this plane and soon consider it an extension of yourself."

Ike smiled at this analogy. "Be careful of steep dives. The Nieuport, if overstressed, will shed the fabric on the upper part of the top wing," DeNard continued. "If you get too violent in control pressures at high speed, you may even loose the wing and, as we all know, that could ruin your whole day." There was a smattering of chuckles from the American pilots before the captain continued. "Its structural integrity is all right, but the aircraft, on the whole, could be stronger. For your first flights, do not exceed airspeeds of 120 miles per hour. Most acrobatic maneuvers are acceptable, but beware of those maneuvers that put great strain on the airframe, such as imprecise loops, power dives, rapid application of back pressure, and any other type of high stress maneuver."

When the captain completed his lecture he looked at the eager faces of his students and said, "Captain Dennison, you are to be the first to fly." Ike was ecstatic and saw the envy in the eyes of the others. "Yes Sir," he said and stepped forward quickly so as not to give Captain DeNard the opportunity to change his mind. As he looked at the plane just sitting on the ground, it appeared to be moving at 100 mph. Next to the Jennies and Rouleurs, there was no comparison.

After visually pre-flighting the airplane, with Captain DeNard at his side explaining what he should look for, Ike stepped up on the lower wing and swung his body into the wicker seat in the cockpit. His adrenaline began to flow. The cockpit was a tighter fit than on any other plane he had flown. He spent a few moments familiarizing himself with the instruments, their position and readings. Next he went through a pre-start routine. He moved the joystick in a circular motion and observed the movement of the control surfaces, ailerons and elevator. Next he pushed the rudder pedals to check the actual movement of the rudder.

Ike grinned, rubbed his hands together, then fastened his leather helmet strap under his chin, adjusted his scarf around his neck, and put the goggles down over his eyes. He fastened his seat belt tightly over his lap and pulled on his gloves. Last of all, he scanned the sky. It was an overcast day with scattered showers and visibility of eight to ten miles. The breeze was out of the west-southwest at about 10 to 15 mph and the temperature was a little above freezing. It was a beautiful day for flying.

He yelled to his mechanic, "Okay Mike, let's get her running."

"Switch off?" Mike called to Ike.

"Switch off!"

Mike then pulled the propeller through two revolutions and positioned it over a compression stroke for starting. "Switch on?" he called.

"Switch on!" Ike replied. As he spoke, he could feel a lump develop in his throat as he tried to swallow.

Mike gave a mighty heave and the engine came instantly to life. Ike leaned the mixture a smidgen to bring the RPMs up. Next, with both hands clenched in a fist and his thumbs turned up, he signaled the ground crew to remove the wheel chocks. He saluted his instructor, who was standing off the starboard wings, and kept the power at high RPM until the plane started moving.

He taxied straight ahead for 10 to 15 meters, then gave full right rudder for a 90-degree right turn in order to parallel the takeoff runway. The roar of the engine was louder than any plane he'd flown before. The feeling was electrifying. The Neiuport, like most planes, had a tailskid, and it took a little speed and a lot of rudder to negotiate a turn on the ground.

As Ike approached the take-off point on the runway, he checked for traffic. Seeing no conflicts, he left the engine at full rpm and pushed full left rudder and swung the plane around 180 degrees for a takeoff to the west. He glanced at the windsock on the maintenance hangar in order to check the wind direction and speed. It appeared to be still out of the west-southwest at about 15 mph, a left quartering head wind.

Without retarding the rpm, he held a little left aileron and left rudder into the wind. The speed came up rapidly and soon, with some forward pressure on the joystick, the tail came up smartly. The torque of the engine pulled the plane left, Ike applied right rudder and overcompensated, and the plane's nose started moving to the right of centerline. He had a little difficulty in finding the right combination to compensate for both torque and the crosswind as the plane wiggled right and then left of center in the takeoff run. Soon the mains broke ground and he was airborne.

He heaved a sigh of relief once he was in the air. The rate of climb was tremendous. He couldn't believe how fast the plane climbed to 700 meters. He held right rudder throughout the ascent, circled slowly to the right, and eventually leveled out on a northerly heading. At this point Ike established straight and level flight in a cruise configuration. The speed quickly came up to 105 mph, and he maintained this power for the remainder of the flight.

The Nieuport was well designed and well rigged, for at this power setting, he could fly, nearly hands-off in the smooth air. After he was situated and comfortable in the plane, he started a routine of familiarization. First, he put the plane in slow flight. This was a process of slowing the plane down to a speed just above the stall, and while holding that speed he did not allow a stall to develop. At the same time, he tried to maintain his altitude. While in slow flight, he made a series of right and left turns. Next, he performed climbs and descents at this minimum control speed, switching the power on and off as needed to maintain a constant airspeed.

After he had a little better feel for the Nieuport, he went through a number of approaches to a stall. He switched the power off and held backpressure on the joystick, slowing the plane down by raising the nose. When the plane started to shudder from the impending stall, he released the backpressure and switched full power on to return to straight and level flight. He then performed a number of full stalls. For these, he held the backpressure until the stall broke and the nose fell through the horizon before initiating his recovery. As his confidence grew in his ability to handle the plane and the solid performance of the aircraft, he continued on and performed a few three-turn spins, two to the right and two to the left.

He loved the plane; it handled as if it were one of his own appendages. His only surprise was the steep nose-down angle in the spin and the rapid increase in speed during the pullout.

He finished the day by performing some chandelles and lazy eights followed by one power dive. In this he allowed the speed to reach 120 mph, and then initiated his pullout. By the time the plane started to level out, the speed had built up to 130. He felt a violent shake as the fabric skin on the upper wing started to flutter due to the high speed, but this subsided as soon as the speed fell below 120. Now he knew why Captain DeNard had warned him and the others of high-speed dives. But this also gave him an indication of the performance envelope within which he had to work.

He spent about fifteen more minutes maneuvering and adjusting to the aircraft before he returned to the field, executing one loop, and a few snap rolls and three slow rolls.

As he approached Issoudun, he put the plane in a shallow dive until he was approximately 100 feet above the field and allowed the airspeed to build to 125 mph. As he leveled out and before he reached the center of the field, he performed a slow roll. When the Nieuport returned to the upright position over the east end of the field, he continued at full power and added back pressure to the joystick in the start of a loop. The airspeed fell off rapidly as he came to and passed vertical. As the plane came over on its back at the top of the loop, he rolled the ship to the upright position, heading in the opposite direction.

"Now, that's aerobatics!" Ike said to himself as he entered the pattern and landed the plane.

Captain DeNard, along with the other trainees, was at the tiedown when Ike shut down the engine and climbed out of the plane.

"What do you mean by performing acrobatics over the field, Lieutenant? You know that isn't allowed," Captain DeNard said in a firm voice. But as he looked at Ike and turned so the others couldn't see his face, he winked and added in French, "Nice flying."

Ike couldn't help but grin. "I'm very sorry sir! It will never happen again."

Regathering of the Rainbow

For the first two weeks of February, the men of the Rainbow Division pursued the finer points of their training. Major Hinkle and his staff also used this time to procure and distribute all necessary equipment and supplies to bring the division to combat readiness, as it was apparent they would soon move onto the line.

They were experiencing the worst weather yet throughout all of France, from the west in Rolampont to the eastern province of Brittany. The conditions were wet and cold; everything was covered or filled with mud. In Coetquidan, the water at the horse troughs consisted of more than fifty percent mud, so the animals had to be watered some five kilometers away.

Gas masks were issued to all of the men of the 42nd Division on February 3. They were soon put to use; the men drilled in the mask's function and purpose on a daily basis.

Unlike some of the regiments, the men of the 149th Field Artillery were issued English-designed masks consisting of a rubberized canvas face piece that was pulled over the head and tightened with straps. They had a mouthpiece and a nose clip, requiring the wearer to breathe only through his mouth. The mouthpiece was attached, through the mask, to tubing, about 1 inch in diameter, which led to a chemical-laden canister that was strapped to the chest when at the ready position. The chemicals cleaned the incoming air of contaminants and allowed the wearer safe passage through the dangerous, gas-filled environment. A clear paste was also provided to smear over the glass eyepieces, inside the mask, in order to prevent fogging and condensation, which otherwise would obscure the man's vision. This proved to be of dubious value in the warmer weather, and it soon became apparent that conversation with these devices in place was nearly impossible.

As the time approached for the men to join the front line battle, practice in the use of this very essential equipment became all too frequent. Each man had to move through gas-filled bunkers in order to perfect the use of this lifesaving apparatus. Artillery practice also took most of the day and sometimes went well into the night.

Each battery was issued two machine guns to be used for protection against enemy aircraft. When Battery F was on the march, the number one gun was to be positioned on the lead carriage of the column and the number two gun brought up the rear. However when entrenched on the front, one gun would be positioned with the firing battery and the other would be placed near the rear echelon.

On February 9, the battery underwent a thorough inspection. The men rolled their blankets with care, then loaded their packs and saddlebags according to army regulation. When all personal items were ready the battery harnessed and hitched and moved to the parade ground in marching order for inspection by Lieutenant Case and the Second Battalion commander, Major Reddon.

The days that followed the inspection dealt with getting equipment and animals ready to move to the front. It was rumored that the regiment would be located somewhere in the Lorraine province. As soon as items were ready, they would be moved to Guer in preparation for loading on the trains that would take the brigade to the front and reunite them with the rest of the division.

On February 11, everyone in the regiment was issued British made trench shoes, all size ten and totally inflexible. To the Americans, it was like strapping lead bars to their feet.

On the following day Major Redden, addressed all of the men in the battalion. "We are moving out to take our position in the battle line. On the sixteenth, Headquarters Company, Supply Company, and Battery A will leave for the front. Then Batteries B, C, D and E will leave on the seventeenth. The rest will leave the next day. We are at long last going to put to use our many months of training. From this time forward we will fire our guns in earnest, not practice. I commend you men for the hard work and may the Good Lord bless our mission. God's protection over each and every one of you."

On February 14, Hank, Pat and the two other mechanics were enjoying their breakfast in the mess hall. "Do you realize that this is the first time we've had wheat cakes since we left Camp Mills?" Tom ventured after a long silence.

"Yeah, really good. It may be one of the last hot breakfasts we'll have in a long time." Hank added. "We'll be at the front in a couple of days."

"Hey, this is what we came for, to fight. It's time to celebrate," Paul said.

"I don't know if celebrate is the word I'd use Paul," Pat said. "It is what we came here to do, but I really don't feel like celebrating. I guess you'd say I'm awfully anxious."

Hank nodded.

"You know we've had a good time up to this point because no one's life has really been in danger," Pat said. "But now it's no longer a game, it's for real. It makes you think about what could happen."

They fell silent for a few more minutes.

"We'll be leaving Monday, and did you hear I can't take my camera?" Paul said. "Why, they said it'd be a court martial offense if anyone's caught with a camera."

"The other thing that gets my goat is that we have to leave a day after everyone else so that we can clean up the camp," Hank groaned.

"Don't fret about that, we're having one wingding of a party Sunday night," Paul said with a grin. "That oughta make up for the extra detail work."

Not much else was said as they finished their breakfast and went to the guns.

It was on this day that all necessary repairs and adjustments were to be completed, and then the guns were to be readied for transport. Their last job was greasing them and then wrapping them in burlap.

On February 18, reveille was at three a.m. It was hard rolling out at that early hour, and particularly this morning as the previous night's party hadn't ended until midnight. There were many hangovers, since the last of the supply of liquor just had to be finished before leaving.

After a breakfast of fried bread and bacon, the men got to work finishing up with their packs and rolls. By six thirty-five, all of the horses were harnessed and hitched and the last column of the 149th Field Artillery marched out of camp on their way to Guer. By seven a.m. the loading was well underway—eight horses plus two handlers per car, and the men were loaded approximately twenty-five to thirty per car. All of the rolling equipment was placed and secured on flat cars.

As the men boarded the train, travel rations for the trip were handed out. The boxes contained some French bread, jam, hardtack, a can of baked beans, a can of tomatoes and a can of corned Willie.

When the train pulled out of Guer, the manifest for Battery F showed 27 carriages, 106 horses and mules, 158 enlisted men and 16 officers.

After the train passed through Rennes, Vitry and Laval, it pulled to a siding for a short stop. Here the animals were watered and the men replenished their canteens with wine, rum and cognac, purchased at a nearby store.

They spent the night on the train and the cold settled deep into everyone's bones. Pat endured a sleepless night. The floor of the 40 and 8 car was hard and cold, with just a little bit of straw between him and the hardwood planking. The train stopped frequently and each time he would sit up wide-awake, trying to determine just where they were. At dawn the guards announced that they were approaching Paris. Most of the men on the car were awake and they opened the doors and windows in anticipation of seeing the great city of light. As luck would have it, the train was switched to another track and they circled around the outer fringes of the city. The men saw very little of Paris.

Next the train stopped at Versailles-Chanty in order to water the animals. Here the French Red Cross handed out rum-spiked coffee that helped to warm the men. Games of chance thrived throughout the train. Pat and Hank passed on the gaming and looked out at the passing scenery most of the day. The towns drifted slowly by, Romilly-Seine, Troyes and Boulogne, but the local inhabitants showed little enthusiasm for the passing Americans.

The troops tried their hardest to flirt with all of the young women along the way, but their hearts weren't in it since the train would not stop. The men's principal cheer was lavished on an ancient Ford sedan that coughed and wheezed it's way along a parallel path near the town of Troyes.

Late in the day they stopped once again to give water to the horses. Here it was announced that they would detrain in the early morning. Those who were anxious for the trip to end rolled up their blankets and sought out sufficient hay with which to cover themselves in order not to freeze during the cold night.

For Pat the night seemed endless; fearing the future he couldn't sleep. What if he ran when they were under fire? What if he were killed? What if he crawled in a hole and refused to come out? Could he stand and fight when under attack? Nothing seemed to bother Hank who was next to him, asleep, and snoring peacefully.

Through a crack in the side of the car, Pat caught a glimpse of the eastern horizon and saw that it was just beginning to get light. As he shut his eyes and tried to force himself to sleep, he felt the train start to slow. He knew that sleep was out of the question and decided to sit up, and punched Hank in the back. "You asleep?" he whispered loudly.

"I couldn't sleep a wink," Hank said as he sat up, rubbing his face and eyes with his hands. "How about you?"

"Not a bit. You were sure making enough noise, you almost drowned out the sound of the train."

"I guess I may have dozed a little. I worried about how I was going to react when we move into the line. It kept me tossing and turning."

"Yeah, me too. I wonder if we're there yet. The train is slowing down."

As he said this, some of the other motionless forms on the floor of the 40 and 8 started to stir.

When the brakes were applied, their ear-piercing squeal awakened everyone. One of the men near the front opened one of the windows and peered out into the darkness ahead. The cold air filled the car and Pat, sitting with his back to the sidewall, shivered uncontrollably.

"What's the matter, Pat? Cold?" Hank asked.

"Freezing. Where are we?" Pat spat out through chattering teeth.

"Who knows?" someone replied.

"What was that? Was that thunder?" asked another voice from the darkness.

"Does this mean we have to detrain in the rain and mud?" someone else said. "I'm sick and tired of the wet and the mud."

"That weren't no thunder," came the unmistakable voice of Sergeant Martyn. "That was the bark of a French 75. You can't miss the sound. We're near the front."

All fell quiet for a moment or two, each man straining to hear the cannon fire.

The train came to a halt at approximately 9:30 in the morning. The men off-loaded with haste, in a quiet and expectant manner. Ever since arriving in France they had been told, and even had drilled into them, that when they reached the front the sound of battle was always present. The cannonading that they had heard earlier in the morning reinforced this notion. But here, a short distance from town, they found little visual evidence that this was a battleground.

Once off of the train, those not tending the horses or moving equipment formed up and marched into the village of Luneville. As the battery moved through the town on their way to their billet, *Quartier Stanislas*, they encountered a large group of German prisoners marching with their hands on their heads and fingers interlocked, under guard, in the opposite direction. These men had been captured during an early morning raid; the artillery fire had made the rumbling sounds that greeted the train at dawn.

From this chance encounter with the prisoners, it was but a short hike to the place the regiment was to be quartered for the next few days. This turned out to be a palace that had been built by the Polish king, Stanislas, after the Russians deposed him. It was an immense and once beautiful estate with well-manicured grounds and stately structures, from the principal dwelling to the servant's cottages. Even the stables and corrals where the animals of the 149th were to stay were lavish in their appointments. The men were to be quartered in the lofts located over the stables.

There was little evidence, other than an occasional shell hole here and there, that this was a war zone. Luneville was a quiet sector, and there had been no serious fighting here since 1914. During the initial stages of the war, the Germans had indeed occupied Luneville and other small communities within a short distance of the town. However, they withdrew to their current trench line position soon thereafter. Luneville had been spared the ravages of the fighting, unlike Ramvilars, another nearby town, which had been utterly destroyed. Since the time of the German withdrawal, there had been an unwritten agreement between the Germans and the French sparing the villages in the area. Neither side had used gas, and in the daytime a shot was seldom heard.

The country around Luneville was a picture postcard setting, with low rolling hills richly spotted with trees and many small farms, all too beautiful to be the scene of battle.

After unloading their gear and setting up their barracks in the garret over the stables, the men of Battery F gathered in groups and went exploring and sightseeing. Pat and Hank went a short distance from town, viewing and discussing the countryside. They took particular interest in the local farms. They felt the soil with their hands and guessed at its fertility compared to that in their home in the Midwest. It felt good to stand in a country setting, though it was just for a brief time.

In the evening, Tom, Hank, Paul, Pat and others gathered over mugs of beer and discussed their situation with some infantrymen of the 167th who joined the battery members at the cafe. Each recounted their trials since they had parted company at St. Nazaire. All soon came to the conclusion that they had mastered the art of warfare and it wouldn't be long before the white flags of surrender would be waving from the German trenches, now that the Rainbow was here.

Jack, who still held the position as company clerk for the battery, came into the establishment about a half hour after the others. By this time the cafe was filled with soldiers from all the various units of the Rainbow. He pushed his way through the crowd over to the table where Pat and the others were sitting and collapsed in a heap on an empty chair across from Pat.

"I didn't think I'd ever find you guys, this town is loaded with troops," he said. "All of the beer emporiums are as crowded as we are here and I have a lot of beer to drink to catch up with the rest of you. The paperwork sure took longer than I thought it would."

"Well we haven't been here that long. We did a little sightseeing before coming to this place," Pat said.

"Oh, and before I forget, Pat, there's a reporter from the *Stars and Stripes* looking for you. Don't know what he wants but said he'd try to catch you in the morning."

"That's got to be my brother. Hey, Hank!" Pat shouted down the table. "I think Roy is here in Luneville."

"What's he doing here?"

"I don't know, I guess he's come to pay us a visit. He said in his last letter that he'd try to get out to see me when he got to France, so I guess he finally made it."

"I didn't know that was your brother," Jack said. "He didn't tell me his name, just said he was looking for you. Otherwise I'd have brought him with me."

"Did he say where he was staying?"

"No."

The major was sitting at his desk just as it was getting dark. He heard the front door of the outer office open and saw a figure enter. It was dark in the room and the only light was on his desk. The men on staff at G-1 had finished for the day with the exception of Major Hinkle, who had worked late trying to wrap up the details of the troop deployment that was to disburse the Rainbow into the trenches during the next couple of days.

"Who's there?" he called out into the darkness.

"Major Hinkle?"

"Yes, who is it?"

"Major Hinkle, it's Roy Littler with the *Stars and Stripes*. Remember, we met some months ago at Camp Mills?"

"Well, of course I do, Roy. Come in my boy, come on in and sit down."

Roy approached the desk and sat down. "I didn't want to disturb you, sir, but I saw the light. I thought you might have a minute?"

"Sure do. I was just finishing up some details, and, as a matter of fact, I was just going to close up for the night and go get a beer. Would you join me?"

"That would be great, sir. I'm here to write a story on the Rainbow, so maybe you could fill me in on what's happening."

"Be glad to, Roy. Have you been in France long?"

"No, sir, just arrived about a week ago. This is the first assignment I've had since coming here."

"Great, then you can fill me in on what's happening in Champaign."

With the dawning of a new day, the men awoke to a fresh, light snow on the ground. But this was hardly enough to prevent the 149th from harnessing the horses, hitching them to the carriages, and going for a compulsory march. After lunch, they joined other units of the division for a parade. On the reviewing stand was none other than General Menoher, the new commander of the Rainbow, and some French general, unknown to the troops. After the review and completion of other chores, Roy caught up with Pat at the evening meal at the battery's mess.

Actually, there was no mess hall. The cooks had set up a field kitchen and the men, once served, sat wherever they could find a place. Pat and some of his friends were sitting on the ground near the corral eating and talking when Pat spotted Roy coming towards him. He set his plate down and rushed over to him, almost tripping over a few of his buddies in the process.

"I knew you were here when Jack said there was a *Stars and Stripes* reporter looking for me." Pat nearly shouted as he reached his brother and threw his arms around him in a big bear hug. "It sure is great to see you."

Roy hugged him back. "Strange place for us to meet, little brother," he said, "out here in the middle of nowhere."

"I looked all over for you this morning before I found out your group was out on a field problem. Then later, I watched you pass in review this afternoon as Major Hinkle's guest," Roy said.

"Well, you've got a lot to tell me, about the folks and all, but first come on over and meet the crew. I've got guard duty tonight so I won't be able to spend much time with you. But tomorrow is Washington's Birthday and we have the afternoon off," Pat explained leading Roy to where he'd been sitting.

After dinner was over, Pat walked a short way with Roy, who was on his way back to his hotel. They discussed where they would meet the next day, said good night and Pat headed back to his guard duty.

Reveille was at 5:30 a.m. on Friday, February 22. The men rolled out and went to the field kitchen in the rain. They stood while they ate and found shelter where they could. After eating they left the stables for this was a market day for the local citizens. Every Sunday, Wednesday and Friday, any of the inhabitants of Luneville and the surrounding countryside, who had goods, vegetables and/or dairy products for sale, would bring them to the stables at Stanislaus to display and hopefully to sell. To do so anywhere else would present an open invitation for attack from roaming German aircraft.

The remainder of the morning was spent performing various chores, from grooming the horses and polishing the carriages to inspecting telephone lines. The mechanics cared for the cannon.

After the noon meal, Pat and Hank met Roy and the three of them walked around the town sightseeing, talking and shopping. Food was scarce in Luneville and so they spent some of the time buying what food they could, then took it to a local restaurant and gave it to the proprietor, who cooked their evening meal for them. Much of the talk revolved around happenings in the states and in particular, the latest gossip in Champaign.

Later, Hank asked Roy, "What's this business with you and Major Hinkle?"

"My primary reason for coming to Luneville is to cover the actions of your division. I knew that the major was heavily involved with the movements you're going through, so I thought I would seek him out first, since he probably had a handle on what was going on. I went to his office last evening and found him there and we ended up going out for a beer and a long talk. Very interesting gentleman. He invited me to the review yesterday afternoon and arranged for some other interviews for me today, and now I'm ready to head back to Paris and file my story. I'll be on the early train tomorrow morning. That's all there is."

"I don't think you're telling us everything," Hank said, raising an eyebrow.

"Well, a lot that he told me can't be printed for awhile, as they don't want the Germans to know you're moving into the line. So I have to wait until they know you're there before I can file the remainder of the story, but that shouldn't be too long."

"What's the deal, I mean for us?" Pat asked.

"When the First Division went into the trenches a short time ago, they moved in with some fanfare, which aroused the suspicions of the Boche, and this brought down a rather deadly burst of fire on the heads of our troops. Therefore they, the French, want to merge you into the line right away without the Germans knowing it. As I understand it, the division will be divided into small units and brigaded with four French divisions of the Seventh Corps already positioned on the line."

"And?" Pat said anxiously.

Roy checked his notes and gave them the particulars. "Now don't pass this around. It's all confidential."

"No one will hear it from us." Hank said.

After eating their meal, they each sat back enjoying a large mug of beer.

"Pat, I don't know what you've heard from home," Roy began, "but Dad isn't real good. He had another heart attack on New Year's Eve. He was in the hospital for over a week. By the time I left the states he was home, but I think he's worse than he or Mom let on."

"I didn't even know he'd been sick. I got a letter from Mom saying he was a little under the weather but all was okay. Nothing about his heart." Pat felt sick in the pit of his stomach and tears came to his eyes. He had known his life was going to be in danger, but he'd never even considered that his mom or dad wouldn't be at home when he returned.

"Well, I thought you'd better know so you won't be shocked if the worse happens."

"Is it that bad?"

"I don't know but I would be prepared if I were you. I know I am."

To the Line

During the late afternoon of February 20, 1918, the 167th Infantry Regiment detrained just outside of Luneville. After gathering their gear and marching a short distance, they established their bivouac about two kilometers from the town, a place where they would remain for four days.

Then, shortly after dark on February 23, the 167th broke camp and marched the remaining 13 kilometers to the trenches and the position they would defend on the front. Their purpose was to move in and set up their watch on the line under the cover of darkness without arousing German suspicions as to the presence of American troops in this sector.

The 167th and the 168th Infantry Regiments were in the trenches, next to the 128th French Division located in the Baccarat sector. This had always been a somewhat quiet part of the front, so peaceful in fact, that the French had calmly smoked their pipes while perched on the very top of the trenches during the evening hours and not worried about becoming a sniper's target. The Germans seemed to enjoy an evening smoke in a similar manner.

There were even some Germans, directly across from Jake's platoon, who would come every morning and wash their dirty clothes in a water-filled shell crater, just as if there were no war, all in full view of the Allied trenches.

On the third morning, after taking up their position not long after dawn, Jake was abruptly awakened from his slumber by his sergeant vigorously shaking his shoulders.

"What the hell you want, sergeant?" he said as he struggled to adjust his eyes to the light.

"They're out there again this morning, Lieutenant. They're washing their clothes in that damned shell hole again. Can we shoot 'em? We sure could scare the holy b'Jesus outta 'em."

At that very moment the sound of rifle fire filled the air. Jake jumped to his feet, hitting his head on the overhead bunker timbers. He ran out, rubbing his head with his left hand and carrying his helmet in his right, and headed toward the firing line where the shooting had originated.

"Cease fire," he yelled. "Who told you to start firing?" he said to the first man he came to.

"Sir, didn't we come here to fight the Germans? You shoulda seen them scatter, like scared rabbits. I think I got one in the shoulder."

"Thomas, you're never to initiate fire unless ordered, you got that?" Jake screamed.

Captain Hammonds came running up, somewhat out of breath. "What's going on, Jake?"

"They opened up on some Germans washing their clothes out in no-man's land, hoping to bag a few," Jake answered.

"You men get any?" Captain Hammonds asked. This came as a shock to Jake, who thought he was going to catch holy hell for letting it happen.

"You bet!" came the reply from Private Thomas. "I got one of the bastards in the shoulder."

"Well, Jake, I think the Boche know we've arrived," Captain Hammonds said.

"But, sir, I thought we weren't supposed to let the Germans know we were here."

"Hell, Jake, they know, and now it's official—we're in this war."

At about this time a field grade French officer, followed by an entourage of lesser-ranking officers, came running up the trench line toward them. In very clear English, he said, "What are you Americans doing? You have done a terrible thing. Now the Germans will be angry and will retaliate with shelling and maybe even gas. What has happened?"

"Sir," Captain Hammonds replied, "we came here to kill Germans, not watch them wash their dirty laundry out in no-man's-land."

"You had better prepare your men for an attack," the French officer said with disgust. "You have violated an understanding between the Boche and us. This will be reported to your superiors."

The period of the quiet war was now at an end. True to the Frenchman's words, on the morning of March 5, the Germans started their retaliation.

At four a.m., the Boche initiated a heavy artillery barrage on the position held by the 168th Infantry from Iowa. They first hit any position they thought would contain artillery in order to prevent counterfire coming from the allied side. Next, their cannon hit the barbed wire in front of the trenches. Simultaneously, they dropped a barrage behind the trenches to cut off any reinforcements that might be sent forward and to prevent any line of retreat of those in the forward trenches.

The 168th was to the right of Jake's position, defending some small, bombed-out, brick buildings just north of Badonvillers known as Le Chamois Farm. This position was at the union of two shallow valleys, and this was the point at which the raid was directed.

Jake watched with wide-eyed wonder as the Germans next laid down a creeping barrage of high explosive shells. Behind this wall of fire he could see, in the bright moonlight, gray-clad troops moving toward the American lines. At the point of attack there was a mere 150 meters separating the trenches. The brunt of the strike on the Iowans was just 100 meters to Jake's right.

The alarm sounded, and all of the troops stood on the firing step in the trench and focused the sights of their Springfields on the advancing Germans. Jake felt the adrenaline flow through his veins. He had never been so alert or so frightened before. Though the attack was off to his right and not directed at his platoon, the enemy was within his men's line of fire.

At the command, Jake's platoon, along with the Iowans, opened up with a blistering fire that felled many of the advancing troops. However, those to the rear kept coming. The Marylanders of the 151st Trench Mortar Battalion cut loose with their mortars, and the Georgians hit them hard with machine guns. Allied artillery countered the German fire, but all seemed to be in confusion as far as Jake was concerned. The smoke from the fight filled the air and the sound was deafening.

At daybreak, the violent sound of battle diminished and then finally the guns fell silent. The line had held; there was no breakthrough, and the Germans were in retreat back to their own trenches. No-man's land was littered with German dead and wounded. The Rainbow had won their first encounter with the enemy.

In front of the Iowans, three bodies in gray uniforms hung grotesquely over the barbed wire. There they stayed as a mute warning to any German that dared to strike at the 42nd Division again.

When the fighting was over, a cheer came up from the men in the American trenches. They had met the enemy head on and they had won, at least for now. The Americans did not win without their own causalities. One officer and eighteen men were killed and twenty-two were wounded. The first bitter blood had been drawn.

Jake put the field glasses to his eyes and surveyed the scene in both wonder and dismay. The battle had been much more ferocious than he had ever imagined.

Captain Hammonds came to Jake's position. "How you doing, Jake?"

"I guess all right, sir, my knees are a little wobbly yet."

"We sure beat the crap out of them today. Your platoon was the only one from our regiment to fire their rifles, but some of our machine gunners got in on it. It was a big win for us."

"Well, Captain, I can't help but think of the men we lost, or that the 168th lost, for someone down there was in the line of fire."

Captain Hammonds frowned. "Jake, that's the last I want to hear from you about losses. We're in a war and everybody is fair game. Keep your focus on the win. Forget about the dead and wounded, your job is to fight. If you think too much about our losses, you'll be a basket case in no time. Now rejoice in our victory, you got that?"

"I think I see what you mean, sir."

On Sunday, February 24, Lieutenant Case and all of the other battery commanders of the Second Battalion were ordered to the front to reconnoiter the sites that had been designated for the regiment. Each battery was being paired with a comparable French battery attached to one of their own divisions, in this case, the 164th. After spending the day at the position with the French regimental artillery commander, Lieutenant Case returned in the late evening. With the aid of Lieutenant Allen and Sergeant Baker, Lieutenant Case selected fifty men to go forward the next day and prepare the position for the cannon, which were to follow in four to six days.

Reveille on the 25th was at 5:30. The morning was cold and, after a month of overcast skies, it was crystal clear. The sky was a brilliant blue and there was a freshness in the air that the men hadn't experienced since leaving the states. Breakfast that morning consisted of bacon, wheat cakes and coffee. When they finished eating, Pat, Hank and the others on the detail went to the stables and gathered their personal belongings. When their packs were ready they headed for the exercise yard out in front and began loading equipment and kitchen supplies into the one wagon that was to accompany the detail to the front lines.

The road to the front was well traveled and well camouflaged with a brown burlap covering. This camouflage had been suspended on wires, which in turn, had been attached to poles located on either side of the road. The burlap was about twelve feet above the ground making passage under it simple and easy for all but the largest pieces of equipment. This covering prevented the Boche from observing movement of troops, ammunition and supplies.

As a further precaution, the men proceeded in six groups of eight men each, with 30 meters separating each of the groups. The two men on the wagon brought up the rear.

Hank and Pat were with the fourth group moving along the thirteen-kilometer route from Luneville to their destination, la Neuveville aux Bois. The hike was eventful, as a number of shells landed in front and to their left as they approached the front, but the impact was far enough away that the men didn't have to dive for cover. A veteran might have termed the trip uneventful.

As they walked, the men for the most part were silent, but they took in everything with their eyes. As Pat walked under the burlap on this bright, clear day, he could have sworn the color of the sky and surrounding countryside had been sucked out by the war. The closer they got to the front, the more the landscape became monochromatic, black, gray and dirty white.

The sporadic shelling ceased as the detail neared their destination around 2:30 in the afternoon. The town of la Neuveville had long ago been the scene of a fierce battle. As the detail approached, Pat could see that every building had either been severely damaged by artillery or leveled completely. Even the trees that once stood in majestic splendor along the streets, reaching their branches to the sky, had been shelled into little more than broken splinters whose stumps stood no more than eight to ten feet high.

The streets had been cleared of the rubble so that the numerous military vehicles and troops could pass, unimpeded by debris from the bombed-out buildings.

All that remained standing showed the ravages of war.

From the streets of la Neuveville aux Bois, which was situated on a knoll, Pat could look down to the front line trenches located to the north and east, some five kilometers away. These appeared as deep, ugly wounds in what had once been a beautiful and colorful setting. They found everything in semi-ruin, occupied only by military personnel. The civilian population had long since fled to safer ground.

The enlisted men were billeted in buildings located in the town. These were for the most part bombed-out structures without roofs, and walls with gaping holes that provided a view of the front. The officers hadn't faired any better as they were placed in a bomb-ravaged parsonage adjoining the demolished church. After occupying their billets and helping set up the field kitchen, no other duties were assigned for the remainder of the day, as it was approaching the dinner hour.

As they ate a supper of cold corned beef and beans, Pat and Hank sat on a pile of rubble with their backs to a brick wall of their bombed-out shelter, looking toward the trenches.

"Well, Hank, here we are. Whatcha thinking?"

"It's hard to take it all in. So far I guess that it isn't what I expected, but it's too soon to judge."

"Yeah, I think I know what you mean," Pat replied. "Here we are, after all the expectations, and, you know, it's just another day. We're at the front and nothing's happening. I think I expected to be under fire the whole time. I guess I really didn't know what to expect. Each day we seem to take yet another step that brings us closer to the war, and this is just one of those steps. The devastation around here is unbelievable, and yet it's so quiet."

Hank nodded. "They said that it gets lively after dark, so maybe things'll change soon."

"Yeah, the sun will be down in a short while."

After eating, the men lounged as best they could on the rubble and talked, played cards or wrote letters to loved ones at home. After dark no fires or lights were allowed and soon the men covered themselves with their blankets and went to sleep.

Late in the night a heavy cannonading awakened these newcomers to the front. All of the men were up in a flash looking to see if they needed to seek shelter in the underground dugouts provided for that purpose. The shelling was to their right and not very close. They all stood in amazement, taking it all in. The artillery was loud and constant and the ground vibrated under their feet. The flashes of the guns and explosions of the guns' deadly missiles mesmerized them all.

After an hour the shelling subsided and the men returned to their chicken wire bunks. These were suspended from walls and posts in hammock style in order to keep them off the ground, out of the way of the rats.

It was on the following day that the real work of the detail began. Reveille was at six and after breakfast, each man was issued a pick or a shovel. They headed off in a northwesterly direction and hiked about one and a half kilometers to the abandoned French artillery position, selected a few days earlier by Lieutenant Case. This position was located on the edge of a small wood, the Bois de Lagrange. The gun pits and dugouts hadn't been in use for over a year and were in a terrible state of disrepair. The rebuilding of this structure was like starting all over. The dugouts were to be replaced, trail pieces salvaged from the mud, and the overall layout altered due to the different direction of fire now to be employed.

The work was distasteful, due in large part to the deep mud that stood in each of the pits. The men dove into the task and made some headway before returning to Neuveville aux Bois for the noonday meal.

After eating and on their return to the digging, they all witnessed French antiaircraft fire, trying to hit a single Boche plane headed for its lines. To the Americans on the ground, it didn't appear that the German had a chance to escape, and little black puffs seemed to surround the aircraft. However, adroit manipulation of the controls took the plane safely over its own lines.

The remainder of the daylight hours was spent working on the gun emplacements.

Each evening, while the battery was on the line and after the meal, two men were sent forward to one of the observation posts, where they were teamed with two French Poilus, to watch for signal rockets.

The next day greeted the detail with drizzling rain. This made the gun pits nearly impossible to dig out. With each shovel full pitched out, two more seemed to stream in from the top.

In the early evening a detail of ten more men arrived from Luneville with a wagonload of lumber for the gun positions. It was early in the morning before they finished unloading the timber, and all came to the billet in the village, drenched and covered with mud.

On the following day the rain came down even harder, creating a mud pool almost knee deep in the positions. The mud was so gooey the men had to push it off the shovel with their hands.

After an hour of trying to dig this muddy goo, Jack threw down his shovel in disgust. "This shit is like glue. All I do is rake it off the shovel with my hand and it flows back in before I can get the shovel back into the ground. This is ridiculous."

Jason Newcum, who had never uttered an expletive heretofore, cursed like a seasoned trooper. "The goddamned Army ought to have given us heavy equipment for this job. The son of a bitch that sent us out here with picks and shovels, must of had his head up his ass."

In addition to the digging, the men had to carry heavy timbers and steel elephant backs from the road to the gun position, some 400 meters distant. In an effort to quicken the crew's pace, Lieutenant Case ordered that lunch be taken to the detail to save the time it took the men to walk from the position to the field kitchen and back. The men, who felt they were overworked and deserved at least the small break of walking to the village for their lunch, received this somewhat coolly.

Finally, on March 1, after four days of backbreaking work, the detail was ready to place the gun platforms on the floor of the gun pits.

At the first position, as the crew was working to bring the timbers into place, a French staff car drove up to where Lieutenant Case and two of his officers were directing the construction. A French major, the artillery chief of the French 232nd Regiment, jumped from the vehicle and approached the officers. He was the same officer who had helped Lieutenant Case select this site earlier in the week. All three of the Americans saluted the major smartly, which he casually returned.

Soon the French major and Lieutenant Case huddled off to the side and began discussing their current strategy. After a few minutes the lieutenant instructed the men of the detail to stop their work. He then went back into a huddle with the major and requested Lieutenants Allen and Wynland to join them. Soon the officers had pulled out a map that they draped over the hood of the vehicle, and all were studying it and looking up and pointing to the front, then back to the map in an animated fashion.

The enlisted men leaned on their shovels and picks and tried to hear the conversation, but were unable to catch any of the words. Pat and some of the others, down in the first gun position, came out of the pit and questioned those who had been at ground level.

"What's going on?" Hank asked.

"It seems that the good major ain't too happy with this here gun emplacement," was the reply.

"What does he want us to do, fill it in and start all over?"

"That may be the case," said Sergeant Baker.

It was decided in the late afternoon to move the positions back some 1200 meters to the southwest. The grumbling was vehement, directed toward the French major, but this turned out to be a blessing in disguise, as the new spot offered superior drainage and less rocks to dig out.

On March 2, the remainder of the battery came forward and set up the portable barracks, corral and kitchen, about 50 meters behind the guns. They then pitched in to help complete the primary digging on the gun positions.

By March 5, the guns had been brought forward and installed in the pits. When the digging was completed, the bunkers were outfitted with ammunition.

Word was received in the late afternoon of the sixth that Battery C had received a terrific shellacking from German artillery the day before and one man had been killed and three others were wounded. These causalities were the first suffered by the 149th since entering their wartime service.

Finally, on March 7, the guns of Battery F were in position and the first shell was fired at 10:20 a.m. for registration. This shell casing was taken from the breech of the gun and given to Lieutenant Case for safe keeping until it could be presented to the University of Illinois in memory of this event.

In trench warfare an artillery battery was effective as long as it could remain undetected and continue to take action against the enemy. The chosen position had to remain out of sight of the enemy observation posts, balloons, and aircraft. As a result, the targets of the battery were not normally visible to the cannoneers and gunners.

Once the guns were positioned and camouflaged, the battery commander had to select a reference point with a known position. Lieutenant Case, used the chimney of a destroyed farmhouse near Mon Laval Ferme. This structure was charted on the maps and its distance and direction from the gun position was determined as accurately as possible.

Each gun was qualified on this reference, and the direction and range to the target adjusted. In the case of the new position for the battery, each gun fired one or two rounds. A forward observer would then record the impact in order to determine the accuracy. If necessary, further adjustments would be made. This procedure allows the cannoneer to make final adjustments to the gun in order to properly register it on the target.

After the battery commander was satisfied with the position of the guns, the aiming stakes would be set at approximately 15 meters in front of each gun. This positioning of the stakes was set through a site positioned on the gun. Once the aiming stakes were positioned the gunners used them as their reference for all subsequent fire.

Thus, the need to survey the position of the guns in an exact location and, taking into account the trajectory and known distance a shell will travel, the battery commander could determine, through mathematical formula, the place where it would land. In conjunction with accurate maps this positioning could, theoretically, be pinpointed and the result, called unregistered fire, may well surprise an enemy without his knowing the source of the cannon fire.

On the eighth, the battery received its baptism by fire, in all probability an answer from the Boche to the registration fire the battery had shot the day before. The first shells landed in front of the guns, the next series behind the barracks. As the first volley exploded in front of the guns, Pat who was just a short distance away working on the barrel of gun number three, immediately dove for cover and no sooner found safety in a nearby bunker than the shelling stopped.

Suddenly Battery F was in the war at the front. In the middle of the afternoon, the battery fired 93 rounds at Salient Poirier, an enemy strong point. An hour later the battery fired 107 rounds at another strong point, Ouvrage Rouge. From then on, the whole regiment was firing on a regular basis, and was subjected to answering fire from the German guns.

The First Patrol

During the time Ike was finishing up his training in the Nieuport 27, he continued his correspondence with Agnes Bovay. Ike liked Agnes more and more and was learning a great deal about her through her letters. Though he had met her only once, he had fallen deeply in love.

His affections for Agnes did not interfere with his love for flying, though. He spent every available moment in the air. When not flying, he sought out pilots who had flown against the enemy and quizzed them at length on the methods they used to stay alive. When airborne, he would practice these maneuvers and if prudent, add them to his own repertoire.

He soon was getting more out of the Nieuport than he originally thought possible. The Nieuport still displayed structural integrity problems, particularly with its wing, so if pushed too hard and too fast, the plane would begin to break up in flight.

He quickly learned that the care of the plane was his overall responsibility. His ears were soon well tuned to the sound of the engine at different RPMs and if something didn't sound right to him, he would question the ground crew in order to determine the problem. He would keep the plane in level flight at the lowest revs possible, an effort to conserve the precious fuel and prevent unwarranted wear and tear on the engine. However, when in simulated combat, he would use that fuel and run full out by demanding the most from the engine. He even had his ground crew change the oil twice as often as the specifications called for, as well as change vital parts, hoses, and spark plugs more frequently than required.

One of the suggestions he took to heart was the need to become more observant of the skies. The Boche had a nasty habit of diving upon a victim from seemingly out of the sun, and he soon learned to use his peripheral vision to detect any movement. His head was on a continual swivel, scanning from right to left and back again. Each time he came to center he would briefly drop his eyes to check one instrument on the panel, and then continue his scan.

Frank Linki and Jon Nelson were working with him as a team and they would fly simulated combat missions on numerous occasions. Both Frank and Jon thought Ike was being a little too practical in his meticulous approach to flying and chalked it up to one of his eccentricities; but somehow Ike always ended up on the tail of whoever he was flying against in mock combat.

As none of the pilots on either side of the front used parachutes, the greatest fear was fire. Frequently a battle-damaged aircraft could be landed without the pilot being killed, or even injured. However, if the plane were on fire, the chances of survival diminished greatly. Ike made frequent practice emergencies that would help him cope with fire. He practiced side slipping both to the right and left as a means of avoiding flames from the fuselage, as well as other tricks used by flyers to bring their crippled, burning planes safely to ground. Many pilots had sworn that they would use their sidearms on themselves rather than burn, but Ike wasn't ready for such drastic action.

Most combat aircraft had been designed and built with the fuel tank as close to the engine as possible, normally located between it and the cockpit. The tanks themselves were neither self-sealing nor baffled. One well-placed incendiary shell could lead to disaster.

At the end of February, Ike, Frank, and Jon were posted to the 95th Aero Pursuit, or Kicking Mule Squadron, stationed near Toule. This was one of the quiet sectors and they ended up flying their new, unarmed Nieuport 28s on patrol, in and around Toule.

The Nieuport 28 was a totally redesigned airplane, though it maintained the same shape and appearance of the 27. The newer and more powerful gnome rotary engine was fully cowled and the plane sported redesigned wings that were braced by parallel struts instead of the old V-shaped strut. The new 160 horsepower engine allowed the plane a top speed of 122 miles per hour in straight and level flight, a full 12 mph faster than the old model. The structural integrity was better, but still not as strong as it should have been.

An advantage that the Boche had over the Allies was that they seldom flew east of the front lines. If they did venture to the Allied side, they normally did so at great altitude and never penetrated deep into Allied territory. Due to the prevailing westerly winds and the nearness of the front, any flyable, battle-damaged aircraft or engine failures would frequently result in the plane gliding to safety in their own territory. The Allied pilots, on the other hand, regularly penetrated deep into Boche territory, and the prevailing wind, ordinarily out of the west, frequently hampered most attempts to establish a glide to safety on the western side of the front.

Shortly after the first of March, the Kicking Mule Squadron started flying their unarmed Nieuports on patrols along the front, but on their own side of the line. This was a dangerous procedure, for without a means to fight back, they could easily be at the mercy of any skilled enemy they encountered.

Their squadron leader was Josiah Wortham. Before he was named commander of the 95th Aero Squadron, he had been a member of the famed LaFayette Esquadrille. In the year before America entered the war, he had established himself as an ace in the Franco-American squadron, with eleven confirmed kills to his credit.

Ike's first patrol included four planes—Frank, Jon and Ike, led by Captain Wortham. The preflight briefing was simple and to the point.

"We'll stay away from trouble, keep away from enemy planes," Wortham said. "If we see any, turn away and head back to the aerodrome. Without guns we're like sitting ducks. We'll stay at least three miles inside our lines and patrol about twenty-five to thirty miles northwest before turning around and coming back. Keep the formation tight. We'll climb to 3000 meters and maintain that altitude till we return. Keep your eyes alert and I'll signal any changes. Got that?"

"Yes, sir!" they answered in unison.

Captain Wortham was a little older than his men, having become 27 just the month before. Prior to joining the French Foreign Legion, he'd been a lawyer in a small town in Michigan. When the war started he left his practice, and headed for France. After spending six months driving an ambulance he applied for duty in the air service and went through flight training during the closing months of 1915. By the following spring he was in the LaFayette Esquadrille. Captain Wortham was rather short, a few inches under six feet, had thinning blond hair, and piercing blue eyes. Ike, Jon and Frank admired the older captain and listened very carefully to every word he had to say.

The captain then reviewed the hand and plane movement signals he would use in communicating with the other members of the flight. When the briefing was completed, they each walked to their own plane.

Ike felt the thrill and excitement take hold of him. Finally he was flying in the war zone, even though his plane was unarmed.

After a quick walk around, Ike climbed up on the lower left wing and swung into the cockpit. He put on his leather helmet, fastened the chinstrap and pulled on his gloves. "Okay, Mike, let's get her started!" he yelled to his ground crew chief above the roar of the engine of Frank's Nieuport.

"Switch off?"

"Switch off!"

Mike pulled the engine through once and placed the prop over a compression stroke. "Contact?"

"Contact!" Ike responded.

One mighty heave and the engine was running smoothly. He allowed the engine to run at high RPM and it was purring like a well-fed tiger kitten. He checked his instruments and everything was ready.

Ike glanced to his left and saw that Wortham was ready to roll. He glanced to his right and looked at his two friends, and saw that they were ready to go. He looked back to the Nieuport on his left and watched the captain give the signal to start moving. He pulled his goggles down over his eyes, adjusted them for comfort, and was ready to become airborne.

The planes had been parked on the tarmac facing into the wind, towards the takeoff runway. Ike signaled the ground crew to remove the chocks from in front of the wheels and started forward, shortly after Captain Wortham had pulled ahead of him by half a plane's length. To his right, Frank and Jon were rolling a little behind him.

Ike felt the speed increase gradually at first as they started bouncing along the grass runway. Soon a little forward pressure on the control column brought the tail up, and before he knew it all four Nieuports were airborne.

This was the part of the flight Ike liked the most, breaking free of the ground and climbing into the smooth air. The fresh air of the slipstream in his face always invigorated him.

The flight executed a slow climbing turn to the right and established a heading of three, zero, zero degrees. The planes flew a triangular-shaped formation, Captain Wortham at the point, Ike to his left and off the tail of the lead plane, Frank in the same position to the right, and Jon in the center directly behind Josiah.

As the flight climbed, Ike looked closely at the landscape below. To his left was the beautiful French countryside beginning to show the new life of spring. Fields of differing colors spread across the rolling land—small stands of trees, fields of brown and tan where the stalks of last year's crops still stood, and black fields where the soil had been freshly tilled. Also visible were some beautiful, light green fields of new alfalfa. He saw numerous small villages clustered around crossroads, as well as small farmhouses and their attendant outbuildings that dotted the countryside.

Off to his right was the deep and ugly scar that was the front line, colorless and potted with deep, round craters that gave evidence to the horrendous struggle taking place.

As the flight approached the base of the clouds, the trailing planes followed Wortham's lead as if all were joined by invisible strings. Up through a hole in the clouds they climbed, Captain Wortham leading them in a wide circle.

Once above the clouds, Ike scanned the sky for other planes. It was a beautiful, crisp, spring like day. The sky above was a brilliant blue and he could see the colorful landscape through the breaks in the bright, clouds now below him.

They continued northeast for about thirty minutes before Captain Wortham signaled them to turn around and head home.

The return flight was just as uneventful. When they were over their field, they did a slow spiral down through the clouds and landed. When Ike finally shut off the engine and checked his watch, he noted he would log one hour and thirty-six minutes of flight time.

The three young aviators followed their captain into the briefing room, exuberant over completing their first patrol.

"How many planes did you see during our patrol?" Captain Wortham asked.

They all shook their heads and admitted they had seen none.

Frank added with a chuckle, "The Germans must have known we were out today and didn't have the nerve to send anyone against us."

Captain Wortham raised an eyebrow. "Well, you're wrong. I saw four different flights of planes, two of French Spads, and two of Boche Fokker triplanes. You men are going to have to do better than that. Keep your mind on the business of war, that's what we're here for." With that said, Captain Wortham left the room.

The three friends stood in the empty operations shack looking at one another, open-mouthed.

Ike turned and walked out without a word, feeling let down after such a beautiful and successful flight. He walked to his quarters to write yet another letter to Agnes to tell her about his day.

Settling In

In the early morning of March 12, Pat and Hank were returning from the observation post after their turn as rocket guards when a German plane flew low over the line of the 149th. On spotting the two men in the open, the pilot turned his Albatross and dove at them in a strafing run, machine guns blazing.

"Hank, let's get the hell outta here!" Pat yelled as he started running as fast as he could in his ill-fitting shoes.

Hank, in hot pursuit, didn't answer, running for his life.

The Boche aviator pulled up from his first run, climbed to an altitude of 500 feet, and turned 180 degrees in a steep right bank, then started down toward the two men, who were running for the nearest ditch.

Almost immediately, a machine gun at the cannon line opened up on the plane.

"Pat, there's a culvert off to your left," Hank yelled from behind.

"Got it," Pat answered as he turned and increased his speed.

Bullets from the plane were kicking up divots of dirt behind them. With one long jump, both Pat and Hank dove for the culvert as the bullets whizzed past their heads. They flattened themselves against the side of the ditch until the plane flew over them and pulled up. They could hear the chatter of their own battery's gun over the roar of the engine. The gun stopped firing then the pilot leveled off from his strafing run and headed back to his own lines.

"Welcome to the war, Pat," Hank said breathlessly. "Is it living up to your expectations?"

"I could have done without that." Pat said, feeling his heart banging against his ribs.

With the passage of time the 149th settled into the line and soon found they were not immune from suffering their own battle casualties. On March 13, German artillery fire hit one of Battery C's gun positions, killing two men, and on the same day, Battery A was hit with gas shells, killing one and wounding two others.

The F Battery troops were thanking their lucky stars that they were not in the original location that had been selected by Lieutenant Case, and instead had moved to the current position. Both Battery A and Battery C occupied old French gun emplacements whose locations were – apparently—well known to the Germans.

In the late evening of March 17, sparks from one of the cannons set fire to the burlap camouflage covering Battery E's position. Men from Batteries D and F were dispatched to help make the repairs before daybreak, before the German observation network could detect the guns.

The batteries of the 149th Field Artillery continued to fire on a daily basis and register an improvement in their accuracy. When they weren't firing, the finishing touches were applied to the dugouts and ammunition bunkers at the gun positions.

The men's awareness of the need for digging the shelters deep was brought home to all of the personnel of the Rainbow when word was received that on the seventh of March, 28 men of the 165th New York Infantry Regiment were buried alive when a Boche shell hit the bunker in which they were sheltered.

On March 19, the 149th received word that they would participate in a large trench raid to be conducted by both French and American infantry. All batteries would be involved in laying down the covering barrage. This raid was to take place the next day at 6:00 a.m.

Reveille was at 2:00 a.m. and the time was a busy one for all of the batteries. The caissons brought ammunition to the guns where the cannoneers stacked and prepared it for firing. Fuses were placed in the ready position while ramrods and buckets of water were readied for cooling the cannon barrels.

At 6:00 a.m. it was announced that the starting time for the attack had been put off until evening, and that all were to stand down. Some of the ammunition had to be taken from the pits for the sake of safety. Finally, in the middle of the afternoon, the hour for the attack was reset once again for 7:40 p.m. that evening.

The men began gathering at the guns early and by 7:00 all were at their designated position ready to start the big show. The cannoneers cut the fuses and greased the shells. The mechanics oiled and fine-tuned the guns for the expected action. The assault was directed at the German trenches positioned in the Bois des Arrieux. The initial barrage, provided by both French and American artillery was to be at ever increasing ranges sweeping from the right to the left. At the end of the first five minutes they were directed to alter their fire to a box barrage, designed to prevent enemy support troops from counterattacking into the targeted area. The infantry would follow the initial barrage to the Boche trenches where they would take whatever prisoners they could find before returning to their own lines.

At 7:40 the order to fire was given and the guns roared into action. The initial rate of fire was four rounds per gun per minute for the first five minutes. Battery F's guns fired at ever increasing ranges, sweeping right to left as they blazed away. At 7:46 the firing rate slowed to three rounds per minute as they began a box barrage intended to impede German reinforcements from moving up to the line.

As the attack proceeded, Pat, at position one, was constantly swabbing the gun, as it was getting hotter with each round fired. After an hour of firing, Lieutenant Case ordered all unnecessary personnel out of the gun pits as a precaution against injuries in case one of the hot guns exploded, which fortunately, did not happen.

Lieutenant Jake Jacobson walked along the trench floor checking each man in his platoon, calling them all by their first name.

"Are you ready, Warren? Everything okay, Tom? Get your helmet on, Henry! Don't let any dirt get in your rifle, Bud! When I blow the whistle we'll go over the top, so be ready, Frank!" and so on down the line.

His heart was racing and he felt that thrill of excitement deep down in his chest, much like a runner before a big race. He looked at his watch as he walked back to his position. It was 7:37; three minutes to go. He stood up on the firing step and peered over the top. All was quiet and dark out in no-man's-land.

Then came the roar of a hundred guns as they opened up from behind him. The noise was deafening. He could see the first shells explode in front of the German trenches before he ducked down below the parapet of the trench. He looked at his watch—exactly 7:40, five minutes to go.

The minutes ticked by quickly, Jake checked his watch every minute and when 7:45 came, he stood on the firing step and put his whistle to his mouth and blew. At the same time, the shrill sound of whistles blew up and down the line and the men started out of the trenches and moved into no-man's-land.

The return fire from the German side was slow in coming as the men moved rapidly towards the enemy trenches.

Pat was conscious of little except the roar of the gun and his almost frantic efforts to keep it cool by constantly swabbing it with water. Suddenly he heard the gun chief of position one, Dan Dreyer, yelling to Pat that the light on the aiming stake had gone out. Pat looked up, and sure enough he couldn't see it.

He ducked low, ran out of the pit, and then ran the fifty yards to the stake to see what the problem was. The sound, out in front of the gun, was amplified tenfold as it fired every twenty seconds.

At the stake, everything seemed to be in order with the wiring, so he jiggled the bulb and it came on. He turned to start back to the position when the 75 fired again. The light went out yet again. This continued for the next three or four rounds and nothing he did would keep it on. He knew the importance of the stake to the gunner and for this particular raid. He stepped back about five yards and lay down on his stomach, and used the beam of his flashlight on the stake and stayed there throughout the battle, with the beam of the light trained on the stake.

Apparently the infantry was on time, as the battery was ordered to stop the box barrage and called to implement the Gouteleine barrage, a technique used to protect the infantry as they withdrew from no-man's-land and returned to the safety of their own lines.

Jake ran as fast as he could in a semi-crouched position. He had been one of the last out of the trench and he wanted to get to the front of his men.

The German artillery was trying to pinpoint the position of the advancing troops. The first bursts were in front of them, and shortly afterward a second burst landed behind Jake. The rifle and machine gun fire was light, but still he saw one of the boys near him crumple to the ground.

He yelled to his platoon to urge them on. "Just another one hundred yards, boys, pick it up," he heard himself say.

Before he knew it, he was at the defensive wire of the first line of the enemy's trench system. The wire had been pretty well chewed up by the allied artillery, and he found a path through it and then leaped into the trench, followed by others in the platoon.

They found three wounded Germans, one who could walk.

"Wendal, take this one back with us, the rest of you on my left, spread out down the line till you run into some of our guys. "Sergeant, keep an eye out for any Boche reinforcements coming from the northeast. The rest of you to my right, keep moving up the trench line until you make contact with the third platoon. Take any prisoners who can walk back with us. Got that?"

"Yes, sir!" came the reply.

Jake was beginning to feel pretty good about this, his first adventure on the offensive. He knew casualties had to be light and, most importantly, he knew he was better than his enemy. This war would be over before much more time passed.

Soon, word was passed along the line to prepare the troops for the return to their own lines.

"At my command we'll start back. Keep a sharp lookout for any of our men who have been hit and bring them with you."

With those words the retreat was sounded and the second platoon climbed out of the German trenches and, again, headed out across no-man's-land. The Allied barrage increased in tempo in order to protect their return.

Jake lagged behind the men of his platoon, who were all to his right. Enemy fire was light and sporadic. As he ran to his lines, he kept looking back over his shoulder to insure that no enemy troops were following.

At midpoint of the return, Jake took one last look over his shoulder and tripped over something soft and went sprawling, face down. As he got to his feet cursing under his breath, he discovered the object was a fallen doughboy. He didn't know if the soldier was dead or alive, but thought he'd better get him back to the safety of the trenches. He quickly got up and hoisted the man onto his shoulder and ran the rest of the distance back to his lines. When he arrived at the top of the trench, the other men of his platoon were waiting and helped him put the soldier down into the safety of the ditch. It was dark as pitch as they laid the man down on his back at the bottom.

"Someone, get a flashlight and call for a medic. Sergeant, get me a head count and give me a status report, pronto!"

Jake felt someone thrust a flashlight into his left hand, and with his right he felt for the jugular vein in the soldiers neck. Nothing. He finally found the switch with his left thumb and the beam fell across two lifeless eyes that stared up blankly at him. It was his friend and confidante, Lieutenant O'Doule.

"John? John!" he shouted.

"He's dead, sir." It was the medic, kneeling on the other side of the body.

Jake said nothing as he switched off the light and struggled to stand up. He felt as if he'd been kicked in the stomach. All he could do was stare at the lifeless form at his feet.

"Lieutenant, all but one are accounted for, and two have minor wounds. A good night, I'd say, sir," his sergeant said.

"Thanks, sergeant." was all Jake could say as he felt tears well up in his eyes. "I must be in hell," he muttered as he turned away.

Ludendorf Offensive

Clint Phelps sat back in the seat and relaxed as much as he could. He had another ten-to-fifteen minute ride before he would get off at Amiens and change trains for his final stop. Vesle, his destination, was the headquarters of the British Fifth Army, now under the command of a General Gough. Weeks ago, his editor had made arrangements for this interview with the general. It was to be the closing article on a series he was writing, intended to further enlighten the American public on the readiness of the various Allied armies.

Clint had been in France for over three months and his news assignments weren't exactly what he had expected. He had come to France to report on the AEF. But, instead of writing stories about the American troops, he'd ended up writing this series on the Allies, starting with the French military, their readiness and deployment. Now, for a change, here he was taking a train north to write about the British.

It was on Friday last that he was finally able to convince his managing editor to relent and allow him to cover some of the American divisions—that is, when he was through with this part of the series on the British involvement.

Clint was what one would call a "people" reporter. His concerns were with the troops, the men that manned the trenches and fought toe-to-toe with the enemy. Certainly he was interested in overall strategy, but the best of plans and campaigns couldn't be implemented and carried to success without motivated troops.

It was while working on his stories about the French that he was made aware of the seriousness of the mutinies that had taken place in the French army during the preceding year. The mutinies, though well covered up by the French upper military echelons and government, had been very serious and nearly jeopardized the Allied cause. They had occurred as a result of what seemed to be a lack of concern for the life and well-being of the soldiers. Literally thousands of men had been sacrificed for nothing more than a few feet of ground. Only through strong leadership and rapid reorganization were the mutinies brought to an end.

Clint felt the train begin to slow for their approach into Amiens. He checked his watch and found it to be right on time, 5:30 p.m. It was Tuesday, March 19, and he wanted to be in Vesle, another 30 miles or so, within the hour. Hopefully he could be finished with this fact-finding trip and be back in Paris by the weekend. Vesle was located some twenty-one miles behind the front. Because of its close proximity, Clint thought that he might be able to wrangle a trip to the trenches before he had to return, in order to see for himself how the English troops, or "Tommies," were faring.

As he stood and waited for the train to stop, all he could think about was a good meal and a good night's rest. He felt overwhelmingly tired. He had worked through the weekend on a story and had had very little sleep. There were constant deadlines. Early the next morning he had to be well rested and alert for the interview with General Gough, the commander of the British Fifth Army and of this whole sector, a trench line of approximately 40 miles.

The long dry spell had finally ended and the overcast skies supplied a light general rainfall throughout the area. Clint noted in his notebook that it was not a good day for aerial reconnaissance.

The train from Amiens to Vesle stopped frequently and it took another hour and fifteen minutes to travel the 30 or so miles. Finally, at five minutes to seven, they came to a quiet and smooth stop. Clint waited his turn to disembark behind a long line of Tommies who were apparently returning from leave. At long last, he found himself in the center of town. He checked into the only hotel and had a meager dinner at a local restaurant. It wasn't much past ten when he fell sound asleep.

In the morning Clint was up with the dawn and found it had brought a steady drizzle and light fog. After eating a quick breakfast, he made his way to the headquarters of the Fifth Army, located near the train station in an old department store. The general's office, he learned from the guard, was on the third floor.

At the top of the stairs, Gough's adjutant met Clint.

"Mr. Phelps, I presume? I'm Major Matthews."

"Yes, Major, I'm Clint Phelps with the *Chicago Globe*," Clint said extending his hand.

"The general will see you now, though as you may have already guessed, he does not have a great deal of time to spare."

"I understand, major."

"Follow me please."

They walked past a number of desks occupied by soldiers of various ranks busily attending to paperwork, pounding on typewriters, or talking on the telephone. The room was abuzz with the business and sounds of waging the administrative side of the war. At the very back of this large and busy room was a door that led to the general's private office. There was a desk just outside and the major deposited some papers on it before moving to the door and knocking.

"These are my digs," Major Matthews said, waving an arm at the littered desk.

A booming voice from inside the room yelled, "Enter!"

The major opened the door and held it for Clint. He stepped through and found himself in a large, austere room dominated by a huge table in the center, covered with maps and surrounded by a number of chairs. There was a series of windows along the right hand wall that provided most of the light in the room. There was a small lamp on the lone desk, off to the left and rear of the table. The desk was massive, and it too was cluttered with papers. Behind the desk stood the general.

At 47, General Gough was the youngest army commander in the British sector. Clint was surprised to find the owner of the booming voice to be a rather short man, about five feet eight, not at all what he had pictured him to be. The general was well known for being a tenacious and courageous soldier. His face was long and lean, his complexion dark. The glint in his steely blue eyes was his most striking attribute, and Clint found he could not look away. This man had the appearance of authority and Clint soon came to understand why he was so admired by his men.

"General Gough, this is Clint Phelps, the foreign correspondent from the *Chicago Globe*. And Mr. Phelps, this is General Gough," the major said. "If you need me, sir, I'll be at my desk."

"Thank you Matthews," General Gough answered, and with that the major was gone. "How may I help you, Mr. Phelps?" He reached out to shake hands with Clint.

"General, I appreciate your taking the time to speak with me and I'll be brief. The American people, particularly my readers in the Midwest, are interested in where the English are situated in the line and what your state of preparedness is, in case the Germans start the rumored spring offensive."

"I feel that we are at a very high state of readiness, and the men on the whole are in high spirits, though we always suffer from the same problem of being understaffed in the trenches. I have a mere 13 divisions to cover forty-two miles of this front and we know that the Germans are building great strength on their side. I also have two divisions in reserve. Right now we are holding the line against increasing odds. As you know, the British are charged with holding the line from Flanders on the left to the Oise River on our right. The Fifth Army makes up the far right of the entire British sector and we join with the English Third Army on our left and the French Sixth Army at the Oise on the right. I'll give you as much information as I can, but you'll have to understand some information will be withheld, that which would benefit the enemy."

"I understand your meaning, sir."

"As you had requested in our correspondence, I've made arrangements for you to go forward to the village of Ham this morning, to meet with some of the troops being held in reserve. I cannot permit you to go to the front, as we are expecting the Boche offensive soon."

"When do you think that offensive will take place, General?"

"I expect a bombardment to commence soon; it could be as early as tomorrow morning, with the enemy infantry jumping off just after daylight. That's why I want you safely back in Vesle by nightfall. Major Matthews can brief you on our deployment and give you an idea of what the enemy has opposing us. He will be the one taking you to Ham as part of a trip he's making for me, in order to meet with General Maxse, commander of my Eighteenth Corps."

"Sir, that is more than I could hope for, thank you," Clint said.

Adolph Krause had been in the German army for nearly six years and was considered a grizzled veteran having fought on both the Western and Eastern fronts. He had been in on the initial invasion into France in 1914 before being sent to Russia in 1916. He loved the adventure of the war as much as he loved the fatherland. As he sat near the huge gun, he peered off to the southwest. The low clouds and rain showers reduced visibility to the point where he was barely able to see no man's land.

"I hope this weather holds through tomorrow morning," he said to his friend Walter Strummer, who was higher in rank than Adolph.

"Yes, the weather has pretty well hidden us from observation. If it stays cloudy and foggy like this, the English won't have the slightest idea of what hit them," Walter replied.

Both Sergeants Krause and Strummer were gun commanders of the large 305 mm Skoda siege guns that were to be used in the great offensive scheduled to begin at 4:40 a.m. the following morning. Their heavy gun regiment had just recently arrived from Russia and, at this moment, the two men were taking a break from the work of preparing their position for the big push.

"General Ludendorf has outdone himself in setting up this attack. The infantry are jammed into the line so tight they are able to move in only one direction, and that's forward, towards the English. And I understand some have been positioned for ten days or more." Adolph said. "The trains keep bringing more troops and equipment. It's rumored our attack will consist of nearly sixty divisions."

"Yes, and the piles of ammunition that we have could last a week, even if we fire round the clock. Think of it Adolph, six thousand cannon all within a fifty-mile front. There have been endless trains bringing in men, horses, wagons, trucks, guns, tools, rations, ammunition, bridging materials and whatever we will need. There is no way that this offensive will fail," Strummer boasted. "We will defeat the English, French and even the Americans within a month! Just think about it, the war will be over and we will be victorious."

"Yes, you're right. I believe the code name for this attack is Operation Michael. Sounds sort of peaceful, doesn't it?" Krause added with a smirk.

Each man fell silent for a few minutes and watched the scurry of activity all around them with almost unbelieving eyes. They could even detect, off in the distance, strains of martial music as a military band played for the arrival of yet another infantry battalion from the east.

By 10:00 a.m., Major Matthews and Clint Phelps were underway traveling towards the town of Ham. There was a lot of activity on the road—military units, truck convoys, and horse-drawn artillery were all moving towards the front. They also encountered numerous infantry regiments. The dirt roads were well worn and potholed, and the rain of the last two days had made them treacherous and slippery. The trip of just fifteen miles took them over an hour.

The staff car, with a canvas top and no side windows, was open to the air. It was wet and cold. Clint was feeling very uncomfortable, but the major could have been out on a sunny Sunday drive through the English countryside. Clint was silently giving thanks for the rain slickers they were wearing, without which they both would have been soaking wet.

"I take it, Major, that you make this trip quite regularly?" Clint said after a period of silence.

"Oh, at least three or four times a week."

"Is it always this busy?"

"No, it isn't. As the general might have mentioned to you, we are expecting a German offensive soon. With these troop movements, we are trying to plug up any soft spots in the line. Our concern is that the Germans have been moving men and materials opposite the Third and Fifth Armies for the past few weeks. We are an obvious target for the attack as we join with the French on our right."

"And why would that necessarily be a weak part of the line?"

"Any juncture between two different nations, even though we are Allies, is the weakest point in the line, because we each have different philosophies on the war. For example, if the Germans do in fact break through the line, the French will curve their defenses south and to the west in order to defend Paris. We will probably move to the north and east to defend the coast in order to protect our eventual withdrawal to the Isles, if that becomes necessary. Now understand that's a worst case scenario. I don't believe it will happen, but Ludendorf is aware of this also and is counting on it happening."

"Then I can assume that this is going to be a big offensive?"

Major Mathews paused thoughtfully. "We don't have the numbers yet, but I would say it will be a big one. Intelligence shows troops and artillery have been moving in from the east for more than a month, so we must be prepared. Ludendorf has been known to attack the strongest sections of the line near known weak junctures. In this case that would be the Fifth Army, near our junction with the French."

"According to General Gough, he feels this attack could come sooner than later?"

"Yes. As you know, the American army is bringing large numbers of troops into France and I think the Germans believe they have to win the war before your people are ready to fight."

"Can you hold them?"

"That's difficult to tell. We will, in all probability, be outnumbered, but by how much we don't know. The numbers will be the determining factor. An overwhelming force and a willingness on their part to take heavy casualties could push us out of our well-prepared defensive positions. I just can't answer that question for you. It'll be answered soon enough after we engage the Germans in battle."

Both fell silent for the remainder of the trip and before long they were in Ham, at the headquarters of the Eighteenth Corps.

"I'll be tied up here for approximately three hours," Major Mathews said, "so feel free to walk around and talk to whomever you please. Be back here at two-thirty and we'll toddle on back to Nesle."

Clint took the major at his word and spent the next hours talking with many of the troops passing through the town on the way to the front. He found them high-spirited, but anxious about the rumored attack that was soon to come. At two-thirty he made his way back to headquarters to wait on Major Matthews.

Soon after his arrival at the car, the major appeared at the door of the headquarters building and walked swiftly to the vehicle.

"Mr. Phelps, I have some more urgent business on forward at Flavy-le-Martel. After that, I assure you, we will be on our way back to Nesle."

"Where is this Flavey-le-Martel?" Clint asked.

"Oh, about six or seven miles on ahead. I tried to find you a ride back, but no one is going that way. So climb aboard and we'll be off."

"I'm glad you didn't get me the ride. The closer I get to the front the better. At least for the purposes of my story."

The road wasn't as crowded with vehicles as it was when they came from Nesle, and they arrived at their destination within thirty minutes.

After the major completed his urgent business, the two men were in the car again, headed back towards Fifth Army headquarters. At the edge of town, the right front tire blew, forcing the vehicle to swerve out of control and into a ditch, bringing them to an abrupt halt. Clint flew forward and hit his head on the windshield, leaving him with a nasty bump.

"Are you all right, Mr. Phelps?"

"I believe so."

"Blasted luck," Major Matthews muttered, climbing out of the vehicle to inspect the damage.

Clint performed a quick check of his own condition as he joined the major at the front of the vehicle.

"Well, Mr. Phelps, we have a broken axle. This vehicle is going nowhere, at least not for a while. Let's walk back to the command post and see what we can do about getting us out of here."

Clint was excited over the prospect of spending the night at this forward position. True, he wasn't at the front, but he was just a mere six or seven miles away. The town was full of British troops and it was an excellent opportunity to do an in depth-story from the soldier's perspective.

After Major Matthews had been unable to obtain a ride back to Nesle, Clint found a room at the local hotel for the night. Following dinner, Clint walked the streets of Flavy-le-Martel, stopping occasionally to enjoy a beer with some of the Tommies, who were relaxing there before proceeding to the front. They were all aware of the impending German offensive, though they seemed nonchalant about it. They all felt confident they could hold the enemy back.

At 11:00 p.m., Clint, with a splitting headache, made his way back towards his hotel. The evening was warm and clear. It was quiet on the front and for all Clint knew, he could have been back in Champaign, enjoying a pleasant spring evening walk.

It was pitch dark in the room, but the rolling thunder awakened him. Clint switched on the light and looked at his watch, it was 4:43 a.m. He got out of bed and walked to the window in order to close it so the rain couldn't come in. What greeted his eyes made him shiver right down to his slippers. To the east there was a constant and flickering light, not from an electrical storm, but from the German guns. The roar at first sounded like thunder, but the rumbling did not end. The crescendo was rapid, and once it peaked, the roar continued unchanging, unaltered.

Clint went to the bed, switched off the light on the nightstand, and returned to the window that faced the front. Though he was six miles away, the light of the battle lit up the room and he could see easily. The sound of the bombardment was tremendous. The vastness of the sound instilled a sense of awe in Clint, for it was something he, a man known for words, could not find words to describe.

After an interminable amount of time at the window, Clint quickly dressed and rushed to the street, then towards the command post. He noted that the sky was cloudy and patches of fog were beginning to form. At the command center, he met Major Matthews.

"I was just on the phone to Nesle," the major said. "The magnitude of this attack appears to be greater than we have ever imagined. All four corps of the Fifth Army are being pounded and the Third Army is being hit at least along the southern ten miles of its line." The major had to yell in order to be heard above the sounds and roar of cannon. "Go to the train station, Mr. Phelps, as I have reserved you a seat on the next train that will take you out of harm's way. It will transport you back to Nesle. It leaves in about two hours."

"What about you, Major?"

"One of the two divisions being held in reserve is moving through here, and I am to join them. Our best estimates are that the German infantry will start moving forward at between 8:30 and 9:30 this morning. We must be there to stop them. I earlier told you that the numbers would determine the outcome."

"Yes, yes, I remember."

"Latest estimates give the Boche a three-to-one edge in manpower. It was nice meeting you, Mr. Phelps. Pray for us."

"I will, major. It's been a pleasure knowing you. I hope we meet again. Good luck."

Clint then found his way to the train station and changed his reservation to the next day at the same time.

The End of Training

On March 21, the 149th received orders to withdraw from the front and directed to return to Luneville in the evening. The regiment had been on the line for a month and the order to withdraw was received with gratitude by the tired men.

In the early morning, Colonel Reilly called on Lieutenant Case in order to congratulate the battery on their superb behavior under fire. "Up until this time your men have been little more than civilians dressed in the uniform of the US Army. However, from this day forward I consider them soldiers," the colonel said.

As the regiment went through their last day at the front, the Boche guns shelled the whole sector with gas and high explosive munitions. The entire front from the North Sea to Switzerland had been subjected to intensive artillery fire, in hope that it would disrupt or even prevent the transport of Allied troops to the Somme to support the British, where the first of the great spring offensives was underway.

In the evening, after firing numerous rounds, the guns of Battery F were pulled out of their pits and hitched to the limbers. At the same time all communication equipment was detached, and everyone readied to move.

By 9:30 p.m. the battery was on the road, and by midnight they were in *Quartier Stanislas* in Luneville. After a brief speech by Lt. Case, extolling the exemplary conduct of the men on the line, all rolled up in their blankets and slept soundly.

The following day, reveille was at 7:00 a.m., which was answered by only fourteen men, those who had served in the rear echelon. A mere bugle call was not going to interrupt the rest of the true soldiers who had served in the gun pits and had missed out on a month's worth of sleep.

The true soldiers of the battery finally arose at eight, and after a leisurely breakfast performed the minimum of tasks for the rest of the morning. Equipment was repaired and cleaned and the carriages were greased in anticipation of their trip to Rolampont for rest, refitting and advanced training.

After lunch, the majority of men had the day off and most spent the time in the cafes filling up on beer and foods of all kinds and telling tales of their stay at the front. Many of the infantrymen were there as well, and all were recounting their stories of the war. The New Yorkers told of the 28 men buried alive in their bunker and of the survivors vain efforts to dig them out during the heavy shelling that followed. Others told of the trench raids by both the Americans and the Germans. All praised the field artillery and the precise barrages that protected them.

Pat and Hank were enjoying the camaraderie of veterans at a table with men of the battery and some of the doughboys from the infantry regiments of the division.

As he was listening to the story one doughboy had to tell, Pat felt Hank tug at his sleeve.

"Pat, isn't that Jake coming in, over by the door?"

"Sure is. Come on, Hank let's go talk to him."

They both got up and headed towards the door, pushing their way through the crowd.

"Do you see him?" Hank yelled from behind Pat.

"Yeah, he's still by the door."

At that moment, Jake looked up and saw his two fraternity brothers heading towards him.

"Why, it's Elmer and Henry!" he said as a broad grin spread across his face. "What are you guys doing here?"

They reached him and shook hands with him warmly.

"We just got off the line yesterday, how about you?" Pat answered.

"Yeah, got back last evening. What a tour!"

"I know what you mean," Hank said. "We got back late last night, too, and really slept in this morning."

"Do you have some time to sit and talk?" Jake asked. "I'm here with some others but I can ditch them for awhile."

"Yeah, we were just sitting and downing a few beers," Pat said.

"Well, let's find a table. I insist that we talk about anything but the war. Maybe reminisce about the old U of I."

They found a table in the corner of the crowded cafe and sat and drank and talked well into the night. The three all laughed until their sides hurt as they recounted numerous stories of their last year at the university.

Late into the night, before Pat and Hank had to return to *Quartier Stanislas*, Jake turned serious. "You two take care of yourselves," he said. "This business in the trenches is no kids' game. I lost one of my best friends a few weeks ago. The Germans are playing for keeps. I've seen a lot of death."

"We've been lucky," Pat said. "Our battery hasn't suffered one casualty. Others in the regiment haven't been so fortunate."

"Well, take care and pray that this war will end soon."

"You take care Jake. We'll be thinking about you," Hank said.

They stood and shook hands again, then went their separate ways.

The next day the 149th Field Artillery harnessed and hitched and began their move towards Rolampont at around ten in the morning. By three in the afternoon they arrived at their first stop, the village of Haudonville some 15 kilometers south of Luneville. In Haudonville, the men were assigned to haylofts, and as there were not enough stables, a picket line was established for the animals.

The men were allowed to sleep late the next morning, until 8:00 a.m. Following the breakfast and a complete inventory of all equipment, the men were given the remainder of the day off. The mechanics walked around the area, more or less sightseeing. The Germans had occupied Haudonville, Gerberville, and the other surrounding towns early on in 1914. Gerberville had been heavily damaged by the war and still bore signs of the occupation.

As they were strolling through the village, Pat saw an old, beautiful church down one of the side streets. "Hey, guys, let's go peek inside the church and see that stained glass window. It really looks old."

The other three, Hank, Tom, and Paul tagged along for the lack of anything better to do. They entered the old sanctuary and were confronted by the brilliance of the stained glass that cast a bluish color on everything inside.

As they were whispering their comments about the beauty of the church a priest came up the aisle towards them.

"May I help you?" he said in accented English.

"We were just admiring the building," Pat said. "Is it old?"

"Oh, very old. It was built in the fifteenth century," he said. "I saw you looking at the window. That too is old. Probably over three hundred years. We were fortunate that none of it was broken when the Germans invaded."

"Did they enter the town and occupy it?" Pat asked.

"Yes, during the fall of 1914. They were here before they withdrew to their current lines," the priest sighed. "It was a terrible time for us during those early days. Over 100 civilians were executed for defending their very own homes. Fifteen at a time were lined up in the center of town and summarily executed by a firing squad. I, myself, was taken prisoner and transported to Germany. But, after a year I was included in a prisoner exchange and returned here to tend to my flock."

The men talked a short while with the priest before thanking him and returning to their quarters.

"I have a greater sense of what these people have been through," Paul said. "To think that people were brutally murdered, just for defending their homes." The others nodded their agreement and returned to the battery in silence.

On Monday, March 25, the battery made preparations to move on to Rolampont, but midway through the packing they received orders to hold fast at Haudonville. It was becoming apparent that the Boche had sustained great success in their initial blows against the English on the Somme. As a result, the more experienced French divisions were to be pulled from the line and sent north to aid the beleaguered British troops.

The Americans would then move into the line, in the sector vacated by the departing French.

The order to hold fast stood for six days. To prevent the men from falling into idleness, they were given the duty of cleaning the streets of Haudonville. The local citizens didn't seem to mind this, as long as their beloved manure piles were left untouched. The officers never ceased to find various projects designed to keep the men occupied, including the cleaning and repair of all of the equipment.

On Tuesday, cootie underwear was issued, a gift of the Women's Regimental Relief Association. These outfits were made of cheesecloth treated with a chemical that was supposed to dispose of the little pests. In appearance the underwear resembled long johns. At about the same time of the arrival of the new underwear and in honor of the coming of spring, summer uniforms were issued with the request that the men turn in their overcoats.

"It seems that the calendar and government know spring has arrived, now let's hope the weatherman recognizes the date and gives us some warmer weather," an exacerbated Pat said to Hank as he took off his overcoat to turn it in.

Miscellaneous duties continued for the next few days and on Wednesday, Pat, Hank, Jack, and a number of the more athletically inclined fielded a soccer team captained by Sergeant Martyn. In the late afternoon they took on a team of French Poilus, who had no idea of what they were getting into. The Americans kicked anything that moved, and occasionally the ball. The French soon forfeited the game in the third quarter, as they were losing 3 to 1 and their number of players had dwindled to six due to injuries suffered at the hands of their American allies. It was deemed the better part of valor to quit before all their players ended up in the hospital.

Finally, on March 30, the battery harnessed and hitched early in the morning and soon was bound for the front. In the late afternoon they arrived at Fontenoy la Joute, some fourteen kilometers southeast of Haudonville where they joined the rest of the regiment.

On March 25, the 95th Aero Squadron finally received their armament for the Nieuports. All of the men were excited by the news and assembled in the hangar to watch the mechanics mount the machine guns on the planes.

Ike, Jon, and Frank were standing around observing the procedure when it came time for their planes to be armed. "This is what we've been waiting for!" Frank exclaimed as he rubbed his hands together. "I can't wait to go out and shoot me some of those Huns."

Before the others could join in on the bragging rights, Captain Wortham walked up to the small group of pilots. "You men aren't going out to shoot anybody, not until you go through gunnery school."

"What do you mean, sir? We can't go out and do what we came here to do?" Frank protested.

"That's right, Lieutenant. You have to learn how to use these things. How to aim, how to fire, how to reload, and most importantly how to fix a jam, this all while you're still flying the plane. We'll leave for Cazaux in the morning and spend about two weeks at the gunnery school."

After Clint left the train station at Flavey-le-Martel, he started walking the main road to the east, towards the front. The way was choked with military vehicles, artillery and troops headed towards the battle. Coming from the opposite direction were the refugees dragging their worldly possessions to safety in hand-pulled wagons, wheelbarrows, horse-drawn carts, or whatever was at hand.

The loud and incessant rumblings of the cannonading increased the nearer Clint approached the front. He walked as rapidly as he could and felt fortunate that he still had the English rain slicker on.

Soon after leaving the town, he picked up an English helmet he found abandoned on the side of the road and thought his presence wouldn't be questioned by anyone because of the emergency. From a distance, he looked like one of the Tommies. The fog was still quite thick and he couldn't see more than fifty or sixty yards ahead. He'd walked for thirty to forty minutes before he checked his watch and found that the time was 9:30 a.m. He surmised that he was about two to three miles from the front.

As he was proceeding eastward, he came upon a company of English infantry taking a breather along the side of the road. At the head of the column, he literally ran into the company commander, who was walking backward as he pulled on the halter of a mule harnessed to a wagon blocking the road. This particular animal wasn't about to go any further. As the captain was pulling, the halter strap broke and the captain lunged backwards into Clint.

"Get out of the way!" the captain snapped as he turned to chew Clint out, then realized that Clint was not one of his men. "Oh, I'm sorry sir. This hasn't been a good morning; I'm being short with everybody. Sergeant, get this fixed and these wagons moving."

"That's all right, sir, I'm not sure where I'm going either."

The captain looked Clint over carefully. "You're a bloody civilian, what are you doing this close to the front?"

"Yes, sir, I am. I'm Clint Phelps with the *Chicago Globe* and I was trying to get a story on what's happening."

"Well, Mr. Phelps, you've landed yourself in one bloody mess. The front is just a mile or so over that rise and if you don't get out of here, you may find yourself dead, wounded, or imprisoned. You're right in the middle of the big Boche offensive."

"That I know, but I didn't think I was that close to the fighting. With the fog and all, I got lost."

"If I were you I would turn around and go back, now!"

There was a sudden change in the German artillery and shells started to rain down on the road about 100 meters from where they were standing.

"What's happening? Have they spotted us?" Clint asked with alarm.

"It means that their infantry is beginning to move, the barrage is being raised as the troops move forward, I must get to the line. "Get out of here this is a dangerous place. I wish I were you. I would turn around and run in a second. Good luck to you."

"God's speed to you, Captain!" Clint yelled back so as to be heard above the sounds of battle.

The captain yelled at his platoon leaders, and soon they were doing double time towards the front.

Clint felt that the barrage was getting too close for comfort and he decided to cut across the fields to the south in order to stay out of the way of the shells that were falling in and around where he had been standing. As he proceeded south, he came upon a squadron of English tanks that were crawling slowly to the front. They were noisy and emitted large clouds of black smoke from their engines as they rumbled along.

Never having seen these creatures before, Clint stood and watched as the monstrous machines, English Mark Vs, filed past. He waved at the tank commanders, but it was impossible to talk or even shout and be heard above the din of the artillery and the clanking and roar of the tanks. They were an impressive sight and Clint watched them for the longest time as they sailed over the countryside, unimpeded by any obstacle in their path. Soon they disappeared into the fog and he continued south. With the tanks, he didn't think the German infantry would have a chance.

Soon, after the tanks disappeared, he felt very alone. He could still hear the artillery but he could not see another soul. He began to walk in a more easterly direction, not wanting to end up in a German prison camp.

All during the morning, as Clint wandered the countryside, he encountered many different British units moving up to the line. He felt encouraged by the bravery of these young men as they advanced into the teeth of the great battle.

As the morning flowed into noon, the fog lifted and the visibility increased to five or six miles. He could see the blue sky directly overhead and caught an occasional glimpse of the sun from time to time. He heard, during various times of the day, the roar of aircraft overhead as they joined in the great battle. Though he was walking away from the line, the sounds of battle did not diminish. In fact, their intensity increased. When he stopped and listened closely, he thought he could detect the distinct sound of rifle and machine gun fire.

At noon, he stumbled upon an artillery unit that had pulled back from the front and reestablished a temporary position at the point where Clint now found them. It was here that he learned that the true weight of the German offensive had begun to push the British out of their defensive system. The artillery unit was trying to make an orderly retreat and would soon be moving back again. The men looked tired and had been through a hellish ordeal during the German barrage.

They had lost one gun, two men had been wounded, and four animals had been destroyed.

Clint observed vehicles and troops moving to the front and, at the same time, long lines of ambulances were heading in the opposite direction. He was now with an artillery unit that was retreating. He was unable to see any great distance and didn't have a map of the area. He had no idea where the Germans were, other than they were west of him and moving in an easterly direction.

He chatted with the battery commander for a while, and as they were preparing to fire the remaining three guns, Clint continued his odyssey off in a southeasterly direction. He came upon a small dirt road that was packed with ambulances and walking wounded.

He soon fell in step with one of the Tommies, whose left arm was heavily bandaged to his side.

The man was a tank commander, probably one of those Clint had seen earlier in the morning. They had come upon the enemy and fired most of their ammunition before turning around and retreating to the west. Soon they had received artillery fire that disabled 70 percent of the machines, including the lieutenant's. Right after the tank commander was out of the monster, a shell hit directly on top, turning the machine into an inferno of flaming fuel and exploding the remaining munitions. The lieutenant's arm was broken and shell fragments had penetrated his upper body.

"I'm just glad to be alive," he stated emphatically. "I know my driver was killed and I don't know what happened to the other crews. Once the tanks are hit by artillery, your life isn't worth much."

At this point, the lieutenant could hardly walk and nearly collapsed. Clint helped him to the side of the road and a place to sit. He tried to wave down an ambulance, but most were loaded down with the wounded. One driver took pity on them and stopped his full vehicle. Clint helped the lieutenant climb up and sit on the hood with his feet resting on the right front fender. That was the last he saw of the man, as the vehicle continued on east to dubious safety.

By the end of the day, the Fifth and Third Armies were in full retreat to the east-southeast all along the fifty-mile front.

* * *

Corporal Krause was elated over the progress of the offensive. Since morning the heavy guns had been moved twice and were now two miles east of the original position. Word was received at dusk that the guns were to be moved another three miles forward during the night. Shortly before dawn the tempo of the barrage was to be intensified.

"Walter, this war will be over before the end of the month," he stated enthusiastically.

"We will be in Paris for Easter!" was the reply.

* * *

It was difficult for Clint to tell that it was dawn. He had spent the night along the side of the road and had finally fallen asleep a few hours before. The fog was dark and yellowish in color, denser than the day before. The smell of gas and cordite lingered in the air. The weather had turned cold and Clint felt he'd never be warm again. He hadn't eaten for a day and a half and eagerly accepted a biscuit from one of the ambulance drivers he encountered.

He learned that the British had fallen back to the west side of the Crozat Canal and their hold there was tenuous at best. With the new day, the German offensive intensified. The artillery continued to pound the defenders and the Boche infantry continued their relentless movement forward.

Clint spent the second day wandering the front and continuing in an easterly direction. Late in the afternoon he found himself back at Flavey-le-Martel. The town was close to being deserted and the last train to leave had been in the morning, the one he was supposed to be on. He was able to find a telegraph office that was just closing and bribed the manager to get a dispatch off to his paper before the man left town with his family for safety, as Flavey-le-Martel was in eminent danger of falling into the hands of the enemy.

Clint learned that General Gough had moved his headquarters out of Vesle and back to Villers-Bretonneux. General Maxse moved his headquarters out of Flavy-le-Martel to Vesle in the afternoon.

Clint stayed close to the lines for the next few days, falling back with the British troops before the relentless onslaught of the German advance. At the beginning of the fourth day, Clint felt that the tide was turning. The retreat didn't seem as rapid or disorganized as it had been. Both armies were worn out and as of yet there had been no major breakthrough. The battle still hung in the balance, but Allied resistance had stiffened. The long-awaited French reinforcements began to show up. The German army had formed a huge salient in the line, but had not broken through.

Clint tried to keep in touch with his editor in Paris through the use of the telegraph and telephone. These contacts were infrequent, but were enough for his stories to get through. He found it necessary to continue moving to the east a little faster than the retreating armies, in order to find lines of communications that hadn't been broken by the fighting.

On March 25, he heard about a big conference of the Allies taking place the next day in the small town of Doullens, located some 20 miles north of Amiens. He spent most of the afternoon and night of the twenty-fifth hitching rides there. At dawn on the twenty-sixth he found a hotel room in Doullens and slept in a bed for the first time in five days. He left strict orders to the proprietor to be awakened no later than eleven in the morning. The meeting was scheduled at noon and though he couldn't attend, he wanted to be near that place to catch any and all of the news he could about the great German offensive.

The meeting lasted several hours, and it was still later that Clint heard the final results. A unity between the French and British had resulted, a unity that just a short time ago would not have been possible.

General Foch, a Frenchmen, had been charged by both governments to coordinate the action of the Allied Armies on the Western Front. With a unity of command, there was now optimism that the Germans could be stopped before Amiens. On a lesser note, and one that distressed Clint, General Gough was to be relieved of his command and replaced by a General Rawlings, the commander of the Fourth Army. Foch's stated objective was to fight a joint battle, British and French, to protect Amiens, the connecting link between the two armies and the pathway to Paris. The command was to yield no further ground.

On March 28, General Pershing, the commander of all of the US forces in France, made his grand gesture to General Foch. In his best French, he stated as eloquently as he could, "I have come to tell you that the American people would consider it a great honor for our troops to be engaged in the present battle. I ask this in their name and my own. At this moment there are no questions but of fighting. Infantry, artillery, aviation, all that we have are yours; use them as you wish… I have come especially to tell you that the American people will be proud to take part in the greatest battle of history."

The French were ecstatic over the gesture. Foch answered with deep emotion that this was truly a noble gesture on the part of Pershing and that he wanted the American First Division to take up positions near Mondidier, the center of the current German drive.

Clint was not present, but he was one of the first American reporters to wire this news to his paper. A short time after this meeting, he accidentally encountered General Gough, who spent a few minutes speaking with him. He was preparing to return to England and was not so rushed as before since being relieved of his command.

As they were parting, Clint asked about the wellbeing of Major Matthews. The answer was a shock.

Gough looked pained to answer. "The Major was killed on the second morning of battle as he was in a rear guard action, defending the withdrawing division. I shall miss him, for he was not only my aide, but also my friend. I have lost many friends over the past week, Mr. Phelps. Now I must go. Good-bye."

"Good-bye, General, and God be with you."

On March 29, Good Friday, the Germans were still moving forward, and the hold of the Allies was shaky at best. Both sides were tired and the rapid movement of the Boche had slowed to a crawl.

Finally, on April 5, the Germans mounted their final attempt to take Amiens, but were once again repulsed by the Allies. This day marked the end of this phase of the Great Spring Offensive.

The Germans had succeeded in driving 40 miles deep into Allied territory, occupying 1200 square miles. In just two weeks, the Boche had captured more territory than the Allies had gained in all of their offenses since the beginning of the war. Over 90,000 British prisoners had been taken, 975 guns captured, and there had been over 164,000 British and 70,000 French casualties. The Germans had suffered heavily, too, and had lost many of their best storm troops while exhausting 70 of their front-line divisions. Worst of all, they had not broken through the line.

Clint jotted these facts down in his notebook as he relaxed on the train during his much-delayed trip back to Paris.

Unterseeboote

In German, the English term for submarine is 'Unterseeboote'. Thus in the English vernacular of the time, the term 'U-boat' was born and used whenever referring to the German undersea fleet.

The Imperial Navy assigned a sequential number to each underseeboote that they produced. Thus, U-46 was created a modern boat that had been launched in October of 1916. She was 212 feet in length and had a 21-foot beam. When submerged the boat displaced nearly 300 tons.

The U-46 was armed with two torpedo tubes in the bow and two aft. She had one deck gun, a 105 mm, high-velocity cannon.

She ran on two propulsion units. On the surface the U-boat was propelled by a pair of 240 horsepower diesel engines and could sail at about seventeen knots. When submerged, she would utilize her two battery powered electric motors and cruise at approximately eight knots. The diesel engines not only propelled the submarine when she was surfaced, but recharged her batteries, as well. This was accomplished through a series of gears that reversed the rotation of the electric motors and, by so doing, the motors became generators and recharged the batteries.

The U-boats of the 1916 vintage were constructed to submerge to depths up to 100 meters, beyond that, the pressure of the sea would begin the process of crushing and collapsing the hull.

The U-46 had a crew of 39 men including her captain. Normally she would be at sea for approximately two months before returning to her port in Heligoland for refitting and rearming.

After her encounter with the English Q-Ship, the U-46 limped back to her base and spent the next three weeks in dry dock having the battle damage, suffered at the hands of the Londonary, repaired.

Captain Links set sail during the third week of February and had been at sea for well over a month on the prowl for more victims.

On March 27, he received a message concerning the location of a slow moving American convoy headed for Europe. He knew he was close and could catch up to it if he sailed at full speed on the surface. His fuel was low, but after carefully calculating his needs, he was convinced he could catch the convoy and get off the three remaining torpedoes, before breaking away from the engagement and still have enough fuel to make the return to Heligoland.

Just at sunset on March 29, Captain links and his executive officer, Hans, were able to make out the smoke of the convoy, which was just beyond the horizon. Captain Links made a rough estimate of the convoy's route including the zigzag turns it would make during the night. The Captain then plotted a straight course for what was hoped to be an interception of the convoy by daybreak or before.

Captain Dennison had been on the bridge since 4:00 a.m. when it was still dark as pitch. Now the sun was just beginning to peak over the eastern horizon. He could just make out the high overcast clouds, and the surface visibility appeared to be unlimited.

It felt good to have a ship under his command, particularly the *Hampton*. She was one of a new class of ship that could outsail all of the other destroyers in the fleet. The *Hampton* had been outfitted especially for convoy and submarine duty. She was heavily armed and loaded with the new hydrosound gear, a super sensitive underwater listening device that was able to amplify underwater sounds. The unit could distinguish submarines by the sounds they made and determine the azimuth, or direction from the ship's bow, the U-boat was located. The equipment could not determine the distance or range. To pinpoint a location, it would take a minimum of two simultaneous readings, one each from two different ships, in order to triangulate the enemy's position.

They had been at sea for eight days and it seemed as if this cruise would last forever. One of the freighters in the convoy was an old rust bucket that should have been scrapped years ago. It was constantly breaking down and holding up the whole convoy. Dan was uneasy about the slow passage and anxious for it to be completed.

Since leaving on this cruise, he often thought of his friend, Robert Montgomery. Shortly before the *Hampton* set sail, he'd received a note stating that Robert had received the Victoria Cross, posthumously, for bravery in a battle with a German submarine. He felt grieved that the war had taken yet another courageous life.

"Captain Dennison!" It was Dan's executive officer, Lieutenant Commander George Keiffer.

"Yes, George."

"The *Bennington* reports a periscope sighting about three and a half miles southeast of our current position, and we're getting some indistinguishable sounds on the hydrophone."

Suddenly, there was a loud explosion to the north. All on the bridge raised their glasses and saw a pillar of smoke rising from one of the ships in the convoy; she was about three miles northwest of their current position.

"It looks like the *Tuscania*, sir."

"Helmsman, come about to a heading of two, five, zero degrees, ahead full speed."

"Aye-aye sir. Turning to a heading of two, five, zero degrees, ahead to full speed."

The big ship responded immediately to the rudder and lurched ahead as the speed increased rapidly. Smoke from the boilers poured from the 4 stacks as the Hampton made a 180-degree turn and sped towards the last known position of the sub.

"Sound battle stations and tell hydrophone to listen carefully. I want this sub."

Lt. Commander Keiffer acknowledged and went below to the radio and hydrophone room. The ship came to life immediately as the crew ran to their battle stations. The speed of the ship was up to 25 knots in no time. Dan felt it would take approximately eight to ten minutes to get to the position from where he surmised the sub had fired its torpedo. But where would the sub go to get away?

The *Hampton* was located on the south-southeast perimeter of the convoy. Dan figured that the U-boat would head due south in order to put as much distance between her and the convoy. He ordered another turn to the left of 15 degrees to a heading of two, three, five degrees. That should lead him to a proper interception angle, if he'd guessed right.

"Any response on the U-boat?" Mr. Keiffer asked.

"No sir, not…shh, I think I hear 'em, sir. Yes, sir, that noise we heard earlier was their propeller. About ten degrees to our port side and here's the *Bennington's* plot on them. We should be on top of them in about 6 to 7 minutes."

"Good work, Thompson." Lieutenant Commander Keiffer picked up the intercom and buzzed the bridge. Dan picked it up immediately. "Captain, we have the plot lines on the sub and we should be over them in six to seven minutes. I'll give the word to drop the depth charges. Turn left to a two, two, zero degree heading.

"Turn left to two, two, zero degrees, helmsman." Dan said and checked his watch.

The seconds and minutes ticked by slowly.

"Prepare to drop charges!" yelled Mr. Keiffer.

Dan raised his arm to signal the fantail crew.

"Release charges!"

Dan brought his arm straight down and the depth charge crew rolled two charges off the rear racks while two were fired out to the sides of the ship.

It had been 15 minutes since the U-boat fired its' torpedo. Captain Links ordered the ship to stop and run silent. All ears strained to listen for any sign of the advancing surface ship. At first all was quiet, then one man heard something, a distant whine, then the others heard it. Fear gripped the sub. Captain Links ordered the crew to prepare for depth charges. The sound of the approaching ship grew louder and soon it was directly overhead. They barely heard the splash of the charges as they hit the water and sank.

First one and then the other charge exploded. A few seconds later the third and fourth charges went off. The U-boat rocked and rolled like a toy in a tub of water. The concussion from the depth charges caused some of the valves to burst or open and water was entering different parts of the ship. The damage crew soon had these shut off as best they could, though water continued to seep into the boat.

As soon as the charges went off Captain Links had the U-46 brought to periscope depth. He immediately saw the destroyer turning and heading back for another run at him. He aligned the boat with the destroyer and fired one torpedo before submerging to maximum depth.

The missile hit a glancing blow to the bow of the Hampton, blowing a hole at the water line in the bow, slowing her up a little but not causing catastrophic damage.

The *Hampton* came over the spot where the submarine had been and released another quartet of depth charges.

After the third one exploded, Captain Links' heard the popping of rivets in the hull. When the fourth charge went off, very near the boat, he heard what appeared to be some tearing sound. Though the charges didn't hit the boat directly they were close enough for the concussion of the water to tear the sub open.

"Blow the ballast tanks, surface, surface," the captain shouted. But it was too late. The torpedo room flooded and the lights throughout the boat went out. The ship was filling fast. As the ballast tanks emptied other parts of the sub were taking on water, they maintained their equilibrium, at least for a short time, then she started to settle. As she went down, the increased pressure of the sea began to crush the hull and the U-boat continued to fill and go down. The conning tower hatch seal blew, due to the ever-increasing pressure of the sea, and the water poured in.

Mr. Keiffer came up to the bridge after the second pass over the enemy. The *Hampton* was completing its turn ready for a third run over the target.

"Captain, I think we got her. Hydrophone reports hearing the sub breaking up and she appears to be going down."

Dan acknowledged his words and pointed to debris and oil coming to the surface. "It looks like we split her open. Good going, George. Now let's check on the convoy. Notify the radio room to contact command and let them know our situation, and that we will stay here for a while to see if there are any survivors. Also verify that it was the *Tuscania* that was hit and see if they need any further assistance."

"Aye-aye, sir."

Word had been received that the Germans had broken through the line near Amiens and were rapidly approaching this vital city in the north. During the immediate crisis, General Pershing changed his demand for an independent army and offered the complete armed services of the AEF to General Foch, the Allied supreme commander.

The Rainbow Division was to return to the front immediately and hold the front line in the Baccarat Sector, to relieve the 128th French Division in order for them to withdraw from the trenches and move north to reinforce the British on the Somme, in the vicinity of Amiens.

The Rainbow thus became the first American division to occupy a divisional sector under its own commander, Major General Menoher. The First and the Twenty-Sixth Divisions, the only other American combat troops to precede the Rainbow to the front, had held only brigade sectors. The Rainbow thus became a part of the French 6th Army Corps under the command of a General Duport. This change took effect on March 31, 1918.

On that day, Sunday, while still in Fontenoy la Joute, most of the men in the battery attended the Easter services conducted by the Reverend James. It wasn't that they were suddenly turning religious; rather, it gave them an opportunity to hear the regimental band perform. The men on the whole were quite fatalistic and even cynical in their religious thinking. The prevailing philosophical mood, though mistaken, was that if they died in this war on the side of right, the Allied side, then they, of course, had earned their way into the heavenly congregation.

In the early afternoon, after eating lunch and receiving their pay, the 149th started the march back towards the front. The morning began with scattered showers here and there, but by the time they were on the road, the skies opened and the rain fell in torrents for the remainder of the day. Their path was no less than ankle-deep in muck and the horses' hooves and the wheels of the vehicles kicked up mud that covered the troops from head to foot. The carriages slipped and slid across the road. The horses and mules had trouble maintaining their footing.

Just prior to reaching the place where Battery F was to establish their echelon, located some six kilometers beyond and to the northeast of Azerailles, many of the carriages became mired in the mud. The men tugged and pulled and cursed as they tried valiantly to reach their destination at the summit of a little hill, some one thousand meters away. When they finally arrived at this place, they found the mud was even deeper, and it didn't take long before the echelon was rechristened "Influenza Ridge."

After a meal that consisted of lukewarm beans and corned Willie, mixed generously with rainwater, the firing battery left for their new gun positions located some two to three thousand meters behind the American line.

Those who stayed at the echelon sought shelter from the mud and rain. A few were able to relax in the supply wagons, though that space was limited. Others wrapped themselves in their shelter halves and sat against the few trees that dotted the landscape. The majority dug elaborate trenches in an effort to direct the water around their shelter halves, which were placed flat on the ground with the intent to keep the man out of the mud. Each man then tried to cover himself with his blankets in an effort to keep the rain off, but to no avail.

Before the firing battery continued forward, Lieutenant Case ordered that one cannoneer from each section stay behind with the echelon in case the battery suffered casualties.

The firing battery finally arrived at its forward position after one in the morning. Lieutenants Case and Allen, who had preceded the cannon on horseback the day before to select a site for the guns, met them. They decided to occupy an old French gun emplacement used during the early days of the war. This position was located approximately 1000 meters east of the sleepy little village of Reherrey.

There were bunkers to the right of each gun pit used for storage of ammunition. On the left were wooden pits covered with corrugated steel roofs that were used by the gun crews for beds. As the ammunition bunkers, were filled with water, the lower shelves of the bunk pits were used for ammunition and the upper shelves for some of the cannoneers.

Those who could not be accommodated at the positions were assigned to a larger shelter built a few meters behind the guns across a small road. This dugout had been built with separate rooms to accommodate officers, enlisted men, and the telephone room.

The quarters were at least semi-dry, though the roof leaked in places and the floors were thick with mud. The bunks were the standard chicken wire hammocks that kept the men off of the ground. The cannoneers shared their quarters with mice, rats, and worst of all, large, soft-shelled snails. The mice and rats often scampered over the slumbering troops and were tolerated to some extent, but to reach out in the night and touch one of the snails made one's skin crawl and the hairs on the back of the neck stand up. It wasn't long before the men learned to shake their bedding vigorously prior to retiring in order to dispose of these slimy pests.

As the walls between the officers and enlisted men were not impervious to sound, it didn't take long for the enlisted personnel to start making loud comments questioning the officers' qualifications to command, as well as to question their virginity. This, of course, was done in a manner of conversation, whereby the officers were unable to determine the offender. These little barbs derogating the targeted officer were usually followed by uproarious laughter, much to the chagrin of the officer named.

Shortly after their arrival, Lieutenant Case ordered the echelon to move back to Glonville, some 2000 meters southwest of Reherrey. This allowed the men at echelon to sleep in the loft of a local barn which afforded them greater comfort and, thankfully, a dry place to sleep.

The cannoneers at the emplacement soon began to dislike the walk into Reherrey for meals, and therefore began appropriating food and small cans of solidified alcohol from the field kitchen and cooked their own meals at the gun positions. All members of the gun crews, including the mechanics, became very proficient at pilfering items from the kitchen; bacon, bread, sugar, jam, etc. Bread fried in bacon grease sprinkled liberally with sugar was a favorite. Of course, if there were a special meal in the offing, wheat cakes in the morning or fresh meat in the evening, they would then make their way to the field kitchen.

Soon, the routine in the Baccarrat sector mimicked the routine established just the month before when they were in the Luneville sector.

To while away the many hours of waiting, the cannoneers took up the hobby of making trays and various other decorative and functional objects from the shell casings they found lying around. The French Poilus had taught these skills to them when they were in the Luneville sector. In furthering their indoctrination by their French compatriots, many took to wearing comfortable wooden shoes and slippers at the positions. This practice was brought to a quick end when the men answered a call to the guns one night. Many were dressed in their slippers, wooden shoes, and underwear. What a sight they presented to Lieutenant Case, who happened to be at the emplacement that evening.

The Lieutenant was enraged. "What are you men doing dressed like this? You are to be in full uniform at all times when on duty. If I wanted to see a bunch of clowns I'd have gone to the circus. If I ever catch any of you out of uniform during duty hours, you will spend the rest of the war in the brig. You got that?"

"Yes, sir," the offenders meekly replied.

"Now go get dressed and get back here on the double!"

Shortly after establishing the gun emplacement, two cannoneers in full uniform from each unit were sent forward to learn the task of being a rocket guard. This forward observation post was located at the junction of the Reherrey-Migneville and Montigny-Migneville roads. The observation post was situated upon a hill that gave a superb view of the American lines, which were between three and four thousand meters distant. The front line stretched from the north and meandered to the southeast.

The post consisted of a trench about ten feet long and four feet wide, and was about three and a half to four feet deep. It dropped off into a five-foot deep dugout at the west end of the trench. This abris had a timber roof and was large enough to hold two chicken wire hammocks. At about the midpoint of the trench, on the side facing the front lines, was a three-foot square board firmly affixed to a post holding it in a flat horizontal position. On the board were various graphics, which Sergeant Baker explained to the cannoneers.

"Look at this board closely," he drawled. "As you can see, there's a map of the front laid out in a semi-circle detailing the position of each of the infantry regiments. This here arm is attached at the center near the edge closest to the trench. Where the arm is attached represents this here post. When y'all see a flare go up, swing the unattached end towards the flare and then sight in on the location along this here groove in the top of the arm. When you set the arm towards the flare and determine where it's coming from, then you look here at the other end, and on the board it tells you what unit sent up the flare. Then above that, you'll see these here patterns and colors, which will tell you what barrage they're callin' fer. You got that?"

"Yes, sir," they all answered.

"Now, Barrage L is way over on the left, next comes Z Barrage, then 14A, then 13, and so on. When you know what barrage they're callin' fer, you telephone headquarters in Rehrrey, who will then notify the batteries."

Each night three men were detailed to stand as the rocket guards working on two-hour shifts. A rotation system was set up between the different batteries of the regiment and once a week Battery F would supply the guard. The cannoneers devised a means of changing this guard without having to leave their post for under no circumstance was an on-duty trooper to leave his assigned station. Therefore, when the guard was to be changed, all he would have to do is pull a rope which was tied around the foot of the next one on duty, who was sleeping in the dugout at the west end of the post. This was supposed to arouse him and get him out to stand his turn for the next couple of hours. On the whole this worked well, until Hank was on watch. He had an uncanny knack of slipping the loop from around his foot in his sleep.

"Next time you do that, I'm going to tie the rope around your neck!" Pat stated with some vehemence after it had happened the second time.

However, the resolution was simple enough. Hank was the first to stand guard each time their turn came around.

On April 5, Lieutenant Case determined that the guns needed to be moved. He felt that the Germans had mapped this position and was fearful of being hit by enemy artillery. First he selected a new site about 500 meters to the south-southeast. Next, he ordered all available engineers and reserve cannoneers to this new site to assist with the digging. First, the engineers erected camouflage over the entire digging area, and then the work began.

As at Luneville, the moment the digging started, the rain began to fall, and worst of all, it soon became evident that once the top foot or so of soil had been removed, the diggers ran into solid rock. Nothing less than drills and dynamite could cut through the obstacle.

The work on the new positions proceeded slowly. A communications trench was to connect the four gun pits, and loose dirt was bagged and put in front of the guns as protection from German fire. The drilling and the blasting away of the solid rock slowed the construction process to a crawl. The cannon continued to fire from the old position until the digging was completed at the new emplacement.

On April 30, Major Reddon came to the battery position. The men were ordered to fall in a short distance behind the guns, and as they stood at attention, the major and Lieutenant Case went to each man and gave him a service chevron honoring six months of active foreign service.

When the presentation was finished, the major said, "You all have done an exemplary job and are to be commended on your spirit and professionalism. I'm proud to serve with you."

Lieutenant Case dismissed the men, and Major Reddon went to his car and drove to the next battery down the line.

Hank's only comment was, "I'd rather have more money than this chevron, and I wonder how many of these things we'll accumulate before we go home?"

Pat, too, was unimpressed and just nodded in agreement as they returned to work on the guns.

The Air War

On April 16, the 95th Aero Squadron gathered once again at their base just outside of Toul. Their planes were at last armed and the pilots were trained in all aspects of air combat. The next step was up to the men. Were they prepared both physically and mentally to fight?

This question was answered in part that very evening when word was received of the first successes of American pilots in the war. Doug Campbell and Alan Winslow, both of the 94th Aero Squadron, had registered the first official victories of the war. Both victories had been scored within minutes of each other and it was difficult to determine who had the first kill, as both enemy planes fell to the ground within a half mile and within one minute of the other. Other Americans flying under the French or British flags had scored victories before this date, but these were the first by Americans flying in US uniforms and attached to US squadrons.

Ike felt a little let down at the news. He wasn't sure why, but he had long harbored a secret daydream of scoring the first American Air Service victory. It really didn't matter that someone else had beat him to the punch; he felt elated over the news and was ready to set out on patrol.

Both Frank and Ike were scheduled to go up with Captain Josiah Wortham the very next morning on their first flight behind the enemy lines. Ike knew he wasn't going to sleep well this night. To help relieve his preflight stress, he sat at his desk and wrote a long letter to Agnes.

The morning of April 17 dawned clear, with a stiff breeze out of the west. Visibility was unlimited.

After breakfast, Frank and Ike walked to the briefing room. "I sure didn't sleep too well last night, and I could barely eat any breakfast," Ike confided to Frank.

"Oh, I slept like a baby!" Frank answered.

"Sure you did," Ike said sarcastically.

"Well, maybe it wasn't a sound sleep, but at least I did sleep some."

"This is so different, I mean from our other patrols. Here we're going out to really stir up some trouble, and we have the means to fight back instead of just turning around and running with our tails between our legs."

They entered the briefing shack where the squadron leader was waiting for them.

"Well, gentlemen, are you ready to fight?"

"Yes, sir!"

"This will be your first patrol behind enemy lines. I want you both to stick close to me and follow my signals. Be alert and vigilant, so come on over to the table and let's go over the map. I want you both to be aware of where we are at all times, and if we do get separated, you need to know how to find your way back here. Memorize the landmarks, rail tracks, towns, and of course the front. We've flown a great deal along the west side of the line, and if you do get disoriented, your best bet is to fly west and cross the front and then return here to base. Got that?"

"Yes, sir!" They answered together in strong voices so as not to betray their apprehension.

Next, Captain Wortham reviewed in detail their planned flight for that morning's patrol. He reviewed his signals so there would be no misunderstanding as to his intentions. Finally, he briefed them on what to look for.

"We need to look for any changes in the German's dispositions along the line and for any heavy concentration of aircraft. Colonel Mitchell wants the 94th and the 95th to prevent enemy aircraft from penetrating our side of the front in order to view our strength. So good luck and stick close. Now let's get airborne."

With that, the briefing was finished and the three left the room and headed for the planes that were about 50 yards from the shack, already facing into the wind, ready for takeoff.

The sun was just beginning to peek over the eastern horizon and Ike shivered, more from the excitement of the moment than from the chill of the early dawn.

They each struggled into their leather, fleece-lined flying clothes. The temperature was still in the mid-forties but at altitude, three thousand meters; the temperature would be around ten degrees.

Ike, as was his custom, did a brief walk around the aircraft and, after inspecting all of the control surfaces, engine, propeller and main landing gear; he finally climbed into the cockpit. The plane sported two Vickers machine guns, one on the cowling in front of him, firing through the propeller arc and the second mounted on the top wing, firing over its arc. Both guns fired simultaneously through the action of the trigger on the cowling-mounted gun.

At the pilots' signals, all three engines started on the first pull-through by the mechanics and soon they were beginning their takeoff roll. The three craft broke ground quickly in the cool air and rapidly climbed to their patrol altitude. It wasn't long before they were over the front lines, and then on into the enemy's territory.

Ike was ever alert and kept his head swiveling, allowing his eyes to sweep the horizon from left to right and back again. He would frequently look over his shoulder, to check the rear.

Once on the east side of the line, Captain Wortham turned to the northwest and flew a course parallel to the front. The others followed close behind.

The flight continued along the front lines for about thirty-five minutes and, at Wortham's signal, started a gentle right turn of 180 degrees, bringing them to a heading of one five zero degrees for the return trip. The flight plan had called for them to be airborne for one and a half hours. If they encountered the enemy during this time, they would still have sufficient fuel reserves for an engagement and the eventual return to Toul.

By this time the sun was up about even with the Nieuports. Ike kept checking to his left, trying not to look directly into the sun. At their current altitude, they were skimming low over the deck of stratus clouds.

He was still on an adrenaline high but a little more relaxed than when they had first taken off. He kept his scan up but was occasionally blinded by the brilliance of the morning sun, which would strike him full in the face from behind the upper left wing when the plane would pitch and roll from the light turbulence. As he was getting comfortable with the patrol and beginning to enjoy the beautiful landscape spread out below him, he suddenly saw at least three high-speed projectiles penetrate his upper right wing – bullets. The first two passed in front of the lower wing but the third one took a chunk of wood from its leading edge.

Ike knew what the objects were and immediately applied full left aileron and the Nieuport responded rapidly, rolling over on its back. He didn't even look for his attacker, for he knew that the German had the advantage. His sole objective was escape. While inverted, Ike pulled back on the joystick and dove straight down into the cloud he'd been flying over.

After penetrating the stratus layer, Ike continued to hold some backpressure on the control column until he felt that he was in upright flight once again, but in a gentle descent. This would put him on a heading in the opposite direction. Without the outside references, it was difficult to tell. He watched his airspeed closely and reduced power as it crept past 120 mph. His compass was oscillating wildly.

After what seemed to be an eternity, he broke out of the bottom of the cloud with the wings in a forty-five-degree bank and the nose pointing down thirty degrees past horizontal. Once his visual references were active again, he overcame the effects of vertigo and carefully returned the craft to straight and level flight. He was still close to the cloud he'd just penetrated and flew on out to the edge, where he immediately started climbing the two thousand feet needed to get back on top.

Once up above the clouds, there were no other aircraft to be seen. Ike loitered in the area for fifteen or twenty minutes looking for his squadron mates, but to no avail. The skies were empty. After searching in vain, he decided to head in a southwesterly direction out over the front.

He was feeling quite alone. He hoped that he could make it back to the aerodrome without encountering any more of the enemy. He was beginning to realize that the lower right wing was flexing more than normal, so violent maneuvering was out of the question. He reduced his cruise speed in order to put less strain on the wing.

When he crossed over the front he turned to the southeast and soon found a familiar landmark, visible through a large break between the clouds. He started to lose altitude and mentally plotted a direct course to Toul.

After landing, he noticed that both Frank's and Captain Wortham's planes were at parking. The two other pilots had just stepped out of their Nieuports. On seeing Ike pull up next to their ships, they both ran to his plane as he shut down the engine.

"Where'd you go, we both thought you were a goner!" Frank exclaimed as he ran up to Ike and gave him a bear hug. "Jesus, I thought I'd never see you again!"

"That was quick thinking, Ike," Captain Wortham said. "You did the right thing by diving into the cloud. We saw the Hun follow you and then it was over. We looked for you, and the Hun, and didn't see a thing, so we came back here. Glad you're Okay! How's your plane?"

"I don't know, he put a couple of bullets through the wings and that's the last I saw. I think he did some damage to the lower right wing but I was able to get the ship back."

The three walked around the Nieuport to inspect the damage. Ike's mechanic came running up and joined them at the wing. Soon many of the other pilots were at the plane.

"Lieutenant, that German sure tore hell outta these wings," Mike said. "There are two ribs in the upper wing shot to hell and one of the bullets broke the main spar in the lower wing. You were lucky she held together."

Ike took off his helmet and scarf. He was beginning to feel awfully warm as he inspected the aircraft. There were over fifteen holes in the wings.

"Ike, if that Jerry had aimed about ten more feet to the left, you'd be a dead man," Frank concluded.

"Thanks for nothing," Ike said with a grin. "I just didn't see him. I didn't even hear his guns."

"You weren't the only one, Ike," Wortham said. "I should have been more alert myself.

"All you pilots, listen up! Ike here is living proof that the Huns don't always attack out of the sun. We all were so busy looking to the sun that we missed this bandit altogether."

Life at the Baccarrat front fell into a monotonous routine. The guns were fired on a regular basis but no movement of the lines was planned or anticipated by either side. There were frequent trench raids that sent the Americans to the German trenches for prisoners, as well as the Boche raids on the American trenches. Little resulted from this stalemate other than death and injury to the participants on both sides.

"This whole thing is stupid!" Hank complained to Pat. "Here we sit in the mud twiddling our thumbs while we try to kill some poor bastard we can't even see a mile or two over the hill. Hell, I might as well be back in school learning something worthwhile. What sort of good am I going to get out of learning how to fieldstrip a French-made 75mm gun? That's sure going to get me a long way in Vet school."

"Yeah, I'm beginning to have second thoughts on this grand adventure of ours, too," Pat sighed. "You have to admit, though, we've been lucky. No one has been seriously hurt or killed. Look what happened to Battery A, and then to Battery C, as well as some of the others. They've all had some men killed and suffered a lot of causalities. I sure hope to hell someone realizes that there's little rhyme or reason for our sitting on our butts in this endless hellhole and then does something about it."

Pat and Hank were sitting under the camouflage of the old gun position playing a dull game of rummy. Suddenly, they could hear the anti-aircraft guns open up, trying to hit some of the German planes flying over the position. Both had to duck into the dugout to escape the falling shell fragments that started raining down on and around the guns.

Once in the shelter with the cards redealt, Pat said, "Even the skies are falling on us."

Soon after Ike had calmed down from his close encounter with the unknown German plane and regathered his wits a short time after the debriefing, he meandered over to the hangar to check on his Nieuport. Even though there were no doors on the building, the mechanics were able to work on the planes under its roof and out of the elements. Although the hangar was open to the east, it still retained the odors of the planes—fuel, oil, and particularly the dope used to lacquer the aircraft's fabric skin. Ike loved the smell of the repair shed and went in as often as he possibly could.

Once inside, he made a beeline for his ship—Miria, as he fondly called it—and was in the process of inspecting the damage when Mike came up from behind him.

"Lieutenant, your plane is going to be down for at least four or five days for repairs."

"Be sure you get the wings as strong as new, Mike. I have a feeling we're going to put a lot of stress on them."

"Oh, they'll be better'n new, that's one of the reasons for taking so long in the repair work. You'll be back in the air by Monday, honest!"

With that said, Ike took one last sniff of the air, gave a quick nod and wave to his mechanic, and turned on his heel, left the hangar, and headed for the mess hall in order to grab a late lunch.

On his way, the squadron adjutant came up to him and, somewhat out of breathe, said, "Lieutenant Dennison, Captain Wortham wants you in his office, on the double!"

"Thanks, Brodrick, I'll go right over."

Ike headed off to the operations shack; back over next to the hangar. "I wonder what I did now?" He muttered to himself as he proceeded towards operations.

Once inside, he told the sergeant in the outer office that he was there to see the captain, at which point he was waved to the captain's door. Ike stopped there and knocked gently. "Come in!"

Ike opened the door and entered.

"Oh, Ike, glad you're here. Are you all right after this morning's encounter?"

"Yes, sir! I would expect that we'd all be in for a lot more than that as time progresses."

"True, true. Well, you handled the situation properly. Did you see the plane that shot at you?" Ike shook his head and shrugged. After a short pause the captain continued. "All I can tell you is that the plane was a brilliant blue Fokker D-VII. You want to be careful with those. They are without a doubt the most deadly planes in the air. It's a new design and all we know is that they're fast and can outclimb the Nieuports, and practically anything else we have in the air. But that wasn't what I called you in here for. We've received a request for you to get a three-day pass to go to Paris."

"To Paris?"

"Yes, it seems your father is there and wants to see you. He's a Navy man, right?"

"Yes, sir. He's the captain of a destroyer. I wonder what he's doing in Paris and what he wants."

"Well, he sank a German sub and is receiving an award of some sort from Premier Clemenceau himself, and he requested that you be present at the ceremonies. Do you want to go?"

"Of course, sir. When do I leave? You know my Nieuport is going to be down for four or five days. It's a perfect time."

"Well, get packed, as you'll be on the one o'clock train for Paris. Now, while you're there, I need for you to do me a favor. I made an appointment for you on Saturday with a Monsieur DuBois. He's a factory representative for the Societe Pour Aviation et ses Derives. He's going to hand a new SPAD XIII over to you to bring back here for evaluation. As a result, I've extended your pass to five days."

"You're kidding! I'm going to fly back here? In a new SPAD?"

Captain Wortham smiled, "That's right. I was going over and pick it up myself, but when the request for you to go to Paris came to my desk; I thought I'd let my best pilot handle the task. So you better get it back here in one piece and before dark on Sunday night."

"Oh, sir, you're breaking my heart! I've dreamed of flying the SPADs. This is great, thanks!"

"Now here's a message from your father. He's staying at the Chatham. I'll see you late Sunday afternoon."

It was dark when the train finally pulled into the station. Ike was fit to be tied—there had been delay after delay before they arrived in Paris.

As he was sitting on the slow moving train, he thought a lot about his father. He was really proud of his accomplishment—to think, he sunk a German sub and then had to proceed on to La Harve for repairs before returning to the states. It was fortunate. It would give him some time to spend with his dad, and maybe give him a chance to see Agnes and even introduce her to his father, the hero.

When the train finally arrived at the station, he picked up his overnight bag and stepped out on to the smokey platform and then headed for the main entrance, dodging around the large throngs of people. He soon found himself on the street. After asking directions from one of the porters, he headed for the American Hospital, only a few blocks away.

Ike hadn't contacted Agnes or even his father regarding when he'd be in town; there just hadn't been enough time. He wanted to see his dad, but he was more anxious to see Agnes and decided to go there first. By the time he reached the hospital, his heart was pounding. Agnes should be off duty within the next few hours if the schedule she'd relayed to him last week was still in effect. He went to her duty station to see if he could find her.

He was surprised to see that he recognized the duty nurse, but he wasn't sure from where.

"Yes, I'm looking for Agnes Bovay," he said when the nurse looked up at him. "Can you tell me where I can find her?"

"Why, you're Ike Dennison, aren't you?"

"Yes. I know you, don't I?"

"We met last December when you just arrived from the states. We were with Agnes when you met her. Oh, will she be surprised! I'm Beth Stern."

"Oh, I remember. I've had somewhat of a different day and I'm having trouble getting all of my thoughts together, Beth. I hope she won't mind my coming here to the hospital to see her."

Beth laughed. "She won't mind, believe me. You can find her in the cafeteria. Go down these stairs and turn left, you can't miss it. She just went on her dinner break."

"Thanks, Beth. It was nice seeing you again, and I'll probably see you later."

Ike turned and hurried to the stairs and went down, taking two steps at a time. At the bottom of the staircase he turned left and found the door that led to a large room filled with tables, chairs and lots of people, mainly dressed in white. Ike guessed them to be hospital staff.

He quickly and methodically scanned the tables looking for Agnes. He didn't see her at first and was disappointed at missing her, and as he turned to leave, he spied her, sitting by herself at a small table, next to the wall at the right of the door. She was engrossed in a book. He walked over and pulled out the chair opposite her and sat down, all without a word or sound.

She was dressed in white and her black hair was done up in a bun with her nurse's cap perched top. Her skin was alabaster white and her dark eyes glistened in the bright lights of the room. She was more beautiful than ever.

When he was seated, she looked up from her reading. She dropped the book and shrieked, loud enough to quiet the large room.

"Ike, where did you come from?" she said in her accented English, and turned a bright crimson.

"It's a long story, but I just got off of the train and I came straight here to see you." Ike wanted to grab her, hold her and kiss her right there. He restrained himself as well as he could. He felt that, just maybe, Agnes felt the same. "I'm in town to meet my father," he said after a long silence. "He had to bring his destroyer into La Harve for repairs after an engagement with a German submarine. As a matter of fact, he's being awarded a medal for sinking the U-boat."

"Oh, Ike, I've longed to see you and here you are and I don't know what to say."

"Would it be better if we spoke in French?" Ike asked.

"No, no, I'm just at a loss for words. I've been practicing my English and I would prefer to use it with you. I'm just so surprised to see you. I have many things to say but I can't think of them now."

"When are you off duty? I'd like to take you to dinner and we can talk then."

"Of all the nights. I'm working a double shift, and I don't get off until well past three in the morning. Maybe I can get away... well, no, I have to assist in surgery."

"That's all right, Agnes, the good news is that I don't have to be back to Toul until Sunday night. We have a whole five days together, if you want."

She smiled and squeezed his hand. "I can't wait Ike, I'll get Thursday off for sure."

They continued talking throughout her dinner hour and then he walked her up to her duty station. As he was leaving he bent down and kissed her gently. She threw her arms around his neck and returned his kiss.

"I'll see you for lunch tomorrow, at eleven," Ike said as he departed. He turned and disappeared around the corner.

He was exhilarated and didn't come to his senses until he was out in the cold night air. He hailed a taxi and was soon on his way to the Chatham. He went directly to the registration desk and got the number of his father's room.

As he climbed the steps to the third floor, he thought that it seemed like years since he'd last seen his dad, even though it had only been six months. Ike paused at the door for a moment before he knocked, then tapped lightly.

"Who's there?"

"Dad? It's me Ike!"

The door flew open and the two men stared at one another for a moment. His father, who stood a good two inches taller than Ike and was more powerfully built than his son, threw his arms around him in a big bear hug.

"Ike, what a surprise. I didn't expect you till tomorrow. How are you? Let me look at you. I'm so glad you're early."

"This is such a great opportunity. When I received the word just this noon I grabbed the first train to Paris."

"Have you eaten?"

"No."

"Well, let's head on down to the dining room, I'm famished. We have a lot to talk about. Come in and wash up and I'll get my coat. Do you have a room?"

"Well, no, not yet."

"We'll get that taken care of right away. Leave your bag here and let's get going. Your mother is certainly going to be envious."

The two men weren't seated for dinner until after ten, and once there they sat and talked for over three hours. It was a grand reunion and Ike couldn't help but think that this was the first time the two of them had ever had a long, heart-to-heart talk.

His father talked of home and of his convoy duty and finally of his victory over the U-46. Ike talked at length about his flying and of his encounter with the Fokker D-VII, just this very morning. Finally, and somewhat hesitantly, he told his father all about Agnes.

"Dad, I would like to bring her with me to the ceremony on Thursday. You need to meet her. I think she's the one I'll marry."

"I'd love to meet her. We'll all go out together for dinner and a show afterward." He paused and looked at Ike intently. "Don't jump too soon into a relationship during these hard times, Ike."

"I know, Dad, but Agnes is different, you'll see."

Ike eased himself gently into the wicker seat of the SPAD. He was ready to go back to the war.

What a week it had been, seeing and being with Agnes and seeing his father. He'd been with the ones he loved the most and now it was over. His father had really liked Agnes, and they had hit it off well from the beginning.

Ike hadn't known that his dad not only spoke French, but spoke it fluently. Agnes and he were carrying on conversations that Ike was hardly able to understand. Well, his dad had always amazed him, and this was just another example. With his father on his side, maybe his mother would be agreeable and open to Agnes, just as his father had been.

"Switch on, throttle cracked?" the mechanic yelled, breaking his train of thought.

"Switch on, throttle cracked," Ike replied.

The mechanic heaved on the propeller and the engine took hold immediately. The engine was rough and shook the whole airframe as it struggled to run. Ike advanced the throttle a little more and with the added fuel, the engine's roughness disappeared and settled down to a smooth idle at 1000 rpm.

The day before had been a learning experience for Ike. The SPAD was a much heavier aircraft, more powerful and much faster than the Nieuport. The ship was armed with twin Vickers machine guns mounted in front of the pilot, firing through the propeller arc as a result of the synchronizing gear. It was powered by a water-cooled V-8 Hispano-Suiza engine with 235 horsepower. The plane could attain a top speed of 135 mph in level flight.

The SPADs did have their vices, though. The landing gear was placed far forward, making landings extremely tricky, as the tail had a tendency to dig in the ground on hard landings. The high rate of descent at slow airspeeds required some power to be carried all the way to touchdown. If not properly attended, it had a propensity to ground loop, as did most aircraft currently being used in the war. The aircraft was not the most stable plane and was difficult for a novice pilot to master. In the hands of an expert, the inherent instability was an asset, making it highly maneuverable.

Ike had been thoroughly briefed on its idiosyncrasies during his checkout by Monsieur DuBois the day before. He fell in love with the plane on his first flight and put it through many a stressful maneuver. Few planes could dive as fast as the SPAD, and it didn't have any of the structural weaknesses exhibited by other contemporary aircraft, especially the Nieuports. The SPAD took some getting used to, but after three hours in the air on Saturday, Ike felt at home and was anxious to get back to Toul.

He already missed Agnes, and he had put his father on the train to La Harve early Saturday morning and that night had been great, as he had spent the whole evening with Agnes. They had dinner and went to a show and then went dancing. Ike admitted to himself that he was more in love with Agnes than before. She was beautiful.

Agnes had told Ike that she had lost her two older brothers to the war and was wary of any firm commitments, and so she had artfully held Ike somewhat at arm's length, but Ike knew she was in love with him too, though she never admitted it. He would frequently catch her staring at him when she'd think he wouldn't notice, and she would catch hold of his hand whenever they were walking. There were other subtle indications that convinced him of her love.

After running the engine up to 1800 rpm and completing the magneto check, Ike gave the thumbs-up signal, and the ground crew motioned for Ike to start his taxi for takeoff. While wending his way to the takeoff end of the airfield, he checked his map to determine his departure heading for Toul. As he approached the grass runway, he checked for other traffic and then swung the plane into the wind. The low throb of the dual exhaust pipes sent chills down Ike's spine. When the plane was facing into the wind, he made one last visual check of the aircraft controls and instruments, then firmly and deliberately pushed the throttle full forward.

The engine came instantly to life with a deafening, throaty roar and the aircraft began moving forward, slowly at first. The speed increased quickly, and soon the tail was off the ground. A little backpressure on the control stick, and Ike was airborne. He initiated a gentle turn to the westerly heading that would take him to Toul.

There was a low overcast so Ike climbed to 500 meters, where he established normal cruise at 480 meters, and was soon on his way home. His power setting of 2250 RPMs gave him an indicated airspeed of 112 mph.

In less than two hours, Ike was circling the Toul Aerodrome. The flight had been uneventful—he hadn't seen another plane until the mains made contact with the grass runway.

He quickly taxied to parking and as he was clambering out of the cockpit, he saw Captain Wortham approach the plane from the operations shack.

"How'd you like the SPAD?"

"Its great, sir! I sort of hate to give it up."

"Well, you might not have to. We have it here for evaluation and I just received five new pilots and three aircraft. I'm giving you the SPAD and one of the new guys will get your Nieuport."

"With the SPAD I'll shoot every German out of the sky. Thanks, Captain."

Captain Wortham patted him on the back. "I'll hold you to that promise."

Three Nieuports pulled up next to the SPAD and shut down their engines. Frank and Jon were two of the pilots, and the third pilot was a young man Ike didn't know, one of the new pilots fresh from the states, a Bill Summers. They all gathered around the SPAD, admiring it as Ike explained some of its characteristics as compared to the Nieuports.

As they started for the debriefing room, Captain Wortham said, "Gentlemen, some news reached us late this afternoon that I think you'll be interested in. Von Richthofen has been shot down and killed late today."

"The infamous Red Baron?" Frank asked.

Captain Wortham nodded. "The very same, he's been a scourge to Allied pilots for a long time. We estimate he's downed 70 to 80 aircraft."

Trench Warfare

Jake was getting used to these come-and-go raids. They were exciting to him in some morbid way, but they also frightened him. There were the inevitable casualties that resulted from their little forays across no-man's-land. He faced death or injury each time, but he enjoyed defeating death, and every time he returned to his own trench, he rejoiced. Lieutenant Jacobson was becoming a soldier's, soldier and had won the admiration of his platoon.

In the early hours of May 3, he walked up and down the trench, getting "his boys" ready for yet another raid on the enemy line. At exactly 3:58 a.m., the cannons began the box barrage around the Boche positions at Bois des Chiens. Upon receiving the word, the second platoon left their trenches and headed out into no-man's-land.

The thunder of artillery was tremendous as the Germans tried to pinpoint the advancing troops. Jake ran to the head of the platoon and urged the men on. The Germans found the range and shells were bursting in their midst, but miraculously there were no casualities in the Second Platoon.

Upon reaching the enemy defensive position, the doughboys spread out along their sector of the line in order to make contact with the flanking platoons. They searched all of the bunkers in their section of the trench and found only an overcoat and a couple of candles that were still burning. This indicated to Jake that the Boche were caught by surprise and had made a hasty retreat to their second line of defense.

"There are no Heinies here! Get the men ready to go back, Sergeant!"

"Yes Lieutenant. I think everyone got here, but I'll have 'em look close for any casualties on the return trip," the sergeant said as he started up the trench line.

The return was without injury, and soon the entire platoon was accounted for and safely in their own trenches.

Jake sat back to catch his breath and thought of Pat and Hank. "Sure glad the artillery is there to save our butts," he said to the sergeant.

Major Donnaldson came into the bunker. "Jake, Captain Hammonds has been wounded. I need you to take over the company."

"Me? Why me? You got other lieutenants with more time in grade. I just made first lieutenant last month."

"You're the one I want, Jake. I need a man I can count on."

Jake took a deep breath. "Well, I hope I don't let you down. How's the captain? Can I see him before they take him to the hospital?"

Major Donnaldson shook his head and rubbed his eyes. "He's not real good, Jake. His left leg is gone, just below the knee, and he's lost a lot of blood. They've got him at the aide station now. I don't think he knows his condition so just be positive."

"I'll go over right away, sir!"

"When you're through, come and see me and I'll bring you up to speed on everything."

"Yes, sir," Jake responded with a salute. Then the major was gone.

"Lieutenant, I'd like to shake your hand," said his sergeant, who was standing nearby and had overheard the conversation. "If anybody deserves a promotion, it's you."

Jake took off his helmet and scratched his head, lost in thought. "Thanks, Sergeant," he said absentmindedly as he took the sergeant's hand.

For two weeks, Ike flew three patrols a day. Dawn patrol was the first and his favorite, for at that time the air was normally clear and smooth. There was a certain detachment he felt when flying above the earth alone, almost as if he were an alien observer viewing the crazy earthlings in all of their madness. No matter the aircraft Ike was in, he always felt exhilarated, and felt this sense of power and separation whenever he was airborne.

The more Ike flew the SPAD, the more he loved the machine, but it took some getting used to. It was heavier on the controls than the Nieuport and if mishandled it would quickly let the pilot know it. The stall developed rapidly and if the rudder wasn't managed properly, she would roll over on the wing where the rudder was depressed and go into a spin. Once the spin developed, the nose-down was at an extreme angle of 70 to 80 degrees. The characteristics of recovery, once properly initiated, would bring the plane quickly to straight and level flight. However, if the pilot misused the recovery technique, he could spin on into the ground or overstress the airframe in the pullout from the resulting dive. Recovery took opposite rudder to stop the turn and then sharp and rapid forward pressure on the joystick in order to break the stall.

All in all, this pursuit ship was faster and could outdive and outclimb anything Ike had ever flown, and he was ready to test it against any plane the Boche had in their inventory. He hadn't yet fired a shot at a German aircraft, and for that matter saw few enemy planes. He was anxious for a fight, but the opportunity had not yet presented itself. The main job of the squadron was to support ground troops and fly cover for the bombers, which flew frequent sorties behind the German lines.

Most mornings, Frank and Ike would go on patrol before dawn. Usually the eastern horizon was beginning to show light when they broke ground. They flew along their side of the line for an hour or so and then returned to the aerodrome for breakfast, and then a second takeoff before noon for another patrol along the front. They would fly the last mission in the late afternoon, generally in support of the ground troops or as air cover for the DeHavilland DH4 or Brequet bombers.

Jon, the third member of the trio, had contracted a bad case of influenza in late April and was in the hospital for over a week. On May 8 he was finally well enough to rejoin the squadron and the three took off for his first patrol since returning from the hospital at 5:00 a.m. on the tenth of May, heading for the line.

The weather was not ideal. There was an unbroken layer of low stratus clouds at 1000 meters and numerous showers throughout the area. The visibility was about six to eight miles and it was still quite dark, even after sunrise.

Ike never felt comfortable with night flying—with an engine out you took potluck on where you landed. Fences and power or telephone lines were impossible to see. Low-level flying was even more treacherous on dark, moonless nights, as hills and buildings were difficult to make out until maybe it was too late. Flying inadvertently into the clouds at night was another hazard.

As a rule, the planes that made up the dawn patrol quickly climbed to altitudes of approximately 5000 meters. At that vantage point, the horizon was usually visible early on, soon followed by the sun. This particular morning, the flight climbed to just 500 meters and headed towards the front. Ike was in the lead, with Jon off to his left and Frank to his right. They flew a tight V formation but when Ike glanced over both his right and left shoulders, he could barely make out the Nieuports. By the time they reached their patrol zone, the sun had risen enough so that the surroundings were at least visible. Ike looked down and noticed that all of the low spots in the landscape were covered with ground fog.

During these low overcast days, the Allied patrols would stay below the clouds, looking for German observation aircraft that would also stay below the clouds in order to observe French positions and movements. As the planes approached the line, Ike started a gentle climb that eventually put the flight at the very base of the cloud layer. The bottoms of the clouds were very ragged and the planes were constantly in and out of the haze, always low enough to see the ground but difficult to be seen from below.

They flew along their patrol zone for more than an hour. As they turned for home, Ike was beginning to feel a little let down again; he'd hoped to find the enemy this day.

Suddenly, and as if by the mere power of his wish, he spotted a Boche Rumpler, a two-seat biplane, about a mile west of his position and two to three hundred meters below. It appeared that the crew of the Boche craft had not seen Ike or the others. The pilot was in the front seat, close to the upper wing. The observer was stationed in the rear cockpit, manning a single-barrel machine gun.

Ike scanned the sky and didn't see any other enemy airplanes. He quickly signaled to Frank and Jon to stay at this altitude, and that he was going in for the kill. They both waggled their wings in response and Ike rolled the SPAD over on its back and pulled the joystick back into his lap. The nose quickly pulled through the horizon, and when the plane passed vertical he added right aileron and rudder. In a few seconds he was diving at his victim, flying a heading that was approximately 200 degrees from his previous course.

In the dive, the pursuit quickly gained speed, the engine screaming and the wind of the slipstream rushing over the windscreen and past his helmeted head. His ship was upright when he saw the Rumpler in his sights. The SPAD was approaching the Rumpler nearly head-on, about 20 degrees off of its nose to its starboard side.

The observer in the German observation plane spotted the SPAD before Ike was close enough to fire his guns. This man tapped the shoulder of the pilot and pointed in the direction of the onrushing plane. The pilot looked up at Ike as the observer swung his gun around and began firing at the SPAD.

Ike could see the tracers coming towards him at an apparent curved trajectory, missing his plane and disappearing off to his left. As Ike was about in range to fire, the pilot of the Rumpler performed a steep left bank and began a rapid turn. Ike pulled the trigger on his twin Vickers and saw the bullets hit the lower left wing of the Rumpler, sending fragments flying.

He continued his dive until he was below the two-seater's altitude. He maneuvered his craft to the same heading as the German's. He looked up and saw the tail of the plane about 200 feet above him, directly off of his nose. He added full power, established a climb, and then pulled the trigger on the guns.

He saw the tracer bullets penetrate the bottom of the Boche plane all along its length. Suddenly there was a large flash of orange as the fuel tank ignited and the plane broke into a thousand pieces and fluttered slowly to earth. As he followed the wreckage down for a few hundred feet, he noticed one large piece in particular, and to his horror realized that it was the observer, who must have jumped free before the explosion. Ike's last image was this man shaking his fist at him as he fell to his death.

The battle had taken Ike's aircraft out over the line, beyond no-man's-land, to the enemy's side. Soon after what remained of the Rumpler hit the ground, Frank and Jon joined Ike. Frank was so excited about the victory; he flew all sorts of aerobatics around Ike's plane—slow rolls, loops, and snap rolls. During this demonstration, the German antiaircraft fire began exploding in their midst. Ike quickly signaled the others to follow and he headed back towards their base.

Finally, Ike was a true combatant in this war, credited with his first enemy plane, but the mental picture of the falling observer was a picture that would not soon leave him.

There was a raucous celebration that evening. The beer and wine flowed freely. There had been a rigid pecking order established in the squadron. The lowest in the line were the Vultures, the newly arrived replacements that were without aircraft, waiting for someone to become a casualty or the arrival of new planes. Once this recruit got a plane, he became a Buzzard. On this day Buzzard Dennison became a Goffer, and to mark this promotion, he was required to down a liter of champagne in the mess while singing the squadron's fight song.

As time passed, the men of the Kicking Mule Squadron encountered an ever-increasing number of enemy aircraft. The 95th held their ground during these encounters, but pilots from both sides were being shot down. The losses were mounting in wounded, captured and killed. The fun of flying had turned deadly, and Ike regarded it now as a grim business. Soon, the celebrations over a pilot's first victory became more subdued.

Ike's flying skills continually improved. He developed a killer's instinct and a lethal style when in combat. He never fired his guns until he was up close to his victim, and never wasted his ammunition.

On the thirtieth of May, he became separated from the remainder of his squadron, which had been on a bomber escort mission far behind the German lines. As he was headed west for home, he came upon an enemy aerodrome where two enemy Albatrosses were in the process of taking off. From his altitude he throttled back and established a glide down over the runway and quickly fell in behind the last of the two fighters, as they became airborne.

He pushed the throttle full forward and closed the gap between himself and his victim. At fifty meters, he pulled the trigger and saw the bullets penetrate the Albatross, which quickly burst into flames. It rolled to the right and dove to the ground. The pilot of the first plane saw the wreckage of his companion and started evasive maneuvers to escape Ike's attack. Ike continued to close the distance, but before he could fire at his victim, his plane was racked with ground fire. He heard a loud crack in the center section of the lower wing and realized his plane had been severely damaged.

He quickly broke off the engagement and headed towards home. Ike nursed his plane back to Toul, fearing every moment that the wings would collapse. He toyed with the idea of setting it down, but he was on the Boche side of the line and that meant almost certain capture, or worse. Finally, he saw the front just ahead and cut his power to a glide, losing altitude until he crossed the trenches. This took the Boche by surprise and few shots were fired at him. Over no-man's-land, he gradually pushed the throttle back to cruise power and continued for home.

After what seemed an eternity, he saw the aerodrome and made a long, low approach and landed. When he pulled into his parking spot on the line, he took a long, deep breath and climbed out of the cockpit to inspect the damage. He and his chief mechanic found that the main spar had been hit by a light cannon shell and was close to collapsing.

He acted nonchalant about the event, but silently thanked God for his good fortune.

At daybreak Battery F ceased their fire. When the guns were cleaned and oiled, Pat went to his bunk and slept soundly, even though his ears were still ringing from the thunder of the cannon.

The trading of fire had continued day after day. On May 9, the number two cannon was moved forward to a place midway between Reherrey and Migneville, to lay down a molesting barrage on Boche supply lines that moved along the Ancerviller-Barbas road, a point where ammunition trains traversed to bring supplies to the Germans. The gun was moved in order to prevent the Boche from pinpointing the normal gun emplacements through the use of sound-ranging equipment. This can result when the cannons are fired at a slow, steady rate over a long period, the sound gear can eventually zero in on the cannon's coordinates and counter the fire fairly precisely.

On the tenth, the gun was brought back to the emplacement.

May 12 dawned a cloudy and rainy day. After early duties were performed, the normal activities were suspended during the morning in honor of Mother's Day. All the men of the battery were urged to write home.

Pat and Hank suddenly got busy in the afternoon, installing the new aiming stake lights that arrived after lunch, but the monotony of the trenches soon set in again. Each day there were duties to perform, and few of the men were even aware of what day of the week it was.

Different pieces from the battery would take turns and go to the forward position every so often to fire on the enemy lines of supply. New loads of lumber were brought in to be used in the construction of the new position.

On May 21, a disabled enemy plane made a forced landing not far from the battery, near Migneville. Sergeant Baker, who was the closest to the site at the time of the incident, brought the two intrepid airmen into Rherrey at gunpoint. For this, he was credited with their capture, though it was evident that the aviators were not going to resist and somehow seemed relieved that they were out of the war.

On May 23, the first and third guns were taken to Cheneviers, some fourteen kilometers west, for general overhauling. Pat went along to watch the ordnance team work on them. At the end of the day, after dark, they returned to the position.

As the days drifted by, it was becoming apparent that the intensity of the fighting was increasing. On May 26, the cannoneers of Battery F watched helplessly as Battery B, off to their left about 300 yards, was pounded for three hours with gas and high explosive shells. Six men, including the battery commander, were hospitalized.

Late that same evening the trenches of the Ohio and New York infantry regiments were inundated with gas in what was called a projector attack. There were reports that the doughboys suffered more than 400 causalities.

On May 27, at exactly one a.m., the Boche subjected the whole sector to heavy shelling using both high explosive shells and a lot of gas. At 1:05, the gas alarms resounded throughout the area and the troops quickly donned their gas slickers and masks. This bombardment continued on into the early daylight hours and ended shortly before sunrise, just as suddenly as it had begun.

Later in the day, Pat, Hank, and the other members of the battery at the emplacement witnessed a burning enemy plane, disabled by antiaircraft fire trying to fly back to its own lines.

"I don't think they're going to make it," Pat yelled to Sergeant Martyn.

At that instant, the pilot lost control and the plane did a slow roll over onto its back and dived straight down. The pilot made one last frantic effort to avoid disaster and raised the nose of the aircraft so that it dove into the ground at about a twenty-five-degree angle.

"Look, something fell out!" yelled Hank.

"That was the observer, he jumped just before impact," Pat yelled back as all three of them ran to the burning wreckage. Others who had witnessed the crash soon joined them.

When they got there, the craft was engulfed in flames and there was nothing anyone could do for the occupants. The pilot had been severely wounded in the head and the impact had in all probability killed them both. Soon they were burned beyond recognition.

The whole scene sickened Pat. He knew he was there to kill Germans, but these were men probably no older than he. He couldn't imagine the horrible pain of burning to death. It was an unthinkable way to die. He tried to avert his eyes from the sight, but even then, the mental picture of these poor men, was seared into his brain.

As he turned and walked away from the gruesome wreckage, some of the others were picking up souvenirs—pieces of fabric, wood and metal. Sergeant Martyn noted that the tires were American made, by the Republic Company. Soon the MPs arrived and cordoned off the area and ushered the men back to the position. The fear of the regimental commanders was that the Boche would soon start dropping a number of rounds on the scene of the crash and kill or wound many of the cannoneers.

It took awhile for Pat to shake the image of the two dead airmen. This was the first close-up view he had of the ravages of war. This first hand view of the violence of war made him shiver each time he thought of it, and the visions of the wreckage were frequent.

On May 30, the men of the battery endured yet another medical inspection to determine if any of them had contracted venereal disease, but all tested negative.

"Who had the time or opportunity to be promiscuous?" Paul asked the doctor.

This exam was followed by a band concert in Reherrey, but this diversion was soon interrupted by another artillery attack all along the front.

The activity was continually increasing. German aircraft were constantly patrolling over the line. Lieutenant Case was concerned that the position would soon be pinpointed by enemy artillery and thus ordered the guns forward to the yet unfinished new position on June 2.

That evening four caissons and four limbers came forward and the whole battery pitched in to move the ammunition and cannon. By midnight, the guns were placed and the shells were safely stacked in the abris.

Rumors were that the 149th would be leaving the front soon. No one knew where they were going or when, but it would be soon.

Shortly before one in the morning on June 6, Pat, along with Hank and Paul, were standing rocket guard in the forward lookout position. Pat was daydreaming about going back to school and all of the activities he was missing. The other two were asleep in the bunker.

Suddenly, he saw flashes of many cannon from the German side of the line. The thunder and roar of the cannon filled the air just before the first shells landed, one not far behind where Pat was standing. He quickly yanked the rope tied around Paul's foot and yelled for them to come out.

After the impact of the first salvo from the enemy guns, he saw rockets go up from the American lines, calling for barrage 13. He picked up the phone and called telephone central in Reherrey and reported the signal.

Paul was at his side within a minute. "What's going on?"

"Looks like a big raid in our sector. Keep your eyes peeled for more rockets." The first salvo of return fire came from Battery F.

"Man, F Battery got the guns going real fast," Paul said somewhat in awe.

"That's the advantage of keeping them loaded at night."

"Yeah, but don't let Colonel Reilly find out, or we're all in big trouble."

The wailing of the gas klaxons could be heard all around them. Soon, rifle and machine gun fire could be heard up and down the front.

"Can't a man sleep in peace?" Hank said sleepily as he stumbled out of the dugout into the trench.

"Get your gas mask on!" Pat ordered, and all three struggled into the clumsy apparatus.

In a short while, Hank lifted his mask and smelling nothing but clean air, motioned to the others to take theirs off. The gas seemed to be concentrated on the trenches.

"That's better," Paul replied.

At that moment, Pappy came into the lookout trench and took control of the phone.

"Have you men seen Baker?"

"No, sir, he hasn't been here," Pat said.

"He took off after me and I lost track coming up here. Hope to hell he didn't get hit by one of the incoming. Littler, go see if you can find him, and be careful."

"Yes, sir!" Pat started out of the trench just as the first sergeant sauntered up the hill.

"We were just going out to look for your remains," Pappy stated matter-of-factly. "Thought one of those German 105s got you!"

"I had to stop and lace up my boots. Those bastards couldn't hit the broad side of' a barn if'n they had to!" Baker replied calmly.

At the rocket guard post the shells from both sides once again whistled overhead. The noise of battle was too loud to talk without shouting, so the five men stood and watched the show without speaking, except when a rocket was spotted. Then Pappy would get on the phone and inform headquarters. An occasional shell would land nearby causing them to duck for cover—with the exception of Lieutenant Allen and Sergeant Baker, who didn't even flinch or look up.

By daybreak, the barrage was over and all five walked back to the emplacement, noting the extensive new network of shell holes all around.

On June 9th, Lieutenant Case ordered that all digging tools be returned to the supply company located in Gelacourt. This was done without complaint and not a man voiced a single objection for not having to dig and move rock anymore.

It was also on the ninth that the 149th was hit hard by the Spanish influenza, a short-lived but painful three-day strain of flu. If not treated promptly, it could develop into a more serious ailment. Each day, more men got sick and were sent off to the hospital. On the eleventh, Battery F had no fewer than twenty-five men hospitalized.

By the fourteenth, a call went out for extra cannoneers, though some of the first to fall to the disease were beginning to return. The rumor that the Rainbow would be leaving the Baccarrat Sector soon became more persistent. Those who had been hospitalized became alarmed by the rumor. If the 149th moved out before they recovered, they might not be able to rejoin their battery.

On June 19, the men who had been incapacitated by the flu were beginning to return in large numbers from the field hospital. On that day, the last day that the 149th was at the Baccarrat front, the four cannon fired 634 rounds into the enemy trenches. At midnight, the First Platoon of F battery was ordered to leave.

On June 20, the Second Platoon and all the rest of the 149th assembled at Azerailles and marched the 31 kilometers to Damas aux Bois. Some of the gunners remained behind for a day to turn the emplacement over to the French regiment that filled the positions formally occupied by the 149th Field Artillery.

The 61st French Division and the 77th American National Army Division from New York were relieving the Rainbow Division.

Belleau Woods

Clint Phelps sat in his room in the hotel trying to put the story together. The US had finally seen its first major action in the war at a place called Belleau Woods.

Belleau Woods was a small stand of trees about five miles northwest of Chateau-Thierry and bordered on the southeast by the Lucy-le-Bocage - Bouresches road. The Germans had occupied most of the wood and the entire small village of Bouresches. They were continuing their spring offensive and were still driving south and threatening Luce-le-Bocage.

By American standards this was just a small stand of trees, about 1 square mile in size and when viewed from the air the woods were irregular in shape. Belleau Woods had been under the care of a forester for many generations and all underbrush had been cut away. The trees were tall and slender, and were so densely spaced that one could scarcely see six or seven meters into them.

The ground was littered with large rocks and boulders and deeply scarred with crags and gullies. It provided perfect cover for the German defenders, who had set up scores of machine guns arranged in supporting fields of fire.

The American 2nd Division had been eager to show the world what they were made of. Even though this division was a conglomerate consisting of both army and marine brigades, it was considered an elite unit. Getting to Belleau Wood had been a race to reinforce the line. If the Germans broke through and took the village of Lucy-le-Bocage, the Boche would be just 45 miles or less from Paris.

The division was transported to the area by approximately 1000 trucks running at top speed both day and night. They passed through the edge of Paris and on through many nameless villages to get to the line in order to stem the German advance.

Paris had been apprehensive all week, as many feared the Germans would be in the city before long. Some Parisians had already given up and left.

Clint, always in search of a story, had hitched a ride in Paris on one of the trucks. He recalled how the boys of the division acted. It seemed as if they were going to a ball game instead of to the war. They stuck their legs out of the trucks and laughed and joked. The weather was hot and dry and the sun beat down on the troops in their open trucks that kicked up great clouds of dust from the dry roadbed. The French were delighted by these brash American boys and waved and cheered them on as they sped past. New life had come to France, a country that had nearly bled to death after four years of war. The confidence of these American troops lifted the spirits of the French and gave them new hope.

As soon as the division arrived, they were rushed into the line just south of the wood to fight under the command of Major General Jean Degoutte of the Twenty-first French Corps. Clint remembered that the French, discouraged and beaten, had advised the Americans to start digging a trench line. The American officers answered, "Trenches are for defending! We intend to attack."

And attack they did. At 3:45 a.m. on June 6, they went over the top. Their objective was to take hill 142, high ground just north and west of the American line used by the Boche for observation. They were soon faced with a withering machine gun fire from the Boche in the woods.

The soldiers hit the ground and the attack would have stopped had it not been for Marine Captain Hamilton of the 49th Company. He ran along the line and got the men up and moving toward their objective. They rushed forward with fixed bayonets charging the enemy, many of who surrendered, while the rest retreated with the main body of troops or otherwise perished at the hands of the Americans.

The situation was critical all morning, with the Germans counterattacking several times. These attacks were beaten off and finally, by noon, the Americans held hill 142. At 2:15 the division commander, a General Harboard, ordered another assault. The objective this time was to take the southern edge of Belleau Wood and the village of Bouresches. Zero hour was to be 5:00 p.m.

Hill 142 had been relatively easy to take compared to what awaited the Marines and doughboys in the woods. The attack was to come in an arc running around the woods' southern edge. Between the Marines and the woods lay a wheat field about one quarter of a mile wide. At 5:00 p.m. the troops started to advance in four ranks about 60 feet apart, one behind the other. When the first rank was close to the halfway point, all hell broke loose. Machine gun bullets scythed the thigh-deep wheat sending the soldiers to the ground.

A fellow journalist, Floyd Gibbons of the *Chicago Tribune*, had been at the scene of the battle since morning. He had started across the wheat field behind the fourth rank during the evening attack and had been severely wounded. He had been with the Sixth Marine Regiment when they went over the top at exactly five o'clock. They were swept with machine gun fire and increased artillery. Gibbons tried to follow the men into the field, but was hit in the arm and face before he reached his goal. He was retrieved later and was in remarkably good condition despite a bullet that had gone through his left eye and crashed through his forehead.

Clint had stopped to see Floyd Gibbons in the hospital before returning to Paris. He found him in much better shape than he had imagined and somewhat talkative. Clint consoled him a short time before returning to Paris.

Clint could still hear the sound of the battle in his mind. The terrific clash had been numbing. He still remembered the sight of one battalion as it marched across the wheat field in attack formation into the sweep of the machine guns. The causalities were heavy but they continued to advance to the wood.

June 6, 1918 proved to be the worst day in Marine Corps history— their losses, 1087 killed and wounded, were more than the corps had lost since its inception, 143 years earlier.

It had now been a week since the battle and all-important objectives had been secured. Still, minor skirmishes were being fought and would probably continue for some time. Small as this action had been, it could be viewed as an important victory for this American division and for the Allies. This battle came as a turning point in the German spring offensives, for they would not get any closer to Paris. Clint felt certain that the Allies would soon start on their own offensive. The reckless courage of the Americans struck a strong note of fear in the hearts of the German defenders. The German high command had to know that there were close to one million Americans already in France and another million on the way. These were fresh, high-spirited troops, trained and ready to do battle. The Germans who had been captured had called the marines *Teufelhunden* or "devil dogs", a sort of backhanded compliment.

Though the skirmish at Belleau Woods was small when compared to the entire Western Front, the Americans proved one thing—they knew how to fight and were here with a vengeance.

Shortly after Ike scored his second air combat victory, he developed an ear infection that kept him on the ground for a little over two weeks.

It was during this time that he received two letters from his mother telling him how impossible it would be for him to marry a French girl and bring her to America to live. She tried to say in a tactful way that wartime conditions can throw two lives together that otherwise never would have been compatible if conditions had been normal.

Ike was a little chagrined by his mother's tone. She had never interfered before, and now she was trying to tell him what he could or could not do with his life. He wondered what his father had told her. He thought that his dad had liked Agnes. He was more convinced than ever that Agnes was the one for him, the one with whom he wanted to spend the rest of his life.

As the days passed he became very anxious to get back to his flying, so he wouldn't have time to just sit around and worry. True, Captain Wortham had him doing a great deal of paperwork for the squadron, but that was boring and led his mind to wandering, usually to thoughts about Agnes and his mother's rejection of the only girl he had ever truly loved. He continued his daily letters to Agnes, but didn't mention that his mother disapproved of their relationship.

During the time that Ike was grounded, Frank got his first confirmed victory on June 8, and Jon Nelson scored a probable on June 10.

When Ike finally was able to resume his flying, things were beginning to heat up for the American participants in the air. Their losses were beginning to climb as more and more new pilots arrived at the combat squadrons. The number of bombing raids behind the German lines were increasing and taking the pilots ever further into enemy territory.

On June 17, Ike finally got back in the air. The flight surgeon wanted him to start slowly to be sure his ears could take the altitude changes without suffering undue pain. For the first few days he flew local, low-level patrols, primarily to check out how he felt in the air and to see if his left ear could withstand the pressure difference at altitude. His first time above 5000 meters was painful until his ear popped and the pressure equalized; then he wasn't bothered anymore and was soon back to his old self, ready for regular patrol work.

During the rest of June the activity was routine, morning patrols and bomber escort flights. There were few encounters with enemy planes. They saw the enemy at great distances, but seldom ended up in dogfights.

Finally, on July 1, Ike, Jon and Frank were on an early morning patrol along the line, cruising at 6000 meters, when they were jumped by a flight of seven Boche Albatross biplanes.

The enemy dove out of the early morning sun, coming upon the three Americans, off and behind the right side of the flight. Ike had kept a sharp lookout for German planes, as his patrol had penetrated a number of kilometers behind the front lines. But on this day there wasn't a cloud in the sky and the enemy had planned their attack carefully, diving upon their victims with the sun directly at their backs.

All three of them were unaware of the German's presence until Jon received the machine gun fire through his engine compartment and fuel tank. Fortunately, there was no fire. Each plane broke away from the tight formation they'd been flying. Ike rolled left over on his back and pulled on the control column that brought him through a half loop and upright, facing the opposite direction. This maneuver placed him in the very advantageous position of being on the tail of one of the attackers.

This plane had flown below the Americans and performed a steeply banked turn to the left. Recognizing his unfortunate position, the Boche aviator started maneuvering frantically. This enemy pilot was good and twisted and turned in a desperate way trying to shake his pursuer.

Ike stuck on his tail, twisting and turning with his prey. He fired short bursts with his guns whenever the enemy plane crossed his sights. Down and down they went, twisting, turning ever closer to the ground.

Ike knew it was just a matter of time and he'd have his third victory. The Albatross could not outclimb the SPAD and had a little wider turning radius.

The cat and mouse game continued for what seemed like hours. Suddenly, the Boche pilot made a fatal error when he maneuvered to avoid an outcrop of rocks along a shimmering stream. Ike anticipated his steep right turn. When the plane fell under his guns, it was a mere 25 meters away. He saw the tracers penetrate the back of the cockpit and sweep forward into the fuel tank and engine. The pilot slumped over the control stick and the plane shuddered and dove headfirst into the ground.

Ike completed his tight turn to the right and proceeded in a low pass over the wreckage. He saw no movement. Quickly, he scanned the area to get his bearings and check for other enemy aircraft.

He felt no remorse, and was rather elated over his victory. His joy was only momentary, though, as he caught sight of a Nieuport desperately weaving in and around little stands of trees, trying to avoid the fire of another Albatross in hot pursuit. The aircraft were about two kilometers off to Ike's left.

He applied backpressure to the stick and pushed the throttle full forward. The resulting climb took him rapidly to 200 meters. A gentle left turn put him in a position directly over the maneuvering Nieuport, whose engine was leaving a trail of thick, black smoke. Ike reduced power and slowed to a near stall, and the Albatross appeared from under his right lower wing.

Again he jammed the throttle full forward and released the backpressure on the controls. The SPAD lurched forward and down in a steep right turn. The airspeed increased rapidly amidst the scream of the engine and the bracing wires.

In no time, he was hot on the tail of the German, who had no idea that he had become the pursued, so intent was he on gunning down the Nieuport. Ike coolly brought his aircraft into position, and when the Boche crossed his sights he pulled the trigger. He saw his tracer's spray across the upper right wing, near the fuselage, which then suddenly folded upward. The plane turned on its right side and spun into the ground.

He quickly pulled alongside the stricken Nieuport. It was Jon. He appeared wounded but waved his thanks meekly. Ike continued to fly alongside Jon, who appeared to be in great pain. By this time, they had flown at least 15 kilometers behind the lines.

Jon nursed his stricken aircraft along as best he could. He was unable to gain altitude and they were no more than 30 meters above the ground.

Ike kept a lookout for other planes and flew to the right and a little above Jon. He had no idea where Frank was; he just hoped that he was safe. His concern now was to protect his squadron mate and get him safely home.

As this thought crossed his mind, the Nieuport's engine quit. The plane quickly sunk into a small clearing in the trees. The initial touchdown was good. Jon controlled the plane well, but the roll was too long and the main gear fell into a small culvert and the ship flipped over on its back.

Ike pulled up in a wing over, and dived back down over the wreckage. He could see Jon hanging upside down from his seat belt and detected some movement; his friend was still alive. He flew over the area and around the wreckage, looking for a place to land. His only thought was to fly Jon to safety.

He saw a field less than 100 meters away, and flew low over it looking for any unexpected hazards, then climbed to 100 meters and began a downwind approach. Opposite his touchdown zone, he cut the power and turned on a short base leg. It was here that he noticed some enemy troops approaching Jon's plane on foot, about two and a half to three kilometers away.

Ike turned left on his final approach. He slowed the plane by slightly raising the nose with backpressure. Next, he applied full right rudder and full left aileron, and slipped the aircraft over the trees at the approach end of the field.

Once he cleared the trees, he slowed the plane by adding a little more backpressure to the control column while releasing the other control pressures. The plane sank quickly and landed hard on the mains and tailskid. He was close to a stall when he touched down, making the landing roll short.

After the SPAD had slowed, Ike applied full right rudder and a burst of power, and taxied back to the approach end of the field, where he again turned around into the wind. He reduced the power to idle, released his seat belt, and clambered out. He left the engine running on purpose, as he needed to make a fast getaway.

He found a couple of rocks and placed them under the wheels to prevent the craft from rolling, then sprinted through the hedgerow and to the adjoining field. Jon's plane lay on its back just a few meters away.

As Ike approached the aircraft, it suddenly burst into flames and his heart sunk to the pit of his stomach, for he knew he couldn't reach Jon in time. He ran to the burning Nieuport, around the tail to the other side, and to his great joy saw that Jon was lying to the side out of danger. Jon had released his seat belts and dropped to the ground and crawled to safety.

Ike ran to him and helped him to his feet. Jon was badly wounded and bleeding profusely.

"Can you walk?"

"I don't think so."

"Here, put your arm over my shoulder and lean on me. We have to hurry as there's some Jerries a short distance away."

Ike practically had to drag Jon back to the SPAD. Jon didn't complain, but Ike could feel him wince in pain. When they reached the SPAD, Ike sat Jon on the lower left wing near the junction with the fuselage.

"Start climbing aboard while I remove the chocks, I'm going to have to sit on you. This would be a great place to have two seats, but we don't, and there's no other way."

Ike crawled under the wing and removed the rocks. He then went to the wing and helped Jon into the cockpit. After sitting as gingerly as he could on Jon, he smoothly applied full throttle. The plane started to move slowly at first. As it picked up speed, he pushed the stick forward in order to raise the tail off the ground. Once the tailskid was up, Ike could feel the plane gain speed.

He brought the tail up so the aircraft was in a normal cruise attitude, streamlined to the wind. The trees were looming ever larger and ever closer. He soon reached flying speed, but kept the plane on the ground till he reached his best rate of climb, then pulled back on the control stick.

As the SPAD climbed, Ike focused his full concentration on clearing the trees. Everything seemed to be happening in slow motion. There was a moment he wasn't sure they were going to make it, and then the plane hit a slight updraft, just allowing the wheels to brush the top branches, and they were clear. Suddenly Ike realized that enemy troops were firing their rifles at the plane.

When they were safely above the trees and out of rifle range of the enemy troops, Ike took a big gulp of air and tried to settle down and catch his breath. His heart was racing and he suddenly felt overwhelmed by the events of this past hour. A lot had happened in a very short time.

"Jon, are you doing all right?" Ike yelled over the roar of the engine and slipstream. He tried to look over his shoulder at Jon, but couldn't see his face.

Jon stretched out his left arm and gave a thumbs-up sign, then passed out.

Ike kept the throttle full forward. He had to get his friend to the hospital. He saw no other aerial activity and though the time passed slowly for Ike, he was back at the aerodrome within twenty minutes.

Flying the plane in such an elevated stance, sitting on Jon's lap, made control handling sloppy. He approached the field from straight in and landed, bouncing before he was able to get it to stick on the ground. He taxied to the parking area and shut the engine off, then gingerly stepped out of the cockpit.

Jon was unconscious and Ike yelled to his ground crew to go get an ambulance.

"Hang in there, buddy," he said, squeezing Jon's hand. As he looked up, he saw Frank's plane land.

To the Champagne

After leaving the Baccarrat front, the 149th Field Artillery marched rapidly to the small town of Damas aux Bois about 10 kilometers south and west of the old battery position, and here they stayed for three days. This time was spent taking inventory of equipment and readying for the move to Chalon-sur-Marne.

It was in Damas the men learned that the Rainbow was now considered an elite fighting division and would be classified in the category of "shock troops." The Rainbow, as a result, would be sent from front to front where the fighting was heaviest. All members of the battery were excited by the prospect of moving to the active sectors, though somewhat apprehensive about what the future would hold.

In the meantime, off-duty hours were spent resting and sightseeing. During the evening hours, boxing matches and band concerts occupied the time of those not involved in making the rounds of the local beer emporiums.

On Sunday, June 23, they began to finalize their preparations for leaving Damas aux Bois for the trip to the Champagne Sector. After a cold lunch of hardtack and bread, Battery F harnessed and hitched, and soon they were on the road for a short hike to the small burg of Charmes, some 12 kilometers distant. Their route took them through the beautiful Foret de Charmes.

Charmes is where the battery entrained, and at exactly 9:30 p.m. the engine's shrill whistle penetrated the gathering darkness, and the train jolted into motion. With the next mighty heave of the locomotive, they were on their way.

The trip manifest specified 11 officers, 197 enlisted personnel, 180 horses and mules, 2 two-wheeled carts and 24 four-wheeled carriages, requiring 50 railcars.

Throughout the night and early morning the train wound its way to the west and passed through Bayon, Nancy, Toul and Bar-le-duc before arriving at Chalons-sur-Marne at noon the next day. After the train came to a halt, Battery F detrained in 45 minutes, breaking the record set by Battery D the day before. As soon as they gathered their gear and harnessed and hitched the wagons and animals, Battery F was soon on another 10-kilometer hike that would take them to that day's destination, Chepy.

The battery's enlisted men were put up in haylofts after completing the necessary preparations to stay the next four nights. Those who had heretofore escaped the ravages of body lice became aware of what itching was all about, for the haylofts were overrun with cooties.

The Marne canal was located close to the town of Chepy and much of the off-duty time was spent swimming in its cool, clear water. It also provided an opportunity for the men to rid themselves of the vermin that had come to call the warm body of the soldier home. The town also sported a dairy where the men could obtain fresh milk, cream, butter and cheese, a wonderful supplement to their regular diets.

During their second day at Chepy, the mail caught up with the 149th. This was the first mail they'd received in over three weeks, and it was greeted with unrestrained enthusiasm.

Pat looked over his pile of letters from home and decided to read them in chronological order, starting with the oldest, no matter who the writer was.

Hank, on the other hand, pulled all of the letters from Betsy and started with those. They were by far the largest pile, as she had written almost every day. When finished with those, he went back and read most of them again before starting with those from his folks.

"Betsy says she's getting fat and very uncomfortable, but seems to be progressing okay," Hank said. "She's experiencing some pain and the doctor has curtailed almost all of her activities. She's due in the middle of July. Wow, I don't know whether I'm ready to be a father yet or not."

"Oh, you'll do all right. Though I think it'll take some getting use too—late night feedings, crying. You'll just need patience. I got a letter here from my mom." Pat said, his smile suddenly gone. "My dad had another heart attack, but she says he's doing fine. Boy, I'd sure hate not to get the chance to see him again. I always felt my parents would be around forever and here there's a chance I won't get to see them again, and there's nothing I can do about it. We need to finish off this war and go home in a hurry!"

Hank nodded solemnly, "Yeah, I'm with you. I'd like to be with Betsy during her delivery. I'm sorry about your dad. I think I know how you feel. If something happened to Betsy or the baby while we were here, I don't know what I'd do." But both men knew that it would be a long time before either of them would return home.

The duties continued each day, from standing gun drill to cleaning the hardware, pistols, cannons, carriages, and harness. There were always stables to clean, and to top it off, the men had repeated practice in pitching their pup tents in straight lines.

"For the life of me I can't figure out what good this duty is for shock troops," Paul Driscoll said dolefully after a particularly arduous day of duty, one that included too many hours of aligning the pup tents.

Finally, on June 28, the battery harnessed and hitched after a late supper and headed in the direction of Chalons-sur-Marne, approximately nine kilometers to the north. Shortly after midnight, they passed through this town and as they walked down the main street, they were aware that French and American officers were closely monitoring their marching order.

The morning of June 30 dawned clear, and the temperature was in the seventies even before the sun came up. Reveille was at 7:00 a.m. Pat had trouble getting up and wished he could sleep for a little while longer. His back hurt and he hadn't slept well because it was so hot and humid. After all of this time in the army, he still had difficulty sleeping on the ground.

Hank was sound asleep, as usual. He never seemed to hear the bugle.

"Wake up, and get rolling," Pat said as he hit him in the backside with a shoe.

Hank rolled over on his right side and lay still again.

"Come on, Hank, up and at 'em. Remember, we have that big inspection today. And don't forget this is the one-year anniversary of our entry into war service."

"You're kidding, you mean we've been having all of this fun for only one year?" Hank mumbled as he began to move and eventually rise to his knees. "You know, if you didn't remind me I'd have thought I'd been in the artillery all of my life."

They both continued to dress in silence, and soon Pat was out of the tent, stretching and heading for the latrine.

After shaving and washing, Pat ran into Jack and walked with him to the field kitchen. There was no joy in eating. Everyone was grumbling about the food, as it had been the same thing every day for over a month. Their only hope was to go to the kitchen and look for something different. When they arrived, they found nothing new.

"Well, Pat, I'll never get fat in the army!" Jack said as they waited in line for the "slop" they called cereal to be thrown on their tin plates.

"Well, at least we have coffee," someone behind Pat said.

"Is that what that brown liquid is?" another voice added from further on back.

After eating, the men began preparing for the upcoming inspection. All of the equipment, cannon, harnesses, carriages and even the horses were given a beautiful sheen.

At precisely 10:00 a.m. Colonel Reilly and Major Redden arrived at the encampment. Lieutenant Case quickly called the battery into ranks and then to attention.

True to his military training, the colonel did a thorough white glove inspection. All went well until it came to George Duddly, who had joined the battery during the training period at St. Nazaire. The colonel felt that George hadn't "stood close enough to his razor that morning."

"Sir, I didn't have enough time to shave, Sir." Duddly sputtered. "The schedule just didn't allow me time to get completely ready."

For ten minutes the colonel lectured George on the West Point schedule, which did not recognize "lack of time" as a proper excuse under any circumstance. It became Private Duddly's duty from now until "doomsday" to see to it that the bugler would be awakened fifteen minutes earlier each and every morning from here on. "This should provide you and the rest of this battery with ample time to shave. You got that, soldier?"

It quickly became apparent to every member that there was no room for slackers in the 149th Field Artillery. Even though they were approaching the time of battle, military discipline would not be relaxed.

After the inspecting party left and because the colonel had not looked closely at the side arms, Lieutenant Case pulled a surprise pistol inspection of his own, which went very badly on the whole. The weapons were filthy and the men were ordered to clean them within the hour for the next sidearm inspection.

The inspection went better this time, and in the afternoon, passes to Chalon-sur-Marne were issued to those who felt the long trek would prove to be worth their while. In the evening, there was a band concert by the regimental band.

During the intermission the colonel spoke to the men of the war and of the arduous days that lay ahead. "Now that the Rainbow division and particularly the 149th is ready to take the field as an offensive unit, I have no doubt in my mind that our cause will lead to ultimate victory over the Central Powers. But the fact remains that there are still many tough days, weeks, even months ahead. Our goal is total victory. Soon we will be on the offensive, so we must be prepared to fight a war of movement. No longer will we be hiding in trenches. Instead we will be moving forward, only stopping long enough to blast the Huns out of our way."

This statement brought the men of the regiment to their feet cheering, whistling and clapping.

When the colonel was through, Major Redden, the battalion commander addressed the troops and lapsed into an emotional speech about the loved ones the artillerymen had left behind and of their high hopes for the 149th.

On July 3, orders were received in the afternoon. They were to prepare to move to the front. However, before the packing got underway, the orders were rescinded.

That evening Sergeant Martyn called the mechanics together.

"The Rainbow and other selected French divisions are to act as shock troops and we will be sent to the point in the line where the principal German attack is expected. You men get these guns in prime working order. They're going to get a continuous workout.

"Be prepared to move out soon, probably tomorrow."

The next day, July 4, the men were given most of the day off in honor of the independence holiday. However, they first had to complete the stable details. Most of the troops relaxed or participated in baseball games or some other form of athletic endeavor.

At 5:30 p.m. the holiday was declared over and by 9:30 the 149th was harnessed and hitched and on their way to the front.

There was a no smoking order in effect and the men marched in silence. As they approached the front, a brief and violent cannonading drew their attention. The flashes of the guns could be seen along the length of the line, in addition to the rockets sent off by the infantry.

After the brief artillery duel, all fell quiet. The only sounds were the tromp of the horses' hooves, the creak of the carriages, and the jangling of the mess kits and other equipment being transported.

Midnight slipped by and they were into July 5. As they marched on, a dense fog began to form, making it difficult for the men to find the emplacement Lieutenant Case had located earlier in the evening. By three in the morning, the battery at long last completed their 20-kilometer hike and found the designated location. It was near Boyeau-Belger that the entire Second Battalion lined up in platoon formation. The cannon extended along a line from Ferme de Jonchery to the southwest, each gun spaced about 200 meters apart. The two platoons of Battery F were positioned on the far left of the battalion alignment.

The battery commander assigned Lieutenant's Allen and Wynland as the executive officers of the First and Second Platoons respectively before establishing his headquarters "Clematite" at a forward observation post near the edge of Bois 65.

After positioning and unlimbering the guns, the men went right to work unloading the caissons of their valuable ammunition. Once this chore was completed, the caissons and animal handlers departed to establish the echelon several kilometers to the south.

At the guns, and still under the cover of darkness, the cannoneers and other forward personnel erected the camouflage over the positions and set up their pup tents under the camouflage. Lastly, just as the sky to the east began to show signs of dawn, the detail section was able to establish visual and telephone contact with regimental command.

The men were all admonished to keep out of sight during the daylight hours and to be particularly careful not to leave telltale signs of their presence around or outside of the camouflage covering, to prevent detection as a result of enemy aerial reconnaissance and photographs.

This area was being reinforced, as the French High Command felt that the German main blow would come at this point in the line. No need to give any indication to the Germans that the line had been strengthened here.

Just prior to sunup, most of the men were in their pup tents sound asleep. Pat was one of those and slept until shortly after 1:30 p.m. It was the best sleep he'd had in a long time and he felt well rested after arising. Though he was restricted to staying under the camouflage he was able to survey the area from where he stood in the pit of the number two gun. The surrounding country, at least as far as he could see, was an immense chalky region devoid of vegetation except for a few clumps of grass and a few small stands of trees. Boyeau Belger was just one part of a complex defensive system constructed to defend the allied line, which was deficient in natural physical obstacles that could slow or stop the German advance. It was even said that these very same plains was where the infamous Attila the Hun had been overwhelmed, so many centuries before. Pat wondered if maybe the great German army could be stopped here once again.

The next few days turned hot and humid. During daylight hours, the men sought the shade and comfort of the pup tents, trying to catch a cool breeze if one would happen by. Before dawn on the sixth, an ammunition train arrived and the men quickly off-loaded 1400 rounds of 75 mm shells before it continued on its way to the other canon emplacements. During hours of daylight the men stayed under the cover of the camouflage and ventured out only for meals. Most work on the positions was undertaken at night.

Late in the afternoon of the sixth, Lieutenant Case called the men together and read an order from the commander of the 21st Army Corps, which said that an attack on the Champagne front would take place within the next week. The order assured the men of the 21st Corps that once again where it stood the German Army would be stopped.

On the seventh, more ammunition arrived at the gun positions, and Lieutenant Case received barrage charts in the late morning. The cannoneers were then instructed to lay the weapons on standard firing pattern. In the afternoon, the men received orders to dig gun pits. This work was done after sundown in order to escape observation and to avoid the terrific daytime heat.

The gunners were not permitted to register their guns by fire in order not to alert the enemy to the strength in the sector. When the attack came, the cannons were expected to lay down accurate fire and an effective barrage based on data given to the commander on the barrage sheets.

By early in the morning of the eighth, the gun pits were complete. It was now a waiting game for the men of the battery. The guns were positioned so as to fire point blank at the enemy in case of a breakthrough. Orders were given to the mechanics on how to blow up the guns in the event they were in danger of capture.

The days slipped by slowly. The weather remained hot and humid, with little or no rain. Each night there were heavy bombardments along the line, though the 149th did not participate. All of the men were on edge, listening for the telephone and the word that tonight was the night. Each night the French were sending out raiding parties to the German lines in order to capture enemy prisoners, in the hopes of getting the final details on the impending attack.

Late in the evening of July 11, Lieutenant Case read an order from Army Commandant General Gouraud to the men under his command. "An enemy assault upon our position is looming just over the horizon. Never has an army been readied for an attack as ours is today. Our defenses are solid and well dug in and we as soldiers are prepared for their onslaught. I ask each one of you to be vigilant and to be on your guard. Our reserve forces of artillery and infantry are in a position to fill any weakness that may develop"

Case paused and cleared his throat, then continued. "You are fighting on the very land you have altered with your own hands into an impregnable stronghold. The barrage will be relentless and dreadful, but all accesses will be closed to the enemy. We will stand with courage and strength as we meet the enemy with superior might and purpose. In us beats the hearts of courageous and free men."

Case paused once more, looking at the men intently, then looked back at the sheet of paper in his hand. "No one will look to the back nor shall you give up one bit of ground. We will destroy the enemy until they can take no more and retire from the field. It will be a glorious day for all of us."

This order cast out any thoughts that when things got tough the guns would be packed up and sent to the rear. All were now thinking, that the day of the attack had to be July 14, Bastille Day. To support this belief, there were ever increasing numbers of reports suggesting heavy activity behind German lines in this vicinity.

Late in the day of July 13, Lieutenant Case addressed the men of F Battery once again.

"Gentlemen, I've just received the division report that states quite succinctly what we are up against. Thirty new batteries have been located opposite the Fourth Army. New battery positions have been discovered within 1500 meters of the first line and at one point in front of the trenches. Their ammunition dumps are full, they have cut new roads, repaired the old ones and new bridges have been constructed over boyeaux and trenches. We know that we face twenty enemy divisions and they're on or just behind the front line."

This announcement was greeted with low whistles and mumbling from the men of F Battery.

On July 14, the men were whiling away the hours by going through the motions of making final preparations for the attack they knew would come soon, and most were convinced that it would be this very night.

Each man privately contemplated his future. What did it hold? And most importantly, would they be around when the battle was over? Their conversations with one another were more casual and confident than their real feelings.

The morning hours slid by slowly. Pat and Hank tended to the guns and said little. When noon finally arrived, they both sought refuge from the oppressive heat in the shade of the number two gun. The summer heat had been terrific for the past few days and today was even worse; the temperature and humidity were higher and there wasn't even a hint of a breeze. The meal of hardtack and bread was uninspiring and they ate in silence. Pat was gazing off to the south, out of the rear opening to the pit, and was shocked, to see his brother walking towards them.

Pat poked Hank with his elbow. "Here comes Roy! I can't believe it."

Hank looked to where Pat was pointing and did not recognize the approaching figure, as he was still some distance away. Before he could respond, Pat had set down his mess kit and was running to meet Roy.

The brothers embraced without a word. Pat then stood back and said, "My God, where in blazes did you come from? Your the last person in the world I expected to see out here, and just before the big battle that's a-brewing."

"Great to see you Pat. I came out here to cover the Rainbow for the paper. And, of course, I planned to cover you men in the artillery. You look great, fit and trim."

"Well, with all of the moving around we've been doing and digging the guns in, we don't have time to get fat and lazy, like some reporters I know," Pat said, laughing. "We've been working on getting the positions ready and completed the job just last night. Now we're just waiting for the Huns to come. Hey, you want some lunch? All we have is some cold monkey meat and bread. It doesn't taste very good but it'll satisfy your hunger."

"No thanks, I ate a big late breakfast with Major Hinkle. I think the officers get fed better'n you guys."

"There's no question about that. How's the professor anyway?" Hank asked as he walked slowly up to the two brothers. "It's good to see you again, Roy."

Roy clasped Hank's hand with both of his and pumped it vigorously. "Likewise, Hank. The professor is fine. I'll get to that a little later. You boys look great, but I'd have to say that both of you smell a little gamy. I guess I can live with that, at least for a little while."

"Well it's hard to take a bath in a teacup," Pat said. "Water is in short supply around here. We don't even have enough to swab the guns when they're in use, let alone bathe."

After a short and an awkward pause, Roy said, "Pat, I came here for another reason. Ah, well, I guess I'll tell you outright. Last week I received a wire from home from Mom. Dad passed away on June 30. I was going to be tactful and all that, but you guys have seen enough death and misery that I thought you needed it straight."

"Heart?" Pat choked on the word as his eyes filled with tears, which he quickly brushed away with the sleeve of his shirt.

"Yeah, Mom said he was peaceful and went in his sleep. She also said that a letter would follow. She specifically asked that I find you and give you the news. I knew I was coming here soon, so I convinced the editor to let me make the trip about a week earlier than originally planned."

"Damn!" Pat said, the tears returning.

"I was somewhat prepared, but it still came as a shock to me," Roy said.

After a pause, Hank said, "I'm sorry for you guys. It's gotta be a terrible blow, particularly, when you're so far from home. But you know that he's with God now and has cast aside all of those troubles of the world. He's in a much better place. I know your dad was a born again Christian. The grieving should not be for him. He is in God's glory. Grief is only for we who are left behind. Rejoice in the good news that you will be with him again and for eternity. Celebrate his life, don't grieve over his death."

They both looked at Hank. He wasn't the type that came up with such wisdom. They looked briefly at one another and felt that what Hank had said was absolutely right, but it didn't take away the hurt.

"Roy, it was good seeing you and we'll talk later, but for now I'll leave you two alone." Hank turned and walked back to his mess kit.

The two brothers went off by themselves as they talked over the new change in their lives and remembered days past.

Pat asked Roy about their mother. They both had letters from her dated the same day, and these had preceded EP's death by two weeks. They concluded that Matilda was in good hands with their older brother, Roger, who lived just down the street from her. Roy said he'd send a wire to him inquiring as to how their mother was doing. There was little else they could do until they returned home. "Heaven only knows when that will be," Pat said.

Before seeking out Pat, Roy had gone through the chain of command, in reverse order.

First, he had visited with Major Hinkle, to get background information for his story about the Rainbow Division and, most importantly, to get permission to visit Pat at Battery F's position on the line.

The Major was very accommodating on both counts. He liked and respected Roy as much as he liked Pat and Hank. It gave him a feeling or closeness, like being home in Champaign-Urbana. Roy was a good listener, and the professor liked to expound on the history-making events that were taking shape at that very moment. He also felt that a family member should give this news about EP's passing to Pat.

Next, Roy sought out the battery commander and explained the situation to him. Lieutenant Case had approved and encouraged the men to take a few hours off, but not to leave the area because of the impending attack.

After an hour and a half of talking and consoling one another, Roy and Pat returned to the gun position and found Hank sitting in the shade of his pup tent.

"Well, Pat, and you too, Hank, I'll be praying for you guys. This offensive sounds like a big one."

Hank sighed and nodded. "Roy, what did the major say about it? You know, he seems to tell you all of the deep, dark secrets."

"Well, he did give me some information about the deployment, Hank. Do you both want to hear it?"

"I guess it'll keep my mind off Dad, so give us all you got. You know they don't tell us a thing; it's like a big dark secret. Just go fire the guns," Pat said.

Roy pulled out his notepad that he had previously stuffed in his shirt pocket. He paused a moment to scan his notes and gather his thoughts. "Well, first of all, the French have placed a small number of companies in the front line trenches. Their express purpose is to convince the Germans that the main army is situated there, while in fact our strength is behind this first system of trenches. These men have been busy over the past two weeks convincing the Germans that our main strength is located in this first line of trenches.

"The term Major Hinkle used for this means of confronting the Germans was 'elastic defense.' The Boche will be expecting to bombard and attack our armies here in the most forward line, while in fact there will just be a few of these sacrifice companies, well dug in and deep enough to survive the initial barrage. After the storm troops start forward, these men will come out of the bunkers and harass the living hell out of 'em and warn Gouraud that the attack is in fact underway."

Hank and Pat nodded. "The resistance from the Allies will start in the second line of trenches," Roy continued, "and they are prepared to fall even further back. The Germans will not meet the main defense until they get to the third trench line; about three miles back from the current German positions. It is hoped that the Boche will be overconfident at this time and be wide open to a fierce counterattack. Artillery has been placed back far enough to be exempt from the initial German barrage. However, when they advance to this intermediate position, this artillery will then be in range and hit them hard."

"Very clever," Hank said quietly.

Roy nodded. "That's why none of the artillery regiments from the Rainbow have been allowed to fire up till now. They don't want the Boche knowing the real strength in this rear area. The Rainbow has been dug in at the intermediate position and starting on the far left of the line and just south of Auberive-sur-Suippes are the New Yorkers, the second and third infantry battalions of the 165th Infantry. Also and to the immediate right of the New Yorkers is the third battalion of the 166th infantry, the boys from Ohio."

He then went on to detail the rest of the troops positioning.

"You guys in the artillery are mingled with French regiments. The 151st Field Artillery from Minnesota is on the right, next to you guys from the 149th. Two battalions of the 150th from Indiana are on your left, and one battalion is on the right, in support of the 151st. The furthest forward American unit is the 117th Trench Mortar Battalion from Maryland covering the far right side. They'll be used to bombard the Germans with showers of mortars as they advance. Behind it all, at

Vadenay Farm, are headquarters for the Division, also guarding the path that leads to Chalons-sur Marne, the objective the Huns are seeking. And that's about all I have. After I leave you guys, I'm on my way to Vadenay Farm, where I'll await news as to the outcome of the battle."

Roy looked at his watch. "Well look at that, I've overstayed my welcome. You look after one another and be careful. I'll look forward to seeing you when this is over." Roy shook Hank's hand, then threw his arm around Hank's shoulders. "Take care, Hank."

"Thanks, Roy, good to see you. Sorry about your dad. We'll talk later." Hank turned and walked away.

Roy and Pat embraced again.

"Pat, I'm sorry my news was so bad. But what Hank said is right. Pray for Mom and her recovery from the shock. Keep under cover, little brother, I don't want to lose you too."

"Thanks, Roy. I think this upcoming fight will keep my mind off of Dad; I'm sure going to miss him. Don't worry about me. Battery F is leading a charmed existence. I'll get word to you when it's all over."

They shook hands, and Roy turned and walked away.

Pat watched him for a while, then turned and walked slowly back to the number two gun.

The Last of Trench Warfare

It was 11:00 PM and Adolph Krause was anxious for the attack to begin. His heavy gun had been in position for over a week now, and he was ready for action.

The Skoda couldn't throw it's shell as far as the other cannon lined up for the great offensive in the Champagne sector and therefore the gun battery had been brought out to the very front line trenches. The shell could now be lobed into the French trenches and back to the enemy's artillery positions.

Adolph was mad and full of hate at this point and couldn't wait until 12:10 a.m. arrived, the time they would start the barrage, some 6000 guns in all.

A French raiding party had captured his friend and mentor of so many years shortly after dark. Sergeant Walter Strummer had been at his gun, making final preparations for the big offensive to begin. Without warning he and the rest of the gun crew were confronted by twelve French infantrymen who took them prisoner and forced them across no-man's-land to the side of the enemy. Before leaving with their prisoners, the French had destroyed the cannon.

Besides Adolph, Sergeant Strummer was the last of the original group of men who had been in his artillery regiment since the very beginning of the war, way back in 1914. The others had been killed, captured or severely wounded.

Adolph wanted revenge on the French, and yes on the Americans too. They, the enemy, sat a mere 3000 meters to the south.

"Kill the bastards, kill them all," he said aloud to himself as he prepared for battle.

Major Hinkle and two French officers sat on three legged stools behind a wooden table. On the other side stood a young German soldier. The bunker was dimly lit by the light of three candles, which cast long, dark shadows against the chalky gray walls.

"What time is the attack to come?" Major Hinkle said in French. "Give us the time and you'll be sent immediately to the prisoner camp, where you can eat and rest."

The French captain interpreted the question in German.

The young soldier shrugged his shoulders and said nothing. His lips were dry and chapped and he tried to lick them, but his tongue was just as dry.

Major Hinkle held a tin cup, filled with water, out to the sergeant and he quickly snatched it and put it to his mouth. However, before he could gulp any of it down, the French colonel hit the cup with his open hand, causing it to sail across the bunker and hit the timbered wall, where it clattered loudly to the dirt floor.

The German soldier felt the cool water drip down his face and tried to lick some of the precious liquid with his tongue. He'd been awake for over 24 hours and hadn't eaten for two days. He was weak and he felt his knees begin to buckle under him. Before he fell, the two Poilus, one on either side, grabbed his arms and propped him up to a standing position.

"You'll answer our questions or stand here till you die," growled the French colonel in his best German.

They interrogated him further, but after twenty minutes, Major Hinkle stood up from the stool he'd been sitting on, said something in French to the two officers, and started to leave.

The young German sergeant said something behind him.

Major Hinkle paused at the door and said in French, "What did he say?"

"He asked that you not leave," the interpreter said.

The German spoke again.

"He believes we'll kill him." The colonel smiled, then turned and spoke savagely to the prisoner.

"What's happening?" asked Major Hinkle.

"I think he is ready to talk, that is, if you don't leave."

Without a word, Major Hinkle returned to the stool and sat down. "When will the attack come?" he asked again in French. As before the French captain repeated the question in German.

"Tonight," was the simple reply.

"At what time will it come?"

"At midnight! The artillery will begin at 12:10. The infantry will move at 4:15."

"Colonel, you have your answer," Major Hinkle said. "I think it's time this man, Sergeant Strummer I believe, be sent to the prisoner compound."

"Very well, major. If you won't let us enjoy his company any more, he can go to the prisoner camp. Sergeant! Come take this man away."

The colonel then called the information to General Gouraud's headquarters. He whispered the code words into the mouthpiece of the phone and then turned to Major Hinkle.

"You can report to your people that we will begin a heavy artillery barrage at 2345 hours tonight. We hope to catch their troops out in the open as they gather in anticipation of their attack. Orders from Gouraud's headquarters will be issued within the hour."

The colonel breathed a heavy sigh and twisted around on his stool to face Hinkle. He was smiling. He had a dark complexion with deep brown eyes and a thick shock of black hair that needed cutting. To everyone around he now looked relaxed and his appearance took on a pleasant countenance. "It's not unlike the Boche to attack on Bastille Day, thinking we'd all be dead drunk from the festivities of the celebration. By surprise, they expected to catch us in complete unreadiness. And they might well have been right in their estimation, for this is the most heavily defended portion of the western front, more than five miles deep, heavily fortified with trenches, wire, dugouts, troops and artillery."

"Why would they want to attack here, in such a strongly defended area?" Major Hinkle asked, perplexed.

"They expect that we will celebrate our Independence Day in the comfort of knowing that we are so well defended and thus be off our guard and, as I said, drunk to the point of unconsciousness. Remember,

Major, that they failed at Chateau-Thierry, for that Marne salient did not afford the maneuvering room for another major attack. They failed at Verdun on the right and Rheims on the left. They've tried to widen their hold on the right near Compiegne and Montdidier, but we have stopped them there, too. I see this as a last great effort to win the war."

Major Hinkle nodded as the colonel continued. "This geographical area, the point they want to attack, offers them many benefits. For example, their lines of communication will be shorter and it also allows them to operate on a straight-line frontal attack, while our own reserves must be pulled from north of Paris and brought to Chalons around the Marne salient via Vitry-le-Francois. Their reasoning is that once they take Chalons, they will have an ideal jumping-off point for their ultimate goal, Paris. They have always, and mistakenly, felt that if the capitol falls the war would be won."

The colonel stood up. "We know their plans and we will be ready for them," he said. "The sacrifice companies have already been sent forward to plan and implement the surprise for these invaders and to also warn of the actual time their troops move forward in the attack. These brave men have been positioned for days, appearing to the enemy as our main army in the very front trenches, while in fact there are few men who have planned this very vicious greeting for the Germans. Few of these volunteers will live through the attack. If they are not killed, they will be captured. They know that they will meet a glorious end. They are surrounded by barbed wire and situated in deep dugouts and will not come out until after the bombardment has stopped. Then they will come up from the tunnels and trenches and delay the German advance."

The month of July brought with it an ever-increasing tempo in the air war. Ike and Frank, as well as the remaining members of their squadron, were in the air every day.

Jon Nelson had been sent home due to the extent and seriousness of his wounds. It had been touch and go for a few days, but Jon was finally on the long road to recovery. The event would leave him with a slight paralysis of his right arm, as some nerves had been permanently damaged.

Ike was greatly relieved that Jon had pulled through. The doctors had been very pointed in telling him that if he hadn't gone in and picked

Jon up, he never would have made it. Now he was on a ship that sailed from La Harve on July 10. Ike knew that Jon was greatly troubled by his paralysis and tried to put on a good show, but only time would tell how complete his recovery would be.

Since the first of July, a majority of the squadron's time was spent escorting French Brequet Bombers over the rail yards in and around Chateau-Thierry. All of the American airmen knew a large offensive was in the offing and the air service was endeavoring to hinder the potency of this certain German attack.

On July 14, the German offensive fell all along the line, from Chateau Thierry, along the Marne River to Dormans, then northeast to Reims around the salient and due east for twenty miles, into the Champagne sector.

At 11:40 on the night of July 14, before the Allied barrage was to begin, Jake trotted along the trench line passing each of the platoons that made up his company. He knew most of their names and he called to each man as he passed by. Their morale was high and they boasted their confidence.

"We're gonna kick some ass tonight, Lieutenant."

"I'm going to kill every Hun that sticks his ugly face over that there rise!" and so on up the line.

Jake wanted the men to spread out more and started spacing them further apart as he moved along the trench. He came to his old platoon at the same time the Allied artillery opened up; it was exactly 11:45 p.m. The sound was deafening. The men shouted and cursed the enemy and laughed to the roar of the pre-emptive strike. They all stood up on the firing step of the trench and cheered the artillery on. Behind Jake the sky was red from the muzzle flashes of the guns and he too felt confident in their ability to repel the German attack. He could see large explosions on the enemy's side of the line.

"It's a fine night for killing, lieutenant," said his first sergeant who came up and stood by him.

"Thompson, we need to keep the men spread out, don't let them bunch up. When the Boche start their bombardment we're all going to catch holy hell. There's not much protection other than this trench. We need to keep spaced in order to minimize our losses."

"Yes, sir. I'll go see to it now," and without another word, Sergeant Thompson was off and running.

The Second Battalion of 167th Infantry Regiment consisted of four companies. G and H Companies were to the right of the Chalons road, and E and F Companies were to the left or west of it. The battalion held the crests of two slopes, one on either side of the road that meandered through the little valley between these gentle hills. The slopes themselves were strewn with old tree stumps and scrubby little pines.

Jake's G Company was at the very top of the hill that gave him full view of the roadway off to his left, and its approaches. The silvery ribbon of avenue shined and glimmered in the moonlight, at least before the artillery barrage started.

The heavens exploded as the Allied batteries began their artillery barrage against the Boche armed forces that were massing their troops in various staging areas as they were assembling for their offensive. The roads were jammed with men, horses and vehicles. Trenches were crowded with troops, and their batteries were preparing the guns for the initial bombardment.

The Friedenstrum, the German offensive for peace, was scheduled to begin at 12:10 in the morning. The Allies hoped that their earlier barrage would catch the enemy troops in the open and hit their artillery before they could fire the guns. Massing centers, woods, ammunition dumps, and observation posts, rail centers—all took a tremendous pounding.

The night had been clear with a few clouds to the east and a bright moon directly overhead. But once the guns commenced their fire, the smoke and muzzle flashes of the cannon paled the moonlight. This chorus of cannon was the largest massing of Allied artillery since the war began. The horizon was bright red, almost like a sunset, from the fire spewed forth by their cannons.

Behind the German lines, large secondary explosions lit the sky as the shells fell on the targeted ammunition dumps, crossroads, and staging areas. All of this dwarfed any of the action the Americans had seen since arriving in France. The cannonading in the Baccarrat Sector had been mere child's play when compared to this onslaught blazing forth from their artillery.

All of the Americans stood at or near their stations admiring this amazing spectacle, maybe even feeling a little sorry for the enemy. Nevertheless, there was joy in their hearts as they thought how this would disrupt the enemy's ability to launch an offensive.

Suddenly, they became aware as to how puny these efforts were, for as the clock struck 12:10 a.m., the German bombardment on the Allied lines began. All along the forty-two-mile front, the sounds of the Allied guns were muffled by an even greater sound, that of six thousand German cannons as they began their offensive. Only on the Somme in March had there been such a concentration of artillery. This effort in the Champagne laid down a barrage that fell like a blanket over the Allied lines.

To the casual observer it would appear that all the sky and earth were ablaze. Rockets, flares, flashes of guns, and bursting shells made a terrifying but spectacular picture, too spectacular for the men to stay under cover for long. Soon all were out taking in this display of brute power. It was spellbinding. Thoughts of self-preservation were tossed to the wind as large shells from both sides roared overhead. Smaller-caliber shells whistled and exploded all along the front. The volume of sound swallowed the Allied artillery as if it didn't exist. The crescendo was instantaneous, as if the very world had gone mad. It continued unabated for nearly four hours.

The once clear night was filled with flying debris, shrapnel, smoke and gas. A rain of deadly steel fell on the lines and behind them. Pat and the cannoneers watched the spectacle without a word. They stood behind the earthen wall that protected the guns, peering over the parapet.

A nearby ammunition dump took a direct hit, lifting the dirt and fiery smoke high into the air while shells exploded in an indiscriminate manner. One shell hit a rocket dump and sent flares and rockets high into the night sky. Enemy artillery targeted all wooded areas with incendiary shells. The resulting fires brightened the sky like daybreak. The distinctive ping of gas shells exploding nearby caused the cannoneers to quickly don their gas gear.

Earlier that night, Clint Phelps arrived in Chalons sur Marne. The trip had been a hectic one and involved numerous modes of transportation and no small amount of walking. Clint had been in the Chateau Thiery region doing a story on the American 26th Division, when he received a telegram from Champaign, Illinois. Now his most crucial quest was to locate Battery F of the 149th Field Artillery. He had received this urgent telegram on the 12th of July and it had caused him a great deal of anguish. Hank's father had wired him to see if he could locate Hank and inform him of the news.

The terse message read:

CLINT PLEASE LOCATE HANK STOP INFORM HIM THAT ON JULY 7 BETSY BEGAN HEMORRHAGING STOP RUSHED HER TO HOSPITAL BUT TOO LATE STOP BOTH BABY AND BETSY GONE STOP BABY STILLBORN AND BETSY SUBCUMBED JULY 9 STOP LETTER TO FOLLOW STOP

FRANK

Clint didn't want to be the one to break the news to Hank. He liked the young man very much, even though he hardly knew him. It had been in college that Clint had known Hank's father; they'd been close friends for four years. Since that time he had had little contact with him.

Clint hoped that Pat could help him in breaking this devastating news as gently as possible.

It had been Clint's intention, upon reaching Chalons sur Marne, to spend the night before proceeding to the front the next morning, but this was not to be. It was during the early morning hours of July 15, that he heard the guns. It was so reminiscent of the great spring offensive he'd witnessed in March that when the dull roar of the Allied canon awakened him, he jumped from bed and rushed to witness the spectacle. As before, he stood frozen at the window of his hotel room. The horizon to the north glowed red from the muzzle flashes. The steady roar of the guns was like a clap of thunder that would not end.

Shortly after midnight, when the Germans began their bombardment of the allied lines in preparation for their offensive, the sky to the north suddenly lit up as bright as daybreak. The sound of the artillery increased tenfold, devouring the sound of the Allied cannon, covering it as if it didn't exist.

Once again, Clint found himself under siege. Not only was the front subjected to a bombardment of immeasurable proportion, but the rear areas were also hit hard by the enemy's long-range artillery.

To Jake, the German barrage seemed endless. On and on it went. One hour, two hours, three hours, when would it end? It didn't take long for the morale to sag. In many men, fear replaced the confidence that had filled their minds a short time before.

The artillery shells landed in and around them for hours. Huge geysers of dirt shot skyward with each exploding shell. Some sections of the trench took direct hits, but most shells fell harmlessly on either side of the line.

Jake couldn't determine how many casualties his company was suffering. He felt fairly certain that the rate was light. Forward of his position, the first and second line of trenches were taking a terrible shellacking, but Jake knew that no men were there other than the sacrifice companies, and that those men were deep underground.

At 4:10 a.m. The violence of the Boche bombardment diminished slightly, indicating that the German infantry was coming. Shortly thereafter, Jake detected an increase in the intensity of the Allied artillery. Batteries heretofore unused began pounding the intermediate zone.

Before the sun was up, the German infantry was moving out of the trenches and starting across no-man's-land. Six veteran divisions made up the initial assault force on the center, held by the American and French shock troops. One division struck at the Allied left, held by the New Yorkers and Ohioans. Three attacked the center held entirely by the French, and two struck on the right, against the Alabamians and Iowans.

Battery F was ordered to commence firing at 4:07 just before the German assault started. The cannoneers wanted to fire at a faster rate and damned the slow pace they were required to maintain. Accuracy was important and required the slower rate of fire.

When the Prussians hit the first line of defense, they found only mines that blew up beneath their feet and a heavier bombardment from the artillery, sprinkled liberally with gas shells.

The French sacrifice companies came out of their deep holes and hit the Prussians hard with rifle and machine gun fire, but the Germans kept on with their attack, even though their casualties continued to mount at an alarming rate. Through sheer disregard for their losses, the Boche reached the first line of defense at daybreak.

Jake stood on the firing step of the trench and peered over the parapet gazing into the darkness, looking for the enemy. His heart was racing and every muscle was tense.

One of his men, off to his right, climbed up out of the trench and crawled forward about seven or eight yards.

"J.T., get back here!" Jake yelled at him.

"I think I see 'em coming, Lieutenant! Yeah, there's thousands of 'em. About 50 to 60 yards out, sir."

There was a pause, and all of the troops stood on the firing step, sighting their Springfields out into the darkness of the early morning. Jake noticed that the eastern horizon was beginning to brighten. Soon they would be able to see the enemy troops.

After what seemed an eternity, J.T. shouted, "I see one, Godd is he big!" With that, he squeezed the trigger. There was the loud crack of his rifle, and all guns of the infantry opened up, devastating the first line of German troops advancing on the Americans.

From then on, no one knew what was happening outside of his own little private war with the onrushing enemy troops. Some Boche troops jumped into adjoining trenches and continued sneaking forward under cover. The battle soon became a hand-to-hand conflict where all tools at hand were used --bayonets, rifle butts, pistols, bare hands and teeth. The pressure from the Prussian advance kept coming. The Americans held onto the positions tenaciously, not giving an inch. The fate of the line was hanging in the balance when Jake could see, in the early dawn light, eleven German tanks moving slowly towards them along the Chalons highway.

"We're in for it now, Lieutenant!" Sergeant Thompson yelled over the sound of battle.

"Give me the telephone, Private," Jake yelled to his communications man, who quickly handed the instrument to him. "We have eleven tanks on the road about two hundred yards from our position," Jake yelled to the man on the other end of the line.

After a pause, the reply came over the static of the receiver. "The major said he'd put the Maryland Trench-Mortars on it right away, they've sighted them also."

Within two minutes, mortar shells were bursting in and around the tanks. The Trench-Mortar Battery was firing their bombs at a furious rate, and soon four of the machines had been put out of action. The rest of the tanks continued moving along the approach. As they neared the trench line, the 37 mm guns of the 167th Infantry zeroed in on them and the threat was soon over as the remaining seven tanks were destroyed.

The Americans' full firepower was hitting the Germans, but they still kept coming. The enemy troops were coming to the ridge at a faster rate than those in front of them were dying. At the height of the attack when Jake was firing his automatic as fast as he could, he felt a tap on his shoulder. It was Major Davidson, the battalion commander. Jake jumped off the firing step, down into the safety of the trench. The major cupped his hands and yelled into Jake's ear, above the sounds of the battle, "Jake, I want G Company to counterattack. H Company will spread out along the trench to take your current position. Pull your men back off of the firing step and move out to the right using the trenches and hit them in the flank. Now!"

"Yes, sir!" Jake replied, and the major was gone.

Men from H Company were beginning to filter across the line, and Jake, Sergeant Thompson, and the platoon leaders began forming the men from G Company for the counterattack. Jake sent the company in by platoons, his old platoon, the Second, leading the way. They followed along the trench line, fighting their way through, climbing over the dead and wounded who filled the trench—French, Germans and Americans. Through the zigzag of the line they went, firing their weapons, throwing their grenades, and using their bayonets. The battle was fierce and deadly. Both sides took heavy casualties, but the Americans were making headway into the Prussian vanguard. The counterattack by G Company cleared the adjoining trenches of enemy troops and helped establish a stronger defensive system for the 167th Infantry.

During the early morning hours of July 15, all of the pilots of the 95th Aero Squadron were awakened by the not-too-distant roar and thunder of artillery. At 3:00 a.m., after eating a light breakfast they assembled in the briefing shack. Captain Wortham was the last to enter and as he moved briskly to the front of the room, the chatter quickly subsided. He slowly scanned the men assembled and after a brief pause, started his preflight briefing.

"Gentlemen, we will fly cover for the doughboys, who will be defending the south bank of the Marne," he announced in a casual and quiet tone. "We will be attacking the German ground forces on the north side of the Marne and, of course, any troops trying to cross the river. The 94th will be flying overhead against any enemy aircraft in the vicinity. We know that we are seriously outnumbered, so be careful and keep a watchful eye out for intruders."

The Captain then turned to the large map tacked to the wall behind him, where he pointed out the patrol limits for each flight. Ike's group was to hit the five pontoon bridges the Boche had erected just east of Dormans.

When the individual assignments had been made, Wortham looked at all of the pilots carefully, and then ordered, "Man your planes."

Ike and Frank walked briskly out of the operations shack and to their aircraft, which were parked close by on the tarmac.

Ike's SPAD was in tiptop shape having just received a thorough check by the ground crew. He had sighted his own guns just the night before.

There was a chill in the early twilight and the sky was broken with a few scattered showers. None of the pilots said much as they struggled into their flight gear. Once Ike got his leather jacket buttoned up, he did a cursory walk around the aircraft before he climbed into the open cockpit. There he fastened his seat belt and shoulder harness, pulled on his leather-flying helmet, and adjusted his goggles. Finally, he put on the soft leather gloves that Agnes had sent him.

"Switch off, throttle closed!" he yelled to Mike.

The mechanic pulled the prop through two revolutions and stood back a step. "Contact!"

Ike turned on the magnetos. "Contact!" He put his left hand on the throttle and advanced it one-half inch and pulled the control stick full back with his right. Mike pulled the propeller through and the engine kicked over once and died. He then gave another mighty heave, the engine sputtered for a few revolutions, took hold, and then smoothed to a deep, throaty throb idle.

Ike could hear some of the other engines catch, and soon there was a cacophony of sound up and down the flight line. Ike signaled the ground crew to pull out the wheel chocks, which they did immediately. As there was little or no wind, the aircraft, on signal, applied full throttle, and the sound became deafening as the long line of planes started bouncing and rolling forward on the grass field on their takeoff run.

In a short instant, all were airborne, climbing up to the base of some clouds floating gently overhead at 500 meters. Quickly, they gathered into their individual flights and headed towards the front.

The weather had been hot, almost unbearable during the past week, and yesterday's rain was a welcome relief. The cooler temperatures also allowed for improved performance for the aircraft.

Ike was tense, anticipating their attack. He never liked the ground support missions. He didn't like firing on the troops on the ground, but worse was the fire the planes encountered from the enemy's ground-based defenses.

At cruise altitude, each flight of four planes headed for their designated patrol area. The flight joined the Marne a little southwest of Reims and continued westward along the river towards Dormans. As they approached the town, Ike saw many artillery shells pounding the south bank of the river. As he advanced he saw the five pontoon bridges spanning the Marne, choked with German troops marching across in anticipation of attacking the south bank. This, then, was their target. Ike scanned the skies and didn't see any enemy aircraft. He signaled to the other pilots in his formation to begin their run on the bridges.

After over flying the targets at altitude, he put his SPAD in a steep left turn, reduced power, and began a steep dive at the first bridge. As he began firing his guns, his plane was racked with ground fire from the north bank. He felt a twinge of pain in his left thigh but didn't pay much attention to it, as he was engrossed on hitting the bridge. He looked over his shoulder and saw Frank off of his right wing firing his guns into the second bridge.

Ike's engine started smoking and he could see fire coming from under the cowling. He detected a severe roughness and the RPMs were dropping off rapidly. He continued firing his guns until he passed the fifth and last bridge. At this point, the engine stopped completely—the silence was overwhelming. The fire engulfed the entire front end of the fuselage, and he could catch only a glimpse of where he was headed. He applied full right rudder and full left aileron, resulting in a forward slip. This allowed him to see ahead a little better and, most importantly, to keep the flames from moving rearward into the fuel tank and cockpit. He discovered he was closer to the ground than he originally thought and that his ship was going to hit the river near the south bank. On impact, a great wall of water engulfed the aircraft.

With the daylight came the German planes that had numerical command of the air. Any Allied planes were either driven off or shot down. Once the Boche established air superiority, their planes began strafing runs on the ground troops and cannon emplacements.

Paul Stuart and his machine gun crew were busy trying to drive off the intrepid airmen with their weapon, which had been positioned just behind the middle of the cannon line. The horse-drawn caissons kept bringing ammunition to the guns. The wagoneers drove the horses hard and did what they could to dodge the barrage as they dashed across open roads and fields.

Pat, between rounds and swabbing the gun with water, could see the caissons coming forward at a gallop, then suddenly disappear into a cloud of smoke and flying debris but miraculously emerge unscathed as they continued forward.

As the battle progressed, the guns were getting hotter with each round fired, and the shortage of water only made matters worse. The possibility of a gun explosion was constantly on the minds of the crews. As Pat swabbed the cannon he could see the oil boiling out through the seams of the locking hoops. All of the mechanics continued to swab their guns between each round as best they could with what water was available. As they placed the cooling liquid on the cannon they had to stand out in the open, unprotected from the flying shrapnel.

Tom Wagner on gun three, after withdrawing the ramrod, looked down the barrel for fragments that might result in an early detonation of the shell. At the same instant, cannoneer Jason Newcum, who was firing by the clock, pulled the lanyard. The explosive force of the shell leaving the cannon tore Tom's helmet from his head, breaking the chinstraps, and sent it flying ten meters out in front of the gun. The resulting flash burned his face, and blinded him for the moment. Hank and Jack ran to his side and led him to the nearest aide station a short distance to the rear. Had not Newcum delayed the pull of the lanyard a fraction of a second, it would have beheaded Tom. After a few hours of rest, a shaken cannoneer returned to resume his duties late in the day.

Many of the enemy's incoming shells that landed near the battery's position were duds, failing to explode on impact.

Lieutenant Case's OP was hit by a shell that knocked everyone to the ground and destroyed the command post, but all escaped serious injury. The battery commander set up his command in the liaison position, located nearby. From here he continued to direct the fire.

Lieutenant Wynland's position was hit by an enemy shell, wounding him in the leg and sending him off to the hospital, the first real battle casualty suffered by Battery F.

As the sun rose in the sky, the fighting continued at a savage pace. E Company retook ground they had previously lost in the predawn hours and another position was taken by the third platoon of H Company, with some French reinforcements sent forward to help. By noon the Americans held the same ground they had occupied when the attack started the night before. Seven times, the Boche gained a foothold in the Allied trenches, and seven times they were hurled back. While on the left side of the battle line, the New York and Ohio regiments fought the same kind of seesaw battle throughout the day.

At six in the evening, the Germans made one last effort at taking some ground, and for the last time were beaten off.

The Germans ruled the skies and their aircraft flew over the trenches with impunity, bombing and strafing the Allied positions. During the daylight hours, enemy planes hovered over the lines like huge vultures, waiting to dive, attacking troops and vehicles at will.

On the night of the fifteenth, the German artillery bombarded the lines and rear areas, including towns, hospitals and roads. At 6:00 a.m. on the sixteenth, the Germans mounted another assault on the left side of the center, held by the 165th. Again they were driven off. On the right, G Company came under attack again and again. After being repelled for the fifth time, many of the enemy soldiers hid behind tree stumps, scrub pine, and rocks that littered the area, waiting to reform for yet another attack.

Jake gathered the men of the First Platoon for one more counterattack. As soon as the enemy came out in the open and started forward, they found not the rifle fire of the Americans, but thirty-five wild Alabamians yelling and rushing at them with bayonets fixed. The Boche troops immediately turned and ran the other way, but most were too late—the doughboys caught and bayoneted twenty-five of them without suffering a single casualty.

Jake and the men from the First Platoon jumped into the trench after the retreating Germans and found another twenty-five. The ferocious attack by the Americans caught the enemy off guard, and the remainder surrendered. All threw their hands in the air, yelling, "*Kamerad!*"

"Thompson, get some men to look out for more Boche while we take care of these fellows."

"Yes, sir! Chandler, Walker, Schultz, get to the wall and see if any more are coming," Thompson ordered.

The men jumped up on the firing step and peered towards the enemy lines.

"The rest of you men, get these prisoners disarmed and ready to take back to our lines."

It all happened so quickly that it made Jake's head swim. In no time at all Jake called to Sergeant Thompson that they were starting back.

"Give us five minutes and then get on back to our trenches."

The sergeant turned and nodded, gave him a thumbs-up and turned back to look for the enemy.

The 149th Field Artillery continued their fire at the preliminary pace until 12:05 p.m. of the 15th. Then the batteries reduced their rate until four in the afternoon, when the cease-fire order was received.

It soon became apparent that the Germans had called off their attack. The men removed the gas protection clothing and found their uniforms were drenched with their own sweat. This pause in the battle brought the men to realize how totally exhausted they were, but the work had to continue. The guns needed cleaning, the water supply had to be replenished, and more ammunition needed to be brought forward and readied for action.

Major Redden appeared at the position and reported that the enemy had been held. The Rainbow had won the admiration of the French through their display of courage and daring. The American presence was now being felt.

During the battle the cannoneers weren't the only ones in danger, for the men at the rear echelon were under considerable shellfire as they prepared for a rapid retreat if called for. They had been harassed all day by Boche artillery fire. In the early afternoon, ten caissons from Battery F were just approaching the ammunition dump when a German shell landed directly on the dump, sending it up in flames. None of the drivers or animals was hit, and they galloped off to another depot in which to secure their shells. It was 4:00 p.m. before they could resupply the guns.

All wooded areas near the echelon were subjected to a probing fire by enemy artillery. Providentially the site where Battery F was located escaped damage. The echelon machine gun crews were the only ones in the rear area who were able to fight back, and they had several opportunities to drive off Boche aircraft. The Indiana Regiment was forced to withdraw the echelon from the wood they were stationed in as the enemy gunners destroyed the wood and many of their animals were killed.

For the remainder of the day, the infantry was embroiled in repelling enemy attacks. The Germans were not above using ruse and deception in trying to infiltrate the Allied lines.

Some had taken uniforms from the dead French Poilus that had been in the sacrifice companies, and by wearing those uniforms got close enough to toss hand grenades at a Wisconsin machine gun crew, killing two Americans. Others had approached Company G with hands upraised yelling "*Kamerad.*" The Third Platoon fired on them immediately, and when they fell, grenades rolled from their hands, exploding harmlessly on the ground, away from the Allied trench.

Another man in a French officer's uniform came running towards the Americans with four Germans chasing him from a distance. Again, the doughboys fired killing all. It was another instance of Boche trickery. The apparent French officer was actually German, with explosives strapped to his back.

In another instance, four German infantrymen were spotted moving towards the Allied lines carrying a stretcher with a wounded soldier covered by a blanket. All were wearing Red Cross bands on their arms. What appeared as a wounded soldier turned out to be a machine gun being moved up towards the American trenches. The wary doughboys were able to pick them off before the gun could be fired.

After dark the 149th resumed fire, but at a very slow pace. Each gun squad was divided into three groups of two men each. One shift would fire the gun as the other four men slept.

A German plane had strafed the cannon shortly before dark and probably reported the position of the battery to Boche cannoneers, who then fired nearly 400 rounds before midnight trying to put F Battery out of commission. Fortunately, no direct hits were recorded.

Late in the evening Lieutenant Case called his men together and read a report from the division's chief of staff, Colonel MacArthur.

"Six first class divisions of the enemy attacked the center corps, of which we are a part, and at least 300 batteries have been engaged in the action between Rheims and the Argonne. By 11:00 a.m. the enemy's first effort had failed and soon they were organizing a second attack. At this time the Boche had been so badly defeated and had suffered such heavy causalities that they were unable to make anything but a feeble effort, which was quickly beaten back late this afternoon. You will be interested in knowing that a map found on a high-ranking officer showed that the Germans fully expected to reach Suippes by noon today and Chalons, still twenty-five miles to the rear of our lines, by 4:00 a.m. tomorrow. I congratulate you men on your courage and your will to win."

Finally, late in the evening of July 16, the Boche ceased their attack on the lines in the Champagne. Though the defender's lines had waffled in and out, they had not broken. The Germans hadn't gained one inch of ground during nearly two days of fighting.

Not happy with defeat, the enemy began shelling the rear areas, as far back as Chalons. They vented their rage most of the night on ammunition dumps, hospitals, and supply depots. All sorts of artillery hit anything that seemed of value.

The next day, the battle ceased but destruction was everywhere. Dead animals littered the roads and byways. Buildings and hospitals were in shambles. Some roads were obliterated and indistinguishable. Trees and vegetation were charred. Everything within twenty miles of the Allied lines was torn and devastated, mute testimony to the ferocious battle that had been fought.

With the battle finally over, Jake sat back and relaxed for the first time in three days. He lit up a cigarette and enjoyed it immensely, watching the smoke slowly drift to the top of the trench and then disappear as the swift breeze carried it away. The victory for the Allied cause was a big one, but the cost had been heavy. The entire Second Platoon had been either killed or wounded. Jake felt guilty for allowing those men, the ones he had entered service with, to lead the counterattack. They had all been his friends and he would miss them terribly. His other platoons had taken heavy casualties also, and he quietly mourned the loss of all the men. There was Warren, Tom, Henry, Bud, Frank, and five or six others. He could see their faces in his mind's eye and said a quiet prayer for each one.

Jake rested most of the day and caught up on some of the sleep he'd missed during the battle. After the midday meal on the eighteenth, the 167th Infantry Regiment was relieved by some Moroccan troops. The regiment withdrew to the rear to await new orders.

That same day, General Gouraud spoke to a hastily gathered assemblage of US troops from the 166th Infantry Regiment. He was a tall, slender man and the empty left sleeve of his tunic was neatly folded into a pocket. He walked with a limp due to a shattered hip. Both injuries had been suffered in previous battles. He stood erect in front of the dirty, scrubby-chinned Americans with his good arm behind his back.

"The Rainbow Division has brought a new spirit to France. Before this battle your mere presence had been like an intoxicating tonic. But your courage and resistance during this great struggle was like a promise of new life. On July 15, you broke the effort of fifteen German divisions supported by ten others. Our enemy intended to arrive at the Marne by sunset on that first day. But you blocked their progress at the spot where we most wanted to confront and ultimately defeat them. Your action was courageous, beyond reproach. Each of you, in the infantry, in the artillery, yes, the aviators, the planning staffs, and the reserve corps, all have a right to be proud. This has been a decisive blow to the Boche and truly a grand day for France."

This last comment was met with applause.

"I know that I can count on each and every one of you every time the enemy confronts you on the field of battle. As a fellow warrior in this monumental struggle I thank you from the bottom of my heart. And because of this great victory, the Allies have started a new offensive, just this very day, between Soissons and Chateau-Thierry. Because of your help, the French will now celebrate July 14, Bastille Day, on July 19."

Officers and men alike, each covered with dirt and blood cheered with joy. Just out of the jaws of death, the survivors celebrated and the champagne flowed freely.

It didn't take long for Clint to learn that no civilians, including journalists, were allowed to go forward during the battle. He also discovered he would have to spend nearly two days in Chalons, gathering as much news as he could. During this time he made frequent trips to the military hospital to talk with some of the walking wounded to learn more on the progress of the fighting.

He sent regular dispatches to his paper concerning the progress of the battle and the attitudes and morale of the men, which proved to be high. Even the severely wounded seemed buoyed by the news that the line was being held.

It was early in the morning of July 16 that Clint spied Major Hinkle near the front of the building housing the staff officers for the

Rainbow. Clint was across the narrow street, now crowded with troops and vehicles. He yelled and waved his arms several times before catching the major's attention. The major returned the gesture, not sure who this strange civilian was. Clint ran, walked and zigzagged through the traffic to the other side of the road and finally approached the major, who was enjoying a cigar with a group of fellow staff officers. They were on a break just outside the main entrance of the headquarters building, which in better times had been the residence of a city official. The major was in his best uniform with his billed cap pushed back on his head. His riding boots were polished to a brilliant sheen and fit neatly over his riding breeches up to the calves of his legs. He wore a brightly polished Sam Brown belt over his dark khaki coat.

"Major, Clint Phelps, it's good to see you again."

"Why Mr. Phelps, yes, I didn't recognize you at first, but I remember our visit at Camp Mills. What on earth are you doing here?"

Clint paused a moment to catch his breath. He was dressed in a light khaki summer shirt and pants and wore the standard issue trench boots. His outfit resembled the soldier's summer uniform, but he stood out from the other soldiers in that he was hatless. He quickly explained his presence and the news that had brought him here to locate Hank. "You know how difficult it is for this type of news to reach the men in a sensitive and timely way. I'm sure that his father felt that I could do this with greater dispatch and with sincerity."

"Yes, I understand what you're saying and I do feel deeply for the boy. But I can't help you now in the heat of this great battle. So many fine young men are being killed and wounded as we speak and my job is to keep as many from being injured or worse. I do this by gathering information and by sending in the equipment and the supplies that they need. As you are probably aware no civilians are being allowed to go forward at this point, but let me know where you are staying and as soon as things settle down, I'll see what I can do to get you to the 149th."

"I would appreciate that very much. It seems you're always doing me a favor." After a short pause Clint asked, "How is the battle going?"

"Our latest reports are good. The enemy has not moved forward and the lines are still intact. Well, I must be going. We have a staff meeting and I must attend. Someday I hope you and I can meet for dinner and have a long talk, but this is not the time."

"Thank you for you help, Major. I'm staying just down the street at the Avion, room 202. I look forward to the time we can meet. Good luck to you."

With that said, a colonel appeared at the door of the building and summoned the staff in. The major turned and disappeared inside with the other officers.

Late in the evening of the sixteenth, Clint helped evacuate the wounded from the hospital, which had come under heavy fire from the Boche long-range guns. When the shelling had begun, he had been standing on the front portico interviewing an infantry sergeant who had been wounded in the left arm earlier in the day. As the sergeant was relating his story to Clint, the first shell hit the west wing of the hospital, knocking both men to the ground. Clint was the first on his feet and helped the sergeant to his.

The first shell had hit without warning and the barrage continued to hit in and around the hospital over the next fifteen minutes before moving away in a northeasterly direction.

"Are you all right?" Clint asked. The young man nodded and both ran to the west wing of the hospital, which had collapsed under the impact of the explosion. Enemy artillery continued to rain down on the structure, killing and wounding more of the occupants. Clint felt the adrenaline flow as he and other survivors frantically threw aside timbers that had collapsed from the explosions. They heard cries for help and screams of agony from the casualties trapped in the rubble of the wooden structure. Numerous wounded soldiers, as well as doctors and nurses had fallen victim and needed assistance. Many had perished. It seemed such a waste to Clint. Such a large number of the dead had barely escaped with their lives earlier in the day now only to be destroyed in what should have been a sanctuary. He and the other rescuers worked late into the night searching for those who were still alive and pulling the bodies of the dead from the wreckage.

It wasn't until one in the morning that the hospital was finally evacuated and Clint was able to leave. He was exhausted and emotionally drained.

On his walk to the hotel, he realized the terrible devastation the German bombardment had brought down on the city. The long-range guns of the enemy had destroyed whole blocks. Fortunately for him, his hotel had escaped the fury of the attack.

When he at last opened the door to his room, he found a note from Major Hinkle that had been slipped under his door. The note told him to report to the aide station at 8:00 in the morning for a ride that would take him to within five miles of the line. The driver of the ambulance was making a morning run to a field hospital located several miles from the 149th's position. Clint was so tired that he collapsed on his bed fully dressed and didn't budge until seven the next morning.

As the driver slowed the vehicle and brought it to a stop, he explained to Clint where he thought the 149th Field Artillery was located. Clint jumped out of the ambulance, slammed the door and yelled his thanks to the driver, who then made a hard right turn at the intersection and sped off. Clint looked around at the bleak landscape, got his bearings, and started his trek towards the artillery echelons.

As he walked along the road trying to find the regiment, he was amazed at the devastation that greeted his eyes. The roads were pockmarked by shell holes and it was difficult to walk in a straight line without falling into a crater. There were numerous dead animals scattered around the countryside and the stench was nearly unbearable. Countless autos and trucks, destroyed by the bombardment, were strewn along the roadway. He could hear a scattering of gunfire both near and far, but the tempo seemed light compared to the preceding days.

Clint passed many vehicles along the way, both horse-drawn and motorized. All seemed in a hurry. From those he asked he found that he was getting close to his destination.

At noon he arrived at D Battery's echelon. The men gave him some lunch as he rested before traveling on. He interviewed the lieutenant in charge for the story he'd decided to write. This would cover the reaction of the men from Chicago to the heavy fighting they'd just been through. Battery D had been a Chicago National Guard unit and the lieutenant was a Chicago native who had graduated from DePaul University in 1916. Before leaving, Clint gathered as many names as he could from the battery's enlisted ranks to publish in his article. His Chicago readers would want to know about their sons, fathers, and husbands.

"Mr. Phelps, Battery F is about a mile northeast of us. I hope that you find them. Be careful that you don't get out into no-man's-land."

"Thanks, lieutenant, I'll be on my guard. I appreciate you feeding me."

Clint then turned and started in the direction of the front. It was 1:00 p.m.when he started on the final leg. He could hear cannon firing in front of him, but it was too distant to be of a real concern. The ground all around was scarred with shell holes, almost as if he were walking on a moonscape. The small copses of trees were devoid of greenery and branches. Few stood taller than eight to ten feet high, having been blown over or shattered by the artillery. The few buildings in the surrounding area were nothing but rubble.

He finally approached the line at 1:30 p.m. and found that the four guns of Battery F were still another half mile ahead. So he continued walking along the back of the 149th's cannon line, and by 2:00 p.m. he finally reached his destination.

The first person he ran into was Jack Bayless who took him to the battery commander's dugout. Jack disappeared into the dark interior of the dugout, and the only words Clint overheard were, "What is a civilian doing in a battle zone?"

Immediately Lieutenant Case stepped out to confront Clint.

Before Lieutenant Case could say a word, Clint introduced himself. "Lieutenant, I'm Clint Phelps with the *Chicago Globe*. I'm here for two purposes, first to pass some very devastating news on to one of your enlisted men, and secondly as a war correspondent. I did stop at division headquarters and was cleared to come forward by Major Hinkle. I apologize for inconveniencing you in this matter, but I felt it essential to personally pass the news on to Private Henry Seiler."

"And what news is it that you have that would require a personal trip?"

"I received a telegram from his father in Champaign that both his wife and new baby died in childbirth."

There was a brief pause as the lieutenant mulled over the information.

"As I was close to this area," Clint continued, "I felt that the impact on this young man, who I know personally, would be lessened if delivered by me, rather than by some curt telegram from the War Department."

"Rightly so, rightly so, Mr. Phelps. I have a wife and two small children at home myself. I can empathize with what must be done. What is it that you want from me?"

"First I'd like to talk with Corporal Littler, Hank's closest friend, and then we need to get Hank alone and talk with him."

There was a short pause, then the lieutenant turned and yelled, "Corporal Bayless, go get Littler and bring him here."

"Yes, sir!" Bayless replied and was off to the first section.

"It appears to have been quite a battle, Lieutenant."

"Yes, it was, Mr. Phelps. We were fortunate in that we suffered no serious casualties. We fired over 4100 rounds on the fifteenth and sixteenth and we gave those bastards hell. If you need anything else from me, I'll be in the dugout," Case said, and he disappeared inside the bunker.

Clint walked a few yards and sat on a large log. It wasn't until he sat down that he realized how tired he really was. The stress of having to tell Hank about his wife and baby finally hit him full force.

In a short time, he saw Jack coming back with Pat alongside. Pat had his helmet pulled down to shade his eyes from the sun. His uniform consisted of a khaki shirt open at the collar and sleeves rolled up over the biceps. His mud-covered trench boots stuck out below the cuff of his wrinkled khaki pants. Around his slender waist he wore a utility belt that held a holstered .45 automatic that hung loosely at his right side. His uniform was sweat-stained and streaked with mud.

Clint stood and started towards them. Pat stopped for a second, pushed his helmet up a bit and peered at Clint, then suddenly recognized him and quickened his pace.

"Clint, what are you doing here? I couldn't believe it when I heard Jack say there was a civilian here looking for me."

They quickly shook hands, and Clint threw his left arm around Pat and gave him a hug. "Pat, it's good to see you, under the circumstances. I've surprised myself by even being here. But we'll get to that later. How are you? You look great!"

"Oh, I'm fine, sir, maybe a little on the grungy side, but all things considered I'm well. Have you met my friend, Jack Bayless?"

"We've talked but haven't had an official introduction. Jack, glad to meet you."

"Likewise sir, Pat I've got to get back to the CP, so see you later." Jack said, and left them alone.

"Pat, I was sure sorry to hear about your dad," Clint said. "EP was a great friend."

"Thanks, I was hoping that he would hang on till we got home, but I guess it wasn't to be. What brings you up here? A big story?"

"I wish it were that simple, Pat. I came here to see Hank. I'm the bearer of some sad news."

"Sad news? Did something happen to his parents?"

"Worse. Something happened to Betsy." Clint dropped his gaze to the ground and paused a moment before continuing. "She began hemorrhaging on the seventh of July and they took her to the hospital. There she gave birth to the baby, who died upon delivery. They couldn't stop the internal bleeding and Betsy died on the ninth."

"Oh, my God!" Pat blurted out, and quickly collapsed on the log, his face turning white. "That can't be. In her last letter to Hank everything seemed to be okay."

It was about four o'clock before Pat and Clint could get Hank alone and sit him down for a long talk. Prior to that there was always someone around. Most of the Champaign men had actually known Clint or at least heard of him when he was editor of the *Daily Herald*. All wanted the latest word from home. It took a lot of convincing to make the men believe that Clint had been in France about as long as the Rainbow had been there.

"Hank, I have something I need to tell you and I don't know where to begin," Clint began after the three were finally alone.

"It's about Betsy isn't it?" Hank answered before Clint could continue.

"Well, yes it is Hank."

"Something's happened. I knew the moment I saw you. I had a premonition that something was wrong. Something's happened to the baby."

"Yes, that's right, Hank. I–"

"How is Betsy? Is she all right?"

"No she isn't," Pat broke in. "Clint received a telegram from your dad asking him to find you."

"Pat, let me finish this," Clint said. "Hank, this is difficult for all of us, but Betsy is gone."

There was a loud gasp from Hank, then silence.

"Here is the telegram from your father," Clint said as he fished it out of his shirt pocket. He handed the folded sheet of paper to Hank and they both watched him open it slowly. Not a word was said. The distant sound of artillery was all they could hear.

The three men were sitting on logs, Pat and Clint facing Hank who was three or four feet away. They both watched as Hank read and reread the note. Tears flowed from his eyes as he stared vacantly at the message. A soft rain began to fall on the three of them.

After a while, Clint stood and said, "I'll leave you two alone. Hank, I'm so very sorry to bring you such devastating news. Use your strength in God and trust that He is in control."

Pat and Hank sat in silence for a long time. The skies sprinkled off and on before turning to a slow, light drizzle. Pat didn't know what to say and sat in silence, watching Hank.

For the next few days Hank would not speak to anyone, not even Pat. He performed his duties without saying a word. Pat worried about him and continually tried to engage him in some conversation, but he was unable to break down the wall of silence.

Client Phelps stayed with Battery F for two more days and even produced a gift, a box of French chocolates, which he presented to Lieutenant Case on the 18th when the lieutenant received word of his promotion to captain. Clint was a favorite of the men. He enjoyed not only spending the time with them, but was able to gather a great deal of background information for his article. Even Captain Case filled him in on the particulars of the most recent battle.

Late in the afternoon of the nineteenth, Clint said his goodbyes to the battery and before leaving, pulled Pat aside.

"Keep your eye on Hank, Pat. Don't let him go off of the deep end. I hope that his grieving will end soon, but it will take some more time."

Pat shrugged helplessly. "I sit with him, but he won't talk. I don't know what else to do. And I surely don't know what to say."

"Just being with him and showing your support is about all you can do for now. Don't let him run off. My fear is that without meaning in his life he may do something drastic, go AWOL, expose himself unnecessarily in combat, sacrifice his life for little cause."

"I'll do what I can," Pat sighed. "Thanks for coming all this way, for Hank's sake. I don't know what he would've done if this news had come by telegram or a letter. You have been a great comfort for both of us."

"Well, Pat, take care. I'm going to catch a ride on into Chalons and get back to Chateau Thierry and finish that story I started before I got that blasted telegram. I did benefit from coming here, though. I got a lot of information about you Illinois boys for the folks back in Chicago. There are few good things that come out of war and we have to make the best of them. One thing is the friendships we develop in these times of adversity. Both you and Hank, for example, hearing news of the death of loved ones at home while engaged on the front. It's quite a contradiction. The ones at home are always getting the bad news of battle causalities. Both of you have suffered losses at home, and so you might be able to reestablish your friendship, sooner than later."

Pat nodded. "Well, goodbye, Clint. I hope I see you soon. The rumor mill has it we'll be moving out of here soon. Don't get too close to the front. You know that I consider you family and I don't need more bad news."

Clint smiled. "I'll keep safe. I'll leave the fighting to you younger men." He gave Pat a big bear hug and turned and walked away without looking back.

At midnight the limbers arrived, the cannoneers hitched up the cannon, and the battery quickly got on their way, heading south through the small village of St. Hilaire au Temple. They continued on south for another 17 kilometers and arrived at Dampierre-au-Temple around 5:30 the next morning. Here they pitched their pup tents, attended to the animals and slept soundly until 4:30 that afternoon.

It wasn't until after 9:00 p.m. that they were again on the march headed towards Cheppes, some 28 kilometers away. They hiked all night through a light drizzle. The clouds hung low in the sky, adding to the gloom that already pervaded the spirit of the men of the battery. It wasn't until 6:30 the next morning that they arrived just outside of town where they pitched their pup tents again and slept all day.

At 4:00 p.m. Pat woke up, rubbed his eyes, and stretched. He looked around and realized Hank was not in the tent. He felt a sinking feeling in the pit of his stomach and quickly dressed. He'd been keeping his eye on him and now he was gone.

As he left the tent, he asked all he came in contact with if they'd seen Hank. No one had. Pat went into town looking for him. He looked at all the faces of the soldiers, but to no avail. The town of Cheppes was loaded with troops and it was difficult distinguishing one uniformed man from another.

Pat searched for over an hour, going from one bar to the other. As he was about running out of places to look, he at last saw Hank sitting alone at a table in the back of a crowded beer emporium on a side street near the train station. Pat pushed his way through the crowded room, pulled out a chair opposite Hank, and sat down.

"I've been looking all over the place for you. Have you been here a long time?"

Hank just stared down into his beer.

"Hank, you're going to have to talk to somebody sometime. I know you've been through a lot, but you just got to pull yourself together and carry on."

This, too, was followed with silence. A barmaid came to the table and asked in French what Pat wanted. He pointed to Hank's mug of beer and said, "Bring me one of those." Without a word the waitress turned around and disappeared into the crowded room.

After a moment or so, Pat said, "Hank, do you remember what you told me when we got word that my dad died?"

Hank, for the first time, looked at Pat. His eyes were sunken and red, with large dark circles.

"You said that we must not mourn for the departed, but instead celebrate their lives."

"But this is different," Hank blurted out. "My child did not get a chance to live! What do I have to celebrate?"

The waitress returned and put the beer in front of Pat, he dug his left hand into his pocket and pulled out some change and put it on the barmaid's tray. Following another short silence after she left, Pat scooted his chair up to the table, placed his elbows on it, and leaned forward towards his friend. "The only thing I know and can say for sure is that your baby is with Betsy. I have this vision in my head and I've had it for the last few days. And the vision is of Betsy holding a baby and looking extremely calm and even smiling. I can't shake the image, but it's one full of love …and happiness."

"I miss her so much, I feel so empty," Hank said and his eyes filled with tears that rolled unashamedly down his cheeks.

"I know you do. Keep the image of Betsy smiling and holding that baby of yours in her arms. Be happy for her. That baby is part of you too, and most importantly, that baby is not alone, but with his mother. When your days are through, they'll both be there to greet you when you cross over to the other side."

Hank put his head down on his arm and wept silently for a long time.

Pat sat quietly; sipping his beer, hoping his being there would comfort his friend.

Chateau-Thierry

After being pulled off of the line on the eighteenth, the men of the 167th Infantry Regiment had two days in which to lick their wounds and to refit before being sent forward for their next encounter with the enemy.

During the two days of rest, the surviving members of the regiment gorged themselves on army rations and whatever civilian foods and drinks they could get their hands on. In all too short of a time, the 167th had to form up and march from their rear rest area to the town of Cheppes. They arrived late in the evening of the twenty-first. The weary doughboys placed their bedrolls on the ground and slept till revelry, which was at the ungodly hour of 3:00 a.m.

It was during these predawn hours in Cheppes that the troops and animals were loaded on the hated 40 and 8 cars while all of the rolling stock, weapons, and miscellaneous equipment were placed on flat cars. Just as the sun was peeking over the horizon in the east, the regiment began their long rail journey to La-Ferte-sous-Jouarre, a small town located about ten kilometers east of the confluence of the Ourcq and Marne rivers and their eventual debarkation point. It was from here they would proceed back to the front.

The Germans had pushed into Chateau-Thierry, forcing the westbound trains from the Champagne sector to take a roundabout route that sent them through the outer reaches of Paris. There they had been able to turn north and return to the 42nd Division's new sector of the front, which was located on the west side of this large salient.

The day of the trip turned out to be beautiful and warm, and many of the doughboys rode on the flat cars in order to avoid the stifling confinement of the boxcars and to enjoy the weather.

Jake found a clear spot and sat on the side of one of these flat cars, dangling his legs over the edge, leaning back against his backpack that he'd propped up against a large crate. His platoon leaders joined him and he even entered into some of their idle chatter. Mostly, though, he just sat back and relaxed and enjoyed the fresh air. He'd had a shower the day before and for the first time in a very long time, he felt clean and at peace.

It was early afternoon when they reached the outskirts of Paris. Here they found that the bridges across the rail yards in Noisy-le-sec, a suburb, were crowded with Parisians, mostly old men, women, young girls and children. They had come out to cheer the victorious troops. It had been four years since these Parisians had had a chance to celebrate a victory. Now, right here, passing close by, were the very same Americans who had stopped the Boche in the Champagne. The spectators on the bridges and byways of Paris cheered and shouted to the Americans, these young men dressed in the olive drab and wearing those strange, large-rimmed campaign hats. The women threw kisses and flowers at the doughboys. The men cheered back, with renewed spirits, after having faced the worst that war had to offer. In the exchange of greetings they were able to relieve some of the pent-up emotion of the past month spent in the killing fields of France.

For the Americans it was like a big party or parade. This trip through the outskirts of Paris made each one feel proud of his part in the war. However, as the train left the City of Light and headed north, the men grew more somber, for they knew they were returning to the front.

They finally arrived at their destination in the early morning of July 23. Here, the 167th was quickly loaded onto trucks and driven to the vicinity of Epieds, some thirty-five kilometers to the northwest. Prior to the Allied assault on July 18, this town had been in German hands.

The recent German offensive had gobbled up a great deal of real estate before it was finally halted at the Marne River. These gains between Rheims and Soissons created a large salient that reached out and threatened Paris itself. This Boche offensive, which the Rainbow helped stop in the Champagne sector, left a large protrusion in the front that extended from Rheims along the east side and ran southwest to Chateau-Thierry. From there the line extended north just east of Belleau Wood and then north-northwest to the Asine river, about ten kilometers west of Soissons. The Boche was now in a pocket that they could neither broaden nor deepen.

With the latest German advance halted, Marshal Foch, the Allied supreme commander, went immediately to the offensive. He hit all sides of the Chateau-Thierry salient. The Germans were bottled up in this pocket in which they had stored vast quantities of supplies they intended to use on their drive to Paris. It wasn't until after the German advance had been stopped dead in its tracks that General Ludendorf, the German commander on the Western Front, realized his army was vulnerable to an Allied counterattack from all sides of the salient. But his realization of this was too late, for the Allies were upon them before Ludendorf could make an orderly withdrawal.

On July 18, the First and Second American Divisions attacked south of the Asine River and just west of Soissions. The Fourth Division, on their right, also applied pressure to the west side of the salient near the town of Lizy.

The momentum of the ferocious attack carried the Fourth Division forward for eight kilometers. The 26th Division, on the right of the American Fourth, drove east before pivoting north of Chateau-Thierry in an effort to block the German pullout.

American units were not acting alone in this massive strike. French, Moroccan, and Senegalese troops, a small number of British units, and one Italian division joined them. As the salient compressed under Allied pressure, the fighting front narrowed. The fierce combat resulted in heavy casualties on both sides and it soon became necessary to take out the lead divisions for a rest. As a result, the 26th Yankee Division and the 167th French Division were pulled from the line and replaced with the Rainbow Division.

Major Hinkle and his staff were burning the midnight oil, cutting orders and providing the necessary transport to get the division positioned in time. The logistics of the move were integral to the carrying out of the battle plan. The 84th Infantry Brigade of the Rainbow, which included the 167th and the 168th Infantry Regiments were to be positioned on the right side of the divisional line while the 83rd Infantry Brigade, including the 165th and 166th Infantry Regiments were positioned on the left side. Each regiment had to be brought from the Champagne sector and positioned with care at the same time the individual regiments from the 26th Division were withdrawn. If the timing was not right it could leave a weak spot in the line.

The artillery batteries from the 26th Yankee Division held their position in order to continue their bombardment of the German troops. The 67th Artillery Brigade from the Rainbow moved up alongside and fired with them, thus doubling their sectors' bombardment capability.

Late in the afternoon of July 24, the Alabamians of the 167th Infantry Regiment marched within two kilometers of the front line. Jake didn't know how far they'd come since getting off of the trucks. All he did know was that it had taken them a day and a half to get here from La-Ferte-sous-Jouarre. There had been numerous delays, as the roads were clogged with troops, equipment and supplies. The regiment had finally been sent across fields and cross-country in order to speed up their movement to the front. Once in position, they found their work cut out for them. Instead of holding the line as they had done at Lunneville, Baccarat and Champagne, this time, they were expected to advance and gain more ground.

As they moved to their final position on July 25, Jake found that his company had been positioned opposite a little farm across a road that was held by the Germans. This piece of real estate was called the La Croix Rouge Farm, and was in a clearing surrounded by trees on three sides. The road on which G Company was positioned ran northwest to southeast, diagonally through the land. The farm buildings were approximately one kilometer northeast of the road. The Germans had placed numerous machine gun nests on the far side of the farm buildings and in the woods surrounding the farm, each with crossing fields of fire.

The Americans sought cover in the trees that lined their side of the road. It was the clearing between the road and the farm buildings on the German side that worried Jake.

All day and night of the twenty-fifth, the division completed all of their dispositions. Early the next morning the 167th Infantry attacked La Croix Rouge Farm.

Before dawn on the twenty-sixth, Jake led the First and Third Platoons of G Company up a narrow gully he had discovered the day before that ran from the road up to the barn. There was a heavy ground fog that covered their advance. Jake and Lieutenant Sands were in the lead as they approached their destination.

At 20 yards from the barn, Lieutenant Sands held up his hand when he heard voices. He put his finger to his lips and Jake signaled the men to hit the ground and stay quiet. There were two German sentries protecting the gully and both were off their guard, enjoying a smoke and a quiet talk. Jake gestured for two lead men from the First Platoon to move up to his position and motioned to them to use their knives by running his forefinger across his throat. They quietly disappeared into the fog and soon the conversation stopped. Shortly they were back and the men started forward again. They climbed up out of the culvert and rapidly ran across the small open area to the barn. The men quietly lined up along the wall of the stone structure. Jake went to the window and peered in. There were about 20 Boche who were using the hayloft for their barracks. They were in the process of getting up, light in the barn being provided by two ceiling-hung kerosene lanterns.

Jake motioned for the Third Platoon to go to the rear door and the First Platoon to enter the front. He unholstered his pistol, which he held in his raised left hand. With his back to the wall of the barn he led the First Platoon around the corner of the building to the front doors, which were closed. He paused and listened at the door for a moment, took a deep breath, took a step back and with terrific force, broke through the door, pistol blazing. The men of the First followed him in, firing their rifles at anything that moved. The battle for La Croix Rouge Farm was underway. The Germans were caught by complete surprise and few had weapons at hand, and soon all of the Boche were dead or wounded.

When the remainder of the regiment heard the small arms fire, it was their signal to start across the open field. The enemy machine guns behind the farm and those inside the house some yards north of the barn began firing on the Americans now out in the open.

After securing the barn, Jake quickly pinpointed the positions of three machine guns near the buildings and ordered the Third Platoon to attack from their rear. In a short firefight they captured the three automatic weapons, which they turned on the enemy emplacements in the woods and the other nearby structures. The barn provided protection, but the incoming fire was fierce.

The concealed guns in the woods were too much for the rest of the regiment, caught in the open field, and they soon hit the dirt, hugging the ground below the two-foot high wheat, trying to avoid the blasts. Within an hour of the initial assault, the Boche in the woods started a counterattack on the barn and Jake was forced to retreat, along with the First and Third Platoons, back to the gully they'd just come up. During this time the remainder of the regiment scurried quickly back to the road, taking the wounded that could be reached.

All morning and afternoon the wooded slopes around La Croix Rouge witnessed a terrific battle. The buildings changed hands several times. The Americans were now confronting the massed firepower of many machine guns for which the Boche were famous. The Germans used these machine-guns in a masterly fashion and by day's end held La Croix Rouge Farm. Causalities on both sides were high, and the day ended in a draw. The Americans had to rethink their plan of attack against these automatic weapons that the Germans used so well.

The men of the 167th and 168th Regiments had given ground that day and ended where they had started the night before.

Late in the evening, the Germans realized that they were in an untenable position. Outnumbered and surrounded on three sides, they withdrew from the farm late that night and fell back nearly six kilometers, across the Ourcq River to its north bank. Here they reestablished their line in a great natural fortress with the little village of Sergy at their back, which was located in a small valley, backed by bare hills that sloped up to eighty meters above the town and onto level plateaus.

A small creek, the Ru Du Pont Brule, protected the Germans' east flank. To the west were wooded areas in which they placed their machine guns. More woodland and a place called Meurcy Farm were situated in the river valley to the west of Sergy and north of the Ourcq.

All during the twenty-third and twenty-fourth of July, one train after another pulled into La-Ferte-sous-Jouarre. After off-loading their cargo the trains would pull out to make room for the next one.

About two hours after the 167th Infantry Regiment had detrained and departed for the front, the train transporting Battery F of the 149th Field Artillery arrived. They immediately unloaded men and equipment and marched to a timbered area near Montreuil-aux-Lions some 10 kilometers away. This position had been the camp of Battery B of the 101st Field Artillery of the 26th Division.

The men found all kinds of equipment scattered about in a helter skelter manner, implying a rapid advance. The troops were ordered to clean up the area and to establish camp. After these chores were completed and a semblance of order was achieved the men were given the rest of the day off. Most slept until late in the evening.

On the 24th, preparations were made to move forward the next day.

Hank had overcome some of his grief but had become more of a recluse, joining in on the drinking but not adding much to the conversation. Pat worried about him, but wasn't able to break through. They no longer had much to talk about and Hank drank himself into a drunken stupor whenever the opportunity presented itself.

Early in the morning, Captain Case received orders for the men to stamp out or otherwise obliterate the battery and regimental designation embossed on the men's personal dog tags, to prevent the enemy from determining the identity of the troops opposing them.

As he was hammering out these designations on his tags, Tom asked the obvious question. "What's to stop the Germans from asking the live prisoners what their unit affiliation is?"

At 10:00 that morning orders were received for the battery to start their move forward. By noon all was harnessed and hitched and underway.

The weather was hot and humid and all were extremely uncomfortable. The previous night's drinking session did not help.

The route of march took them through recent battle zones, Marigny-en-Orxois, Lucy-le-Bocage, Bouresches, and Bois de Belleau. Each step bore evidence of the savage battle that had engulfed the Second Division just the day before. Castaway and battle-damaged equipment covered the ground as far as the eye could see. Worst of all were the newly dug graves, marked by rifles stuck in the ground capped with the previous owner's helmet.

The scorching sun and dust-covered roads made the march a miserable experience. There were no songs; it was all they could do just to keep the pace. It didn't take long before their canteens ran dry and there were no prospects of filling them.

The men had just had tapioca, bread and coffee for breakfast and it wasn't long before their personal supply of food ran out and they felt they couldn't take another step. With scorched tongues and blasphemous observations they continued on for twenty-five kilometers to their destination, a small wood east of Biznety and south of Epieds.

The battery commander allowed the men to sleep late into the morning. Before eating they fed and groomed the horses, then sat down to an unappetizing breakfast of lukewarm tapioca, bread and coffee. Few had the stomach to eat, as the stench of dead, unburied men and horses filled the campsite.

Following breakfast, Sergeant Baker formed a detail of six men whose duty was to bury two members of Company K of the 104th Infantry. Both had been killed the day before just a short distance from camp. The intense heat brought with it almost instant decay and infestations of maggots. The remains of George Monroe and Henry Laiolette were buried with honor.

At twilight, Captain Case received orders to proceed to the front, just north of Epieds.

Soon after the battery was underway it began to rain. In no time it was a virtual torrent making the roads nearly impassable due to the oozing mud. The carriages slipped and slid across the road. E Battery, in the front, became bogged down and held up progress for hours. When the command to get underway was finally heard, those who had flopped on the ground for some sleep got up and trudged on.

Jason Newcum slowly got to his feet and nudged the person next to him and said, "Time to get moving, buddy!" There was no response, and he grabbed the man's shoulder and rolled him over, only to discover that he was a dead French Poilus who'd had half his face blown off. Jason screamed and Pappy, who was nearby, came to his aid and consoled him as they started the march.

Once they reached the position they learned that the Germans had retreated and were now out of range. There was nothing to do but to turn around and go back to their starting point. The battery arrived at the original camp at 2:30 a.m. All were soaking wet and bitterly cussing out the army and all those in charge. Although there was not a dry spot to be found for miles around, the rain didn't stop the men from falling asleep when they finally rolled up in their blankets at 4:00 a.m.

At 4:15 p.m. the call to "harness and hitch" echoed throughout the camp and by 5:30 Battery F was on its way to the front once again. It had rained all day and the roads were in worse condition than the day before. The night was pitch dark; so dark that one could barely see the man or wagon directly in front.

Shortly, everything was covered with mud; mud splashed up by the wheels of the vehicles and the hooves of the horses and mules. Few words were spoken, as all efforts were devoted to helping pull the carriages forward. The only sounds were of the battery making its way through the rain and mud. The quietness was broken by an occasional cry for "Cannoneers to the front" or "Cannoneers to the rear" and the profane replies to these commands.

Shortly after daybreak the column came to a complete stop when they encountered a steep hill that appeared impassable. Battery E, which preceded Battery F in the line of march, had bogged down and was unable to move. Sergeant Baker, because of his many years of service and military knowledge, was able to speak his mind to his superiors without reprimand. "Get that there damned outfit off'n the road and let us show 'em how to climb the grade," he told the major.

Immediately, permission was granted and the battery started up the hill. With ten horse hitches it took highly skilled drivers and superhuman effort to keep the animals pulling at the traces to get the carriages of Battery F over the top. They then went back and helped E Battery to the top.

When Ike opened his eyes, all he could see was a blinding whiteness that made him blink and squint until his eyes adjusted to the brightness.

His body hurt all over, especially his head, which throbbed and ached in spasms. The pain he felt in his left leg was almost unbearable.

Slowly, his eyes began to focus on his surroundings. He could see that he was in a bright room and that he was on a bed. There was a table and chair nearby and the bright sun was streaming through the one unshaded window. The smell of disinfectant permeated the air. It finally dawned on him that he was in a hospital, but he had no clue where that hospital was.

The last thing he could remember was flying over the bridges near Dormans. Everything else was blank. He couldn't determine if he was in an enemy hospital or a French one. He tried to get up, but the pain in his left leg was excruciating. His head throbbed even more and he lay back down and passed out again.

When he came to the second time, he remembered that he was in a hospital, but it was now dark. He felt the presence of another person, but had no idea who it was.

"Ike, are you awake?"

This familiar voice sounded far off, as if she were lost somewhere in a fog.

Ike tried to answer, but the only sound he could make was a gurgling, almost grating noise deep in his throat.

"Ike, are you all right?"

Ike cleared his throat and whispered in a raspy voice, "Where am I?"

"You're in the American Hospital in Paris. It's me, Agnes!"

"Agnes? Paris?"

Agnes got up from the chair where she'd been napping and grabbed Ike's hand and held it. "I'm so grateful you're awake. You've been in a coma for nearly eight days. They brought you here from the field hospital when they couldn't get you to wake up. We knew you had been awake for a short time yesterday, but I will tell you more about that later. Right now I must go and get your doctor."

When she left the room, Ike tried to rise up on an elbow, but the effort and pain were too much and he fell back, unconscious.

When he awoke the third time, there was a strange man taking his blood pressure. He was an older man, very bald and quite short.

"Well, Lieutenant, when they first brought you in we thought we might lose you," the man said. "It's good to see you awake and out of the woods, so to speak. When your nurse came to get me last night, you had fallen asleep before I could get here, but your blood pressure has returned to normal and your color is back. How do you feel?"

"Hungry and thirsty," Ike replied.

"Good, that's a good sign. We'll have something for you soon. That's some nurse you have. She's taken extraordinary care of you ever since you got here. Says she knows you."

"When can I get up? I need to move around."

"Don't push it too fast, maybe later today. You've had some pretty serious injuries. You banged your head pretty hard and you took a bullet in your left thigh, which fortunately missed the bone, but you lost a lot of blood. You also suffered some superficial burns on your feet and right leg. Nevertheless, you've been healing quite well. Now that you're awake we can get some nourishment down you and get you out and about."

"Agnes said I'd been unconscious for over a week. Has it really been that long?"

"As I said, you had a head injury, a concussion. However, you seem to be off of our critical list now. Today is the twenty-fourth of July and you crashed on the fifteenth. Well, you seem to be doing much better. I'll stop back to see you later in the afternoon." The doctor quickly opened the door of the room and disappeared into the hall, leaving Ike alone again.

He lay back on the pillow and tried to remember how he crashed, but it was all a blur.

Within the hour his breakfast arrived and he wolfed it down and drank nearly a pitcher of water. When Agnes came in he was beginning to feel a lot better. They talked for an hour, before she had to return to her duty station.

Ike's recovery went well for the next four days, and his head no longer ached. Agnes spent every moment she could with him, even though her duties kept her extremely busy elsewhere in the hospital. By the 27th, he was up and hobbling around on his crutches, exploring every nook and cranny of the building.

As long as Ike had been flat on his back, Agnes spent the early evenings in his room, sleeping in the chair. She only went home to bathe and change. He felt closer to her every minute they were together, and his love for her seemed to grow each time he saw her.

On August 1, Frank Linki and Josiah Wortham showed up in the hospital. The reunion was an exuberant one, filled with jokes and laughs.

Ike was incredulous when they first burst into his room, and after a long pause he finally sputtered, "Where on earth did you guys come from?"

"We had to come in to get a couple of new planes," Captain Wortham responded.

"SPADs, to be exact," Frank added. "They're finally equipping the entire squadron with them. We're going to be here for a few days for orientation and then fly back to base on Tuesday."

"There's one waiting for you, when you're ready," Captain Wortham said. "Do you know when you're getting out of here?"

"The doctor says I'll be able to return to duty in a week or so. Man, I can't wait to get out of this hospital."

"Yeah, I bet you just can't wait to get away from your little French nurse, Ike." Frank added sarcastically. "By the way, I fixed the captain up with Lisa Wagner and I'm taking Beth Sterns out. Will you and Agnes be able to join us tomorrow for a night on the town?"

"I wouldn't miss it for the world, even if I have to sneak out of this place."

After Frank and Captain Wortham left, Ike spent the rest of the day relaxing, storing up energy. Agnes was excited about going out and was able to rearrange her schedule. Even his doctor approved, after some ardent pleas Ike made during the morning checkup. Once that hurdle was crossed he spent the remainder of the day preparing for his night out. More than anything, he wanted to spend all of the time he could with Agnes, particularly away from the hospital.

At precisely 5:30 p.m., Agnes showed up in his room. She was dressed in her best evening gown and was a sight to behold. Ike was speechless when he first saw her and all he could do was whistle. After a moment of ogling, he put on his uniform coat and she assisted him down the stairs and out to a waiting taxi.

Their night out on the town was a fantasy come true for Ike. The group ate and drank their fill, laughed until they cried, and most importantly, they forgot about the war. Later, they went to a show and finally to a club for some dancing. Ike sat at the table as the others twirled around the floor. Both Captain Wortham and Frank danced with Agnes, and as she floated lightly by on her feet, Ike knew that he loved her. She was so beautiful that he wished the night would never end.

Later, as they all sat talking, he learned that Frank had become an ace, downing his fifth enemy aircraft just two days before coming to Paris. The captain had increased his kills by two and was now credited with seven enemy planes and two balloons.

As the talk turned towards the war, Ike asked the question that had been on his mind since he came out of the coma. "How did I get out of that plane and here in the hospital? I don't remember a thing except flying over the bridges, and then nothing."

"Two doughboys saw you crash," Captain Worthem said. "Your plane was burning pretty bad but the flames were extinguished when you hit the water. Then, under heavy enemy fire, they waded out to the wreckage and pulled you to shore. You must have loosened your belts just before you hit the water because you were thrown clear. They sent you to an aid station and then on into Paris. As a matter of fact, they tell me that you've had some excellent and very personal nursing."

Agnes turned bright red.

As the night extended into early morning, Ike was rapidly tiring, and at 2:30 a.m. Agnes told the others that she'd better get him back to the hospital. He was weary after his first excursion and was glad to be on his way back.

Agnes helped Ike up the stairs and left the room as he changed and crawled into the bed. As he was just about to drift off, he heard the door of the darkened room open and before he could say a word, Agnes slipped into bed with him.

The Ourcq River

After they discovered that the Germans had pulled out of La Croix Rouge Farm, the infantry of the 42nd Division moved forward, north towards the Ourcq River.

In the late evening of July 27, armored cars, scouting in advance of the 42nd's infantry, drew fire from German machine guns dug in on the north side of the river. Due to the close proximity of enemy positions, the infantry established their camp for the night approximately one kilometer south of the Ourcq, out of sight of the Boche emplacements.

After dark, Jake and ten select men from G Company moved forward to the river on a reconnaissance patrol to probe for a point for the infantry to cross the rushing water. The retreating Germans had blown up the two bridges near Sergy. This only exacerbated the problem, as the heavy rains of the past few days had swollen the Ourcq to a width of 14 meters and it was estimated to have a maximum depth of four meters.

Jake called for volunteers to enter the water with him to test the current and the depth. Without hesitation, all hands went up.

"Jones, strip down to your shorts and follow me," he said, pointing to the trooper standing closest to him.

After shedding their clothes, each placed mud and dirt over his body and then ran in a crouch to the river and entered the stream, Jones a few steps behind Jake. They stumbled on the rocks until they were at a depth up to the chest. Even though the temperature of the late night air was warm, the water felt cold to Jake and he shivered a little, whether out of excitement, the cold water, or fear, he didn't know. Before they reached midstream, Jake could no longer touch bottom. He had to swim against a pretty strong current in order not to be swept away. It was at this point he discovered that Jones could not swim.

"Jones, why did you raise your hand for this job?"

"Well, sir, I didn't think this little ole stream was that deep."

"Keep going downstream and see if you can find a place to cross that isn't over your head," Jake whispered back in disgust, and then continued swimming across.

He came out of the water just west of Sergy and quickly ran to some underbrush along the north bank. He could just make out Jones still working his way west in waist-deep water, looking for a shallow crossing point.

Jake studied the north bank as best he could in the dark. He made mental notes of the incline of the bank and of visible obstacles, as well as places of shelter from enemy fire. He knew he had to find a place or point that wasn't too deep and that would provide cover once across the river, or the men would be slaughtered as they struggled through the water during the attack scheduled for the early morning. He walked west, parallel with Jones, for about 500 feet. It was here that Jones was able to cross in waist-deep water.

Jake entered the water to join Jones as Jones approached the north bank. As soon as Jake had taken only three or four steps into the water, he heard a loud voice.

"Halt!"

This was followed immediately by rifle fire. Both men ran as rapidly as they could against the current to deeper water and dove under the surface and headed back towards their side of the river. Jones soon panicked in the middle of the stream. Coming up for air, he'd stepped into a deep hole in the river's bottom and was in over his head. He was thrashing about, screaming and gasping for air. When Jake reached Jones, he swung with both his right and left fists as hard as he could, knocking him cold. He swam a sidestroke as best he could, holding Jones with his right arm. When he could touch the bottom at waist depth, he hoisted him to his shoulder and staggered back to shore and behind the safety of some boulders.

All of this time he could hear rifle fire and saw water, divots of dirt, and debris flying around him. He stumbled or was thrown off balance once, then quickly regained his feet and continued for the protection of the boulders and underbrush along the bank. The men of his patrol answered the German fire immediately, disrupting the Boche gunners' aim.

Soon the rifle fire subsided and the members of the G Company patrol made their way to Jake, who was huddled with Jones behind the embankment.

Jones had been hit by one slug that penetrated his back, killing him instantly. Jake felt terrible, for if he hadn't been carrying Jones, the bullet would have surely hit him. Jones had saved Jake's life by giving up his own. This was an image that would remain with him a long time.

As Jake struggled into his clothes, the men rigged a stretcher with some branches and Jones' shirt and trousers and carried him back to camp for burial.

Jake reported his findings to Major Davidson and with the remainder of the company commanders fixed the point Jones had found as the primary crossing for the 167th Infantry. At this point Jake described, as best he could, the conditions of the north bank and the defenses.

"It was awfully dark, but what I did see was a steep bank, the top of which is about ten feet above the river. There are numerous boulders and a few small trees and bushes. We'll be in the open till we get to the bank, which should provide adequate cover. I didn't see any enemy emplacements below the bank. It's going to be a tough crossing, but once we're on the far side we should be able to establish a line of defense there."

The major laid out the plan for the attack and went over the disposition of the companies for the next morning's approach to the far bank with each of the commanders.

"This crossing is going to be difficult," he said to the whole group after he'd finished with the individual commanders. "As Jake here has already pointed out we'll be in the open for some time. Since we're going just before dawn, we might escape detection, but I doubt it. Move the men across as rapidly as you can, for as long as we are in the water we're easy targets. God bless you all!" And the men were dismissed.

Before dawn of July 28, the infantry regiments deployed for their attack across the Ourcq River. At 5:30, the artillery started pounding the north side of the Ourcq from Sergy on the right to Foret de Nesle on the left. At 6:00 the infantry started forward. The return fire from the German machine guns was fierce and it wasn't long before the Ourcq ran red with the blood of the Rainbow.

The New Yorkers were the first to gain a foothold on the north bank, and by 11:00 a.m. all of the regiments had reached the other side. The struggle for Seringes, Hill 220, Meurcy Farm, and Sergy was underway and lasted all day and night and late into the morning of the 29th.

Once the 167th had established a toehold on the north bank, they, along with the 168th, rushed the little village of Sergy and established control of the south end of town in the early afternoon. However, heavy concentrations of machine gun fire from the woods on the left and concentrated rifle fire from in front and on the right forced them to retreat back to the Ourcq.

The 167th immediately started another counterattack and entered the outskirts again, the 168th on their right.

Company G, with Jake in the lead, took the first house on the edge of town. The first platoon held the house while the remaining platoons ventured up the street. At about 50 meters from their base, they ran into the vanguard of the Fourth Prussian Guards, and a firefight ensued.

All afternoon, the 167th and 168th Infantry regiments rolled into Sergy, only to lose their grip from another German counterattack. As dusk was falling in the evening of July 28, the Americans rushed Sergy one more time and held.

The fight for Meurcy Farm and Hill 220 was running into the same stubborn resistance. All night and into the early dawn of the next day, the enemy subjected the Americans to a tremendous artillery and aerial bombardment. The men huddled closer and closer to the walls of the bomb-ravaged buildings in Sergy.

After the sun was up on the 29th, the Prussian Guard attacked the little town again and in a terrific hand-to-hand, building-to-building fight, drove the Americans back to the north bank of the Ourcq. After two days of heavy combat and carnage, the Rainbow hadn't made any effective gains and their casualties had been heavy.

Major Davidson called his company commanders for a conference in the late morning.

"Gentlemen, we have a problem with these machine guns. The 166th has come up with a plan that I think may resolve the problem and cut down on our casualties. Instead of rushing the guns all at once with the men exposed, they have been sending one man at a time. Get a platoon as close as you can and try to encircle the weapon or at least form a semicircle around it. Then one man on the left or right can stand and rush the target for two or three steps before hitting the ground. Then another man will stand and rush from the other direction; only two or three steps at a time. By rushing one man at a time and only for a short distance and from different sides, the gunners won't have time to take aim. When you get in close, toss grenades or use your rifles. I know it'll work and it'll reduce our causalities."

Within a very short time, Company G was able to put the new tactic to work. It was their objective to move to the west side of the little town and enter from the northwest end in a pincer movement, with the other companies entering town from the south. In order to do this, they had to clear three machine gun emplacements blocking their objective.

It wasn't long before the German gunners would see one khaki-clad trooper jump up from the tall, golden wheat and run three or four steps towards him. By the time the gun was swung towards the target and fired, the man had disappeared in the wheat. Then another figure would pop up from the other side and rush towards the gun, doing the same thing, tightening the ring around the position. Before they could react the gunners were confronted with blithering rifle fire or hand grenades.

Jake was elated over the success of this strategy, as his company only suffered two casualties in taking out the three machine guns. By noon, the Rainbow had established control of Sergy, Meurcy Farm, and the edge of Foret de Nesle. It was a great victory.

At the end of the day on July 29, the Rainbow now controlled Seringes, Meurcy Farm, Hill 220, and Sergy, where they had established a foothold on the plateau above this small river town.

On Sunday, July 28, the batteries of the 149th Field Artillery moved into position in order to provide support for the infantry, who were preparing to cross the Ourcq and attack the German defenders. Battery F was in an open field near the Preaux Farm, just a little east of the Bois de la Tournelle.

They arrived shortly before 3:00 a.m. after an eight-kilometer forced march. They had been up since 7:00 a.m. of the day before and most were exhausted, but rest wasn't in the cards, at least not yet.

Camouflage had to be placed over the guns, flop trenches and train pits had to be dug and the guns positioned for firing, as well as ammunition readied for use. The support echelon for the firing battery with its combat train and ammunition caissons was positioned in the woods immediately behind the cannon.

The stench of the dead men and animals from the previous day's fighting was overwhelming, and most of the troops wore bandannas over their mouths and noses to help filter the air.

By 6:00 a.m. the batteries had completed their preparations and precisely on the hour began their bombardment. F Battery's target was a series of machine gun nests located in the southwest corner of Forret de Nesle, which were impeding the infantry's efforts in crossing the Ourcq. The targets could not be seen from the gun positions and all fire was based on the barrage maps. The battery commander used the remains of a church steeple in Seringes et Nesle for the laying of the guns.

Late in the afternoon, during a lull in the fighting, Pat had gone to the echelon in the rear to retrieve some tools he needed for adjusting the number one gun. On his way back he stopped to talk to one of the drivers, all of whom were engaged in grazing the horses. Out of nowhere, four shells from enemy guns fell in their midst, killing two animals, wounding three others, and slightly wounding two drivers.

This brought Sergeant Baker and the unit's medical officer quickly to the field. The medic tended to the wounded men, while Sergeant Baker examined the wounded horses. He concluded that they needed to be destroyed.

"Littler, go shoot that there mare on the far side and I'll take care of these."

Pat looked at the sergeant in disbelief. "You mean, shoot the horse?" he stammered.

"You're the only other one with a sidearm besides me, ain't ya? Now go do it, put the poor bastard out of her misery!"

Pat had seen enough dead men and animals in the past few days, but he rationalized that he hadn't been responsible for their deaths. Now he was to take a life, from up close. He slowly drew his .45 from his holster and slid back the ejection slide with his left hand as he approached the mare. He heard the sergeant's pistol fire the first round. He didn't look up.

The nag lay on her side. Pat could see the pain and agony in her eyes as he lifted the automatic and placed it just a few inches above the right eye. He hesitated a moment and started to close his eyes when the sergeants pistol went off the second time. The report of the nearby gun startled him to such an extent that he squeezed the trigger from reflex reaction, and the weapon discharged.

He saw the spark of life quickly fade from the animal's eyes. Pat turned away, and went to his tools lying on the ground where he'd dropped them when he first heard the incoming shells. He holstered his sidearm, gathered the spilled tools in his hands, and started towards the number one gun without a word. He knew this sight would remain with him a long time.

After he finished fine-tuning the sight on the cannon, Pat sat down with Hank and told him about the incident with the horse.

"I've never killed anything up close. You know when I went bird hunting; I shot them from a distance. But this was different. The way the warmth in the eyes suddenly grew cold," he explained to Hank. "Why do these poor dumb animals have to suffer so? They didn't start this war. I just hope I never have to kill man or animal again."

Hank, who was slowly coming around to his old self, sympathized with Pat. But before they could dwell on the subject they were called back to the guns for a twilight barrage on the Germans' machine guns in Forret de Nesle.

The next morning at 4:30 the battery began another barrage targeting the area just north of Seringes. This bombardment lasted only a half hour. After this the guns remained silent until the afternoon. During this lull in the firing of the cannon, the men tried to catch up on some much-needed sleep.

During the evening hours, after a meal of cold monkey meat, another heavy bombardment was again aimed at Forret de Nesles. This wooded area north of Seringes had become a refuge for the retreating Boche. The Germans had set up a line of defense that included numerous machine guns. Prior to attacking the woods, by American infantry, tremendous fire fell on the enemy emplacements. During the day the battery fired 806 rounds.

The cannoneers had trouble keeping the guns properly laid on their targets, due in part to the long range at which the battery was firing. This distance required a quadrant for measuring the elevation of the muzzles when targeting at maximum distances. The cannoneers didn't have the luxury of circular trail pieces and wooden platforms that would ensure accuracy. But the fire fell on target, due to the expertise of the gunners.

At 3:00 a.m. on July 30, the battery began another harassing fire directed at the enemy machine guns positioned in Bois Brule, north of Meurcy Farm. Three men tried to sleep as the other three members of the crews continued the fire.

The Boche cannon were also active. All during the day shells fell all around the position, uprooting trees and sending great chunks of earth skyward. A French six-inch rifle located behind the battery's echelon exploded around noon and killed all of its crew of seven. There also had been little or no rest for the members of the combat echelon. The caisson drivers expected the command to "Harness and hitch!" at any moment day or night.

When the call did come the air was soon filled with their cursing and shouts as the horses were harnessed and then led from the corral to the wagons.

"Move over, you four-legged bastard!"

"Come on, back up, you daughter of a whore!"

This was followed by the familiar sound of the trace chains being pulled into position, the thumping of the animals' hooves on the ground and as they kicked against the carriages while they were backed into place and finally, the whistles and calls of the drivers as they urged the animals on with the accompanying rumble of the wheels when the caissons moved forward toward the ammunition dump.

In single file the carriages moved up to the dump. Once there the drivers jumped to the ground and released the locking pins, this was followed by the clatter of the wooden boxes being dropped to the ground. Next came the scraping sounds of the shells being shoved into place.

When all were loaded, the echelon commander shouted, "Forward yo!" and the deadly cargo started for the return trip to the guns.

All through the night of the thirtieth and on into the next day, the guns continued their harassing fire at the Prussian Guard holed up in the woods. Soon after sunup, the call for the Redden barrage was received. The infantry would soon attack Foret de Nesles.

The enemy resisted this advance and soon counterattacked, and the heavy fighting continued throughout the day.

The guns were blazing hot. As Pat swabbed the number one cannon, he was in a constant cloud of steam, the water vaporizing as soon as it touched the blazing hot barrel.

The German planes had control of the air over the battlefield and constantly strafed and bombed the gun positions. Fortunately, there were no injuries or equipment damage, at least at F Battery.

Corporal Stuart, at the echelon position, became the first to bring down a Boche plane that was orbiting over the position at about 1,000 feet. The machine guns attached to the battery weren't expected to down enemy aircraft, and this feat by Paul Stuart was greeted with great celebration and joy on the part of his compatriots.

It was during this time that word was received that the division surgeon had treated over 3275 wounded men from July 24 through 8:00 p.m. on July 30. There was no way to count the dead troopers as many still lay where they'd fallen, and many had been swept downstream by the swollen Ourcq River. The infantry regiments had suffered so many causalities that the 117th Engineers moved into position as infantry.

In the afternoon of August 1, the entire 149th Field Artillery fired in support of an infantry attack on Bois de Brule. When the bombardment concluded, Battery F had fired 1216 rounds for the day, or as Hank liked to say, "Over 1200 rounds sent forth to disrupt the enemy's beauty sleep."

During the bombardment, Pat and the others of the gun crew witnessed an enemy plane fall from the sky as a result of some accurate anti-aircraft fire. This plane crashed within 20 meters in front of the gun and burst into flames. The crew was incinerated on impact and the remains of the wreckage fell victim to subsequent enemy shelling. So complete was the devastation that after the battle nothing remained of either the plane or her crew.

The evening turned quiet, as the Boche was now in full retreat. This gave the entire battery an opportunity to get some much-needed shut-eye.

On August 2, Captain Case and Lieutenant Allen went forward to find a new position for the guns. However, the infantry was moving forward so rapidly that this turned out to be more difficult than it initially appeared.

The first place selected was soon abandoned, as the targets were out of range. A second position was selected and the battery marched forward, but as they were pulling up a Boche fighter appeared out of nowhere and bombed and strafed the site. Finally, a third position was selected just six kilometers northeast of the previous one, near the ruins of a chateau southeast of Fame du Donavon and forward of the infantry's second line.

As the battery moved forward they all were struck by the effects of the terrific battle that had taken place in capturing Fere-en-Tardenois and Seringes et Nesle. Devastation was all around them. Bodies of the men from the 42nd Division covered the ground, packs still on their backs, lying where they had fallen.

No one said much. All of the battery members took in the sight in silence, in reverence to these men who had given their all for freedom.

During the approach to the new site they were greeted enthusiastically by weary doughboys of the 165th Infantry Regiment, whose numbers had been decimated by the fighting of the preceding days. Once companies, their numbers now approximated those of platoons.

After establishing the position, the battery only fired 51 rounds at a distant crossroads. Soon the enemy was again out of range.

August 3 brought no firing at all. The men took most of the day off. Pat and the other mechanics joined the cannoneers in inspecting the ruins of a chateau, looking for souvenirs. Tom Brooks found a German Lueger that he quickly tucked away in his bag. The enemy, prior to the destruction of the chateau by American artillery, had used the building as a headquarters and observation post.

During the afternoon many men from the battery watched in wonder while a Boche plane attacked and shot down a French balloon. The lone occupant quickly took to his parachute and the Americans watched him float safely to earth.

It was 9:00 a.m. on July 30 and the 167th Infantry Regiment was once again on the offensive. The day before, they and the Iowans of the 168th had secured the river town of Sergy as well as the heights above the town. Their next objective was to attack the Chateau de Nesles, located north of town on the plateau, and back from the slopes that led up from the river bottom.

After a thirty-minute preliminary bombardment provided by the 26th Division's heavy artillery, the 167th Infantry started through a large wheat field towards the chateau. It didn't take long for the German machine gunners to zero in on the advancing troops, and the men were forced to hit the ground after reaching a point a little beyond halfway. The 26th's artillery searched out the Boche emplacements and soon silenced many of the guns.

The casualty rate was high as the infantry continued its advance across the wheat field. The men used their new tactic of moving just a few men at a time from different sections of the line of advance. Two or three men from the left would jump up and run a few yards before diving from view on their bellies under the tall stalks of wheat.

Jake couldn't believe he was unhurt when he reached the stone fence that surrounded the yard of the chateau. The constant chatter of the enemy's guns had swept the field from the right to the left and back, again and again. Those few who made it to the wall with him started pouring rifle fire into the windows of the now bombed-out house.

One by one the Boche guns in the chateau were silenced, but rifle and machine gun fire from the woods to the rear of the property remained intense. As the time clicked slowly away, more and more troopers reached the fence and showered more fire into the enemy's stronghold. The artillery continued to level the building, wing-by-wing and room-by-room. It wasn't long before the Boche started evacuating to the rear.

Jake, with the third platoon in tow, jumped the wall and started to advance on the house. The men took refuge where they could find it, behind trees, rocks, machinery and debris.

Slowly they advanced under the enemy's machine gun fire. One or two at a time would pop up from their hiding place and advance to another protected spot while the others directed their rifle fire on the windows and the enemy's hiding places.

The 168th Infantry Regiment to Jake's right had to dig in when they had gone only 400 meters across the wheat field. The Germans extracted a heavy toll in casualties on the Iowans, forcing them to keep low and to dig small flop trenches for protection.

In the late afternoon, the men from G Company reached the first shattered rooms of the chateau. The men of H Company reached the stables at the same time. Together they deluged the remaining Boche with rifle fire.

From room-to-room, wall-to-wall, and yard-to-yard, they slowly drove the Germans from the chateau and surrounding grounds.

By six in the evening the fight was over. The chateau was in American hands and the Boche were withdrawing slowly northward, towards the Vesle River.

During the next day, the 167th and 168th rested in the ruins of the chateau. Jake and the other company commanders spent the time redistributing what troops they had left amongst the platoons.

Finally, on August 1, the 168th Infantry Regiment fought their last engagement of the Ourcq campaign, while the 167th was held in reserve. Following heavy and bloody fighting they took control of Hill 212, high ground situated to the northeast of the chateau that a few German companies were using in an effort to stop the American advance on their withdrawing army.

This pitched battle raged most of the day, and in the early evening the Third Battalion finally gained a firm grasp on the hill. Early in the nighttime hours the Boche retreated, giving up the entire Ourcq Valley, and continued their retreat to the north, towards the Vesle River.

Shells rained up and down the whole of the valley of the Ourcq River all day and all night of August 1. After that shelling, the valley was once again in Allied hands and began approaching a semblance of peace.

The German Army was now in full retreat, and beginning in the early morning hours of August 2, the Americans and French were in hot pursuit.

The decimated ranks of the 168th Infantry Regiment, those courageous men from Iowa, were withdrawn from the line and replaced with the 117th Engineers from California, who had trained and were now fighting as infantry. Beginning with the first light of August 2, the Alabamians joined the pursuit of the Boche with the rest of the division and advanced nearly five kilometers by nightfall.

Great caches of ammunition and weapons were captured during the march. The retreating Boche had blown up some supply dumps, but not all of them. The Americans were hot on their heels and the Boche couldn't destroy all of their stores, for the division that day alone captured nearly thirty thousand shells.

At ten p.m. on August 2, the Rainbow was finally relieved from front line action as the American Fourth Division moved into position. During their turn on the front, the 42nd Division had advanced from La Croix Rouge Farm to a line running between Chery Chartreuve and Mont St. Martin, or a total of seventeen kilometers. This was the furthest advance by any single division attacking in the Chateau Thierry Salient.

The 42nd Division's artillery remained on the line until August 11, assisting the Fourth Division's artillery in maintaining its hold on the south bank of the Vesle River. The Rainbow's infantry was pulled off of the line and held in reserve for another week. During this time, sickness—mainly dysentery—broke out.

For the men of the 167th Infantry the rest was welcomed, but they did not get much chance to clean up. The men were bone weary, underfed, and susceptible to illness. Spirits were at rock bottom. Then into this dirty and smelly part of the war came one of America's sweethearts, Elsie Janis, a star of the stage and screen. She had come to France to entertain the troops.

The men's spirits rose immediately. They pulled a flatbed wagon out into a field and Elsie danced and sang for a vast crowd. They were happy to remember happier days and pretty American girls.

As she sang "Oh, You Dirty Germans," a Boche aircraft made a low pass over the field, so low that all could see the black Maltese crosses on its lower wings. But no one cared or paid much attention to it as it flew off to the north, as the men couldn't take their eyes off Elsie.

Finally, on August 12, the Rainbow was pulled out of reserve and with weary feet marched out of that war-ravaged land located between the Ourcq and Vesle Rivers. They left behind them a trail of fresh graves marked by little wooden crosses. Those who could walked to the La-Ferte-sous-Jouarre area for a long-awaited rest.

For the first time in over a month, most were able to enjoy a long, hot bath and a haircut. Those who were unable to locate a hot tub or shower bathed in the nearby rivers and streams. After a day or two of rest, many of the men were able to wrangle passes and rides for a few days leave in Paris.

At 6:00 in the morning on August 4, the main body of Battery F finally pulled into their new position, located near the Ferme des Dames and about two kilometers west of Chery-Chartreuve.

They had been on the road for over thirteen hours in the pouring rain and the march had covered only eight kilometers. The men were exhausted from the effort, as all of the rolling stock had become bogged down in the muck and mire more than once. Every hand pitched in, pulling at the prolongs and at the spokes of the wheels just to keep the carriages rolling. All were covered with mud from head to toe.

After the field pieces pulled into position, the limbers and the rest of the combat echelon, moved off to establish their camp in the Bois de Dole, immediately behind and south of the guns. The battery's rear echelon camped near the town of Nesles, close to the ammunition depot.

At the cannon, the men placed camouflage over the guns. They then grabbed their blankets and headed for some much needed rest.

Shortly after their arrival at the new position, they learned that the infantry had captured Soissons and that, for all practical purposes, the Chateau Thierry Salient was once again in Allied hands. Further, the Rainbow's infantry had been pulled from the line and replaced by the American 4th Division. After all of the hurry in getting the guns set up and readied, it turned out that they were not fired at all during the day.

The next day, August 5, the steady rain of the past few days finally ended and again the hot sun beat down on them as they languished in the heat and high humidity. The battery fired 1224 rounds throughout the day, mainly in answer to German fire into their sector. Normal firing range was 4,500 meters and all targeting was visual, reported by phone from a forward observer.

August 6 brought with it a renewed offensive effort on the part of the infantry from the 4th Division. In the early afternoon, a three-hour preparatory barrage was rained down on the Boche defenses in and around St. Thibaut, a small town just south of the Vesle River.

For the first hour the battery fired into some rail yards just west of town. The second hour of firing was to the north of Bazoches, targeting the Rousen-Reims National Highway. The third hour focused on a wooded section a little further north of the road. The cadence throughout the afternoon was twenty rounds per gun per hour, delivered in a sweeping and progressive pattern.

The creeping barrage was begun in anticipation of the infantry's advance, and lasted for nearly forty minutes each gun firing at a rate of 100 rounds per hour. However, due to a snafu on the part of the 4th Division's command, the troops did not advance. This error resulted in a repeat of the barrage. For three more hours the cannoneers poured hundreds of high explosive rounds into the enemy's stronghold.

As Pat was returning to his pup tent after the barrage was finished he ran into Jack Bayless. "Did you hear the latest scuttlebutt?" Jack asked. "Ole Colonel Reilly was so mad at the 4th Division that he read the riot act to the commanders."

"Why was that?" Pat asked.

"He told them that the American taxpayers who are paying for this war shouldn't have to cough up the money for the wasted shells," Jack said, unable to contain his laughter.

"I bet he'll send a bill for the shells," Pat joked in response.

"Well, it sure would have been a great conversation to listen in on."

They walked a short distance further in silence then Jack said. "See ya in the morning," and took a right turn and headed for his own pup tent.

On August 7, beginning just after noon, another 1000 shells were fired into enemy positions on the north side of the Vesle River, just east of Bazoches. This fire continued for two and a half hours. Word was then received that the time to move forward had again arrived.

The drivers and horses, with the limbers in tow, appeared at the position at two in the afternoon. Once harnessed and hitched, they traveled four kilometers to a point just north of the slope of a hill west of Mont St. Martin, some five kilometers southwest of Fismes. The guns were now within four kilometers of the enemy's line, situated directly north of the regiment's emplacements. From this location, the battery was to support an infantry attack on the heights above and north of Bazoches. This action was set to start shortly after the dinner hour.

As they picked at their cold beans and bread, Hank and Pat sat off alone from the others and ate in silence.

After finishing his meal, Hank set his mess kit down and leaned back against the large rock supporting his back. "You know, I've never been so tired in all my life," he groaned as he stretched and yawned. "This dysentery has hit everybody in the battery. God, Paul made me laugh this morning and I barely made it to the latrine. I've never been so miserable in all my born days.

"Did you know that last night the captain charged Tom with committing a vicious nuisance outside the command bunker?"

"No, what'd he do?" Pat said.

"He tried to make it to the latrine, and found he wasn't going to succeed, so he just dropped his draws where he was." Pat laughed. "Every time I think about it I'm afraid I'll lose control myself. He explained to the captain that his intentions were farther removed from where he was, but just couldn't make it. The captain finally relented as long as Tom got a shovel and buried the evidence."

"Please, enough, don't make me laugh or I won't be able to hold it either. Let's talk about more serious subjects."

There was a short pause in their conversation and Pat contemplated the food still on his plate. "We haven't had a bath for over a month and I almost dread eating anymore," Hank said. "Cold beans and monkey meat followed by a piece of moldy bread. Do you think they'll ever pull us off of the line?"

"Hell, I don't know. I guess if we live long enough, we'll get pulled. I guess they decided the infantry had had enough and they got pulled."

"Those poor bastards deserved it. They say the casualties in some of the companies took 'em down to platoon size."

"Yeah, I often wonder how Jake is doing."

They both fell silent again. Pat decided against eating anymore and scraped the leftovers from his plate onto the ground behind the rock on which he was sitting.

"He's a survivor, though," Pat said. "I feel he's still going along. You know, I still think we're lucky to be in the artillery. Seeing all those bodies as we moved forward made me wonder what the hell we're doing still walking around and why we haven't experienced more casualties."

"Well, we still haven't suffered a battle death. I can't help but to think about poor Bedowski though, at least from time to time."

Pat nodded. "Yeah, after going through all that we've been through and end up drowning in the Marne when we were just resting and relaxing and enjoying a short swim. He always acted as the tough guy, but he was a fair guy, when all was said and done."

They both fell silent until the call to the guns was heard.

"Well, here we go again!" Hank added as they wearily got up to go to the cannon.

It wasn't long before the position came under fire for about ten minutes, which the battery answered with fifty-nine high explosive shells. Then the captain went to each gun position to tell the cannoneers that the attack had been called off and they were to stand down from the guns.

For the reminder of the night there were numerous bursts of gas and other enemy artillery fire hitting near their position, close enough for them to seek shelter at times and enough gas for them to wear their gas gear for the remainder of the night.

All during the next day the regiment was subjected to heavy and sporadic shelling. Boche observation balloons appeared in profuse numbers on the enemy side of the Vesle. This was the more probable reason the shelling was so close to the position. Battery E took a hit close to the number three gun, resulting in two wounded and one killed.

It was apparent that the enemy had command of the skies, as no Allied planes had been seen for a number of days to challenge the balloons.

Behind the 149th's cannon line, the 4th Division was moving numerous troops forward, which drew considerable fire from the Germans. One of the combat echelon's machine gunners suffered a slight head wound that knocked him unconscious and earned him a quick trip to the aid station.

During the night the drivers at the forward echelon were subjected to numerous gas alarms, sounded by the 4th Division's echelon. It soon was pointed out to these newcomers that they were mistaking the heavy aroma of dead horses and mules as an attack with gas whenever a fresh breeze carried the scent before it.

At daybreak on the ninth, the incoming shelling from the enemy increased in intensity. This prevented the 4th Division's infantry from carrying out the planned attack. The 149th proved to be too close to the front line for accurate firing and Battery F along with the entire regiment was ordered back to its previous firing position.

In the middle of the afternoon, just as the limbers were moving into position to hook up to the field pieces, a daring air battle unfolded above. An American SPAD was hot on the tail of a Boche Albatross. The planes approached from the northeast and then circled over the position at low altitude, sometimes so low that the aircraft would disappear from view behind the low hills and trees. They would suddenly reappear and continue their battle. The men on the ground could see the tracer bullets as they bounced off of the planes engines.

All along the Allied line you could hear cheers for the American, as he would suddenly jump on the tail of the enemy. No matter how the German maneuvered, the American would eventually end up on his enemy's tail again.

The battle continued for nearly fifteen minutes, and finally the SPAD caught the German in a climbing right turn. The American was a mere fifty yards away and slightly above and his guns caught the German's fuel tank after a long burst. The plane's fuel ignited and the Boche, recognizing his peril, quickly brought the stricken aircraft to earth, barely escaping with his life, only to be captured by the 4th Division's infantry.

After the air battle, the cannoneers quickly loaded their equipment and ammunition, harnessed and hitched, and were on their way at dusk. By 2:00 a.m. they arrived at the new location and in a short while the guns had been laid on their targets and all except those on guard turned in.

Pat was dead tired and found it difficult to walk his post, as he had drawn the first shift. He knew he would be relieved by daybreak, but he was having difficulty keeping his eyes open. The front was relatively quiet and the only sound he heard was distant artillery, or was it thunder? Finally his relief showed up—Paul Driscol. Pat could hardly say a word and staggered to his blankets and fell asleep immediately.

After only six hours of fitful sleep, Pat was awakened by the sound of artillery and joined the others from the firing battery in witnessing a heavy German barrage as it fell on Chery-Chartreuve. They also witnessed several French balloons, located behind the position, brought down in flames by Boche aircraft, which seemed to have complete control of the skies. During the twilight hours, the position received numerous rounds of sneeze gas and the men donned their gas gear. Rumors abounded that the 149th Field Artillery was to be pulled from the line and replaced with the 4th Division's 77th Field Artillery.

August 11 dawned a glorious and clear day. A dry cold front had passed through the area late the night before, and the men felt more invigorated than they had in a long time.

In the early morning, the battery fired 482 rounds at the enemy. Again, the whole of the regiment's line was subjected to heavy shelling,

At their noon meal, they received the word that they were leaving the front for a rest in the rear. This good news was received with subdued cheering, as the men were just too tired to shout. At 4:00 p.m. all of the carriages left the forward echelon, followed four hours later by the limbers. The remaining carriages that made up the supply train had been moving since noon.

The tired and exhausted cannoneers were allowed to ride on the trails of their guns. The men felt that Colonel Reilly must be getting soft to allow such a thing to happen and, just maybe, the men were worse off than they thought.

The march to the rear was rapid and their path took them through Nesles, Fere-en-Tardenois, Villemoyene, Beuvardes and Brey.

A Long-Earned Rest

Ike sat back in his seat of the coach compartment and closed his eyes as the train began to move out of the Paris station on its journey to Toul. This past week had been glorious, to say the least. Not only were his wounds mending at a rapid rate, but he had also spent a lot of time with Agnes.

He was now more deeply in love with her than ever. The time he'd spent with Agnes was incredible. The night she had come to his room was unforgettable. Their lovemaking was filled with an unsurpassed passion, and it was the night he had asked her to marry him. This was not just on a whim; he'd thought it out completely and objectively, even before that night.

He knew she wanted to say yes, but she was afraid that the war would take him as it had her brothers. She avoided giving him a straight answer until she had more time to analyze the situation.

The thought of dying as a result of the war was not even a consideration to Ike. He knew he'd see the end of the fighting and not give his life here in France, but he had not been able to convince Agnes of this fact. Then, of all the luck, in the late afternoon of August 3, he received orders to return to the base at Toul by no later than August 5. Here he was to pick up his new SPAD and fly it over to their advanced airfield at Saintes, near the Chateau Thierry sector.

He felt that Captain Wortham was at the bottom of this, but he also realized the need the squadron had for combat-trained pilots. He'd talk to the captain when he got home.

Ike's last day with Agnes had been a day spent sightseeing and just spending time together, walking in the park, riding in a taxi, sitting together at lunch and dinner. They talked and they laughed and enjoyed one another's company.

It ended at 8:00 p.m., as Agnes went on duty for a double shift. When he was ready to leave she was preparing to assist in surgery, and with a quick kiss and a wave, she was gone behind the closed doors of the operating room.

He limped back dejectedly to his room, gathered his things, and hobbled down the stairs and out the front doors of the hospital. There he flagged down a taxi, which took him to the station. At the depot, his wait was long and the hard wooden benches were uncomfortable. He found an English paper and read the entire thing. The rest of the time he spent looking at the people as they hurried past.

Finally, the call for his train was announced and he was on his way, back to the war. He did feel a lot better, at least physically. He felt he could sit in his aircraft and fly it without too much discomfort. He just had to overcome his longing to be with Agnes. The best way to overcome that was to stay busy and that meant a lot of flying, which he was sure was on his agenda.

Ike slept fitfully on the train, as it stopped frequently to take on and let off passengers. At each stop he would look out into the rainy darkness to see if he could tell where he was. When he saw a sign with the name of the town on it, it meant little or nothing to him. But as they approached his destination, he began to see names that were familiar to him. Many of the small whistle stops were familiar landmarks that he had seen on his flight charts.

It was close to dawn when they finally pulled into Toul. After collecting his things, Ike stepped off of the train and walked into the station. Only a few other passengers disembarked with him. One, he noticed, was in US uniform.

He walked through the station and out into the damp, breezy darkness. After getting his bearings, he started walking towards the transportation pool to seek a ride to the aerodrome. On his way, he stopped in a little cafe that had just opened. He ordered a breakfast, as he was famished and needed the nourishment before searching out a ride to the air station.

As the waitress delivered his breakfast, he noticed the American from the station enter the cafe. This individual wore an American uniform, but the insignia was one Ike did not recognize.

Ike approached him." Excuse me; I noticed that you're wearing a US uniform. What outfit are you with?"

"Oh, I'm not with a particular unit, so to speak, I'm a reporter with the *Stars and Stripes.*"

"I noticed that you got off of the same train I did and I thought you might belong to one of the squadrons out at the aerodrome."

"No, sorry, I'm just on my way out to cover the activities of the Aviation Section. Are you a pilot here?"

"Yeah, I've been in the hospital and I'm on my way back to rejoin my squadron, the 95th. Our permanent base is here at Toul, but we're positioned closer to the front for the time being. I'll pick up my new ship this afternoon and fly it over to Saintes where the rest of the squadron is parked."

"The 95th? That's part of the First Pursuit Group, isn't it?"

Ike nodded. "It sure is. The group consists of the 94th, the 95th, the 27th and the 147th Squadrons. We also have three observation squadrons that fly with us and they tell me a bomber squadron now operates out of the Toul aerodrome. By the way, my name is Ike Dennison. Why don't you join me here at my table?"

Without answering, the man got up out of his chair, carefully balancing his coffee cup on its saucer, and moved to Ike's booth and sat down. "I'm Roy. Glad to meet you, Ike," the man said as he stretched out his hand in greeting. "Where do ya hail from?"

Ike shook his hand. "I guess you'd say I was from Illinois, at least I spent the last four years there before the war."

"That's a coincidence, I was born in central Illinois. My last residence was in New York, though. Whereabouts in Illinois?"

"I graduated from the University in Champaign/Urbana in May of '17 and from there entered the flying service. I completed my ground school at the university and then got my wings up the road at Chanute Field in Rantoul."

"That's interesting. I was reared on a farm near the little town of Tolono just south of there."

"No kidding. One of my fraternity brothers was from Tolono. Pat Littler. You know him?"

"I should, he's my little brother. What a coincidence, to think I have to come all the way to Toul, France to run into a neighbor."

Ike smiled. "The last I heard was that he was in the artillery. Where is he now?"

"He's with the Rainbow Division. They're in the fighting over on the Ourcq."

"Whew, I've heard that it's been pretty rough in the salient. I was shot down just south of there along the Marne, near Dormans."

From that moment until they went their separate ways at the aerodrome, the two men were in constant and animated conversation. After Roy and he separated, Ike checked in with the commander of the base. He was required to sign numerous papers and to undergo some orientation on the SPAD. He just wasn't able to convince anyone that he'd been flying the trial aircraft, a SPAD XIII, for over a month. It wasn't until the late afternoon and a short flight from Toul to Saintes that Ike finally arrived at the 95th Aero Squadron, where he was greeted by all as a long-lost brother.

He spent the next day catching up on the changes that were taking place in the air service and how it would affect the mode of flight operations. On the sixth he was assigned to his first patrol, which was to take place the next morning.

Ike felt good about getting back in the air. He'd missed flying, but his closeness to Agnes had distracted him enough to forget how much he'd really missed it.

The night before his first patrol, he spent a long time looking the plane over with Mike at his side. This SPAD XIII was brand new and had only thirty hours on the engine and airframe since rolling off of the manufacturing line just two weeks before. It was painted in the standard olive drab colors currently being used by the US Air Service. The armament consisted of two forward-firing French-made Lewis machine guns mounted in front of the pilot that fired through the propeller.

During their walkaround, Ike resighted the guns to his liking and had Mike make several adjustments as well as change the engine oil and spark plugs.

"I don't want it quitting on me in the air!" he stated emphatically to his crew chief.

After his critical inspection, he stood back and admired the lines of this beauty. The plane was spotless and nearly glowed in the fading evening light. The unique scallop at the trailing edge of the wings and tail surfaces made her look as if she were doing 100, here on the ground.

After his flight from Toul to Saintes the day before, Ike had his ground crew make some further adjustments to the aircraft's rigging in order for him to fly hands-off in straight and level flight at normal cruise. He needed every edge he could get. He knew that the Boche pilots were good and that since the advent of the Fokker D.VII they had one of the best combat aircraft in the air. The D.VII was extraordinary in its climbing ability and in its resistance to stalling. This led to the exaggerated view, held by many Allied pilots, that this enemy pursuit could hang on its prop in an almost straight-up attitude and shoot out the belly of its adversary.

Ike wanted to at least match their skills and equipment. He knew his piloting techniques were—at the very least—on a par or even better than those of his opponents. The fine-tuning of his aircraft for maximum performance would help him in attaining the edge in combat.

One of the changes instituted since Ike's forced stay in the hospital was an increase in the size of the patrols. Colonel Mitchell had determined that the enemy, who flew in flights of 20 to 30 planes, too easily overwhelmed the small Allied patrols of five or six aircraft. This discredited defensive tactic of the French proved costly to the American pilots. The losses were staggering and escalating with each passing day. The expected longevity of new pilots just from training was no longer than a week or two. Since requiring larger numbers of airplanes on the patrols, the 1st Pursuit Group began to hold their own against the Boche.

At sunrise on the seventh and after a night of restless sleep for Ike, a flight of ten SPADs from the 95th Aero Squadron broke free of the ground and climbed rapidly to their patrol altitude of 5000 meters. The aircraft flew in a west-northwest direction towards the front. Ike was in the second position on the left arm of the V formation.

Once at cruise altitude, he set his machine up for best fuel economy and scanned the skies for enemy aircraft. It felt good to break the bonds of the earth and fly miles above the surface once again. It was exhilarating.

The flight had been airborne for approximately thirty minutes when the leader, Captain Wortham, motioned that he'd spotted a flight of twelve enemy aircraft at four o'clock about 500 meters below their current altitude, headed in the opposite direction. This gave the SPADs perfect position for diving upon the enemy from behind, with the sun directly at their backs. One by one, starting with the trailing aircraft on the right arm of the formation, they performed a steep right turn, diving towards the enemy's Fokker triplanes.

As his turn to peel off approached, Ike felt the adrenaline flow throughout his system. Aerial combat was dangerous and unpredictable, but he loved it.

It took forever for the enemy to realize they were under attack.

Captain Wortham held his fire until he was a mere 50 meters from one plane before letting loose with a long burst. The enemy pilot was a goner before he could take evasive action. One other plane fell to the earth before the formation broke up in order to take on the charging SPADs.

At this point each pilot started looking out for himself. Ike flew through the formation just as it was breaking up and fired his guns on one plane, which quickly turned and dove out of the way.

Once below the enemy, Ike pushed hard right rudder and aileron, resulting in a steep turn of 180 degrees. Ike felt himself being pushed hard down in his seat as a result of the centrifugal force from the steep turn. As he pulled out of the dive, he added full power and back pressure on the control column as he leveled the wings and started to climb just in time, for another Boche plane flew directly in front of his sights. When this machine was within 50 to 60 meters, he pulled the trigger on his guns for a short burst that tore the top of the vertical stabilizer off the triplane.

The German, recognizing his peril, initiated a steep diving left turn. Ike followed. He was convinced that this Boche pilot was a novice to the front, and had little trouble anticipating his moves. They rolled right, then left, they climbed and they dove. The Boche pilot performed all sorts of maneuvers trying to shake Ike from his tail. No matter what maneuver the enemy performed, he could not shake free of his pursuer. The Fokkers were not fast but they could normally outturn the SPADs. Ike knew this and anticipated the German's moves.

As a last resort, the pilot of the Fokker put his plane in a spin. Ike followed suit. He cut his power, brought the nose up smartly, and as the plane began the stall he applied full right rudder. The plane stalled with a shutter and began a slow roll to the right. Suddenly the right wing dropped to vertical and the nose fell rapidly through the horizon into a steep nose down spin. The ground was all he could see as it whirled past his view, nothing more than a blur before his eyes. He located his prey, about 100 meters in front and below him. One turn, two turns, three turns, down and down they spun, losing a great deal of altitude.

As soon as the enemy started his recovery from the spin, Ike recognized it and initiated his own pullout. He applied rudder opposite the turn, neutralized his aileron control and, as the spinning motions stopped, he released backpressure on the control column to break the stall. This brought him out on the tail of his prey, just 50 meters behind. Again the German was in his sights, and he fired a long burst that caused the right upper wing of the German plane to collapse upward.

The triplane rolled over onto its right side and reentered the spin, and continued down until it struck the ground.

At long last Ike was an ace. He'd registered his fifth kill.

Ike watched his victim fall for a short while, then initiated a climb in order to rejoin his comrades, who were several thousand feet above his altitude, beginning to reform into the original formation. He saw that the remaining Boche aircraft were heading north, running from the encounter.

Ike was elated over his kill. It had taken a long time, but there was no question that he had at last joined the ranks of the aces.

On the ninth, Ike claimed his sixth victory over an Albatros in a low-level dogfight over the American lines just south of the Vesle River.

This plane, though badly damaged and burning, managed to land inside Allied lines where the pilot was captured by some doughboys of the 4th Division.

There was a collective sigh of relief as the 149th Field Artillery was pulled from the line and marched back out of earshot and out of range of the enemy guns. It meant a well-earned rest but an otherwise unknown future. The troops were tired, underfed, and weak.

It was time to refit and revitalize the regiment's equipment, which was in as sorry and as poor a condition as the men were. The animals also suffered from the effects of fatigue. They too were overworked, underfed, and all showed the open sores and exhaustion developed from pulling at the harness and trace.

The last section of F Battery arrived at Bois de Chatelet near the small town of Brecy a little after 3:00 a.m. where they joined the rest of the regiment. Prior to the retaking of the Chateau Thierry salient by the Allies, this wood had been the emplacement that the Boche had used in the spring, to position the large Paris cannon. These huge guns were used by the Germans to hurl their 380 mm shells up to seventy miles into Paris and Meaux, terrorizing the inhabitants of those cities. The gun positions were solidly constructed with steel and concrete, as were the dugouts. They even had tracks laid to bring ammunition directly to the guns via a wheeled cart.

In their hasty retreat the Germans had attempted to destroy the position but they had failed for the most part, as many of the explosive charges had not been detonated. Each man of the battery spent some time that day studying the uniqueness of this cannon emplacement. When not checking the emplacement, there were numerous crap games to join in, or sleep to catch up on.

After Pat, Paul and Tom had thoroughly gone over the amazing structure that had once held the world's largest guns, the trio headed back to camp. Paul and Tom stopped to join in on a game of chance while Pat headed back to the pup tent to catch up on some sleep and letter writing. From a distance he saw Hank outside the tent sitting on a rock playing a solitary game of mumblely-peg with his pocketknife.

As he approached, Hank looked up and Pat could see that his face was stained with tears.

"Are you all right?" Pat asked.

Hank quickly wiped his face with his sleeve as he picked up his knife. "I guess so. Because of the fighting, I haven't had time to think and dwell on Betsy and the baby until now. With the mail finally being delivered today, I was just overwhelmed by the thought that I wouldn't be receiving letters from her anymore. I don't know if I'll ever get over the emptiness and grief I feel inside. If only I had been there…"

"If you had been there, there still wasn't a thing you could've done about it, even the doctor was helpless. This was in the Lord's hands, Hank; just as Betsy and the baby are now. Turn it over to Him. He has promised to carry our burdens. Let Him have yours."

"I try to, but it's so hard. What you say is true, I know, and I'll keep on trying." He shrugged and lowered his head.

They sat in silence as Hank continued his game, but he had stopped crying.

The next day the captain ordered all of the rolling stock to be taken to a nearby stream and thoroughly washed and cleaned, including the cannon. All enjoyed the work, for the water was cool and refreshing, and many couldn't remember their last bath.

Late in the morning, Jack Bayless and Paul Driscol borrowed as much money as they could from Jason Newcum, the battery's "banker" who always seemed to have an abundance of cash at hand. They then walked to the YMCA store in Chateau Thierry and spent all they had on snack foods and sweets. Once they got back to camp, they sold it all at a decent profit and paid back the loan. All seemed happy with the arrangement, as the food was devoured in a short time.

Friday, August 14, the camp was roused at 4:30 a.m. At 7:30 they were on the road again. The march took them through Chateau Thierry, along the Marne to just outside La Thialet, where a two-hour halt was called for the noon meal.

At one in the afternoon, the battery was underway to Courcelles, where they arrived at 8:00 p.m., a march of thirty-three kilometers. The men were exhausted, but once camp was set up, the captain announced that he did have a certain number of passes available for Paris. No one hit the sack until after he had submitted his own personal request for one.

On the fifteenth, after careful consideration by Captain Case, Lieutenant Allen, and Sergeant Baker, all of the available passes were issued to twenty men, primarily NCOs and a few deserving corporals and privates.

Hank was one, along with Jack and Jason. Pat and the other mechanics had to stay with the battery. Pat pulled Jack and Jason aside shortly before they left for the Paris train and asked that they watch Hank closely.

"Make sure he's constantly doing something and having a good time."

"Don't worry about it, Pat. We're not going to Paris to just sit around and sleep, for God's sake. See you in thirty-six hours," Jack said.

"Yeah, bye!" Pat added somewhat dejectedly, privately thinking about the great time the men were going to have.

Soon after those with passes headed for the train, the battery harnessed and hitched the animals and carriages in order to hit the road again. They marched to La Ferte Sous Joiuarre, some eight kilometers to the southwest.

The battery stayed there for two and a half days. Work and training were put on the back burner and when the necessary chores were completed, the majority spent the afternoon frolicking in the Marne. The water was cool and refreshing.

When Jack, Jason, and Hank returned, they had many tales to tell of their trip. After settling in and with a hot cup of coffee in hand, they filled Pat and the other mechanics in on their stay in Paris.

"We had about three hundred francs, among the three of us," Hank began. "We barely got the 10:30 train from LaFerte, which got us into the Paris station at around 1:00. What a huge and busy city."

"Yeah!" Jack jumped in. "We stopped at the first restaurant we could find. Paid only eight francs for all you could eat. What food! And to top it off, you should've seen all of the beautiful women wandering around, Oh, I'll tell you, I thought we'd died and gone to heaven!"

"After that we went and got a hotel room, for only twelve francs, and it had a bathtub down the hall. It took almost a half hour to get Hank out of it," Jason added.

"It was great, Pat. I coulda lived there forever—hot running water, sweet-smelling soap, a dream come true," Hank said.

"Yeah, and after lounging around for a couple hours we went out and ate again."

"Then to finish the day off," Tom butted in, "we all went to the Follies. Talk about beautiful women! And the way they danced, wow!"

"We finally hit the hay at midnight. What an adventure! Too bad you guys couldn't have come."

"To think we slept in beds with a mattress and real sheets and pillows," Hank sighed.

"You mean you didn't have a special rendezvous with one of those gorgeous ladies?"

"Get serious!" Jack added.

"What did you do today, then?" Paul asked.

"Well, we got up at 6:00 a.m. and went to see the town. Took a taxi ride for over an hour and then went shopping in some of those nice shops," Jack said.

"Yeah, then went to eat again," Hank grinned. "After that we took another long taxi ride, ended up at the station at 3:30, climbed aboard the train, and here we are."

The next day, Saturday, the men relaxed and swam or washed their clothes in the Marne. The same activities were undertaken on Sunday until orders were received to pack up and harness and hitch.

By early that evening the battery was underway for a twenty-two kilometer hike that took them to Trilport, where they were to entrain once again. Upon their arrival, around midnight, they found that the 117th Ammunition Train was in the process of loading their equipment, so F Battery tied the horses to some nearby fences and settled down for a short snooze without getting out their blankets.

At 4:00 a.m. Captain Case woke the bugler in order for him to sound revelry. The job of loading was underway. As there wasn't a platform, the work of loading the carriages was formidable, as the men had to manhandle them up ramps. At 6:30, following three shrill toots of the engine whistle, the train pulled out of the station amid clouds of steam, smoke and noise.

The day had turned out to be beautiful. The sky was clear and the temperature hovered at eighty degrees. The two-hinged windows on either side of the freight cars, as well as the one sliding cargo door on each side, were left open as the train proceeded on its way, paralleling the Marne for a good part of the trip.

Pat sat on the floor with his legs dangling out the door. As the speed increased, the fresh and cooling air filled the car blowing away the musty smell of his fellow travelers. They sped past numerous towns: Chateau Thierry, Epernay, Chalons, Vitry-le-Francois, Chaumont and Langres. He daydreamed as he took in the sights.

Hank was asleep somewhere in the car, as were many others. There was a big poker game going on at the forward end of the car, a few were talking, but most were riding in silence, staring blankly at the passing countryside.

In the afternoon there was a brief stop at St. Dizier, where many bought some bottles of cognac, powerful stuff that required sipping in order to preserve the linings of one's digestive system. The men were met at the stop by the French Red Cross, who supplied them with swigs of a rum-and-coffee combination that proved to be mainly rum. The train continued on only to stop again, this time in Eurville in order to water the horses.

After a ride that lasted exactly twenty-four hours, the train pulled into its destination, Damlain, in the Neaufchateau area. Here the battery detrained. After gathering their gear they harnessed the animals and were on the road again, heading in a westerly direction. They marched 16 kilometers at a somewhat leisurely pace to the small village of Huilliecourt.

It was this small village that housed Battery F for over a week. Quarters had been established in unoccupied houses and barns for most of the men. However, most negotiated arrangements with local villagers whereby they could sleep in the villagers' houses.

These agreements proved to be far superior. The locals loved having the Americans stay, and in most instances provided feather beds and meals. There were numerous fruit trees heavy with plums and cherries, and the men were welcomed to help themselves.

During the first week there were few duties for the men, and most took advantage of the time to rest and eat. By far, the favorite meals were the chicken dinners provided by the woman of the host house on a daily basis. Duties included policing the streets, repairing the harnesses, repairing and greasing the carriages, and most importantly, overhauling the guns. The farriers spent a great deal of time working on the animals, applying their salves to the open sores that troubled most of the horses and mules.

During their off-duty times, Hank and Pat sat around. The family they were staying with treated them like royalty. Madame de Ville would not let them lift a finger; she fed them and even washed their clothes for them, with the help of her two young daughters.

On the twenty-fourth, the men went through a comprehensive medical checkup. A number of them were sent to the field hospital for treatment of scabies, brought on by a lack of bathing over the past two months.

On the following Sunday the Reverend James held the first formal service since they had taken the field in the Chateau Thierry salient, giving the men time to practice up on their singing. In the evening the regimental band held a concert, playing numerous classical selections, an assortment of popular music and patriotic songs. The concerts ended on an inspiring note when a young woman, who was visiting the village, sang the "Marseilles." Her beautiful voice brought many a tear to the eyes of those in attendance.

During this time, the division was rebuilding its strength. Replacements were coming in every day—men, animals and equipment. Finally, on August 26, a regimen of drill was instituted in earnest. This scourge of rest camps brought the men to the realization that maybe they were ready to go back to the front, as this "Rookie" exercise was worse than a Boche barrage.

On August 28, the men from the field hospital returned to the town with the news that the battery would be leaving the comforts of home soon. Early the next day, the caissons left for the ammunition dump in Levencourt before proceeding on to the front.

Those who had been quartered in homes made requests for one last chicken dinner. Madam de Ville not only cooked a chicken dinner for Pat and Hank, she also baked a cherry pie for them to take on their journey. Finally at 9:00 p.m., after all had said goodbye to the good people of Huilliecourt, the order "Forward yo" was given and the battery was underway.

The destination was not officially acknowledged, however the local citizens had knowingly pointed in the direction of the St. Mihiel.

The Beginning of The American Army

Major Hinkle and Clint Phelps were silent for a few minutes after their meal was delivered. They'd talked almost constantly ever since they met at the bar more than an hour before, and they then continued their conversation when they moved into the dining room.

"You know, Clint, I'm beginning to feel ashamed for eating so well. Some of our guys would kill for food like this!"

"It's my pleasure to take you out. I'm sure glad you called. I've wanted the opportunity to talk with you. I don't think the old *Chicago Globe* will mind paying for this we deserve it. It's been a long and arduous war. I've enjoyed reminiscing on the good old days back in Champaign. It seems so long ago, and a different time. The world has changed, and I believe changed forever. I truly believe the Allies will win this war and the monarchies of old will disappear. We'll start a whole new life; maybe see the end of war itself. Man cannot view this carnage and even consider going to war again. I hope that we'll see the universal need for democracies being established throughout Europe."

Major Hinkle considered this for a moment. "Clint, I think you're forgetting about the new Russia. I fear that they will become a closed and repressive society. I agree with your assessment that permanent change will come to the world, but being less warlike? More democratic? I doubt it. Men's memories are short, and those ruthless souls who desire—no, those who crave power—are willing to do anything just to get their own way. Such men exist in Russia today. We know that

Germany is going through some terrible strife at the seat of government in Berlin. The end of fighting on the fronts will surely lead to the end of the Kaiser's rule, but it will bring on a terrific struggle for power in that nation. The radical revolutionaries could take over there too."

Clint nodded sadly.

"I truly wish you're right," Major Hinkle continued. "I think your assumption is correct, but maybe a little naive. I don't think that democracies will prevail in all countries. True, past history has shown us that democratic governments have been less aggressive towards other nations, particularly their neighbors, but the people of Europe are not ready for the type of democracy we have in the States. The demigods will usurp power and exercise tyrannical control through force. No, we'll see wars continue, although hopefully not on a global scale as this one."

"Well, maybe you're right, but I hope not," Clint replied. "I've viewed many of these battlefields and I just can't believe anyone in their right mind would ever set out to do this again. We have already come too far in the development of our weapons of terror. Gas, machine guns, aeroplanes that can take bombs deep behind enemy lines, cannon that can throw shells seventy miles or further, land mines, submarines, and on and on. This is resulting in not only the soldiers killing one another on a localized battlefield, but bringing death and destruction to civilian populations far removed from the front lines. It's genocide in its purest sense."

"You won't get an argument from me on that point, but as I said, memories are short when it comes to the struggle for power."

They paused to reflect a moment, and Clint was the first to continue.

"I guess this is like arguing about religion—we could go on all night and we both would end up not changing the other's views and we both could be wrong."

"I agree, Clint. Hopefully, though, you're the one that's right!"

Again they were silent as they finished their meals.

"Would you like a cognac with your dessert?" Clint asked.

"That would be a tonic. I'll pass on the dessert, but if you don't mind I'll have my cognac with a cigar."

"Sounds like a spectacular idea." Clint signaled the waiter and ordered the drinks.

As they waited Clint took the cigar that the major offered. "Well, where are we now in the conduct of this war?" Clint asked as he sat back comfortably in his chair. He quickly blew a mouthful of blue smoke towards the ceiling and lightly tapped the ashes of his cigar into the ashtray.

"Well, as of this date, September 1, I can safely say that the Boche are in retreat. Not a general one, mind you, but their fighting will has been weakened by a considerable degree. If you remember, it was just a year ago, at Camp Mills that I said it would take six months or more before the full weight of the American contribution would be felt. The Germans are now feeling that strength. We were able, in a small way, to help the Allies hold during the spring and summer offensives by taking a position in the line so the French could release their troops from trench duty and move them north to reinforce the English on the Somme, who were taking the full brunt of these Ludendorf offensives."

"I well remember," Clint said. "I was there at that front during those terrible days, an experience I'll never forget."

Major Hinkle nodded. "Those were terrible days. Since that time our initial training and organization is pretty well finished, we are now able to form our own army and take the field somewhat independent of the French and English. This is being accomplished as we speak. The American First Army is now being gathered together under the command of General Pershing. We will take the field in the southeast next to the French."

"I have had some interaction with both the French and English," Clint said, "and in the spring they were barely able to hold on. I would say things have changed drastically in the past four months."

"Indeed they have. The Germans fully expected a victory and a finish to the war during the spring. They expended a great deal of resources in the effort. Their armies are worn out and psychologically beaten. Marshal Foch has taken advantage of this and turned the tables on them by going to the offensive. This does not mean that the Germans aren't able to inflict serious injury to the Allies. On the contrary, they are still a potent military force, but somewhat less robust than earlier in the year. I believe this turnabout has been the direct result of our presence on the fields of France."

"How so?" Clint asked.

"From the beginning, Marshal Foch and Field Marshal Haig have wanted to insert the Americans into the line in a helter-skelter manner. A division here, a brigade there. Maybe an artillery regiment on the Somme, or wherever they felt a need. Essentially, this meant that Americans would be under the command of foreigners. Not what General Pershing, or the President had in mind when we entered the war. The general has fought desperately for an American Army under American leadership, and it's finally happening." Colonel Hinkle paused a short time to relight his cigar.

"I can tell you that things are going well in the North for the English," Clint interjected. "As you probably know, they launched a large offensive east of Amiens on August 8. I was fortunate enough to be there at the time of the attack. It caught the Germans by complete surprise and before the day was over they'd advanced over three miles. They had 430 tanks, thousands of artillery pieces, command of the skies, and an overwhelming number of troops.

Major Hinkle whistled. "Quite a scenario."

"It was an inspiring sight. I stood on a hill just west of the line and viewed the events through some borrowed field glasses. It was just after daybreak and I saw the mist lift, magically, as if by some giant hand. There, in the Somme valley, were endless columns of English troops, cavalry, tanks and artillery all in parade formation. At that time they were meeting little Boche resistance. Suddenly the German artillery began exploding in their midst and the war was on. Nothing stopped the advance and I watched till the fog settled in again and cut off my view. Many of the tanks were hit by artillery and went up in flames, and soon ground to a stop. But the infantry, artillery and remaining tanks continued to move forward."

"Perseverance," Major Hinkle said with a wry smile.

Clint nodded. "Throughout the following days the advance continued. The Boche withdrew in an orderly fashion, but suffered heavy casualties and many more were captured. They appeared weary, and that's why I personally feel the war will be over soon. I was fortunate enough to interview some of these prisoners and most seemed content to spend the remaining days of the war as internees. The latest dispatch, which I read shortly before coming here, was that the British continue to push the Boche back and they are now at the Somme. Australian troops have captured Mont St. Quentin. They have captured over 50,000 Germans and 700 guns. Truly a blow to Ludendorf's pride."

"This is good news, Clint," the major said as he raised his glass in salute. "From here it seems that the character of the conflict will change. No longer will we fight a defensive war in the trenches. We will be engaging the enemy out in the open in offensive operations. Field Marshal Haig has long argued that ultimate victory will come from a series of coordinated attacks all along the front from Flanders in the northwest to the River Meuse in the southeast. Day before yesterday, Pershing was given command of the entire St. Mihiel sector. Therefore, we have the British in Cambrai and St. Quentin, the French at Mesnil, and we are at St. Mihiel. There is still a great deal of resistance to the formation of an independent American Army, but it will happen. As to where we will attack I can't say for sure, but I think first at St. Mihiel and then probably at the Argonne. That's only a guess from an old history professor, so please don't publish any statements till you hear it from official sources."

"That will be our secret," Clint replied. "I appreciate your taking me into your confidence."

"I'll try to let you know when the word can be printed so you can get a little jump on the competition," the major added with a chuckle.

After the eighteen days of rest the 149th Field Artillery had enjoyed, they received orders from on high to march once again. No one in the battery, other than Captain Case and no doubt Lieutenant Allen, knew the ultimate destination, but many felt they were headed for St. Mihiel, the part of the front the local citizens had pointed to during the past week.

St. Mihiel was a town located on the Muese River, 33 kilometers south-southeast of Verdun on the southwest corner of a large salient or bulge in the line that had been a thorn in the side of the French since the early days of the war. The Germans had fortified the trench lines on their side of the river and had made the line nearly impregnable.

The men of Battery F left Huillecourt on Thursday night, the twenty-ninth. The march took them through Doncourt, Chaumont-la-Ville, Vrecourt and Bois de Riaux, which was just outside of St. Quen-lez-Parc. A total distance of 22 kilometers was covered in six hours. After tending to the animals and getting their own breakfast, the men rolled up in blankets and slept till noon. At 8:30 p.m., the call to harness and hitch was heard throughout the camp and soon they were on the road again.

On this day they hiked 18 kilometers, which brought them to the small town of Circourt at a little before three in the morning. Here, the personnel were put up in haylofts while the carriages were parked in a nearby orchard. The horses and mules enjoyed the freedom of a large grassy field, fenced on four sides. The troops slept till noon and after a bite to eat they tended to their chores. In the late afternoon many headed for the town's one and only tavern, thinking that they would stay put in Circourt for a few more days. However, that evening, the call to harness and hitch again sounded throughout the encampment. This caught some of the men totally off guard, as they had expected to stay the night and as a result had spent too much time in the local brewery. The inebriated troopers drank to the constitution, the flag, the Rainbow, and to anyone else they could think of.

The good captain was not pleased with these antics and placed these carousers at the head of the column, carrying full field packs for the 8-kilometer hike to Rebeuville, the next stop on the march. They arrived at eleven that night, and the captain put the delinquents to work polishing the carriages and harnesses. The rest of the men slept in some old barracks at the edge of town.

Hank and Paul were two of the offenders, and didn't finish the job of cleaning and polishing till after three in the morning, at which time they collapsed into their bunks, swearing never to touch the golden nectar ever again.

The next morning, September 1, Captain Case had the troops clean the mess hall, tend to the animals, and grease the carriages. In the afternoon, he issued some passes to a number of the men and they all headed to Neufchateau, a town of 20,000 located just two kilometers to the north. A number of different units of the American effort in the area were headquartered here. As Tom put it, "Loaded with too damn many officers that required saluting."

It was during his pass in Neufchateau that Pat ran into Roy, quite by accident. Pat had become separated from Tom and had gone looking for him. As he was entering the third bistro, he literally ran into Roy, who was backing out the same door as he held a briefcase in one hand and a sandwich in the other.

"I sure meet you in the strangest places, big brother," Pat said after he'd recovered from his shock. "Do you have time for a beer?"

"Sure do! I have a meeting in an hour, but I guess one beer wouldn't hurt. I'd intended to eat this as I waited for the colonel I was interviewing, but I might as well eat it here. Have you been in town long? Where are you guys headed? Or are you just camped here for a short while?"

"Whoa, hold on Roy, too many questions for a lowly corporal to answer. I'll tell you what I can though. We arrived late last night and I have no idea where we're going or how long we'll be here. The captain doesn't consult me on those issues for some reason or other," Pat added with a chuckle. "What's happening with you?"

"We got wind of a big offensive somewhere in this sector. It'll be an entirely American affair, or so we've heard. That means it will be planned and executed by the American General Staff. So here I am, trying to find out what's happening and writing an article about the participants." Roy had to almost yell in order to be heard above the noise of this busy bar.

At this point, the two walked to a table just vacated by some doughboys and sat down. Roy signaled the waitress and ordered two steins of beer.

"Say, Pat, I ran into an old friend of yours two or three weeks ago, an Ike Dennison. Remember him?"

"Oh sure, great guy, an old fraternity brother. He's in the air service. How's he doing?"

"He's doing fine and asked about you and Hank. He was shot down over Dormans during the Chateau Thierry battle and spent several weeks in the hospital, but he's back flying now. I think he said he'd shot down four Germans, and if I'm not mistaken, I heard that he got his fifth last week. That would make him an ace."

"Wow, that's something. I can't wait to tell Hank. I sure wish I knew where Jake was. He'd be interested in knowing that too. You remember Jake, he was with us at the party at camp Mills?"

"Yeah, I remember him. Ike had mentioned him when we talked. I guess they were best friends in college. That brings me to Hank. Clint told me about his wife and baby. How's he doing? Is he coming through this all right?"

"He seems to be improving steadily, but it's been an almost impossible cross to bear. He slips back into his grief and depression now and again. Like yesterday, he and a bunch of the guys really tied one on in the afternoon, just before we began to march, and he caught holy hell from the captain. That's why he isn't here now. I didn't know if he'd ever pull out of it, but he's getting better. I think that's the reason for the drinking, so he'll forget. He knows that I'm not going out to get totally zonked, so he gets some of the others to go with him."

The two brothers continued talking for the full hour, covering all things they could—home, their mother, Roy's work, and Pat's job with Battery F.

Soon, Roy stood and readied to leave. "I have this interview, and then I'm on a train back to Paris. If that offensive takes place in this sector, then I'll be back. I'll look you up as soon as I can. Say hi to Hank and tell him I've been praying for you guys!"

Pat nodded and stood. "It was good seeing you, Roy, and I'll write home this week. Take care."

"You too, little brother. I'll be in touch."

With that, Roy hugged him, then turned and headed for the door.

Pat sat back down and slowly finished his beer, then renewed his search for Tom. He found him about thirty minutes later, and the two walked around for about an hour buying various needed items and sightseeing. When they grew weary of that, they set out to find a restaurant. Their search didn't take long, and once there, they ordered a grand and expensive meal.

The next two days were spent at the barracks site just outside Neufchateau. Passes were few and far between, but the duty was light. The nights had turned cold and fall was in the air.

The battery and the rest of the regiment were in for some entertainment during these two days. The YMCA had brought in some performers that put on a series of shows. One featured the famous singer, Helen Davis, of the New York Winter Garden. Many of the men were beginning to get wary of the fine treatment they were getting, as they saw it only as a prediction of coming disaster. They knew they were going to the front.

After dark on the third, the drone of four enemy bombers could be heard as those planes approached the encampment. All lights were quickly extinguished before the Boche aircraft were overhead. The bombers flew over the camp and on over Neufchateau, where they dropped sixteen bombs before turning around and heading back to their home base.

On September 4, preparations were ongoing in order for the regiment to move forward. As the carriages were being readied the drivers took the animals to Neufchateau for a much needed sulfur bath at the remount station. All equipment was checked and rechecked, carefully packed and loaded. In the late afternoon, after all the arrangements were complete, a pickup game of baseball was played between the cannoneers and drivers. It ended in a draw, as the call to harness and hitch was heard before the final inning. By 8:30 p.m. the regiment was once again on the road. As they moved north through Neufchateau, their order of march was closely observed by the division's staff officers.

The weather for the previous week and a half, had been dry and sunny, but during their ten-kilometer hike the sky became cloudy and just as they reached the night's objective, Brancourt, it started to sprinkle. The men of Battery F rolled up in their blankets in the shelter of some local barns. By morning the rain had ceased, but the day remained cloudy. Brancourt was a mere six kilometers southeast of Domremy, the birthplace of Joan of Arc.

Pat and Hank stayed in the comfort of the barn and played a spirited game of bridge with Jack and Tom, while Jason and Paul hoofed it to the historical site of Domremy.

"If it were the Kaiser himself being hung from a tree I wouldn't walk a hundred yards, let alone view the birthplace of this Joan of Arc," Jack stated quickly as he dealt the first hand.

Regimental orders arrived at 4:00 that afternoon, mandating that all be underway by no later than 5:15. Shortly after they were on the move, a steady rain began to fall. They marched till 5:00 the next morning covering a total of 46 kilometers.

During the darkest part of the morning, shortly after 3:45, a hitch from Battery E carrying three men and pulled by six horses slipped off the road into a deep ravine, injuring one man seriously. Two of the mules had to be destroyed and the carriage was little more than a pile of rubble. The accident happened because the men were dead tired and had fallen asleep.

The tired troopers of F Battery finally arrived just outside Pierre-la-Treiche. Exhausted and wet to the skin, the men set up their tents, established a picket line, and finally groomed the horses and mules before falling into their blankets. There was little said, for even those who normally tried to raise the morale of the cannoneers through song knew better than to start singing, out of fear for their lives.

During the afternoon of the sixth, the majority of the troops sought out the local eateries and taverns. The break ended all too soon, and at 7:30 that evening they were on the road continuing north through Toul.

At 4:00 the next morning, the column halted in the Foret de la Reine after a hike of twenty-four kilometers. They quickly established their camp, rolled up in their blankets, and slept until eleven the next morning. It was soon after dawn that it became evident to the cannoneers that the offensive was to start here in the salient, for the woods were crowded with American infantry.

The regiment was to stay put for the next three days. After the morning duties, cleaning the equipment and caring for the animals, the battery had the remainder of the day off.

Jack Bayless, on a late morning walk found a bathhouse not more than six kilometers from the encampment of F Battery. During the day most of the men took advantage of this find as a means of relaxation, and as a means of ridding themselves of the cooties. Unfortunately this was done somewhat in vain, as the pests seemed indestructible. Even though the men washed away all they could see and examined their underwear and popped all the eggs they found over the flame of a candle, every man was still infested with the creatures; an occupational hazard.

During their forays to the bathhouse, the Chicago members of the battery discovered that the 122nd Field Artillery of the 33rd Division was camped nearby, waiting to enter the battle for the first time. This regiment had also been formed at Fort Sheridan and consisted of many Chicago boys. Those from F Battery who had friends in the 122nd told lurid tales of their past engagements as only an old campaigner can do when dealing with amateurs new to the front. The colonel, under whose command the 122nd fell, soon declared his regiment off limits to the men of the 149th.

Once through with the taunting of the rookies, the men of Battery F turned to other diversions. The cannoneers voted on and then selected names for each of the four cannon. The first piece was named "There's a Reason," and German trooper with his hands raised to the sky, painted under the name on the shield plate located in front of the breach. The second gun depicted a shapely woman in a scanty red dress aptly named "Hell's Belle". The third gun bore the name of the "Kaiser's Kurse," with an illustration of the Kaiser on his knees. Finally, the fourth piece exhibited the figure of death wielding his scythe over the title, "The Grime Reaper."

After Ike had claimed his sixth victory he hit a rather long dry spell, but not because he wasn't confronting the Germans. On the contrary, the squadron was flying on a day-to-day basis, and even though Ike had no confirmed victories during the last two weeks of August, he was indeed engaging the enemy in combat.

There was more than one Boche that had a taste of his guns and two of those were seen spiraling down, trailing smoke before they disappeared into the lower cloud layer. Still, there was no confirmation from ground observers that these enemy planes had indeed crashed, and without independent observers viewing the craft fall to earth, there was no credited kill. One of these planes was a Rumpler observation aircraft returning to his home base, deep behind the German lines. Ike caught the Boche from the rear as the plane was preparing to descend through a hole in the low stratus layer. After he fired on the unsuspecting craft, it rolled over on its back and nosed down through the clouds. It was so far behind the lines that it made it nearly impossible for any ground-based Allied personnel to see the Rumpler crash and thus assure Ike his seventh victory.

He was alone with Bill Summers at the time after they became separated from the DH-4s they had accompanied to a nearby target. Due to the low visibility and layers of clouds, they lost sight of the bombers and were headed for home when they came upon the Boche plane. They didn't take the time to look for the aircraft and continued on back to Saintes, as Bill's engine had been running rough and they were still a half hour flying time from home.

It was also during this time that Ike had more than one narrow escape of his own. Two times he fell under the guns of the Boche aviators. On each of these occasions his craft received numerous hits; one even left a big hole in his flight jacket as a bullet passed through the right sleeve just in front of his bicep before crashing through the instrument panel. In both instances he was unhurt and able to return home and fly again, as the hits did little structural damage to his plane. The maintenance crew quickly repaired what damage there was and Ike was back in the air the very next day.

On August 28, the 95th Aero Squadron was ordered to move from Saintes back to the Toul Aerodrome, in anticipation of the American strike into the Saint Miheil Salient.

This process took about five days, during which the 95th did not fly any combat missions. The duties involved the transferring of the aircraft and the attendant job of moving their personal affects and ground crews, which had to be loaded onto trucks and driven to Toul. Ike, because of his seniority, was put in charge of the move and had to accompany the trucks back to the aerodrome, a type of duty he abhorred and which left him anxious to get back in the air.

Finally, on September 2, the 95th returned to their regular patrol duties.

On that morning Ike, Frank Linki and Bill Summers completed their briefing shortly before daybreak. At 6:00 a.m. they approached the planes for the pre-flight check and after a cursory inspection, each mounted their cockpits in the early morning twilight. The three entered their SPADs in unison. Next, each pulled on his leather helmet and gloves. They fastened their belts and harnesses and placed their hands on the controls.

Each yelled to his ground crew chief, "Switch off!"

The crew chief then pulled his plane's propeller through twice and positioned the downward moving blade for starting before calling to his pilot, "Switch on!"

Each of the pilots repeated the command and the props were pulled hard through the compression stroke. All engines caught and started on the first try.

Next, after a quick engine instrument check, each looked up to observe his fellow flight member. Ike, who was the leader of this particular sortie, held a short time to allow the water-cooled engines of the SPADs to warm up. After several minutes of running the engines at a higher rpm than idle, the engine coolant gauge began to register an increase in temperature. At this point Ike raised his right arm and brought it down, signaling to the others to begin their takeoff run.

Ike smoothly pushed the throttle full forward with his left hand. The throaty roar was like music to his ears and the plane started forward, slowly at first, as the propeller bit into the air. The speed increased rapidly as the SPAD bounced and jousted across the ground. He applied forward pressure on the control column and soon the tail was raised. The airplane's speed accelerated even more and soon the main wheels broke free of the ground. Immediately the bumpy ride smoothed out in the quiet, cool, still air of the early morning.

Ike felt a rush as he started a maximum performance climb. He looked over his right shoulder and he could see Frank's aircraft off of the starboard horizontal tail surface, sticking to his position as if he were glued there by some invisible appendage. He glanced to his left and saw that Bill was off of his port side holding as well as he could. Bill would never be the flyer that Frank was, but in his undisciplined manner, he had been able to hold his own in combat, or else he'd been incredibly lucky.

The flight quickly reached its assigned altitude of 200 meters. Ike throttled back to cruise rpm and soon turned towards the objective. The targets this morning were two tethered observation balloons located a short distance south of St. Baussant and just a little north of the

Boche forward trenches. Ike had never been too crazy about attacking these hydrogen-filled airships, as they were well protected with archie and machine guns. How the English had ever come up with the term "archie" for anti-aircraft fire, he didn't know. He'd always left this balloon busting business to pilots like Frank Luke, of the 27th Aero Squadron, who had made an art of destroying the observation balloons and had a number of them to his credit. Today, neither the 27th nor Lieutenant Luke were available at the moment and Captain Wortham had said that it was urgent that they be brought down, or flamed.

Bill was to fly the high cover and draw the ground fire, and Frank and Ike were to attack the first or the one farthest east. Ike was to come in low from the north while Frank approached from the south. After dispatching the first balloon, they were to attack the next one located about five miles to the west.

The flight to the target was a short one, and within fifteen minutes Frank was on station orbiting just south of the front, waiting for Ike to fly the six to seven kilometers north and then turn around in order to attack the balloon from the opposite direction. At precisely 6:40 a.m., both pilots began approaching the first balloon as Bill Summers flew, overhead trying to distract the enemy gunners.

At the designated time Ike raced in from the north, just above the trees, raising and lowering his altitude with subtle movements of the controls as he followed the contour of the land and height of the trees. His object was to keep out of sight of any ground-based gunners until it was too late for them to fire accurately at his plane. He soon saw the balloon above him out on the end of its cable, about 300 meters above the ground. He had a little more than a kilometer to go before reaching the target.

He added full throttle and pulled back hard on the joystick in order to start his attack from near ground level, to nose up in a steep climb. Immediately the balloon was in his sights, looming ever larger as he sped towards it. He pulled the trigger on his guns when he was a mere 100 meters away, feeding a long burst of incendiary bullets into the hydrogen-filled gas bag.

The air was filled with flak and bullets as the ground emplacements fired on the speeding aircraft. He saw Frank's plane just to his left coming in from the opposite direction, firing into the balloon. Suddenly there was a huge orange flame that quickly consumed the balloon in a monstrous ball of fire. Ike could feel the heat of it on his face.

He continued at full power, held backpressure in order to come up and over on his back in a half loop, and then flew in the opposite direction, away from the exploding bag. As he rolled the plane upright, he felt the concussion of the explosion and acceleration as the expanding gases pushed his aircraft forward. He immediately started a left turn to the west. He saw Frank's plane a kilometer or so off his left wing heading towards the second target.

He angled his craft to the right so that he could also approach this second target from the north. He reduced his power a little and began descending down towards the ground as he let his airspeed increase.

Ike felt the adrenaline surging through his veins. The attack was quick and the results were spectacular. He'd never seen an aircraft explode like that. Maybe Lieutenant Luke had known something that he didn't, at least until now.

Ike flew into the same relative position that he'd been in before attacking the first balloon and immediately banked into a steep left turn to start racing for his second target at treetop level. He hoped that Frank would begin his attack at the same time.

He saw the balloon from the moment he started for it, and immediately came under enemy fire. Luckily, the gunner's aim was not precise and missed his speeding aircraft. At a mile out he applied full throttle and his airspeed increased to 130 mph. His attention was on the target, as it loomed ever larger in his sights. At one kilometer from the airship he pulled back on the joystick and pulled the trigger on his guns. He could see the tracers penetrate the bag. He also noticed, that the observer jumped from the gondola and his parachute opened immediately. Ike continued with the attack, waiting for the bag to explode. When this didn't happen, he pulled over in the half loop, inverted, and flew away from the target. Suddenly he saw a bright flash of light, akin to a lightning strike. The gas in the bag had ignited, and as he rolled to upright, he looked over his shoulder and saw a huge fireball.

"Frank must have finished him off!" he shouted aloud to himself, jubilant over the success of the mission. "Now, all we have to do is return safely home."

Ike reversed his flight direction in a wide circle to the northwest before turning south, in order to stay away from the ground-based guns, and then started climbing for altitude to join Bill, who was approximately 500 meters above him heading south.

Ike scanned the skies for enemy aircraft but couldn't see any. He thought of Frank and was unable to find his plane. He was suddenly gripped with fear. He couldn't stand the thought of losing his best friend. Frank should have joined them by this time.

Within minutes, he pulled along side of Bill's SPAD, and saw that his plane had taken numerous hits from the enemy ground fire. He signaled for Bill to return to base and that he would loiter in the area for a short time to look for Frank.

With a wave, Bill started a slow descent and turned towards home.

Ike flew up and down the line, just south of the Allied side, waiting and looking for Frank. He flew along the line as long as he dared, for fear of running out of fuel. He finally returned to Toul and landed, with little more than fumes left in his tank.

Ike pulled up next to Bill Summers' parked airplane and he could see gaping holes in the fabric from enemy ground fire which would probably need a couple of days for repair. Ike also noted a trail of blood on the lower wing. Mike told him that Bill had been taken to the infirmary. No one had seen or heard from Frank.

Bill was lucky once again, as some shrapnel had grazed his right thigh, drawing a great deal of blood, but only superficially wounding him. Ike saw Bill lying on his side on a gurney out in the hall of the small ten-bed infirmary. He approached him slowly, at first, asking how he was doing.

"Oh, I'll be all right, it just grazed me. I'll be flying in a day or two."

"Bill, what happened to Frank? Did you see him get hit during the attack? Or crash? Where is he?"

"I didn't even see him attack the second balloon. I saw you coming in and firing, then a small fire on the south side of the envelope as you came up and over then suddenly it was a ball of fire. I was so glad to see it blow and that I could get out of range of the guns that I forgot about Frank. Then I felt a kick in the ass from the shrapnel that landed me here. Jesus, I bled like a stuck pig."

"You mean Frank didn't even make the attack?"

"That's right, at least as far as I could tell."

After seeing that Bill was going to be all right, Ike completed his debriefing with the operations officer and continued his search for his friend. He and Captain Wortham called as many of the front line companies as they could but the answers were all the same.

"We haven't seen a thing."

The squadron continued the rigorous flight schedule for the next two days. Ike, feeling a deep sense of loss, continued his search of the front line companies when time permitted, but to no avail.

When he landed from the early patrol, on September 5, immediately after the debriefing of the mission, Ike went to Captain Wortham's office, as ordered by the operations officer. He paused at the open office door and tapped lightly. The captain was engrossed in some paperwork and looked up at Ike, and motioned him into a chair opposite the desk, then went back to the stack of papers in front of him.

Ike walked to the chair and sat down quietly, waiting for him to say something.

Without looking up from the work, Captain Wortham said, "At least in the Escadrille I didn't have all of this administrative crap to bother with! But that's the American way, isn't it?" He penned his name to the last sheet of paper on his desk.

Ike merely grunted a reply and continued staring off into space.

When Captain Wortham was finished shuffling his papers, he looked up at Ike and placed his elbows on the desk, clasping his hands in front of his mouth, and spoke softly. "Before you ask me about Frank for the one hundredth time, I wanted to tell you that Frank has been found."

"Where is he?" Ike gasped bolting to his feet.

"Don't get your butt in an uproar and let me finish."

Ike nodded and sat back down in his chair.

"He wandered across the line south of St. Baussant before sunrise. The army people took him to a field hospital for evaluation," the captain continued, "I heard from the hospital about an hour ago and he's doing fine, so well that I'm driving over to pick him up. The doctors want us to take him off of their hands as he is getting to be a real pain in the ass for them. I thought that you might like to go?"

"Are you kidding? Of course I want to go, when do we leave?"

"Give me a half hour and we'll be on our way."

"Where is he, anyway?"

"Not far, about an hour's drive. Meet me here outside the office at ten hundred hours."

"I'll be here!" Ike bellowed as he jumped to his feet and left the office.

He went outside and rushed over to his barracks and quickly got out of his flying clothes, washed, and then put on some khakis. Soon he was out in front of the operations shack waiting for Captain Wortham. He thought of Agnes as he paced back and forth and started to compose a letter in his head, telling her about Frank. He'd barely started when Wortham stepped outside, just as the motor pool sergeant pulled up with the car, an old Ford sedan with a canvas top and no side windows.

"Captain, I threw a couple of rain slickers in the back in case of a downpour."

"Thanks, Sergeant, we should be back late this afternoon. Go ahead and get in, Ike. Let's roll."

Most of their talk during the ride concerned Frank and some of the pranks he'd pulled on the new airmen. The one that they loved most was Frank's way of making the newcomer stand at the mess for dinner and sing the squadron's fight song while chugging a stein of beer. Both Ike and Captain Wortham got a big laugh as they recounted these stories. The fact that the captain had brought along a bottle of scotch added to their merrymaking.

Soon their talk turned more somber as they discussed the men who'd been killed during the recent past; finally they talked of the upcoming offensive into St. Mihiel.

"You know, for the first time we're going to have air superiority. Colonel Mitchell is going to have command of over 1500 aircraft."

Ike whistled. "That's an incredible number. All American?"

"No, there will be a number of French as well as some English. This also means a lot of ground attack."

They both fell silent again as Captain Wortham concentrated on the rough road. He gripped the wheel tightly with both hands and swerved the car frequently as he tried to miss the deepest holes. He drove just as he flew, fast and with reckless abandon. He didn't slow for the potholes and at times they both were nearly thrown out of the vehicle. They continued on without saying much.

As they approached their destination, Ike broke the silence.

"I sure hope Frank isn't hurt very bad."

"Oh, I don't think so. He should be back flying in less than a week."

"Well, that too, but I don't think he could ride with you, the way you drive, and survive even a minor injury," Ike added with a chortle.

"What's wrong with the way I drive? I got you here, didn't I?"

"But that's only half of the trip," Ike retorted as they clambered out of the stopped sedan.

They entered the makeshift hospital and found Frank waiting for them out in a hall that was just outside of a large dormitory filled with empty beds just waiting to be filled when the offensive started. As Ike and Captain Wortham entered the hall from an outside door, Frank was on his feet hobbling down the hall to greet them.

"Christ, where the hell you been? I've been waiting here for over two hours to get outta this hellhole!"

"Well, hello to you too, Frank," Captain Wortham countered.

Ike turned to the captain; "Maybe we oughta just leave him here and go back to Toul."

Each hugged Frank and clapped him on the back.

"I'm sure glad you're okay," Ike said. "We were worried that the Germans had you and that they'd get so sick of you they'd just as soon shoot you than have to put up with your antics."

"Now I don't feel that I've been missed, guys."

"Well, you don't make it easy. What happened anyway?" Captain Wortham asked.

"Let's get outta here before the docs decide I need to stay and then I'll fill you in on the details."

They quickly went out the door and Frank and the captain climbed into the sedan as Ike took the crank handle, positioned it and turned the motor over. It started on the second crank, and Wortham started down the drive to the road immediately, as Ike grabbed a roof support and swung into the backseat.

"It's all very simple," Frank began. "As I started my low-level approach to that second balloon, my plane was racked by ground fire and my engine started to conk out. I circled to the west and no sooner had I done a 180 than the engine quit altogether. I couldn't go much further so I tried to land in a field. The landing was a great one, but there was a small, dry creek bed I hadn't seen and my wheels dug into the sand and I flipped over on my back."

"Jesus, Frank," Ike said softly.

"I heard some voices, German, approaching the plane. So picture this, here I am hanging upside down in my shoulder harness with the whole Boche army coming to get me. I released the belts and fell to the ground on my neck - which hurt like hell anyway - trying to figure out what to do. Give up or run away. I chose the latter. The fuel was dripping out of my tank, so I threw a lighted match in the brew and headed down the streambed. Boy, did that stir them up!"

Just then, the car hit a pothole.

"Jesus, Josiah, slow down. You trying to kill me?"

Ike laughed, "I told you so, Captain. Go on, Frank."

"Well, that burning plane distracted them so much I was able to make it to some trees about 100 hundreds yards from my wreck, and I've been heading for the lines ever since."

The captain handed Frank the half-empty scotch bottle, which he took greedily and drank from deeply as they sped on down the road.

"Well, Frank I gave you credit for the first balloon," Ike said, "but that second one was mine."

The two weeks of rest enjoyed by the 167th was quickly over. The regiment had spent much of the time in the La-Ferte-Sous-Jouarre area. While there, Jake had been fortunate enough to get three days in Paris.

During his stay in the city with his close friend, Tom Sands, now a company commander too, he drank a lot, spent a great deal of the time sightseeing, and much more time sleeping and relaxing. He spent some time alone just sitting on a bench in a park located near his hotel, observing the people who lived and worked in this great city. It seemed incredible to him to think that an immense struggle for life and death, and for eventual world domination, was going on less than 100 miles from where he was sitting, yet these people continued on as if they had no cares.

The three-day pass was over in what seemed to be just a blink of an eye, and before any of the men could adjust to the easy life, they were back to the hard work of bringing the regiment up to combat strength. It wasn't long before the 167th received their marching orders.

August 31 found every man busy packing and readying to move out. All motorized vehicles left at noon, using the roads that would take them to Toul. In the late afternoon the doughboys of the regiment began their march to Trilport where they were to entrain one more time.

At the station the train was loaded quietly and efficiently, and just after seven that evening they were underway. As the locomotive chugged its way eastward to the Neaufchateau area, Jake thought a great deal of what had happened over the past year. He was now considered a grizzled veteran by the standards of the new men arriving in France. These rookies looked up to the veterans and thought them to be unaffected by the war. But Jake could never get over the sense of great loss. More than a half of the men he'd known when the 167th arrived on foreign soil were no longer here. Many were dead and a greater number had been wounded. It was a costly loss, almost as if these men had been family. Many were like brothers.

These vast vacancies that existed in the ranks when they were pulled from the line just two weeks before had been filled with eager, though frightened, new faces. These young men had a better idea of what they were getting into than Jake had had when he first arrived in France. Their apprehensions were apparent, and they hung on every word the veterans had to say.

The whole character of the war had changed over the past few months. No longer were they defending trenches in well-prepared positions. The momentum had swung to the side of the Allies. Now they were out in the open advancing forward against a well-entrenched enemy. The goal was to keep moving ever northeastward, pushing the dreaded Hun back into his lair in Germany.

Jake didn't fear for his life, but he didn't want to die either. There were aspects of this great conflagration that challenged him. He most of all felt the thrill of this great chess game and that he was cheating death day in and day out. He'd learned to live with his fear and had come to terms with it. His belief in Jesus Christ gave a meaning to his life that he carried with him during the stress of combat.

He liked his position as a company commander. He felt for his men and was protective towards, and deeply aware of the loss of each and every one. However, under his care he knew they were safer than they would be under anyone else's. It was Captain Hammond's comments, prior to being wounded, that he kept at the forefront of his mind: "War is hell! The difference between life and sure death for your men is in the heart of their commander." Jake had the heart of a winner and those under him would, therefore, be victorious, too. Jake was aggressive in combat, but not reckless. He took the necessary risks but they were calculated risks, with the advantages weighted towards G Company.

Most important to him was to end the war, so that they could go home and get on with the rest of their lives.

The train ground to a noisy, stuttering stop at Damlin. It was late in the evening on the first of September and the sun was low in the sky, just touching the horizon. The day had been warm and as they stepped from the train they could feel the oppressive high humidity and temperature, as there was no breeze to cool them.

After a quick meal, the regiment formed up and hiked ten kilometers to an area just outside of Neaufchateau, where they set up camp and stayed for twenty-four hours.

At 7:30 p.m. on the second, the 167th started their march towards their staging area, the Foret de la Reine, located seventy-five miles to the north of Neaufchateau. Here final preparations would be made before moving onto the line of attack.

During the early morning hours, a dry cold front moved through the region. As a result, the weather for the first part of the march was pleasant. The roads were dry, the temperature during the day didn't get much higher than the mid to high seventies, and the nights were cool, making it pleasant for the night marches. The doughboys, on the whole, were in good spirits. The veterans bantered back and forth as they marched while the rookies, for the most part, kept silent or talked among themselves.

On the fourth, there were difficulties with the movement of troops and supplies as the congestion increased. With the gathering of nearly six hundred thousand men in a rather small geographic area in and around the city of Toul, which was serviced by a limited number of dirt roads, the inevitable traffic jams brought the movement of the First American Army to a near standstill.

Jake felt the movement slow to a snail's pace during the predawn hours of September 5. The regiment spent more time waiting than they did marching. Adding to the difficulties was the need for the army to move only during the hours between sunset and sunrise in order to conceal the buildup for the impending offensive against the Boche.

Major Hinkle, shortly after his return from Paris, was promoted to lieutenant colonel and put in charge of the logistics of moving the entire First Army into their attack formation against the salient. The task was a monumental one, as he had to sort out the congestion that had developed before he took command of the situation. The Americans could not afford to initiate a campaign without sufficient supplies and ammunition, to sustain the drive over a period of time.

After a short while, Colonel Werner Hinkle had to report the bad news to his superiors that it would require more time before the men and supplies would be ready. The success of the offensive was essential and all troops and supplies had to be in place to assure victory. Therefore, after careful deliberation, the time of attack was put off from September seventh to September twelfth.

Back in August, Marshall Foch had warned General Pershing that he must attack during the first week of September or not attack at all, as the fall rains would start during the second week and make movement nearly impossible. The rains began on the eighth.

The Germans had also assumed that the Allies would initiate not attack after the rains started and therefore relaxed their vigilance, a grave error.

The Rainbow Division was now part of the First American Army's Fourth Corps, located on the southern boundary of the salient east of Mont Sec. Their sector extended to the northeast from Beaumont to Flirey, which included the town of Seicheprey. They were the center division of the Fourth Corps, with the 89th Division on their right and the First Division on their left.

The 167th Infantry Regiment had just set up their camp in the Foret de la Reine, when Jake received a summons from Major Davidson, the battalion commander, to come to his tent.

When Jake arrived, he stood at attention in the doorway and saluted his superior. The major returned the salute casually and motioned for Jake to sit, which he did on one of the two cots in the tent. The major sat opposite him on the other cot.

"How are things going, Jake?"

"Fine, sir."

"How are the new men shaping up?"

"They're going to be all right after they get into combat. They seem to have adequate training, but they're scared to death."

"That's true throughout the regiment. I think if I found one that wasn't, I'd commit him to the loony bin. Jake, you've done a great job since taking over for Captain Hammonds. So good that I put in for a promotion for you over a month ago. It finally came through yesterday. So, Daniel Jacobson, I hereby declare you, through an act of Congress, to be promoted to the high rank of captain. I also have this old set of bars of mine you can wear."

He presented them to Jake, in a small cardboard box tied shut with string. Jake slowly and carefully untied the string and lifted the lid. The pair of bars was protected with two layers of cotton. They had been polished and glowed in the dim light of the tent.

Jake took each one out individually and inspected it briefly before returning them to the protection of the cotton and box. He was genuinely moved by the gift.

"Well, sir, thank you, I guess. I just don't know where I'm going to spend all that extra pay," he added with an embarrassed chuckle.

"You've been filling the slot of captain ever since Hammonds was wounded. I wish I could at least give you the back pay. You sure earned it, but you know how this army works. I'm proud to have you on my team. This next offensive is going to be tough, so keep your head low, son."

"I will, major. I appreciate your trust in me and hope I can live up to your expectations."

"You already have. I guess I'll have to continue to put up with your perverted sense of humor, though?"

"That's the only way a man can keep his sanity under these conditions, sir. Thanks for the use of the bars, I'll take good care of 'em."

"I know you will, Jake. We have more tough fighting ahead of us. Soon we'll jump off and hopefully end this war for good. Keep up the good work. That's all I have for now, so I'll let you get back to making your preparations."

"Yes, sir! And thank you," Jake said as he stood up and saluted the major. He quickly turned and left the tent.

Colonel Reilly announced at the battery commanders meeting early in the morning, that he needed one battery for special duty.

"Division headquarters has requested that I send a unit forward with the infantry during the initial attack. Their job will be to move forward with the infantry and fire on all strong points encountered during the attack."

He paused a few moments for effect before continuing. "They will also fire in defense against counterattacks and upon any enemy reserves observed moving forward to join in the battle, or to aid in the defense of one of the positions. The battery will be expected to move forward with the ground troops and, of course, be in the open during the greater part of the offensive. Your vulnerability to enemy fire will be considerable."

The colonel paused a second time and everyone present held his breath. There was a deathly silence in the bunker as each commander anticipated his battery being selected.

"I have given this very careful consideration and I have selected Battery F to fulfill that role."

Captain Case was taken aback by the announcement, as he really didn't think that his battery would be the one selected. The other commanders were obviously relieved.

Captain Case was well aware of the risks this mission entailed, but he also knew the honor being bestowed. He felt that this could lead to the eventual destruction of the battery, as it would come under fire by all elements of the enemy's defensive efforts. The battery's horse-drawn caissons and field pieces were slow and cumbersome, and therefore conspicuous and susceptible targets to the Boche gunners. He didn't know how the men would react to the news. Before he could respond, the colonel added a one last proviso.

"This is an all-volunteer mission on the part of your battery, Captain, and I'll give you a few minutes to think about it."

Without hesitating Captain Case replied, "I fully appreciate the risks the battery will be undertaking, however we're damned proud of being the one selected and will not let you down, sir."

Without another word being said about the mission, the colonel closed with a few remarks and dismissed the men and they all started back to their encampments. As Captain Case was preparing to leave, the regimental adjutant grabbed his arm and motioned for him to wait.

When the others were gone, the colonel spoke directly to him.

"Captain, this will be a risky business for you and I appreciate your willingness to accept the mission without hesitation. At noon tomorrow I want you to report to the commander of the 83rd Infantry Brigade for final instructions. I wish you well during the coming offensive."

"Thank you, sir."

"If there are no questions, carry on!"

"No questions, sir." Captain Case snapped to attention, saluted the colonel, and turned on his heel and left the bunker.

That day had started out cloudy with a few scattered showers, and on his way back to the camp a steady light sprinkle started to fall. As the captain walked to the encampment, he wondered how the men of the battery would accept this assignment.

Immediately upon his return, he called an assembly of the men. As he waited for the battery to form in ranks, he explained the situation to Lieutenant Allen and to Sergeant Baker.

"After I explain our status to the men, I want you two to select from the volunteers those who should go forward as the combat echelon. I just pray to God that enough men will step out for this task."

Soon the men were standing at attention in ranks and all were silent. The captain had the men stand at ease before he announced that he had accepted the mission on behalf of the battery and that only the guns, cannoneers, mechanics, and other necessary personnel would move forward, the others would stay at the rear echelon.

"This mission is voluntary and it will entail numerous risks, as we will be out in the open. Therefore, those of you who are willing to become part of the combat echelon, I would like for you to take one step forward."

To a man, all stepped forward.

The captain was visibly overcome by the response and his voice wavered just a little when he spoke. "I'm deeply touched and gratified by your response. We will be leaving at 5:00 p.m. So stand easy as Lieutenant Allen, Sergeant Baker and I select those of you who will form the attack team. This will take only a few minutes. Once selected, we need to get to it and be underway in two hours. Again my thanks, and may the good Lord bless our mission."

Just after five that afternoon, the combat team started for the front in a heavy rain. On their way they passed some six-inch rifles and a short time later they came upon a number of naval guns, permanently mounted on some rail flatcars. These all were being readied and positioned for the offensive.

The battery first passed through Mandres-aux-Tours, which was occupied by a large number of doughboys of the first battalion. They then proceeded northeast on the Beaumont-St. Dizier road.

This road was awash in mud and pockmarked with shell holes that were filled with water. The absolute darkness of the night made for an unforgettable trip. The horses were still in a weakened state and more than one fell during the short trip of just nine kilometers. Many of the water-filled shell holes were much deeper than they appeared and the carriages would slip down to hub depth and had to be manhandled to free them from the sludge.

The hike had been a difficult one for all of the combat echelon. Pat was exhausted by the time they arrived at their jump-off position, about one kilometer northeast of Beaumont. Pat, Tom, and the chief of section, Sergeant Martyn, were the only mechanics selected to go with the team. The others, Hank and Paul, were to stay with the rear echelon.

After setting the guns and adjusting the camouflage, Pat and the other mechanics and cannoneers spread out their shelter halves on the wet grass and rolled up in their blankets under the netting, which did little to stop the pouring rain.

The drivers of the caissons were underway to the Bois de la Hazels to get ammunition for the cannon. The Germans shelled a portion of the road where it led into the woods, between the position and the ammunition dump, which quickly became known to the drivers as "Bloody Bend." During the early morning hours a hitch from another battery was blown over from the impact of a shell, wounding four men and killing two horses.

The drivers from F Battery finished their work without mishap and at daybreak finally rolled in for some much needed sleep. It wasn't till nine that morning that the rain finally ceased. This had not prevented the men from sleeping, as they were just too worn out to be bothered.

After arising and under the cover of the camouflage, the cannoneers dug flop trenches while the mechanics poured over the guns, making last-minute adjustments for the upcoming offensive into the St. Mihiel Salient.

All movements of the American First Army had been made at night to keep the enemy from gaining any knowledge of the impending attack. This was the first real test of the American leadership.

On September 11, the low overcast skies and scattered showers resulted in very limited visibility. As a result, the men of Battery F observed an increase in troop movements.

After making the final adjustments to the guns sometime in the late morning, Tom and Pat sat back to await the attack. They both were nervous about being out in the open and had speculated as to whether they'd be playing harps or shoveling coal sometime during the next twenty-four hours.

As they were talking about their prospects, a French motorized battery pulled up next to the battery's emplacement. All members of F Battery were awed by the ease with which the French operated their four 75s. Many longed for the day when they could trade the horse and harness for a can of gas.

At noon, Captain Case reported to the 83rd Infantry Brigade for last-minute instructions. There, he was told to talk with the commanders of the 165th and 166th Infantry Regiments. Major Hardwick of the 166th was interviewed during the afternoon by the captain and Lieutenant Allen, but they were unable to reach Lieutenant Colonel Donovan of the 165th until after ten that evening.

Neither of these commanders were of much help as they didn't have any detailed plan in mind, other than for the captain to use his own judgment in order to deal with the situation as it developed while keeping as close to the infantry as possible.

Word of the time of the attack reached the combat echelon that evening. The offensive would start at daybreak, September 12, at 5:00 a.m.

All during the evening hours, a number of tanks rumbled forward from the rear and established their battle line to the right of Battery F. Their loud engine noises were covered or masked by the very active air service, whose aircraft made numerous excursions up, down, and over the line.

On the night of September 11, Captain Daniel Jacobson sat on his haunches with his back against the dirt wall of the bunker. Jake was only half listening as Major Davidson continued with the final troop dispositions with each of the company commanders. His company had been the first to receive their instructions. His thoughts now jumped from one thing to the other, from concern for his own safety to that of his men. Jake quickly perked up when the major finished with the last company and began addressing the group as a whole again.

"The artillery bombardment will commence at zero one hundred hours tomorrow and continue for four hours. At zero five hundred you're going over the top. Our objective is to enter the woods and seize control of the first line of the German defense. This must be done by zero eight hundred. Any questions?"

No one spoke.

"Remember, they will use an elastic defense. So when you're in the first line of trenches, secure it quickly and prepare for a counterattack, unless ordered otherwise at the time."

Jake raised his hand.

Major Davidson, a Baptist preacher in his former civilian life, responded, "Yes, Captain Jacobson".

"Sir, can I resign and go home?"

There were a few chuckles from the others and the tension and apprehension abated a little.

"Jake, you always got a comment, don't you? Men, if you believe in God and accept Jesus Christ as your Savior, then consider yourself already dead. Why do I say that? Let me tell you. By taking that fateful step over the top in the morning, it's one step into glory. If you're killed you will be with the Father in heaven enjoying all those beautiful things that the mind of man can't conceive. If you aren't killed, then you will bask in the glory of being an American hero. Men this is the big push to end this war. We cannot fail. Use your skills and keep the men moving. The artillery will knock out those machine guns. Stay low and spread out. And to answer your question Jake, no. Maybe next time."

"Promises, promises. Major, we need more ammo. Can we get it tonight? Tomorrow we'll be pretty busy."

"I'll see that you have it. Do any of the rest of you have needs? Let me know now. I will pray for each and every one of you. God be with you."

The St. Mihiel Offensive

During the evening of September 11, the cannoneers of F Battery learned that the initial artillery bombardment on St. Mihiel would begin at one the next morning.

When the preparations for battle were complete shortly after 10:00 p.m., the men who comprised the combat team went to their flop trenches, rolled up in their blankets, and tried to sleep. This was an exercise in futility, as the noise all through the night starting from early in the evening was tremendous. Numerous motorized vehicles were moving forward as the commanders took advantage of the darkness to position them for the upcoming attack.

The rain fell intermittently throughout the night and all, still weary from a fitful rest, were up prior to the preparatory fire that started right on the hour. The battery did not take part in this initial bombardment, and the combat team spent their time readying to move forward. The sounds of the cannon thundered throughout the predawn hours and the flashes of the guns made it appear as if the morning twilight had arrived early.

Finally at 5:00 a.m. the battery joined in on the bombardment and began zone fire for forty minutes, on a region just east of St. Baussant. At 5:45, the four limbers and eight caissons galloped up to the position and the drivers began the job of hitching up the guns and providing necessary assistance in the final preparations for the battery's advance.

As the guns and caissons were readied, the kitchen crew prepared a breakfast that included steaks and eggs. A prophetic sign of bad things to come according to the boys from Chicago, for as they had heard, men condemned to die at the Jolliet prison were given steak for their last meal before being marched to the gallows.

Not one of those readying for battle was very hungry and did little more than pick at the food, an unusual event indeed, as this was the best meal they'd had prepared for them by the field kitchen in over six months.

At 6:32 a.m., the order to move was received from regimental command. The battery started forward immediately, and fell into their position in the column. While the cheers of the other batteries resounded in their ears, the men of Battery F moved in behind the tanks and started up the slope to a small rise in the road.

Their route followed the Bois de Jury and continued on up to the second row of Allied trenches. The road was a dirt one, filled with ruts and shell holes, making advancement slow. The previous night's heavy rain didn't make the going any easier and the cannoneers toiled at the wheels and prolongs. Amidst the drudgery of traversing the rugged country, the enemy artillery was landing nearby, causing some to flinch as the shells shook the very ground beneath their feet.

Soon they crested a small hilltop and the scene presented to the men was both magnificent and inspiring. Montsec, off to the left and far to the front, was being heavily shelled by the American artillery. Directly in front, at the bottom of the hill and then onto the right, they observed row upon row of doughboys moving forward in an orderly fashion, their bayonets gleaming in the early morning sun, which was beginning to break through the high deck of broken clouds. As the limbers and cannoneers waited for the caissons to catch up, the men stood speechless as they watched the troops move towards the German trenches. The advance continued even though gaps would develop as Boche shells burst indiscriminately along the line. This did not stop or even slow their forward progress. As they beheld the scene before them, a full double rainbow rapidly formed in the clearing sky above the sector over which the Rainbow Division was advancing. Most saw this as a premonition of good luck.

Tom, who was standing next to Pat, saw it first and he grabbed Pat's shoulder. "Look at that rainbow! Nothing can stop us now."

They both stood awed by the experience and the others that reached the top of the hill stopped and stared. Soon the voice of Lieutenant Allen could be heard above the sounds of battle, "Are you waiting for hell to freeze over? Get moving, we have a war to win!"

This jogged them out of their inertia and soon the column proceeded down the slope. They continued in a straight line for about fifteen minutes and then turned north on the Seicheorey-St. Baussant road.

About one thousand meters to the southeast this road was crossed by what had once been the little town of Lahayville, leveled by an artillery bombardment in the distant past. Within ten minutes of turning onto the road, the column ground to a complete stop. They were just southeast of Bois de Remieres and their path was blocked by three tanks that had become bogged down in the muck in a failed attempt to cross the trench line that cut through the road. All members of the combat team, along with a group of "pioneer" engineers, set to work for over an hour building a road across these long narrow ditches. It still took nearly superhuman effort to move the battery across and it would still be more time before the tanks would follow. The animals were as exhausted as the men and refused or were unable to pull.

After all finally traversed this section of the road, Pat stated matter-of-factly to Tom as they continued the march, "There ain't no way that a motorized battery could have crossed these trenches. It would take bridges or a complete regrading of the trench walls and that'd take a lot of earth-moving equipment. Otherwise we would still be sitting there with the tanks."

Tom grunted his agreement as they fell in behind the number one gun.

It was 9:00 a.m. and the battery was underway again, but this time, avoiding the main road that was badly torn up from the enemy shelling and the rain. The battery traveled cross-country and took advantage of the cover of the low country between Lahayville and St. Baussant. The column moved in a northerly direction till they reached the Rupt de Mad Rue and then followed the river to a bridge. There they came upon a First Division caisson stuck on this hastily constructed pontoon bridge that spanned the river.

Unable to move his battery, Captain Case ordered the cannoneers to push the offending vehicle over and off of the bridge. The men of Battery F immediately complied amidst the vehement protest of the lieutenant in charge of the immobile caisson blocking the battery's path to the front.

The captain's parting words to the bewildered lieutenant were simple and to the point. "A lone caisson cannot, and will not impede the advance of a combat battery!"

After thirty minutes of relatively smooth going, the battery reached the outskirts of St. Baussant. Here they maneuvered around the body of a headless Boche trooper that lay in the middle of their path. This sight caused Pat to feel queasy and he quickly averted his eyes. From this point on, they took the main road that led to Essey.

Soon they came upon their second major obstacle, a point where another line of trenches crossed their path. Here the battery was forced to stop for forty-five minutes while all the men took to their shovels and picks to dig a road by grading down the sides of the trench. During this wait the drivers unhitched the horses and watered them in the muddy Rupt de Mad Rue and then tied them to wheel in a nearby hollow before pitching in with the grading.

After grading the trench, the battery was underway and had traveled no more than two kilometers when they came upon a spot in the road that had been strategically dynamited by the Boche. This caused another stop in their march, as they were unable to go around due to the rugged country on either side. Again it looked as if they'd need to spend another hour of hard labor to make it passable.

Just as they broke out the picks and shovels, some doughboys came down the road with a column of prisoners. Captain Case convinced the sergeant in charge of the POWs that he needed them to grade that section of the road for the battery to get underway as soon as possible. Quickly, the prisoners were forced to take shovels and picks and start the grading, albeit under heavy protest. However, they soon were convinced that this was better than the pointed end of a troopers bayonet.

As the enemy prisoners graded the road the cannoneers hastened about taking rations from the packs of the dead doughboys and items of value from the enemy dead scattered about the area. The road was soon readied and the doughboys started south with their prisoners. The battery continued north for three kilometers, where they entered the small town of Pannes.

It was in Pannes that the captain called a short halt to the march while he, Lieutenant Allen, and Sergeant Baker proceeded north of town to scout the area and determine the direction of march. Shortly after their departure, someone discovered an abandoned German canteen. Fatigue was soon a thing of the past as the men vanished into the shop taking cigarettes, postcards and whatever items of value they could carry. Some barrels of beer were soon found in another room and the hunt for souvenirs was abandoned in favor of the beer. After consuming as much as they could, they returned to their hunt for items of value.

During this impromptu looting binge the 83rd Infantry Brigade commander had entered the town with his staff, and seeing the frantic activity in and around the canteen, dismounted and walked in the door.

"All of you men stop where you are!" he commanded. "You're under arrest!"

No one seemed to care for the general's opinion and rapidly evacuated the building through the nearest windows and doors, leaving the commander and his staff the sole occupants of the canteen. After their pillaging of the store and surrounding buildings, the men returned to the guns and awaited the good captain's return. Had there been a call for the battery to fire, Captain Case would have found it difficult, as his cannoneers were off looting the town on their self-appointed leaves. Fortunately the captain was away, or there would have been hell to pay.

Soon after the return of the scouting party, the battery proceeded through Pannes. Just north of town they met up with some infantry commanders and the march halted again. As they waited, four aircraft with American insignia passed overhead at a low altitude. They quickly turned around and fired their guns on the column. The troops, including doughboys, dove for cover as the aircraft swooped low over Pannes from the south to the north before turning around for another run. This time they were greeted with return fire from rifles and machine guns.

Pat and Tom dove for the cover of a caisson trying desperately to curl up small enough to hide behind their helmets. For the first time since being issued the heavy, wide-brimmed headwear, the men felt that the cumbersome steel hats seemed way too small.

The return fire drove the planes away and the men came out from under cover. Private Newcum received a flesh wound in the leg and Jack Bayless had a hole through his blouse. Two doughboys along with Jason were taken to a nearby field hospital.

As the battery paused, they could hear the cleanup crews behind them, flushing out the dugouts of any remaining enemy troops. The sound of small arms fire and hand grenades was drawing closer. Just as the battery got underway, a courier from the 165th Infantry Regiment caught up with them to advise that they were getting ahead of the infantry.

At a short meeting of the chiefs of each section Captain Case explained the current situation, and asked if they were ready and willing to continue. There were no dissenters. Another courier from Colonel Reilly arrived informing the captain to report to regimental command in Essey. Instead of continuing north to Lamarche-en-Woevre, the battery was directed to wheel around and return to Essey and take up a position southwest of this small village for the night. Their roll as an infantry battery was at an end, without having fired a shot.

When the battery finally reached the position, everyone was dead tired and thirsty. The day's march had been only fifteen kilometers, but the whole trip had been demanding on the men and animals. All quickly tried to satisfy their thirsts in the mucky Rupt de Mad Rue. After the camouflage had been placed over the guns and the animals bedded down, the men gathered cabbage, cucumbers, and potatoes from a nearby field as they waited for the field kitchen to catch up with them. These vegetables were cleaned and fried and eaten in great quantities.

It was evident that the Boche had not anticipated the American attack. The resistance was weak and the Germans had left a large cache of arms and ammunition. The battery relaxed for a day before moving north during the night of September 13, to Lamarche-en-Woevre, where they rejoined the second battalion.

On September 7, Captain Josiah Wortham called the members of his squadron together. At this point in the war, morale was sagging and nearing rock bottom. The men were weary of the fighting and particularly of the ever-mounting casualties. Their hours in the air had increased to new highs and the men were worn out. Josiah knew he had to do something to lift the pilots' spirits.

The only two old-timers that were left from the original group were Ike and Frank, and they were also dispirited. If something wasn't done soon, he would lose more men, many, no doubt, to careless accidents. It was time for a good old-fashioned pep rally.

As the men shuffled into the ready room on this chilly September morning he could see the discouragement in their faces. When all were seated he stood in front of the men, ramrod straight, and began.

"We've had a bad run of luck, at least that's what you gentlemen are telling me. Is that true?"

There was a buzz from the men and many nodded.

"Well, I'm here to tell you that's a crock!" He paused a moment and paced back and forth in front of the group. The room became silent; the only sound heard was the tread of his boots as he walked from one side of the room to the other before returning to his original position.

"We create our own destiny," he stated in almost a shout, "and it is not, I repeat, it is not created by happenstance or luck. In this room, at this very moment, are the best pilots in the world. Our planes are superior to the enemy's and we have received top-flight training. When are you men going to learn that we can win in the air? I know that you're tired but if you aren't careful, your own carelessness is going to beat you, not the Germans." Wortham paused a moment to let that thought sink in before continuing. "I have some uplifting news for you. No longer are we going out in small flights of ten to twelve planes, but more on the order of twenty-four."

This brought an even louder buzz from the pilots, even some low whistles.

"On or about September 10, we will begin an assault on the St. Mihiel Salient. In this endeavor we will have a great deal of help. At this very minute, the American Air Service is assembling the largest air force the world has ever seen. This force will consist of more than 1500 aircraft."

He paused another moment in order to let that thought settle in. As before, there was a buzz of excitement.

"The majority will be American squadrons, joined by a few of our English and French Allies. All of these aircraft are to be under the command of our own Billy Mitchell. I consider Colonel Mitchell a visionary in matters of aviation, and his ultimate goal is complete aerial supremacy in St. Mihiel. The 1500 aircraft will give that supremacy to him and, ultimately, to us. Don't let me hear anymore grumbling about being outnumbered every time we take to the air. It is time that we go, and I mean enthusiastically, on the offensive. Any questions?"

"Sir!" One of the new pilots near the back of the room raised his hand.

"Yes, Courtney?"

"Does this mean a decrease in our flying?"

"No, I don't think that's in the cards at this time. We may even be in the air a little more. However, I would imagine that with the larger number of planes in the individual flights, we'd have fewer confrontations with the enemy. That is directed at both of you, Frank and Ike. I don't want anymore lone wolf patrols. All operations will be regulated out of my office. Men, this is the beginning of a big show. We are truly starting on the offensive, an offensive I believe will lead to the end of this war." He paused as the pilots mulled it over.

"In closing, I want to make one other point. If you for some reason don't feel up to speed for a particular day, head cold or what have you, see the flight surgeon. Now this doesn't mean we're giving shirkers trying not to go on patrol a way out—for the surgeon will only let you off if your claim is legitimate. But I don't want losses due to incapacity or impairment. If you are truly unable to fly, then don't force it. There is no reason to jeopardize yourselves, your equipment, or your squadron mates. If there are no more questions, I'll turn the proceedings over to Captain McAllister, who will detail today's operations. Just a reminder, we will all meet here every morning at 0430 hours for our assignments."

After the meeting, Ike felt buoyed on his walk to the plane and more confident about the flying, maybe even enthusiastic. He felt fortunate to have a small part in this great air armada, even though it meant more flying. He'd write to Agnes about it to help bolster her spirits, too.

As the days of the next week passed by, Ike seemed to be constantly in the air. Captain Wortham had been right; he and the others flew no less than three patrols a day. His logged time aloft for each of his flights kept on hitting new highs.

However, because of the large flights that usually consisted of twenty or more planes, the American pilots frequently chased away enemy aircraft before they could be engaged in battle. There were fewer confrontations during the week prior to the offensive and ultimately there was a reduction in losses. Even the number of non-combat accidents declined.

Their frequent sorties consisted of escorting bombers into the salient in an effort to demolish rail and road centers, patrolling the front to discourage enemy observers from viewing the buildup, and acting as escorts for Allied observation planes. There were also some runs on the enemy balloons. The object was to blind the Boche in his efforts to determine the Allied preparations for the coming offensive, particularly as to its size and ferocity.

Ike still loved the flying but it was beginning to wear him and the others down. Even though there were fewer confrontations with the enemy aircraft, there were always losses to contend with, friends or acquaintances killed in combat or in accidents. There was always the wounded and the not knowing what had happened to those who had been shot down and captured.

At the end of each flying day, Ike barely had the strength to eat and write a short note to Agnes before hitting the sack and sleeping five or six hours. This sleep was fitful and anxious. The stress of battle was beginning to show its effects on all of the pilots, but there was a new positive spirit amongst the flyers.

All of the crews were awakened at 0400 hours and had a quick breakfast followed by a short operations meeting before taking off by 0500.

On September 8, the 95th Aero Squadron, as well as the many other squadrons, began night patrol over the front lines. They flew low, normally below the cloud bases, in rain and fog. Their object was to help shield the sound of all the mechanized units, including tanks, being moved forward for the attack. Already frayed nerves were drawn even tighter.

After a postponement, the great American offensive began on September 12 at 1:00 a.m. The artillery barrage started on time, and at 4:30 the infantry started forward, with the first third of the aircraft of the great air armada paving the way by strafing and bombing the German positions. Soon the remaining aircraft from the other squadrons began their operations. They flew to the rear of the German lines, bombing and strafing the German efforts to resupply the front and even some of their units who were already in retreat.

As the first wave left the front to rearm and refuel, two other waves of five hundred aircraft each followed in sequence, one after the other, leaving the German supply depots a smoking ruin. Once the pilots bombed and strafed all vehicles in their specific zone of operation, they were free to attack any other Boche targets of opportunity, until the ammunition or fuel ran out.

The 95th Aero Squadron flew in the first wave. As the early morning twilight began to show on the eastern horizon, Ike applied full throttle to his SPAD and began rolling over the rough, dark grass strip outlined only by numerous orange flames dancing in the countless smudge pots placed at fifty-foot intervals around the field. The wind was ten to fifteen knots out of the west and gusty. Soon the tail was raised and as flying speed approached, Ike added backpressure to the control column while holding slight aileron into the quartering head wind. Soon the mains pulled free of their earthly bonds and the plane was airborne, burdened down with ammunition and bombs. Ike was leader of the second section of eight pursuit airplanes. The other seven planes, off to his left, quickly formed their V formation and followed Ike as he climbed to 500 meters and fell into formation to the left of Capain Wortham's flight of eight. Frank, leader of the third section, formed his flight on the field and began their takeoff roll, and soon followed the others.

Once the squadron was together, they flew west along the line to their sector before turning north. The air was rough, making it hard to hold position in the flight. The pilots flew as close to their squadron mates as they dared, always fearful of a mid-air collision. The target for this early morning was the little town of Essey.

By the time the Kicking Mule Squadron reached their sector, there was enough daylight for the pilots to discern their targets. The squadron attacked the town in three waves of eight planes each. Captain Wortham led the first wave, Ike the second and Frank led the third. Wortham's flight dove straight in as the second and third waves circled overhead. Once the last plane of the first wave began the run on Essey, Ike signaled his flight to begin their attack.

Return fire from the ground was light and Ike drew a bead on a convoy of ten trucks facing south. The vehicles were stopped, as the drivers and passengers had jumped out to seek shelter in the surrounding buildings and ditches. As Ike pulled the triggers on his guns he could see the tracer bullets penetrate the trucks, beginning with the one in the lead and moving rearward towards the last vehicle. As his bullets penetrated the third truck from the end, there was a tremendous explosion and ball of fire.

He added backpressure and full throttle to climb above the great conflagration and ended up flying through the top of the smoke, fire and debris. After he was in the clear, he checked his aircraft to be certain that the plane hadn't caught fire or been damaged. Once convinced that all was well, he turned to make another run on the town.

Off to his left, as he made his second run was Captain Wortham's plane. They both dived in unison, machine-gunning the streets that were crowded with Boche equipment. This time the ground fire was heavy and the air full of flying iron and steel. Ike released his six Cooper bombs slung under the wings. He saw the captain do the same, just as thick black smoke started pouring out of the captain's engine compartment. Ike knew that the hit Captain Wortham had taken was catastrophic.

He immediately fell in behind him and followed him as the captain tried to climb and turn to the east. Wortham's engine stopped and he set up for his landing. He put it down in a field about a kilometer northeast of Essey and clambered out, just before it burst into flames and the fuel tank exploded.

Ike kept at low level and circled around to the south, then back to the north. As he came upon the smoking ruins, he saw the captain off to the right of the burning wreckage with his arms in the air. He'd crashed near a German infantry bivouac. There were ten or more soldiers holding their guns on him. Ike couldn't use his own guns on the troops for fear of hitting his friend.

He circled overhead another time and came under intense small arms fire from the Germans. There was nothing more for him to do but leave the area and head back to base. He felt sick to his stomach, but at least the captain was alive.

Jake kneeled in the trench on the firing step below the parapet, waiting for the time to move out. He looked at his watch and saw it was just a few minutes away. The sound of the artillery barrage was constant and so loud he could hardly hear his own thoughts. He dug his helmeted head into the wall of the trench, closed his eyes, clenched his teeth, and said a short prayer. Shells were exploding all around him. Some of the incoming were gas, and he ordered those near him to put on their masks.

The last minute ticked away swiftly, and it was time to go over the top. He lifted his mask, stood on the firing step, and shouted to his men to move out. Over the top they went, out into no-man's-land.

He could hear the Allied guns behind him as the barrage continued. The explosions were just in front of his men and kept creeping forward toward the enemy trenches. The Americans were spread out to his right and left, running in a half-crouched position. There was no rifle or machine gun fire coming from the enemy trenches, and the confidence of the advancing troops grew as they approached midpoint of no man's land. The field that they were crossing was badly scarred with shell holes, but Jake noticed that the grass was still knee-high in places and that there were pretty little orange and red flowers growing profusely. As he jogged along he stooped down with an opened hand to grab a small bunch that he quickly positioned under the strap of his helmet. Just then, the German defenders opened up with all they had.

The Huns fired at them with mortars, rifles, and machine guns. Jake continued to run, though it was difficult to see through the gas mask. He lifted the mask to test the air and detecting only the stench of exploding shells and death, pulled it down from his face. He was out in front of the men of the Second Platoon and as he glanced to his left he saw one of the men disintegrate in the explosion of a mortar. He glanced to his right and the man next to him crumbled to the ground like a rag doll after taking a bullet in the face.

Still they continued to run. Jake couldn't understand why he hadn't been hit. Others around him were falling right and left, and still he ran on.

The barbed wire in front of the first line of the enemy's trench had been chewed up by the artillery barrage and he found a path through. He could see some of his men behind him as he jumped into the first trench. With his pistol drawn he started firing at anything that moved. He was filled with rage and hatred for the Hun and didn't care who he shot. Too many of his men had fallen in their run across the open ground. As he ran along the trench, he turned and saw three Germans coming toward him. He fired his pistol with such fervor that even when it was empty he kept pressing the trigger. All three enemy soldiers were sprawled dead at his feet. He turned and looked behind him and saw some familiar faces of the Second Platoon. He stepped over the bodies of the foe and continued to run the zigzag of the trench. His men were firing and tossing grenades at those Germans who had the misfortune of staying behind in their bunkers. As he ran he put a new clip into his .45. The defenders were scrambling out of the trench and running to the rear, stumbling over one another to get out, and left numerous dead and wounded behind.

At the next turn of the trench he ran into a wounded German sitting on the floor of the trench with his back against the north side. His left arm was gone, blown off during the Allied barrage. As Jake raised his gun to fire, the man pleaded for water. Jake lowered the pistol and pulled out his canteen and gave it to him. The man drank deeply and before he finished, it slipped from his hand to the ground. The man then fell to his left side and died. Jake stared at him and thought that he was a man just like anybody else, not a hated barbarian.

More of his men had caught up with him; all were out of breath. Even though only 30 minutes had passed since leaving their trench, it seemed like a lifetime. For many, it had been.

As Jake was establishing his defensive perimeter on the newly acquired trench, a runner from the battalion commander approached him at a trot. When the trooper was within hearing distance, he stammered, "Captain, the major wants to see you at the command bunker, that's just east of here, about 200 yards, sir!" The soldier took a deep gulp of air.

"Thanks, private. Tell him I'll be there in about ten minutes."

"Yes, sir!" The private politely saluted and turned around, heading back along the trench line.

After Jake had completed the defensive disposition of his company, he took inventory of his men. He was saddened to learn that six had been killed during the assault and nine others wounded and no longer capable of fighting, at least for a while.

"Sergeant, secure the position against any counterattacks, I'm going to dig out the major."

"It's in the works, Capt'n!" was the simple reply from Thompson as he hustled along the line, helping to place men from the Third Platoon.

Jake took a last look at his deployments, then turned and ran along the zigzag of the trench towards the command bunker. The enemy shelling was sporadic and not well aimed. The constant sound of artillery was from the Allied barrage that was pounding the German positions off to the north.

He arrived at the command post just as the major emerged from the underground bunker. As he approached, the major looked up at him and nodded. Jake saluted casually. "Sir, we're secure in our sector and resistance was fairly light. We suffered about fourteen casualties and we're ready to continue with the attack, sir!"

The major returned the salute and motioned for Jake to follow. He retraced his steps and led the way back into the bunker. The underground dugout was dark, lit by numerous candles that flickered, giving an eerie glimmer to the room. As the light was dim, it took a short time for Jake's eyes to adjust to the new surroundings. There were a few others in the dugout, communications personnel as well as a few staff officers.

The major stepped to the center of the room to a rickety handmade table, probably hewed by some German soldier. Now this table held a large American map of the sector. This curled chart was held down with large candleholders made from brass shell casings, one placed at each of its four corners.

As the major stared intently at the map he finally acknowledged Jake's report, though it was obvious that his mind was elsewhere. "That's good news Jake."

He paused for a moment, lost in his thoughts. "Now I'm going to send you on forward for another type of mission. I need for you to test the strength and will of the Germans on to the north. Take your signal flags and some carrier pigeons with you, as you're going to be too far forward to lay phone lines. Establish a position here, on this little rise in the St. Benoit-en-Woevre area up near hill 220, right here. Our observers in the balloons can see that rise, at least after the clouds clear, from here." The major pointed to the place on his map laid out in front of them.

"You want me to take the whole company?"

"Oh no, this is a reconnaissance patrol. Take your most experienced men, probably no more than a squad. When you're set up, get word to me so we can see where the best route to the area is for our advance. We think there's a weakness over east of the road and we want to be able to take advantage of it. If you can get around to this hill and signal the info to us, we might be able to save some lives and some time. If the skies don't clear, send a runner back in addition to a pigeon. Jake, I need your judgment on this. That's why I'm not sending one of your platoon leaders. They're still too green to give me what I need. Get this information to us by no later than tomorrow at zero one hundred. This will determine our advance in the morning. In the meantime, we will continue north and be in Essey or Pannes for the night. Here is a smaller map that you can take with you."

The major handed Jake a case that could be slung over his shoulder. "Now get going, I'd really like to hear from you in twelve hours or less. We need time to plan our attack for tomorrow morning."

"I'm on my way, major. I'll leave Charley Caldwell in charge of the company." Without waiting for a dismissal, he turned on his heel, was out of the bunker, and running back to the position.

Once there, he called his four platoon leaders together and explained the assignment.

"I'll take three good men from each platoon, so give the names to Dave here, he'll get them together. And Dave, you're coming with us, so get 'em ready to move," he said to Lieutenant Workman, who quickly got the names and disappeared out of the bunker without a word.

"Charley," he said to the third platoon leader, "you're in charge while I'm gone. The rest of you, get your men ready to continue the attack by noon, or sooner. I guess that's all. We'll see you later tomorrow. Dismissed."

The men quietly filed out of the dugout and Jake, the last to leave, took one quick look around, spied a Springfield on the one lone table, and picked the rifle up. He had to duck his head in order to leave through the low overhead doorway. He went to his backpack and took the necessary ammunition and canned food. Finally, he walked over to the recon team. The men were assembled along with his first sergeant; who had joined them with a field pack, ammunition, and weapons.

"Sergeant, you're staying here. You gotta help Lieutenant Caldwell run the company while I'm gone."

"Sir, he can do it without me. You'll need my eyes and ears."

Jake started to protest and thought better of it. He knew that Thompson was the best-damned soldier in the regiment. He'd grown up in the bayou country of the south and was well known for his tracking ability. He could move through any kind of country undetected. Jake knew he would need Thompson's stealth as the scout for the squad.

"All right," he said to the sergeant, then turned and addressed the men of the team. "The lieutenant told you about our patrol, so be ready to move out in fifteen minutes. We'll travel light. Bring only weapons, food and ammunition, and wear enough clothes—it may be cold tonight. We have nearly eight miles to cover, and that's as the crow flies. We'll go over the top from the command bunker and head for the trees over on the right. Obradivich, go over to supply and get four pigeons. Warren, bring your signal flags. Sergeant, take point and two others with you so you can keep in touch with us. Remember, we'll be working behind the German lines, so keep quiet."

The men of the reconnaissance party quietly gathered the necessary gear and met with Jake outside the command bunker at 8:25 a.m.

In the meantime, Jake finished his briefing with Sergeant Thompson and the other two scouts whom he had sent on their way just a minute earlier.

At exactly 0830 hours, the squad of nine men including Jake went over the top and headed for the little wood to the northeast, just a short distance behind the three scouts. Most of the trees had been striped bare of their vegetation, but the trunks and debris provided good cover and protection. The condition of the ground slowed their progress at first due to the multitude of shell holes, parts of downed trees, and mud from the previous night's barrage and heavy rain.

The Americans soon came upon some Boche troops who were also moving north. The team skirted around the enemy troops in a wide arc before returning to a more northerly track.

Jake had gone over the map with Thompson, who set the path for St. Benoit-en-Woevre. Private Bliss was the go-between and was in constant contact with the column and Thompson, whose information kept them from being detected by the enemy. They stayed off of the roads and made frequent detours around other pockets of enemy troops who were too preoccupied with their retreat, trying to keep just in front of the American onslaught.

The men of Company G traveled for a number of hours without detection while covering more than five miles. As they continued in their northward movement the going became easier as the ground had not been potmarked so heavily from the shelling. Cover was easier to find, as the small stands of trees had not been so totally stripped of their foliage by the fighting.

At noon, Jake called a halt to give his men time to eat their ration of canned "monkey meat," [aptly named as no one else in the AEF couldn't think of anything better.] Fire or smoking of any kind was out of the question, as it would probably lead to their eventual detection. The small troop of men huddled along a stone fence that separated a small wood from a field of wheat. Three men acted as lookouts while the others ate.

Towards the end of their rest, Thompson returned from scouting. "I didn't find any troops directly north and we can move that way, but there are a lot of open fields. It'll probably be better for the infantry when they begin to move in the morning. We need to stay west along the tree line. We're getting close to their main body of troops."

"I agree," Jake replied. "We'll head north along this wood for about a mile and then turn northwest. Here?" Jake asked as he pointed to the map that he'd pulled from its case that he'd been carrying over his shoulder.

"That oughta do it, Capt'n. Them trees here should keep us outta sight from the Boche. It's when we get through those woods here to the north when we'll be in the open for a short while."

"We'll solve that problem when we come to it, Sarge. Let's get moving. Wait for us at the end of the woods. How long will it take to get there?"

"Oh, about an hour or less."

"See ya then. Okay, men, let's get moving," Jake whispered as he moved along the fence, "and keep the noise down."

The Sergeant disappeared into the woods and the men quietly got up and prepared to continue their northerly march. They moved along under the cover of the trees and stayed off the roads. They could hear the Boche infantry and artillery units as the Germans continued their retreat. The enemy stayed on the roads and had no idea that an American infantry squad was so close.

Jake made notes on his map—as well as mentally—of the best route the 167th could take the next day as they started north out of Essey.

Sergeant Thompson kept in touch through the runner, Private Bliss. The scouts made it possible for the column to skirt numerous German units without the Boche even knowing the Americans were nearby. The enemy was apparently making preparations to retreat further north or was already in the process of doing so.

Jake knew that they would leave a rear guard as protection for the main body of troops who were in retreat, but he was convinced that opposition would be light. There was always concern for the Boche artillery and particularly the Boche machine guns that the Americans would have to contend with. As they continued on, Jake made other notes as to the points that would be most heavily fortified and when there was time he highlighted them on his map.

At 1:00 p.m., the platoon met Sergeant Thompson at the edge of the trees. In front of them lay a large grassy field that would require them to be in the open for about two or three kilometers, roughly fifteen or twenty minutes. The weather was good and there were scattered clouds, with the sun shining about a half of the time with the visibility being greater than five miles. The American barrage had lessened and was aimed more to the west.

Jake decided to take an aggressive step. He had the men put on their rain slickers and march at a fast clip across the field. He hoped that, at least from a distance, they would look like just another Boche unit in retreat.

The plan seemed to work, as they weren't confronted for at least two thirds of the distance. However, as they neared the protection of the wood on the north end of the open area, shells started raining down on them.

Jake yelled to the men. "Head for the cover of the trees. We've been spotted." All broke into a run, trying to dodge the shells as they fell and exploded around them. One shell hit near a group of four just before they reached the safety of the trees. The explosion tossed them about like rag dolls.

Jake was the last to reach the trees before the shelling ended. He lay on his stomach in a small culvert looking towards the men that had fallen victim to the shell. Two were moving and two, he was sure, had been killed. He felt sick inside, but knew he had to control his emotions.

One of the men behind him, who had made it safely to the trees, called to one of the still forms lying in the field, "Randy, Randy are you all right?"

Soon the shelling stopped and Jake ordered four men to retrieve the dead and wounded soldiers and bring them to the cover of the trees.

The man who had called to his friend Randy was the first one out and discovered that Randy was dead. He sat down next to the body and wept silently. The others brought the three remaining victims into the safety of the trees.

Lieutenant Workman examined each trooper as he was brought in. Two were dead and one was seriously wounded, while the third suffered only superficial cuts and abrasions.

"Damn!" Jake said to Lieutenant Workman and Sergeant Thompson, "we'll have to leave a man here with Private DuKane, he's too seriously wounded to take with us. The Allied attack force should be here tomorrow and DuKane needs to be looked after, particularly as long as he remains unconscious. Dave, can we leave Corporal Levies here to take care of DuKane?"

"I would say that he'd be perfect for the job, he seems to be all right even though that shell tossed him about. He's helped with the wounded in the past. What do ya think sergeant?"

"I'd agree, I think he'll be Okay."

"All right then, see that it's taken care of, and I'll send the sergeant and his scouts on ahead."

When the lieutenant was gone, Jake said to Thompson, "I didn't want to alarm anyone, but those bursts were from American guns. That's all we need, casualties from friendly fire. And worst of all, it takes our numbers down to nine."

"You're right, Capt'n, them was our guns."

"How far are we from our destination, Sarge?"

"Less than an hour."

"All right, let's get moving. When we get there I want you and one of the scouts to go back with the info and I'll send a carrier pigeon also. I don't want to use the signal flags, as that might give our location away. I think we have the route worked out and we need to get the word to the major. Do you feel up to it?"

"Sure do, Capt'n. I'll take Private Bliss and leave you Smalley. He's a better tracker and you guys will need 'em."

Jake nodded, "Okay, that does it. Let's get underway."

Prior to this incident the men had been treating this scouting trip as a big adventure, frequently joking about it. As the reality of its danger sunk in, the men turned quiet and sullen.

As Jake gathered the men together, he stopped by the wounded Private Dukane and Corporal Levies. "It won't be long and our guys will be here, corporal. Dig yourself in, as there could be some artillery near here in the morning. The private has lost a lot of blood but seems to be stable for the time being. Sit tight and keep your head down. Good luck."

"Thanks, Captain! We'll be all right. See you guys tomorrow."

Each man in the squad said their goodbyes and fell into line in the column. They continued forward without much being said. Jake continued to take notes, always thinking in terms of the next day's attack.

At three in the afternoon they were drawing close to their objective. The going was more difficult, as they were trying to filter through various units of enemy troops. As they approached their destination, the scouts rejoined the platoon.

"Capt'n, our objective is about five hundred yards straight ahead. There's a German artillery battery taking a breather right there at the moment, but I think they'll be pulling out soon."

"Are we safe here?"

"Yes, sir."

"Dave, have the men take a time-out. No noise or smoking. And post some lookouts."

"Got it, sir." The lieutenant went to have the men settle in and set up two as guards.

"Okay Sarge and Bliss, let's go over the map and get you on back to the major," Jake said.

They quickly reviewed the trip and determined the best route the 167th would take the next morning. Jake wrote as much as he could on the small piece of paper that would be placed in the container attached to the carrier pigeon.

"I'll wait till you and Bliss get out of here before we release the bird. Both of you commit this to memory and don't get caught. I don't want to jeopardize the attack. You'll have nothing on you that tells the enemy what you're up to other than the map?" Jake said. They both nodded.

Jake asked Private Smalley to check on their ultimate destination, to insure that the Boche artillery battery had indeed moved on. As he was releasing the pigeon, Private Smalley returned with the news that the battery was digging in and setting up to fire to the south.

"This puts us in a bind," Jake said. "Are there other batteries in the neighborhood? And is there a safer place for us to dig in?"

"Don't know, sir, but I'll go check." He abruptly disappeared into the surrounding underbrush.

Jake called for Lieutenant Workman, who quickly came to his side.

"I think we've moved into a hornet's nest, Dave. There are more German units around us than I first thought. We're going to have to seek out some cover."

"What are you planning on doing?"

"I sent Smalley out to check on things. Hopefully he can find a safe place for us to hole up for the evening. Then tonight we'll try to retrace our steps and move a little further south. Get the men prepared to move; the scout will be back in a minute."

They heard the sound of gunfire and some shouting off in the distance. The Germans had found Private Smalley.

Jake put the glasses to his eyes and searched the general area from which the sound had come. The trees weren't thick and there were numerous rocks and gullies in the area, and he soon picked out Private Smalley as he ran towards the position, crouched low and dashing from rock to rock. When he was a mere sixty yards away, a German sharpshooter put his sight on him and carefully squeezed the trigger. He caught Smalley in the back and Smalley fell forward, killed instantly.

Jake swallowed hard. He felt panicky but kept his cool. "Dave, get the men up and moving off to the east. I think we've been discovered."

As they started their retreat, mortar shells began falling on the position. One landed in the midst of the squad, killing three outright. Jake, Dave, and the third man started running on to the east. Machine gun fire caught the lieutenant and this third man, and suddenly Jake was alone.

He ran through the underbrush as fast as he could. He heard rifle and machine gun fire behind him but he kept on running. He came to an open field and started across, carrying only his rifle and field pack. He quickly took off the pack and dropped it and threw down the rifle. He needed speed to get away. He still had his handgun strapped to his side.

His men were all dead and here he was, running for his life. The rifle and machine gun fire stopped, but the mortar shells were falling all around him. When he felt that the enemy was too far behind him to catch up, he slowed the pace a little. He felt totally drained.

Just as he was beginning to feel safe, a series of shells fell all around him. One threw him into the air, and he lost consciousness before he hit the ground.

Jake had been unconscious for more than an hour. When he came too, darkness was setting in. It took him many minutes to determine where he was and how he had gotten there. He hurt all over. He started to take a personal inventory and discovered he'd been wounded in the right shoulder. He also knew that he had some shrapnel in other body parts, but he couldn't determine where.

As it was almost dark and he didn't know where his company was, he prepared to spend the night. He was determined to stay awake and to stop the bleeding. He discovered that he was lying on his back in a deep shell crater. He could see the sky but was unable to see any landmarks. He tried to sit up but his pain and fatigue were too great, so he lay back down.

Jake was afraid that if he slept he might never wake up. He'd also heard some gruesome stories about the rats in the battle zone. Some, it was said, were as big as small dogs and that they could pick a body clean to the bone in a matter of minutes.

Darkness came quickly, but the hours of night passed slowly. He tried to ignore the pain and tiredness, but it eventually caught up with him. Jake's first fear was that the Germans would find him and take him prisoner. He pulled his service automatic from its holster and held it in his left hand. At least he was still strong enough to fire it if things got worse. He laid the gun on his stomach and reached into his left pocket and fished out three wooden matches. He placed one in his right hand, which still functioned all right, though the arm and shoulder hurt when he moved them. The other two matches he laid on his stomach. He then picked up the .45 again with his left hand.

Jake couldn't stay awake and would sleep fitfully for a short time, then wake himself up. He hallucinated as he struggled to stay awake. He heard sounds in the night. At first he thought he heard voices speaking

German nearby. Then he heard voices out of the past. One sounded like his mother calling him, just as she had when he was young and lost in the woods. But his mother had been dead all these years. How long? Ten, fifteen years? Then he started to hear the voices of some of the men in his platoon. But these were the voices of men who had been killed in earlier actions. Soon he lost consciousness altogether.

Sometime later, Jake felt a tugging at his foot. At first he thought it was another dream, but then the pain in the shoulder let him know he was awake. He could feel the tugging and vibration on his left foot. He froze in fear. He couldn't imagine what it was.

He finally got hold of himself and started to fumble with the match in his right hand. Quietly and without undue movement, he felt for the head of the match with his thumb. He gripped its long handle between his fingers and the palm of his hand and quickly ran his thumbnail across the top of the match. It sparked brightly, but didn't burn. The vibration on his left foot ceased for a moment. Jake held his breath, and then it resumed. He struck the match with his thumbnail again. This time there was a blinding flash as the match came to life.

As the flame died down to normal, Jake raised his head as far as he could to see what was tugging at his boot. All he saw at first were two bright, glowing red coals close together. As his eyes adjusted to the light he made out the shape of the largest rat he'd ever seen, its eyes glowing brightly in the flame of the match. The rat stood perfectly still with its front paws holding onto the outer soul of his shoe. The rat was trying to eat his boot. The sweat stood out on Jake's brow, and he felt the presence of other rats. He held his automatic with his left hand, took quick aim and fired. He caught the rat right between the eyes and it flew back out of sight. He could hear the others scurrying about, so he shouted as loud as he could and waved his left arm around, trying to scare them off.

When he had time to reflect on what had just happened, he gave thanks to God he hadn't shot his foot off or something worse.

Before the match went out he looked at his watch and saw that it was ten minutes to four. Almost two hours before daylight. He doused the light and knew he had to start moving. First, the rats would come back and secondly, the Germans may have heard the pistol shot or seen the glow of the match. It wouldn't take them long to zero in on his position. He looked up into the black, starry sky and located the Big Dipper. From there he found the North Star. He felt that if he headed south he would have a better chance of finding the American lines.

With great effort he sat up. The shoulder was not as painful, but felt awfully stiff. He couldn't see the shoulder, but he rubbed the area with his hand and felt blood, though the bleeding didn't seem to be serious. He rolled over onto his left hand and knees and started to crawl out of the crater. It seemed that his feet and legs were all right, though his knees were wobbly.

After reaching the top of the crater, he looked around. Seeing nothing to fear, he got to his feet and started walking south in a crouched position. It was too dark to see anything, but he felt that was a blessing. No one would see him.

St. Mihiel in Allied Hands

Soon after Battery F established its position on the south bank of the Rau de Naujupont just north of the village of Lamarche, all activity came to a near standstill. The Boche had retreated further north and were just a little too far out of range for effective fire from the battery's 75 mm cannon. This lull in battle gave the men time to catch an extra forty winks wherever they could. All they needed to do was pitch the tents and place their bedrolls.

Battery F stayed put for the next two days. Taking advantage of the situation, the battery members did only the necessary chores, such as cleaning and repairing equipment and those other duties deemed vital to the battery's continuance as an effective combat unit.

It was during this interval, and on the afternoon of the fourteenth, that Pat and Hank happened upon a cow not far from the guns. The animal had become entangled in barbed wire in a gully and its cries had drawn their attention. Their first thoughts were of fresh milk, but once they'd cut her free from the snares they determined that she had been wounded and that it would be more humane if the poor beast were slaughtered in order to put her out of her misery. It wasn't a bad exchange, though, for as the thought of fresh milk faded from view it was quickly replaced by the vision of steak.

The field kitchen was glad to collaborate in the endeavor, but instead of steak and beef roast, as envisioned by the two mechanics, the inept kitchen crew came up with stew which was fed to the whole battery. The meat had been overcooked and was as tough as leather.

"Oh well, at least the meat was fresh and there sure was plenty for everyone," Hank lamented after the meal.

"If we find another one," Pat added, "I'll slaughter and cook it myself instead of leaving it for those so-called cooks."

"Oh yeah, just like you killed the horse, without remorse."

"But that was different, Hank," Pat responded, somewhat in self-defense.

"Sure it was."

The following day, September 15, during the early morning hours, the men on guard duty became inadvertent spectators of massed Allied planes bombing the city of Metz, a German stronghold located some miles to the northwest of their position.

Tom and Pat were on duty at the time and watched as the long fingers of numerous German searchlights sought out the planes flying high overhead. When one of the planes was caught in the beam, the anti-aircraft batteries concentrated their fire on the target, but none of the planes were hit. The guards were close enough to hear the bombs detonate on their impact with the ground and they even heard the planes, but were unable to see much more than the lights scanning the darkness and the air bursts of the antiaircraft shells in the cold blackness of the predawn sky.

Sometime after breakfast on the fifteenth, Captain Case and Lieutenant Allen took a couple of the riding horses and searched to the north for a new and permanent position for the guns. Late in the afternoon, the two returned with the good news that the new encampment was only four kilometers to the northwest. The battery spent the rest of the afternoon packing their belongings, then harnessed and hitched. They began their forward progress shortly before sunset. The road was a terrible mess, a fact the captain hadn't mentioned prior to their start. The mud was as sticky as paste.

Though the new position was just a short distance away, it took nearly four hours to traverse that stretch of road. Each vehicle became mired down in the mud more than once.

After setting up camp and the laying of the guns on their targeted zone, the battery returned to a more normal schedule. They remained at this position for two weeks. Duties included digging the guns in and concentrating on various tasks, which included some firing. On the whole the days were quiet and the duty continued to be light.

All during this time the rumor mill was grinding away. The first rumor was that they would dig in for the winter. This was not a welcomed piece of news, not for the men who had been designated as shock troops. No one wanted to return to the days where shovel and pick were more important than movement. The next rumor revolved around the notion that the division would be packed up and returned to the states.

As the work schedule continued to be on the light side, some of the men, during their off-duty hours, soon discovered that the position was located in a blackberry patch. These were eagerly picked and presented to the cooks, who quickly used them for baking pies and for jam. Finally, they had food that was a joy to eat and something the cooks could handle without ruining.

They cooked down some apples from a nearby orchard for sauce. As the cooling racks were used for the pies, the sauce was set off to the side to cool. A couple of enterprising drivers found the pot and scurried off with it and its contents. The empty saucepan was later retrieved from the garbage pit minus the applesauce.

As the days passed, the men were continually engaged in solidifying the guns in shallow pits and building light gun platforms from lumber scavenged from a nearby sawmill that, until recently, had been in the hands of the Germans. The battery did some firing, but on the whole it was not intense. Fewer than a thousand rounds were fired over the next five days.

On September 21, Captain Case was summoned to the regimental commander's dugout. Upon his arrival, the colonel was a little perplexed—he thought he had sent for the commander of D Battery.

"No time to locate Captain Higgins now," Colonel Reilly said angrily to his orderly "We'll send a platoon from Battery F, now that Captain Case is here." He turned to Captain Case and the commander of A Battery and said, "I need a platoon from each of your batteries to move forward and support an infantry attack on the Marimbois Farm and Haumont. The attack will take place just before dawn, tomorrow. You are to go forward into no-man's-land and select a position this afternoon, then move the guns into position tonight. Captain Case, I want you up here on the heights to the right, firing into Marimbois Farm, and you, Lieutenant Harkins, here over on the left firing into Huamont." He tapped each point on the map laid out in front of them with his swagger stick.

"These positions will allow you a line of fire without jeopardizing the infantry. You will begin your fire at 0400 hours. And for pity sake, have your cannoneers keep close watch and not hit our own infantry. Any questions?"

Both men shook their heads.

"All right then, get to it. If any changes come up in the meantime, I'll get word to you. Once you've chosen your position, get the information back to the adjutant."

Both men replied with a "Yes, sir!" and were dismissed.

As soon as Captain Case left the bunker and conveyed his wish for their good fortune to Harkins, he started back for the position. On his way he determined that he would take the First Platoon under the command of Lieutenant Allen.

Upon arrival at the position, he gathered Pappy and Sergeant Baker together and advised them of the mission. As the lieutenant got his platoon ready, the captain and the sergeant took two riding horses and rode north towards the line, in order to scout out the most advantageous position for the guns. The men made numerous trips into the unoccupied territory before the ideal spot was located. It wasn't until dusk that they arrived back in camp.

Just before nine that evening, Captain Case had Jack Bayless take a message to Lieutenant Coffey at echelon requesting two limbers and one caisson be sent forward immediately. He specified that each team consist of strong and sturdy animals and that the men were not to bring packs or blanket rolls and he emphasized that the prolongs be included.

Captain Case next assembled the participants for the upcoming action and quickly explained the situation to them.

"Now that the St. Mihiel Salient is history, we must convince our enemy that the American First Army will stay put in this area for the winter, though in truth the Army is marching west in order to attack the Boche in the Argonne region. Tonight's operation is a come-and-go raid. We'll take up our position and fire into the Marimbois farm to cover an infantry company from the 167th Regiment. Their purpose is to create as much havoc as they can and to take some prisoners. Once they withdraw we will pull out and return to the position here. All carriages will maintain a twenty-five meter interval to avoid the enemy artillery fire in case we're spotted. Get some sleep. We'll be leaving at 1:00 a.m."

Hank and Sergeant Martyn were the only mechanics chosen to go on the raid. Pat and Tom both had succumbed to serious colds and were spending a couple of nights in the field hospital to recuperate. Paul was left with the other two guns.

The men of the raiding party were awakened at midnight and began their trek at five minutes to one on the morning of September 22. After they had been underway for more than a half hour they were forced to halt northeast of Louiseville Ferme due to heavy German shelling of the road and the nearby woods.

The shelling ended as abruptly as it had begun and within fifteen minutes the platoon was able to continue the march. They soon reached their next obstacle, a barbed wire barricade placed across the road. It had been placed by G Company of the 167th infantry. The captain ordered the cannoneers to get out the wire cutters to clear the way. The infantry lieutenant in charge protested, but soon relented. The captain further instructed the lieutenant to leave the road open until the platoon returned, which would be before daybreak.

"If we aren't back by then, you can go ahead and replace the barricade, since we'll probably be dead or captured."

Soon the platoon was underway, out into the unoccupied zone to their firing position. The guns were quickly unlimbered and laid on the target, the ammunition off- loaded, and the horses and limbers returned to the safety of the woods located just to the south. The empty ammunition caisson started its return to the echelon encampment.

The men dug flop trenches and made final preparations for the barrage as they awaited H hour. While they were waiting, the infantry detachments involved in the proceedings marched quietly past the platoon of cannon and were somewhat amazed to see artillery this close to the battle zone and in fact precede them into no-man's-land.

At 0358 hours, a battery of American guns opened up from somewhere in the rear with their fire directed on the farm. At exactly 0400, the platoon's two cannon started their fire. Behind the battery's guns and on higher ground were three American machine gun units, which also fired a barrage into the farm.

The Boche were taken by surprise and immediately sent their caterpillar rockets high into the air, calling for artillery support from their own guns. Within five minutes, German artillery shells began hitting near the platoon's position. The return fire from the Boche was close and heavy for the next twenty minutes, but landed around the platoon and not on it. At 0425 the Boche fire shifted to the left of the guns and allowed the limbers to come forward and hitch up the weapons and withdraw. Once again the battery had luck or the good Lord on their side, it just depended on who was asked. Sergeant Martyn was the only one who suffered a wound, a shell fragment burned the skin on his right hand, an inch closer and he'd lost that hand at the wrist.

After the limbers had left the position, Captain Case rode back to be sure everyone had left. He met Hank carrying some shovels and picks.

"Are you the last one out?" he shouted to him, above the sounds of the battle.

"Yes, sir!" Hank replied.

"Give me some of the equipment and grab hold of the saddlehorn and let's get the hell outta here."

Hank handed the captain the implements and grabbed hold as the horse started a slow gallop. Some enemy shells landed near them and Hank ran as fast as he could, keeping up with the horse, and soon they were into the protection of the woods.

It wasn't long before the platoon was on its way, back to the battery's original position.

During this time, the Second Platoon under Lieutenant Wineland had not been idle and had fired over four hundred rounds into the targeted area.

Later in the day, and after events turned to a more normal routine, it was learned from Division that a number of enemy troops had been killed and that nine prisoners had been brought back. The captured Germans stated that they had been taken by complete surprise and that both strongholds, Haumont and Marimbois Ferme, were utterly destroyed.

The following week, numerous artillery duels took place and the lines held firm. Both Pat and Tom were released from the field hospital on the twenty-fifth.

All during this time, the food, what there was of it, turned from bad to worse. The Army had been supplying the units with dehydrated vegetables, and to the men they had a foul, spoiled taste.

Everything was in short supply. Batteries for flashlights were used up, so gunners were using the glow of a lit cigarette to check the bubble gauge on the cannon. Broken and worn out equipment was jury-rigged or fixed with whatever material there was at hand. This included no small amount of leftovers from the battlefield.

The aerial activity over the front had been heavy. The observation balloons had been primary targets for both sides. One intrepid American, Lieutenant Frank Luke of Arizona, would fly over the lines and flame at least one balloon nearly every morning, much to the joy of the cannoneers. Rumors continued to fly as the men worked diligently to harden the position in anticipation of spending the winter.

At 1400 hours on the thirtieth of September, the men were told to prepare to move out. This confirmed other rumors that had been gaining momentum for the past few days. Many of the divisions just in from the states were not doing well in the Argonne and that the old reliable Rainbow Division would have to step forward to gain yet another victory.

At 1800 hours the battery began packing and at 2100 the call to harness and hitch was heard throughout the camp. It was 9:30 that evening when the battery was beginning their trek to the Argonne that two large-caliber shells landed on the now abandoned position. Again luck was with Battery F.

As Jake continued moving southward along the Rau de Naujupont, he noticed that the eastern horizon was beginning to show some signs of the approaching dawn. He increased his pace, as it had been his intent to find the American lines before sunup.

The tremendous crash of artillery stopped him dead in his tracks. He knew he was too late, that after a nighttime pause, the Allied advance was once again underway. He recognized that he needed to seek shelter, fast. A series of large-caliber shells landed all around him. He started to jump down the bank to the river bottom just as the shells hit. The concussion of the nearest one blew him off of his feet. The impact threw him into the air and he tumbled to the bottom, where he hit his head on a large boulder. He lost consciousness, and along with it went the pain and agony of his physical and mental wounds of the past two days.

When he awoke he saw three strange men standing around him, all in American uniforms. He noted that the sun was high in the sky and its warmth felt good. He surmised that he'd been out for hours.

One of the men, a corporal, knelt down beside him when he noticed that he was awake.

"Take it easy, captain. You've got a nasty looking wound in your shoulder. We're lucky we found you before you bled to death. These guys are the stretcher-bearers and are going to get you back to the first aid station, so it may hurt a little bit getting you moved. I think I've stopped the serious bleeding, at least for a while. There's a medic back at the station and he'll get some information from you and then get you into an ambulance that'll take you to the field hospital."

Jake nodded his understanding. The corporal stood up and addressed the other two men. "Okay, Sandy and Jim, he's all yours. I'm going on up ahead to look for some more, so after you get 'em to the aid station, get your butts back!"

Jake didn't say anything as the two men put him on the stretcher and carried him out of the ravine. The pain was excruciating and all he could do was grit his teeth as hard as he could. The men were having a difficult time getting to the top and onto level ground, and almost dropped him twice. After reaching the crest of the gully, they moved easily along the flat ground of the wheat field and soon arrived at the road, where they set him down near some other survivors awaiting the next ambulance.

They departed and another soldier stopped by to get some information. As he asked the questions he offered Jake a cigarette, which Jake took.

As the man lit a match and held it to the end, Jake took a deep drag, "Where am I? Where are the lines?"

"Slow down a minute, Captain. Let me get the rest of your personal info, then I'll answer all of your questions."

The man wrote as Jake responded to inquiries about his unit, his name, and so on.

"Well, captain, first of all I'm Harold Magnus and I'm with the 168th Infantry medical services, and some of our troopers found you over by the river about an hour ago. Our lines are moving northward very rapidly and so it's hard to say where they are at this very minute. Somewhere north of here oughta be right. At the very least, you're safe and we'll be transporting you back to the field hospital in La Marché."

Jake nodded. "Now before I send you on I'm going to examine you thoroughly, so let me know if you have any injuries I don't find." The man went about the task of checking Jake out and redressing his shoulder wound.

Jake felt tired and passed out before the man finished.

When he came to, he was inside an ambulance that was jolting its way back to the hospital over a very rough road. Even though the men were belted down to the stretchers that were in turn lashed to the vehicle, Jake held on for dear life, feeling as if he'd be thrown to the floor at any time. The three other wounded soldiers were moaning loudly from their pain each time the ambulance hit a deep pothole or made a sharp turn.

After an indeterminable amount of time, the ambulance arrived at the field hospital, where the patients were placed on the ground awaiting diagnosis before treatment could be started. Jake noticed that there were numerous other unfortunate wounded troopers awaiting attention from the field medical staff. He could see from his position, flat on his back on the stretcher that his shoulder was bleeding again. The red spot on the white bandage was increasing in size, minute by minute. He felt dizzy and the sight of the bleeding didn't help.

An American nurse soon came by and examined his wounds and redressed his shoulder. She called a doctor over and as the man approached, Jake passed out again.

This time, when he regained his consciousness, he found that he was in some sort of operating room with the doctor, nurse and some others, also dressed in white, standing over him. Before he could protest, the nurse placed a mask over his nose and mouth and he could detect the strong odor of ether. Soon he was out cold again.

He heard voices before he opened his eyes. This was difficult; it was like his lids were glued shut. First he popped open his left eye, blinked, then finally opened his right one. He felt a dull ache in his shoulder and had a fierce headache.

The voices were from across the aisle.

He figured he was in a large room or ward and the voices he heard were from some people standing around a bed across the way. He tried to speak but choked on his words and started to cough, which hurt like hell. He felt nauseous and started to retch as his empty stomach convulsed.

This got the attention of those across the way, and the nurse came over to calm him and held a pan to his mouth.

Jake soon felt better and relaxed.

"Where am I, what's happened to me?"

"You're in the field hospital at La Marche. You had a large shell fragment surgically removed from your right shoulder, plus some other minor wounds patched up by the surgeon," the nurse said calmly. "You'll be up and around in no time, Captain."

Jake didn't feel ready to get up; he just lay back and stared at the ceiling as the nurse redressed his wounds. As she worked on him they exchanged some small talk about the war and the number of patients in the hospital.

After a pause of a few moments, he asked, "How long have I been here?"

"You've been out of surgery for about six hours. It went well, according to the doctor, as the wound wasn't too serious. He said that you lost a lot of blood but that you should be able to rejoin your unit in about a week or so. We'll get you up and walking tomorrow."

"That's fine with me!" Jake said. "I sure don't feel up to it today."

The nurse finished her work and walked away.

Jake felt overwhelmed by the events of the past two days and sank back into his pillow. He was soon sound asleep.

He felt a hand on his arm shaking him and a woman's voice calling him.

"Captain?" There was a short pause, followed by a more vigorous shake. "Captain, you have a visitor."

Jake opened his eyes and saw the nurse standing at his side. "A visitor?" he repeated somewhat groggily.

"Yes, a Major Davidson is here to see you. And when he leaves I'll get you something to eat."

"Send him by," Jake answered weakly. He had a sinking feeling in the pit of his stomach as he thought of his dead comrades who he had left behind.

The major stood a number of feet away, and when summoned by the nurse he stepped forward. "Great to see you alive, Jake. We'd given you and the others up for dead."

Jake felt a cold chill flow through his body as the events of the past few days flooded back into his mind. "How are Sergeant Thompson and Bliss, did they make it back okay?"

"Yeah, they made it back."

"How about Private Dukane and Corporal Levies, did you find them?"

"Yes, they were picked up by the 168th yesterday. Dukane was hurt pretty bad. As a matter of fact, he's here in the hospital and Levies is back with his platoon."

"Thank God!" Jake said.

"The others are dead."

Jake nodded and nearly choked on his own words. "We were discovered and I was the only one to get away. It was just bad luck and maybe bad leadership."

"Jake, I know you and I know how you act under fire. Don't blame yourself. What you did was save many more lives, for your maps allowed the offensive to move forward with little resistance and we were able to encircle and capture a great number of enemy troops. I'm putting you in for a medal."

"A medal? Major, I don't deserve that. Men died because of my actions."

"And many more did not die because of what you and Thompson did. There are men dying at this very minute all along the line. This is war and nothing that we do is going to change that fact. You moved into enemy held territory and did the job. Feel fortunate that some of you returned. Those that didn't make it knew the risks they were taking. We accomplished a splendid victory and much of the credit belongs to you and your men for doing such an exemplary job."

"Thanks, sir. I just have to assess the results to get it clear in my mind."

"You'll see that the results were good. I don't need to dwell on it and neither do you. As a matter of fact, the primary reason I'm here is to tell you that your company is ready for you when you return. Get some rest and I'll be seeing you in about a week to ten days."

"Thanks, Major. You've helped me more than you can know."

"I'll be in touch, Jake. I need you back, so God be with you and bless you."

The major turned and left, and Jake lay back on his pillow and relaxed. He felt better about the mission, but he knew he would never get over the loss of the men. At least the reconnaissance had been a success.

Ike couldn't get the sight of Captain Wortham's capture out of his mind. His friend and mentor was now in the hands of the enemy. He felt guilty over the event, though there wasn't a thing he could have done to prevent it. He just hoped and prayed that the Boche treated the captain well.

All of the pilots had heard rumors of airmen being shot on the spot by their captors, but that hadn't happened in this case. Ike had lingered over the area long enough to see the captain put on a truck and driven away. He was tempted to think that by flying close to the crash site after Captain Wortham's capture he may have played a small role in preserving the life of his friend. He felt the Boche didn't want to suffer the sting of a strafing SPAD and had treated their captive with respect. Ike ultimately concluded that capture was better than death and that the war would end soon.

Three days after the captain's capture, a new man from the 94th Aero Squadron was brought in and placed in command of the 95th. This man, Captain Joseph Mendell, did little to endear himself to the men. He was a spit-and-polish career officer of mediocre flying skills who had a record of six kills. The men soon concluded that Mendell, in all probability, was extremely lucky or that he had shot the planes while they were on the ground. This scenario actually proved to be closer to the truth than anyone had originally dared to believe.

Apparently, one day Joseph and his wingman happened upon a German airfield and fell in behind four Boche planes that were in the process of their takeoff roll. Joseph and the wingman came in at a slight angle across the field and shot three of the planes, which crashed before becoming airborne. Somehow Joseph took and received all of the credit, even though the wingman had contributed substantially. Two other kills had been lightly defended unmanned balloons, being towed by trucks to the front. His sixth victory was an unarmed observation plane. Captain Mendell had friends in high places and was given command more through influence and military finagling rather than through flying abilities. This worked to the advantage of the squadron, as the men still declared their loyalty to Captain Wortham and were fighting their hardest to finish the war in order to free him from captivity.

The new commander flew as little as possible and stuck his nose into the administrative end of the squadron. This was fine with the pilots and the staff officers, as long as the new commander didn't try to direct the tactical aspects of the missions.

The pilots continued the three missions a day. Encounters with Boche aircraft were not as frequent and ground support was still their primary mission up through the sixteenth.

On the seventeenth, when the salient had been officially declared in Allied hands, the squadron had a change of venue and began flying frequent sorties as bomber escort and support for strikes against German supply depots to the northwest, which included frequent night missions over the city of Metz.

The squadron still suffered losses and the daily grind was wearing down the pilots' edge. Combat, equipment failures, and careless accidents took their toll on pilots and crews. The glory of being a fighter pilot had long ago lost its glitter in Ike's eyes. The grueling reality of day-to-day combat had also taken its toll on him. He no longer believed so strongly that he would live to see the end of the war. Ike and all of the pilots were superstitious to some degree, and the question of how long luck would be on their side was always with them.

In the early afternoon of September 22, Ike set out on a solitary mission, an administrative flight for the new commander, to deliver some important papers and maps to the airfield at Bar-de-Luc. Ike enjoyed this type of flight, as he could relax and enjoy the purity of flying without having to worry about the fighting. His route of flight took him west and south of the line in what was considered safe and secure airspace.

After takeoff and initial climb, Ike established a leisurely cruise at one hundred meters below the cloud bases and fell into daydreaming as he relaxed in the seat of the plane. The air was bumpy, but it only took minor control inputs to keep the craft in straight and level flight. As he flew along he looked at the beautiful colors of the early fall countryside as it slid slowly by under the wings of his SPAD. It was a beautiful sight, and it wasn't long before his mind slipped into thoughts of home and of Agnes. He wondered how she would like the midwestern countryside of the United States, so different from what he was now viewing.

His next thought was of his mother, who in her last letter had relented a little from her hard stand against his marrying "this French girl." He knew that his mom would grow to love Agnes once she met her and came to know Agnes's tender heart.

He also thought of his father who was still plying the Atlantic with his destroyer, escorting the supply and troop ships headed for the continent. His father had related in a recent letter that he had had a long talk with Doris and had convinced her that Agnes would be a good and loyal wife for him. Ike sort of chuckled to himself as he remembered his father's last comment in that same letter, as to how boring the duty had become "now that the U-boats were few and far between."

"Dad, you ought to get in a plane and come with me on a few missions if you're bored," Ike said aloud to himself.

As he daydreamed and watched the countryside below, he became aware of a shadow that shot across his own plane's shadow projected on the landscape below, just before he flew under a large cloud.

He was instantly alert. He looked all around and above but saw nothing.

"I'm losing it!" he said aloud, "Here I am, jumping at shadows."

But that gut feeling was there and he determined in his mind that he was being stalked.

"Just as well be prepared. If Jerry is there above me, I'd better be ready for him."

Ike added a little power and eased the nose up with slight backpressure on the control column. At the same time, he started a shallow left turn and came to a heading of two six zero degrees, approximately forty-five degrees to the left of his initial heading. He positioned his aircraft at the very base of the cloud. He continued forward for three minutes on the new heading. When he was within a few minutes or less of reaching the edge of the cloud, he returned to his original heading of three zero five degrees.

"Now that oughta put the Hun off of my right wing."

Ike felt the adrenaline pump throughout his system, ever alert and ready to do battle. He anticipated coming out from under the cloud and scanned the area where he thought his enemy would be.

As the cloud thinned he caught a glimpse of the stalking aircraft for just a second before it disappeared again, above the cloud.

Ike immediately began a climb into the cloud and started a gentle right turn. As he lost sight of his visual references, he made all movements with minute pressures on the joystick and rudders. This was not a place to lose control.

As the sky continued to brighten as he neared the top of the cloud, he returned the plane to straight and level at his original heading. He broke free of the cloud into the full brilliance of the afternoon sun. There, two hundred meters in front of him and no more than fifty meters above, was a brilliant blue Fokker D.VII.

Ike applied full throttle and started closing the gap. He could see the other pilot's head swivel as he looked for Ike's SPAD. As the gap closed to one hundred meters, Ike gave a short burst into the tail of his advisory. He would have waited longer but he sensed that this was a veteran pilot, maybe even the one that had nearly shot him down last spring. He also felt that he would be discovered before he got close enough for an accurate shot.

Ike could see some of his bullets hit the rudder and elevators of the Fokker and the pieces of wood and fabric fly off into the air.

The German immediately went into a vertical right bank. Ike followed suit. The German was a good pilot and knew his aircraft well. After the hard right turn he dove the aircraft to gain speed and then entered an Immelmann turn. Ike stuck to his tail as best he could. The Fokker had the advantage in the climb, whereas the SPAD was superior in the dive. The damage Ike did to the tail surfaces of the German reduced the D.VII's performance slightly, making the two aircraft similar in turn characteristics. Twisting and turning, the planes climbed ever higher, Ike always following and dropping further behind as the maneuvering continued. At six thousand meters they leveled out and circled around in extremely tight turns, to the left and right. At this altitude the Fokker had the advantage, as its engine and wing design allowed for superior flight characteristics in the thin air at altitude. Ike continued the attack with the thought that if things turned for the worse, he could use his superior dive capabilities to escape.

Nearly fifteen minutes had passed since the cat and mouse game had started and Ike had only fired his guns twice. The second time, he missed the target altogether. The Boche was constantly trying to gain the advantage over the SPAD. Ike noted that his adversary would take some risks in trying to gain that advantage. This led him to believe that the German pilot would establish a steep left spiral then pull out in a high-speed dive immediately followed by a tight loop, at which time he would try to establish a position on the tail of the SPAD.

In his previous try he had nearly caught Ike in this kind of trap, and it wasn't long before he tried the maneuver again. The agile D.VIIs could turn inside of the heavier SPADS and the loop would allow the D.VII to reverse the position and get on the tail of Ike's plane.

As the German entered the spiral, Ike reduced his power and purposely fell further behind, and when the Fokker was pulling up into the loop he was directly in Ike's sights. Both guns fired but one or two shots, and then jammed. He pounded them both with the heel of his hand and his clenched fist, but he could not free them. The diversion soon put him in the position of being in front of the enemy. Before he knew it he heard the German's guns and bullets were whizzing past him. Realizing the danger, Ike put the SPAD in a steep dive in order to escape his pursuer. The plane quickly reached its designed speed limit, which Ike exceeded a little as he turned and twisted in his earthward plunge. The fabric on the wings shuddered and vibrated violently as the bracing wires screamed in defiance.

More bullets zoomed by as the planes continued their downward plunge. Ike could see a few large holes in the wings where the fabric was tearing from the structure due to the tornado-force wind of the dive. Ike looked over his shoulder and noticed the D.VII had fallen way behind, but the enemy pilot still enjoyed the advantage of altitude.

Ike reached the clouds and descended into the largest one he could find. Here he brought the aircraft to as close to straight and level as he could without visual references. As his airspeed reached normal, he initiated a slow turn to a heading of one two five degrees and continued a slow descent until he broke free of the cloud. He looked all around but couldn't see the blue Fokker.

The clouds once again saved his life. Ike took a deep breath and soon returned to the heading that would take him to Bar-de-Luc.

"I'll get that son of a bitch!" he kept saying over and over to himself.

On To The Argonne

Jake arrived in Paris on the twenty-fourth of September. He'd been rousted from his hospital bed and given a train ticket and told to go to Paris where he was to receive his medal, the Silver Star. He felt guilty about receiving this honor, particularly on the backs of his dead comrades, but there was little he could say to stop the process.

"Oh well," he said aloud to himself as the train sped along its way, "I'll at least get to spend a few days in Paris before going back. There I can relax for a little while."

The award ceremony was set to take place on the morning of the twenty-seventh and involved numerous other recipients from the division. After the ceremony he was to grab another train for his return trip to the regiment.

In the late evening, when he finally arrived in Paris, he had to push his way through the crowded station and out the front doors, where he was able to hail a taxi. The ride was a short one and soon he was at his hotel, which proved to be nothing special. But to a soldier who'd spent the last couple months out in the field, it was paradise. The bed was more comfortable than the one in the hospital and the bath was just a short distance down the hall. Best of all he had privacy, not a large crowded ward that he shared with countless others.

Jake spent the first morning lounging around the hotel, reading the paper as he ate a large breakfast in the small coffee shop. Next he took a very long, very hot bath. In the afternoon and evening he ate in a nearby restaurant where he met another medal recipient, a Lieutenant

Dickerson, from the 165th Infantry Regiment. Sammy Dickerson had been wounded in the leg and was getting around on crutches. They talked and drank copious amounts of the best champagne into the wee hours. It wasn't too long before dawn when they headed back to the hotel. They found they needed to support one another in order to keep their balance.

After assisting Sammy to his room, Jake stumbled to his. There he went immediately to the bathroom where he became terribly sick to his stomach and threw up. He stumbled to the bed, still partially clothed. It wasn't until early that afternoon when he awoke and found he was suffering from the worst hangover he'd ever had. He finally concluded that after being without an alcoholic beverage for such a long time, his body just couldn't tolerate the amount he had consumed the night before.

He took some clothes to a local laundry; followed with a long walk around a nearby public park, breathing the fresh, clear air. After an hour of indulging himself in strolling in and around the park, he went back to his hotel. It was late afternoon and he was beginning to feel more like his old self. As he got his room key from the front desk clerk, he found he had a message. It was from Roy Littler, who had dropped by to see if he'd join him for dinner. The note specified that he'd also have the professor along.

Jake read and then reread the message. His thoughts went immediately back to those days, so long ago, when he was at Camp Mills, where he'd met Roy and Major Hinkle at the big party just before they left to come to France. It seemed as if many years had passed, but when he counted the months up on his fingers, it'd been just short of twelve.

Jake had made plans with Lieutenant Dickerson for this evening and was trying to determine what to do when Dickerson approached the desk where Jake was reading his message.

"Oh, Captain, glad you're here," Dickerson said as he hobbled on his crutches up to the counter. "I have an invite from some of the boys from the 32nd for dinner tonight, want to join us?"

Jake felt relieved at the question and quickly declined. "Thanks, Sammy, but I also have a reunion of my own. I was going to ask that you join me."

"I guess that we go our separate ways then. See you tomorrow, I've got to go grab a taxi."

"Yeah, have a good time," Jake yelled after him.

Then Jake went directly to his room to ready himself for the upcoming dinner. He took another long bath before he dressed and went out in search of some transportation.

He arrived at the hotel's restaurant early, but he was immediately ushered to an alcove just on the perimeter of the large main dining room, where he found Roy sitting alone at a table set for six.

"Jake, I'm glad to see you. I really wanted you to come," Roy said as he stood to shake Jake's hand.

"It was a surprise seeing your note, Roy. I thought immediately of our last meeting, just a year ago."

"Yeah, in a way it seems like a lifetime ago, doesn't it?"

"Brother, you can say that again. How've you been?"

"Well, I've been lucky, as I haven't had to confront the realities of war the way you have. How are your wounds? Mending, I hope?" Roy said.

"Yes they are, they weren't anything to keep me out of the fighting. I'll be traveling back to the front as soon as the ceremonies are over. By the way, how are Pat and Hank?"

Roy told Jake all he knew and related the news of Hank's wife and baby.

"Wow, that must've been some tragedy for Hank," Jake said.

"Pat told me he had trouble keeping him from going off the deep end. He's still depressed and he drinks quite a bit, but hopefully he's coming out of it."

Jake could empathize with Hank's plight for he had lost so many friends over the past year. They continued talking for a few more moments until Roy spied Clint Phelps and Colonel Hinkle approaching the table.

Jake and Roy immediately stood to greet and shake hands with the other two men.

Jake saluted him. "Well, Professor, I didn't realize that you'd been promoted to colonel. Congratulations!"

"Thank you, and may I say the same to you, Captain, and also on your Silver Star. It'll be my privilege to pin it on you tomorrow."

Jake's eyes opened wide. "You, sir?"

"Yes, it is truly an honor to be able to do this for you and the others from the Rainbow. I've read the citation and you did a very heroic thing."

"I don't feel very heroic. Too many lost their lives, and I barely escaped with mine."

Colonel Hinkle shook his head. "Your battalion commander told me you'd disclaim any glory pushed at you. But I'm proud to know you and to serve with you."

"Thanks," Jake said, as his face flushed red.

"It's a pleasure to be with you all again," Clint Phelps said. "A lot has changed since we left Camp Mills."

After the initial greeting the four men quickly found nearby chairs and sat. They continued with their small talk. When the conversation slackened a little, Clint asked Roy about the other two empty chairs at the table.

"Well, this is a surprise for Jake."

"A surprise, for me?" Jake stammered.

"Yes, sir, they'll be here in a second, I just saw them come in."

Jake turned in his chair and looked towards the front of the restaurant, where he caught a glimpse of his old friend, Ike. He couldn't believe his eyes.

After a short hesitation, Jake bolted from his chair and ran through the room.

"That's Lieutenant Dennison and his fiancée, Agnes Bovay," Roy explained to the others at the table. "Ike was a college chum of Jake's. They haven't seen one another since graduation. I ran into Ike a few months ago when he was heading back to his squadron. He called me the other day to tell me he was going to be in town to pick up a new plane, so I put two and two together and arranged this dinner."

"I remember Ike, I ran into him at Chanute Field," Clint put in. "As a matter of fact, I've followed some of his exploits as the name of all-American aces comes across my desk. I believe he's shot down seven or eight Germans. He's quite a pilot."

Jake reached Ike and without a word, they quickly embraced.

"Where in the world did you come from?" Ike asked in bewilderment.

"I was about to ask the same," Jake replied, "and tell me, Isaac, who's this beautiful women with you?"

"You can put your eyes back in your head, Jake. She's spoken for. I want you to meet the future Mrs. Dennison. Agnes, this poor excuse for a captain is my old college buddy, Daniel Jacobson, better known as Jake.

"And Jake, this is Agnes Bovay. Agnes is a nurse from St. Nazaire."

"Pleased to meet you, Agnes. If Ike here doesn't treat you right, you come and see me."

Agnes, a little embarrassed, held out her hand, which Jake took gently. With a flourish, he bowed and kissed it. Agnes flushed at the gesture.

Jake winked at them and said, "Well, come on, you two, there's a table of people waiting to meet you, so follow me."

When the new arrivals approached, all of the men stood and Roy went through the introductions.

"Mr. Phelps, it's so good to see you again," Ike said. "I often think of our meeting at the club at Chanute Field. One of the prettiest sunsets I ever saw."

"I well remember, Ike. You've done well for yourself, both in your flying and in your lovely friend here." And in perfect French, Clint added, "Agnes, it's a pleasure to meet you. Ike and I met before he came here to France."

"Well, shall we all sit?" Roy said as he pulled out a chair for Agnes.

As everyone sat and pulled their chair to the table, a waiter arrived with some wine, which Colonel Hinkle quickly poured, into the glasses. He then held his glass up and gave a toast for the evening. "Ike and Agnes, welcome. I have not had the privilege of knowing you but I welcome you to this gathering from the University of Illinois. This can be considered a time of celebration, as I firmly believe all of this madness will soon be over and we'll all be able to return to our homes. So let us drink to the swift defeat of the Boche armies and let peace rein once again in this your land, Agnes."

"Hear, hear!" They all replied in unison, and each took a sip of the wine.

The waiter came to the table and they ordered their dinners. The conversation developed around Agnes and Ike. They talked of their meeting and the closeness they'd developed over the past year. This included some stories of Ike's adventures in the Air Service and details of his crash and eventual hospital stay. Agnes talked, in her limited English, of her childhood and of her training as a nurse.

As they ate their dinner, Jake related some of the stories around his duty on the line, and the colonel talked of the citation Jake would receive the next day. Jake, somewhat reluctant, spoke about the event in the St. Mihiel.

As they were completing their wonderful meals, Clint Phelps related news about the action taking place in the northwest along the English portion of the line. His remarks were directed more at Colonel Hinkle, but the others listened intently.

"Since the middle of August the English have been forcing the Germans in a northeasterly direction, back towards the Fatherland. They've moved them approximately twenty miles and have come up against the Hindenburg Line, a massive fortified defensive position that must be breached to insure the defeat of the Boche. These gains have come at cost, as the Allied losses have been high. They've suffered no less than 180,000 causalities. I do know that General Haig started an offensive against this Hindenburg Line this morning, and initial reports are mixed, but indicate that the Boche will be driven back. I will be leaving for that front tomorrow morning, as there are two American divisions involved in this attack that I need to report on, so how can we fail?"

There were some brief chuckles from the others and soon the dinner dishes were removed from the table. Roy then produced some cigars for the men and all but Ike lit up. Next, the waiter brought the dessert, and Colonel Hinkle continued the conversation on the offensives.

"To go along with what Clint has said about the north, an American offensive was started this morning in the Argonne. The planning for this attack has been ongoing and is to work in conjunction with the English attack on the Hindenburg Line. We have had the monumental task of taking 220,000 French troops off of the line and secretly replacing them with 600,000 Americans. We now have nine divisions in position and four in corps reserve.

"The Argonne has been in German hands for over four years and is well fortified. These defenses, like those on the Hindenburg Line in the north, will make the going very tough. This is why secrecy was important. Our intent was to catch them with their guard down. The movement of troops has been primarily at night and resulted in traffic tie-ups that have been unbelievable. Many of these troops were pulled from the St. Mihiel region and moved the sixty miles to the Argonne. Fortunately for you, Jake, the Rainbow is staying put for the time being, though you'll eventually go there. By midnight last night, all was in readiness and the attack started this morning. Movement has been slow and only time will tell of the progress that will be made. The hopes are high and success is assured. Timing is the only element in question."

Once the dessert dishes had been cleared from the table, Clint ordered cognac cordials for everyone.

Ike and Jake fell into a conversation more or less reviewing what had happened since their graduation. Agnes listened with great interest, interrupting only when she didn't understand something said. She had always had trouble with the American slang. The others listened as the two younger officers recounted days gone by. They sat at the table talking, laughing, and relaxing in a way they hadn't been able to relax in nearly a year.

During their second cordial, Agnes excused herself to powder her nose, and all of the men stood as she left. As they sat down Clint said, "That's some young lady you've found, Ike. Are your intentions honorable? If not, I might just steal her from you."

"Yes, Mr. Phelps, they are. I intend to marry her and she's finally agreed, just tonight, on our way here."

"Then congratulations to you two. We all drink to your long life and good health." Clint raised his glass and the others followed suit. "Long life and happiness!" Clint concluded.

"Thank you," Ike said. "I just wish my mother could meet her and have those same sentiments."

"I would be proud to send a letter to your mother," Clint replied. "I think if she could meet Agnes her fears would be allayed. So before we part, give me the name and address and I'll send a note off tomorrow while I'm heading north."

"Dennison." There was a short pause and Clint said softly, "Dennison, Dennison. That name rings a bell. I know we met last year at Chanute, but the name also came up in a dispatch last spring."

"You may be thinking of my father, Captain Dennison. His destroyer sank a U-boat."

"That's it, I remember, he received a the *Croix de Guerre* from Premier Clemenceau for his action."

"That's right, sir, my father is still sailing the Atlantic, shepherding the convoys. Since the U-boat threat is nearly non-existent, I think he's getting bored."

"Well, I seem to be in the midst of very courageous men," Roy said. "You all are men that we civilians can be proud of. And that doesn't exclude Agnes. What she has confronted in broken bodies and broken men is far more than I think I could stand."

At this time Agnes returned to the table, and the conversation extended on into the early hours of the morning when the restaurant closed at 2:30 a.m.

As Ike had to leave shortly after daybreak, they all said their good-byes outside the front door of the Hotel Chatham. Ike and Agnes headed off in one taxi and the other men shared another taxi that dropped them off individually. Roy and Jake were the only ones in the cab as it pulled up to Jake's hotel.

"Roy, I can't thank you enough for making this all possible. It was great seeing everyone, and particularly Ike. Thanks again."

"It was my pleasure. You take care of yourself and we'll see each other again."

With a handshake and a nod, Jake got out of the cab and went to the desk for his key.

It had been nearly three weeks since Jake was wounded, and now he was on his way back to Company G. Once again he was to take the reins and lead them into battle.

The Rainbow had not been in on the initial attack into the Meuse-Argonne, but some of the divisions that had started that offensive were fresh from the States and had shown their immaturity and were badly mauled by the experienced German divisions. It was now time to throw the tried-and-true Rainbow at the enemy in order to break the stalemate.

The battle for St. Mihiel had essentially been won on the second day of the offensive and the 167th Infantry Regiment had seen limited action since that time. There was one attack on Marimbois Ferme and Haumont on the twenty-second, and that sort of did it for them as they settled in to hold the line, which was under constant enemy artillery fire. The previous two weeks had seen numerous replacements brought in to bring the divisions back to combat readiness, and on October 1, all the men were loaded on trucks for the trip to the Argonne.

On his way back to the 95th Aero Squadron, Ike felt buoyant and enthused. Seeing Agnes was always a thrill, particularly now that she'd agreed to be his wife. But the most meaningful event had been the last evening's dinner. Seeing Jake again was more than he'd ever expected, and he was glad Jake had been able to meet Agnes. For some reason Ike always felt better when he had Jake's approval, and he certainly had that now. Jake had been impressed. Ike was also thankful for his friendship with Roy. What extraordinary effort Roy must have exerted to bring this marvelous group of people together.

On top of all of this, he was able to reacquaint himself with Clint Phelps, truly a kind and knowledgeable gentleman. And then there was the colonel, or Professor Hinkle, whom he had not known at the university, but whom he had heard about. He was impressed with the colonel's intelligence and especially his keen sense of humor.

It didn't take long for him to feel like he was back home and the craziness of this war had just gone away. He'd laughed and enjoyed himself as never before. And Agnes had become a part of the group. It was all so wonderful.

He had to pull his mind from his thoughts of the evening before as he groped the floor of the cockpit with his left hand to retrieve his map, which had slipped from his knee. He quickly found it and checked his position. His aircraft was cruising at an altitude of 3000 meters, and with the tailwind component he estimated his ground speed at 130 miles per hour.

He soon saw some familiar landmarks and changed his heading ten degrees to the right. He was about sixty miles from the temporary field at which his squadron was based, located just south of Montfaucon, another twenty to thirty minutes away.

Here he was on his way back to the war and he dreaded, more than the war, this wretched man who had taken Captain Wortham's place. The man's lack of leadership skills was amazing. He shrank away more and more from the combat role and had no qualms about putting all of his pilots in dangerous situations, particularly the new pilots, those just in from the States. This was tantamount to murder, at least in Ike's eyes.

Ike and Frank continued doing their own thing as their status, as aces left them somewhat immune to the inept leadership. Ike felt sorry for some of the new pilots who were not given an opportunity to gain the necessary combat skills before being thrown into the fray. Both Frank and he led and taught their new men as much as they could, but the rigors of the fighting left precious little time for that.

Ike had never been a complainer, but since Captain Mendel arrived, that attitude had changed. He forced himself to think of Agnes. Hopefully the letter coming from Mr. Phelps would help his mother to more readily accept Agnes. Since he was an only child, his mother was overly protective.

Ike knew deep in his heart that the war was still going on and that he needed to be even more vigilant now than before. This was not the time to go get shot down. He had a marriage to look forward to.

It wasn't long before he spied the airfield. He reduced his power and began a long descent into the pattern. As he began his final approach, he mentally noted those things that needed to be attended to by his ground crew. The airplane was faster than the others, but the rigging needed some adjustments so that it would fly better hands-off. He needed to sight the guns and he wanted to check out the left magneto, as the rpm drop had been more than he liked. The list went on, but the items were minor, and they would have to be attended to this afternoon. He would be in combat tomorrow.

On the twenty-eighth, after a short night's rest, all of the pilots assembled in the ready room at 0430 hours for the morning's briefing. As usual, Ike sat with Frank, who was not very talkative. What he did have to say was interrupted by a yawn and a stretch brought on from a lack of sleep.

The two had talked for hours the previous evening as Ike had to tell Frank of the dinner party and particularly of his official engagement to Agnes. They had talked well past midnight before turning in.

As soon as the captain entered the room from the rear of the hut, his orderly yelled, "Attention!" The men gradually fell silent and stood as the captain walked to the front of the room.

Without much fanfare, the captain put the men at ease and began the briefing.

"We have been ordered to participate in an all-out attack on Montfaucon. I will be leading the third flight and fly high cover. Ike, you will take the first flight for the ground attack on the trenches just west of town and Frank, you take the second for the attack on the eastern edge. Lieutenant Richter will brief you from this chart." The Captain stepped to the side and pulled off a cloth draped over a map of the target composed of aerial photographs, that had been set up on an easel just behind him.

As the lieutenant approached the map, Frank quickly whispered to Ike. "Just like the good captain to stay out of the ground attack, so he won't get his ass shot off."

"I'm surprised he's even going!" Ike replied. "It must be a big push to really get him in harm's way."

They both chuckled quietly as the lieutenant went over the individual targets with the flights.

It was a little after five a.m. when the pilots left the briefing and headed for the planes. Ike and Frank parted, as always, with a wish of good luck for each other.

As Ike approached his plane, Tim, the ground crew chief, joined him. "Lieutenant, we got all of the changes completed. I replaced that left mag and played a little with the rigging."

"Good, I'll let you know of any further changes when I get back."

Ike performed a quick pre-flight walk around as he pulled on his flight jacket and helmet. Then he climbed up on the lower wing and slipped into the cockpit. He buckled his lap and shoulder harnesses, checked the mag switches in the off position, and called, "Switches off!"

"Switches off!" the chief replied as he pulled the prop through twice and positioned it for starting. "Contact?"

Ike reached for the magneto switch and turned it. "Contact!"

The chief pulled the right blade downward past the compression and the engine roared into life, as did many others all up and down the line.

Ike let the engine warm up for a short time, and while it ran at a higher rpm he checked the mags. "That's much better," he whispered to himself.

Once he knew the plane was running at peak condition, he looked up and glanced to his right, then to the left as he pulled on his gloves. He saw that his flight was ready. He raised his right arm over his head and brought it down quickly. He pushed the throttle full forward and the plane immediately gathered speed. The other planes of his flight of eight were moving right along beside him. A little forward pressure on the control column and the tailskid was off of the ground. He added backpressure and the craft was airborne.

He climbed at maximum power and leveled off over the field at 500 meters. He pulled back on the power to set up economy cruise as the other planes positioned themselves in the formation. He glanced down and saw that Frank's flight was airborne and climbing and that Mendel's flight was beginning their takeoff run. The flight finished their last circuit of the field and headed for the target.

Ike and his flight of eight SPADs were again on the prowl over the forest of the Argonne. Their primary mission this day was ground attack. According to the other pilots, the Germans had been around in force the day before. One of the squadron's planes had been brought down and two others severely damaged, but Frank had scored his eighth victory, bringing him even with Ike.

The flight to the target was a short one. As soon as Montfaucon was in sight, Ike reduced the power and pushed the nose of his aircraft over in shallow dive as the other planes fell in behind him. The run on the enemy position drew light return fire from the ground. All of the planes and bombs were on target, which was left a smoking ruin.

As he pulled up and away, Ike noticed that the third flight had been engaged in aerial combat with a large number of Boche fighters. He signaled to his flight to follow him and they climbed to join the struggle. The climb seemed to take forever. The third flight was outnumbered and Ike could see one of the SPADs twisting and turning, trying to shake a Boche D.VII from its tail. As he drew nearer to the battle, Ike noticed that it was Captain Mendel who was in trouble.

He maneuvered as quickly as he could in order to get in behind the German that had the captain in his sights. The process seemed to be in slow motion and before he could get his sights on the Fokker, he saw it put another long burst into the SPAD. The captain's head snapped back before he slumped forward over the stick and the plane then entered a steep dive, leaving a long plume of black smoke in its wake.

Though he had no love for Captain Mendel, Ike was mad as hell at this Boche pilot, and wanted to put an end to him for what he had done to the captain. The German, unaware of Ike's presence, followed the Captain Mendel's plane down. By this time Ike was on his tail and soon had him in his sights. When he closed the range to around fifty meters, he pulled the trigger and fired a long volley into the Fokker. The enemy pilot looked back in total surprise, just before the plane's gas tank exploded and the aircraft disappeared into a ball of fire and small fragments.

Ike looked over his shoulder and saw that he was not being pursued. He didn't want to fall victim to the same ploy he'd pulled on his ninth victory. He put his plane into a climb in order to rejoin the fray, but the battle, as if by mutual agreement, was ending, and the antagonists were beginning to form up and head for their respective aerodromes.

As Ike joined the flight, he noticed two planes were missing; the captain's and that of one of the newer pilot's who'd joined the squadron just a week earlier. He hoped that the new pilot was all right, but he knew that the captain had to be a goner. All of the way back to the field he felt guilty about the bad things he'd said about Mendel, as he never meant for any harm to come to him. But that was war, he concluded as he touched down on the home field.

By evening, the news filtered back that the bullets of the Boche aircraft had definitely killed the Captain. The other pilot had crash-landed his plane near the American lines and had been rescued by the doughboys. He would be spending a long time in the hospital, though, as he had numerous broken bones.

During the days following, the aircraft of the 95th flew constant missions of ground support for the Americans of the First Army in the Argonne. Finally, on the third of October, Ike was appointed to take temporary command of the 95th Aero Squadron.

On October 1, the 149th Field Artillery started their march out of the St. Mihiel sector. Their initial route of march was in a northwesterly direction, first towards the old battlefields of Verdun, then on to the west to the Montfaucon region, located at the southern end of the Argonne Forest.

The trip through the pasty mud had been a nightmare. At one time or another, every carriage had become stuck as they tried to navigate the sticky goo. To make matters worse, the animals were in frightful condition, underfed and overworked. Many refused to pull while others collapsed in their harnesses. The men finally left one piece and one caisson in the mud until fresh horses and men could be found to haul them out.

It wasn't until long after daylight that they made it to the echelon position for sleep. All were totally spent and many fell asleep on the ground, too tired to set out their blankets. Few got more than two hours of rest though, as orders were received urging all batteries to be underway by 7:00 that evening. Preparations for the long journey had to be made. Equipment needed to be repaired, cleaned and greased, and the stuck carriages freed from the mud. All items, both personal and belonging to the battery, had to be gathered and packed before they began their march during the early evening.

Shortly after 1900 hours the battery was harnessed and hitched and underway. They followed the road that took them through Lamorville, Lacrois-sur-Meuse, Troyon-sur-Meuse and finally to their destination for the day, Ambly-sur-Muese. The walk entailed thirty kilometers and they didn't arrive until after 3:00 a.m.

It was another two hours before the horses were rubbed down and the campsite set up. Most of the men could have slept standing up, but somehow managed to get their blankets out and roll up for some rest. For five whole hours the troops were allowed to sleep undisturbed. At 10:30 a.m. revelry was sounded and the battery was once again preparing to march.

By 9:30 on the evening of October 2, the regiment was once again on the road. That night they traveled only thirteen kilometers due in large part to the heavy traffic of the other divisions of the First American Army also wending their way to the Argonne. On the third, at 6:00 a.m., the 149th arrived at Camp de la Fourche located just outside of Rambluzin et Benoitmor. Here the cannoneers were allowed to sleep for over five hours before being awakened in order to make preparations to continue the march. During the afternoon the regiment was informed that they would complete the march during daylight hours and were not to leave until the following morning. This little reprieve was truly a blessing for the men of the regiment, providing them an opportunity to do as they pleased during the late afternoon and evening.

The four mechanics went into town in search of some food and drink. There they found the shops crowded with cannoneers from the regiment. The stores were so crowded that few were able to tolerate the long lines to pay for their purchases. Many just walked off without paying.

As they were walking through the town, Pat heard the exciting news that Bulgaria had surrendered and that they were no longer a belligerent on the side of the Central Powers.

"Does this mean that the war is going to be over?" Hank asked.

"I don't know. I'm sure that we'll still be fighting the Germans forever. Well, at least through the winter. Bulgaria hasn't been that much of a factor."

Hank nodded. "You're probably right, but it'd be a good time to run into the professor. He'd give us the straight poop."

"Yeah, him or Clint," Pat added.

After a long night's rest the regiment left Camp de la Fouche at seven in the morning of October fourth. The march took them through the town of Souilly before they turned to a more northerly direction towards Verdun. During the afternoon they passed a large French cemetery where they saw row upon row of crosses marking the final resting place of thousands upon thousands of French Poilus who had died defending that city in 1916. The sound of artillery could be heard and would continue unabated, as they turned west to parallel the front.

At five that evening, on the fourth, after another thirty-kilometer march, the regiment arrived at Camp du Bois de Brocourt. Here they were treated to a regular barracks and even lean-to stables for the horses. The Regiment stayed for thirty-six hours and during that time enjoyed three good meals. On the sixth, the regiment left the good food and quarters and were on the road again, pushing ever westward along the line to their ultimate destination.

They passed through what had once been the town of Avocourt. It had been in no-mans-land for over three years. Not one stone or brick stood upon another and what had once been houses and buildings were now piles of rubble.

The day's march of fifteen kilometers ended at the Bois de Montfaucon, where they set up camp. The devastation of this territory was nothing like they'd encountered before. The forest was little more than splintered stumps and debris that littered the ground. There were so many shell holes that they overlapped one another. Even the town's small cemetery didn't escape destruction as the ground was cluttered with bones, shattered tombstones and coffins.

The troops began to set up their camp, interrupted only as they watched the antics of a nearby balloon company trying to save their airship from the attack of two Boche planes. The observer quickly jumped out in his parachute and the men nearly got the balloon safely on the ground before it ignited in a large fireball. The ground crew ran as the fire consumed the bag. Fortunately, no one was hurt, but the truck that had towed it was burnt to a crisp.

The gun crews quickly set up the guns, erected the camouflage, and dug flop trenches. The caisson train soon began trips to the ammunition dump hauling shells for the cannon. The rain was heavy throughout the afternoon and evening. The drivers could only see when the lightning flashed, making it difficult to follow the road without running into the numerous ditches and shell holes.

After dark and after the guns were set, the men sought sleep in a dry place, an impossible task—the rain did not let up throughout the night. The next morning the rain continued and the visibility remained at less than two than miles. As there were no enemy planes out, the men scouted around looking for souvenirs.

The position was located in a shallow valley southeast of Nantillos. This had been the scene of a terrific struggle, and dead bodies of the Boche, doughboys, and animals littered the landscape.

Pat and Hank had worked on the guns for most of the morning, and shortly before lunch Tom and Paul relieved them and took over the maintenance detail. Pat and Hank took one whiff of the air around the kitchen and felt they would be better off if they just skipped the meal. Instead of eating, they decided to take a tour of the area in and around the cannon. They first stopped and looked over a German battery of guns abandoned by the Boche just a few days before. They also noted that the engineers were placing barbed wire traps behind the gun position.

"All of this wire must mean that the higher-ups expect a German counterattack," Pat said as they paused and watched the engineers from a distance.

"Oh, that's great news. All we need is for the Germans to come rolling through here today," Hank added sarcastically.

"Let's get back to the position. The stench is enough to make me sick," Pat said as they started their return to the guns.

"Yeah, I know what you mean. I hate to look at them. I start to think that just a day or so ago they were like us, wishing this foolishness was over. I also think of Betsy and the baby. Maybe I'm wishing I was one of 'em. Then I'd be with my family." Hank fell silent as they started their return, his eyes full of tears. Pat said little more as they walked back to camp. He'd learned that it was best to let Hank work this out by himself.

As they returned to the position, they found most of the men staring at the sky. Another full, brilliant rainbow appeared over the sector being held by the 42nd Division.

"An omen of good luck!" one man said.

"The Germans have asked for peace terms," was whispered around the camp.

This brought no end to the bombardment. The men's spirits rose despite the shelling. With the rumor and the appearance of the rainbow, new hope was instilled in their hearts.

In the late afternoon, the caissons began to arrive at the position and unload their deadly cargo of 3600 high explosive shells before returning for more. On the third trip to the ammunition depot an enemy shell hit a caisson from the 121st Field Artillery that was in the process of being loaded. Several men were killed and others wounded, and there was nothing left of the hitch of six horses except a bloody mass.

The road from the dump was constantly under fire, making the trip a dangerous one indeed. During the late afternoon two F Battery horses collapsed in their harnesses, which were removed, and the animals were left where they'd fallen. In the evening during their last run from the dump, the drivers helped them to their feet, and tied them to the carriages, and took them back to the corral.

No one got more than one meal that day and this might have been a blessing, as the food had been wretched. On their return to the line the caisson crew found some bread that had been dumped on the ground out in the open. They picked up as much as they could and stuffed it into the carriages' oat bins. At least now there was something to fill a man's stomach.

During the evening the battery went back into action and fired 256 shells into Bois de Cunel. Even though the battery's guns fell silent for the night, the Boche guns continued unabated. The sound of distant artillery was constantly with the men. No one could sleep.

The morning of October 9 turned out to be foggy, with a slight off-and-on drizzle. At 5:00 a.m. the battery commander and the first sergeant moved forward to the observation post to direct the fire of the guns. In the low visibility, due to the fog and light rain, they became lost and found they had traveled too far forward. Soon they found themselves pinned down by Boche machine gun fire and therefore waited under the cover of some fallen and splintered trees.

It wasn't long before the infantry of the 32nd Division, in their forward movement, found them. The doughboys were surprised to find that some artillery personnel had moved into no-man's-land ahead of the infantry. Once Captain Case finally reached the OP, he found the fog too thick to give effective directions.

In the interim, the batteries of the regiment began their rolling barrage based on map coordinates. From morning until noon, Battery F fired 1473 rounds of high explosive shells into the region just south of Romagne-sous-Monfaucon.

It soon became necessary to move the position forward, as the advance of the infantry was putting the targeted area out of range. Lieutenants Allen and Wynland called for the battery to harness and hitch. They came under constant shellfire from the enemy artillery as they were packing. It continued as they moved along the road.

The skies were clearing and the Boche aviators were out in force. Battery A, which was on the road behind F Battery, suffered a few casualties from some bombs. A lot of gas shells fell near the line of march and all quickly put on their gas gear. The high humidity and physical exertion caused the glass goggles of the mask to fog up and made it difficult to see the road. To add to their misery, movement slowed to a snail's pace as the traffic congestion tied the flow in knots.

The rear echelon was also under attack. They were constantly ducking for cover as German planes made numerous strafing runs at them. During the morning they were treated to a heroic effort of a Boche aviator, in a brilliant blue Fokker D.VII, who attacked an observation balloon and shot it down while he had no less than seven Allied planes on his tail. The observers quickly took to their parachutes and made it safely to the ground as the Boche plane escaped into some low clouds after igniting the gas-filled bag.

The bombardment from the German artillery discounted any belief in the rumors that they were requesting peace terms from the allies.

All during the day the air was filled with the sound of artillery and the constant chatter of machine guns.

The battery, as they continued forward, met an endless line of wounded coming back from the front. Some were able to walk. The others were literally piled on ambulances and other vehicles, moving to the more permanent hospitals far to the rear. As the ammunition trains passed field hospitals located closer to the front, they observed numerous blanket-covered bodies of doughboys awaiting last rites before interment. The grave-digging details were constantly at work.

At 6:00 a.m. on the tenth, the guns arrived at the new position on the Nantillois-Cierges road, approximately three kilometers northwest of the previous position. The region surrounding them showed the signs of the terrific battle that had taken place. Dead Boche troops were stacked like cord wood, four deep in places. American dead also dotted the landscape; anywhere an enemy bullet or shell had found them.

Pat tried not to look at the scene. This proved to be impossible for at one spot a headless torso lay to the left of the road and the head to the right, like a discarded doll torn apart by a careless child.

Many more bodies had been literally dismembered by the horrific blast of the shells. Arms, legs, hands and feet were scattered about. A few of the men were not able to keep anything down, the sight sickened them so. The sight, as devastating as it was, didn't affect most men as much as it would have had they not been so exhausted. Little or no sleep in nearly forty hours deadened every man's senses.

As the cannon were being readied, the battery came under fire from the Boche guns, forcing all to seek cover in hastily dug flop trenches. German aircraft seemed to have control of the skies and were constantly attacking the regiment's line.

An official communiqué arrived at the position stating that Austria and Turkey had surrendered unconditionally and that Germany had sought peace terms from the Allies.

No one really believed it.

"That's a lot of bullshit!" Paul said upon hearing the message. "We'll all be long dead before this goddamned war ends."

No one argued his point.

Late in the day the cannoneers watched as a Boche plane downed another American balloon. Again, both observers took to their parachutes.

The next day, October 11, the guns of the 149th Regiment began firing a rolling barrage into the region a little north of Romagne-sous-Montfaucon. Battery F fired 1521 shells during those five hours in support of a 32nd Division assault into the region. The Germans were well dug in and the American infantry made little or no progress.

At 4:00 that afternoon the German artillery found the range of the regiment's line and began a heavy shelling of the area. A French battery next to Battery A took a direct hit on the third piece that completely destroyed the gun and a subsequent volley killed some Poilus at another nearby battery.

Another series of shells next landed in and around Battery F. Tom and Paul were working with the cannoneers at the time, trying to maneuver the number two piece into position for normal barrage. As they were making their final adjustments Tom heard an incoming shell and yelled for the others to take cover. All dove for the flop trenches just as two shells landed within a few feet of the piece.

After the explosion and the debris settled over the men, Corporal Bayless whistled and said, "That's too close. Everybody all right?"

All answered except one, Paul. He moaned and rolled over on his back. Tom took one look at him and began to yell, "Medic, Medic, we've got an injured man!"

He crawled over to his friend. "Paul, hang in there. How ya doing buddy?"

"I'm hit bad, Tom. It hurts like hell!"

Paul's voice was weak and before the others could say anything, Lieutenant Allen and a medical orderly reached the position. Pappy took one look at Paul and shook his head.

A large fragment the size of a baseball slammed into Paul's upper chest and penetrated to the other side before coming to a stop.

After the orderly bandaged Paul, Tom picked his lifelong friend up in his arms and carried him to the aid station. The lieutenant in charge called for an ambulance, but Paul protested. "I ain't going to make it, Lieutenant, it hurts so much. Just shoot me and put me out of my misery," he moaned.

Tom cradled Paul's head on his lap as Paul dictated a final letter to his family and friends.

"Tom, tell my folks that they were the best. Tell 'em I have no regrets for joining up and fighting for my country. I know I did the right thing," Paul choked and coughed as he grimaced in pain. He closed his eyes and said, "Tell Pat and Hank goodbye, they were great buddies and I'll miss 'em," he opened his eyes again, and looked intently at Tom. "You were the best friend a guy could ever have, goodbye."

He took a few short breaths, convulsed a little, and died.

The men stood silently as the tears streamed down Tom's face. This was the first battle death in the battery. They had come to feel that they were invulnerable, but now the reality of it all began to sink in.

"Men, we're at war," Pappy said. "This is to be expected. Now say your goodbyes and get to the line. Tom, you stay here with him 'til the burial detail comes and then get back."

Tom nodded as he gently put Paul's head on the ground and slowly stood up. "Yes, sir," he responded in almost a whisper. Those nearby came over and walked by Paul's body, and then quietly went off to their station on the line.

Pat and Hank were not far away when they heard the news and quietly went over to where Paul lay. They each were so shocked by the news that they had to see Paul to believe it. When they got there, they could no longer doubt that he was gone.

Hank immediately went to Tom and embraced him. "Tom, I'm sorry, I know he was your best friend. I know how you feel over the loss."

"Thanks. He and I grew up together. I don't know how to handle it."

"Tom, you have to pull yourself together. You'll handle it. We'll talk later."

Pat just stared at Paul's body, then grasped Tom's hand and mumbled, "I'm sorry, Tom, he was the greatest." He walked away.

The battery's charmed life seemed to have ended.

Late in the evening Captain Case sent orders to the rear echelon for the limbers and caissons to come forward to get the ammunition and guns. It took awhile for the men to get up and get going as they had spread out in the woods in order to not bunch up because of the shelling. They also wanted to be out of sight whenever the section chiefs were in need of men for bothersome details.

Soon they were on the road with the caissons and limbers, but it wasn't long before traffic congestion brought them to a dead stop. The American Fifth Division was also moving to the front and the roads were clogged tight with the congestion. The lieutenant sent Private Newcum ahead to notify the battery commander of the delay. It was upon his return that the men of echelon learned of the death of Paul Driscol.

At dawn, Lieutenant Coffey decided to pull the carriages off of the road and out into the shell-torn fields north of Septsarges where they made some progress towards their goal. Once they got around the traffic, they got back on the road. Prior to reaching a crossroads in Nantillos, they were held up by German guns targeting the intersection.

"Is there any way we can get through?" the lieutenant asked an MP holding traffic from crossing.

"Well, sir, I think if you wait until they land four shells, you have about four minutes before another volley comes in," the sergeant said matter-of-factly.

The lieutenant took out his watch and timed the volleys, and decided the MP was close to right. "All right, the first two carriages start across the intersection at a gallop after the next volley, then wait for us about a kilo on beyond," he yelled to the drivers. "Then we'll wait and do it again."

It took nearly an hour to get across, but they all made it safely. It wasn't till seven in the morning that they arrived at the position. It had taken a little over nine hours to travel nine kilometers. It didn't take long for the guns to be readied, and within an hour, they were on the road, back through Cierges and Montfaucon.

To their surprise, a real dinner that included steak awaited the men at the battery's mess when they got back to the corral. But the gloom of Paul's death still hung over the battery and no one enjoyed the meal.

Opposite the American lines in the Argonne lay the heart of the new Germany, built on the ruins of the defeated lands of Belgium and France. Here, since the early days of the war, the Boche had stockpiled the munitions and supplies needed to feed the armies that were trying to bring the allies to their knees. In this section of northern France situated behind the Kremhilde Line, they had even built munitions factories, this to shorten and speed the needed ammunition to their troops in the field.

Their focus was on two railroads that met and crossed in an area approximately 25 miles behind the line. Both of these railroads were essential to the rapid movement of troops and supplies for all of their efforts along the Western Front. One set of tracks, those to the north, which started at Cologne, curved southwest and ran through Liege and Namur. The southern line started at Coblentz and ran through Longuyon, Montmedy, and on through Sedan. This line curved south before turning northwest to meet and cross the northern tracks just east of Cambrai. If both or even one of these lines fell into Allied hands, the Boche efforts in France would soon collapse, forcing their pull back into the Fatherland. It therefore was the Allied objective to either cut or capture these lines, near the city of Sedan.

The guns of the St. Mihiel offensive had not stopped firing before the first units of the victorious American First Army began disengaging from the battle and moving in a northwesterly direction towards the Argonne. Since the Rainbow Division had been part of the initial attack force, they were designated as one of those to stay at St. Mihiel in order to secure that victory. Those divisions that had been held in reserve were the ones moving to the northwest for the new offensive.

The last units had barely been positioned when, in the early morning hours of September 26, 1918, the Allied offensive in the Argonne began. All along their twenty-four-mile front, the American Army started the initial bombardment using 3,800 guns ranging in size from 75 mm field pieces up to the formidable 14-inch American-made railroad guns.

With the Meuse on the right and the French Fourth Army on the left, the bombardment started by spewing forth $1,000,000 worth of shells per minute. More ammunition was expended during this three-hour preparatory fire than had been fired by both the North and the South during the entire Civil War.

The attack was into an almost impenetrable enemy stronghold. To the right of center of the American lines were the heights of Montfaucon,

Cunel, Romagne and Barricourt. These fortresses rose at least one thousand feet above the lines, affording the enemy excellent observation and fire control.

To the left stood the Argonne Forest. This ground also pitched upward to nearly a thousand feet above the First American Army. This deep and thick wood provided defensive positions that were difficult to see and worse to attack. The land was marsh ridden and swampy in the rainy season and was serviced by only three primitive roads, thus leaving the tanks impotent. These slow and cumbersome machines were used only in the center, before Cheppy to the right of the Aisne River and to the left of the Montfaucon Heights and woods.

The Boche had spent the previous four years fortifying this area for such an assault. The defensive positions had been reinforced with concrete, which were protected with fields of barbed wire. It was estimated that five German divisions manned the twenty-four-mile front, but fifteen others could be transported quickly to augment the defense.

Due to the urgency of launching the attack in concert with the British attack on the Hindenburg Line to the northwest, and because most of the battle-seasoned divisions were still tied up at St. Mihiel, only four of the American assault divisions had seen any fighting at all. Many of the men involved in the offensive had been drafted during the summer months of 1918, and most of these had only been in the army for six weeks. Some had never fired live ammunition.

The first two days saw the German line falter and fall back approximately seven kilometers, then dig in and hold. Losses on both sides were heavy. The Argonne forest lay before the Americans as hill behind wooded hill, each being heavily fortified by the Boche. Ten kilometers beyond the initial jump off position lay the famous Kremhilde defense; the fortified line the Germans had built to protect the Fatherland from invasion.

The battle-seasoned 32nd Division battered at Romagne and Cunel without taking these vital strongholds. The experienced First Division to the left of the 32nd had captured a strategic position, given the unpretentious name of Hill 212, and then found themselves battering fruitlessly against the Kremhilde Stellung, at whose center lay Cote de Chatillon.

By October 13, the great Argonne-Meuse offensive had ground to a near standstill.

Jake was a little apprehensive about his return to the company. It'd been nearly two weeks since he'd seen any of the men and he hoped that they would understand about the losses he'd suffered in the reconnaissance mission back on the seventeenth.

He was greeted like a long-lost brother. Sergeant Thompson was especially elated over his return, and when they were alone, expressed his view candidly. "Sir we sure missed you. The lieutenant did okay but not the way you woulda done it. I think we took more casualties than we shoulda. Now that we're going back to battle, I'm just glad you're here to lead us."

"Well thanks, Billy Joe, I hope I can live up to your expectations. You know I was really worried about you and Bliss getting back to the major with the info we'd gathered and, wham, the Boche hit us with mortars and machine guns. So it was some time before I heard about you two."

"Well, sir, we didn't run into any trouble, though we had to skirt around lots of Boche. Piece of cake, capt'n, piece of cake, at least compared to what yous guys ran into."

"As I recovered from my wounds in the hospital I got to thinking about you and the private. Then the major came to visit and told me you were all right and I sure was thankful for that. The Lord must have been with ya?"

"There ain't no question about that, sir." The sergeant paused a second. "You ready to get back to work?"

Jake smiled. "Good question, Sarge. It's going to be tough getting back in the saddle, but I think I'm ready. I'm particularly glad you're still around to keep things running. We have a lot of new men who haven't tasted battle yet and I'm depending on you to get them ready. I understand that we'll be getting on the trucks day after tomorrow?"

"That's what the major said. I guess those new men jest in from the States ain't doing too well in the Argonne. They been getting chewed up purty bad from what I hears."

"Yeah, I think you're right. It's the same old story, the Rainbow to the rescue once again!"

The next day Major Davidson held an early morning briefing for the company commanders. Jake then spent the majority of the day meeting the new men and reacquainting himself with the others, and in the late afternoon he had a conference with his platoon leaders. The packing and preparing for the trucks was an ongoing process and he had to catch up on a great deal of paperwork.

Finally just before dawn on October 1, the regiment was ordered to go aboard the long line of waiting vehicles that had pulled into the town of St. Mihiel during the night.

Three days later they were in Reicourt and on October 6, transported to the Bois de Montfaucon, a small forest that had been ravaged by four years of continued trench warfare in the defense of the citadel of Verdun. Here they languished for a week. The 32nd Division was on the line just in front of them and their efforts against the Boche brought barrage after barrage down on the heads of the Rainbow. The stench and the filth of the battlefield soaked into their spirits and into their clothing. When the word finally came for the 42nd to move, they quickly shifted to the line north of Fleville and Exermont, relieving the brilliant but tired First Division.

The stubborn defense put up by the Boche at Hill 288 and the Cote de Chatillon had held up the entire American Army in the Meuse-Argonne offensive. The Rainbow's part in this fighting started on October 14, resulting in two days of hard combat.

The 168th Infantry from Iowa was placed on the right while the Alabamians of the 167th were on the left of Cote de Chatillon. In front of the Iowans was Tuilleries Farm, behind which sat Hill 288, both enemy strongholds that needed to be taken before they could enter into Cote de Chatillon.

When the attack commenced, the 167th was on the left slope of the Cote in the Bois de Romagne. Jake's company, part of the Third Battalion, was on the right side of the line. The First and Second battalions were just to the rear and in support of the Third.

The barrage started at 10:00 a.m. on the fourteenth, and at 10:30 the infantry began their attack. G Company had been positioned at the edge of a small wood and when the signal to attack came, the infantry started forward across a small clearing towards the Germans who were dug in at another wood across the two-hundred-meter-wide wheat field.

The return fire from the Boche was fierce, killing or wounding nearly every man in Jake's lead platoon. The others hit the ground and were pinned down by heavy rifle and machine gun fire. Before long, Jake found Major Davidson's messenger on the ground at his side and quite out of breath after his dash across some open ground.

"The major says you need to keep moving, Captain."

"I would if I could. They nearly knocked the whole platoon out."

"He said if you move to your right to those woods there," the messenger said as he pointed with his right hand, "there isn't any fire coming from that part of the trees."

Jake took out his binoculars and scanned the woods over to the right. The major had seen something that he had missed.

"I think he's right. Tell him I'm taking the third platoon and we will attack," Jake took a quick look at his watch, "in ten minutes."

"Right, sir, I'll tell him, and good luck, Captain." The messenger had to yell to be heard over the sound of battle.

Jake turned to his first sergeant who was lying in the grass close by. "Go tell Lieutenant Durgovits that we'll move out to the right as soon as I get there."

"Yes sir!" and Thompson was gone.

Jake turned to his messenger. "Tell Lieutenant Caldwell to take charge of the company. I'm going with the Third Platoon to attack the Boche from the right. When he sees us move across the clearing, have the rest of the company open up with all we have, straight ahead to distract them. Got that?"

"Yes, sir."

"Then get going."

When the messenger left, Jake picked up his rifle and started in a low crouch run towards the Third Platoon, keeping to the trees. He spotted Durgovits and Thompson lying on the ground near the line of trees on the edge of the clearing and quickly plopped down beside them. "Okay, withdraw your men back to the trees and then have 'em move to the right one hundred yards. It's at that point we'll make a quick dash across the opening over to those trees over there," Jake said, pointing. "Sergeant, go set up a place where we can gather and we'll be right behind you."

"Yes, sir!" Sergeant Thompson replied, and was gone like a wisp of smoke.

"Doug, get your men up and moving and I'll meet you there."

The lieutenant nodded and started collecting his platoon.

Jake paused a minute as he said a short prayer. "Lord, here I go again, please protect us."

He got up and ran down a shallow ravine to where Thompson was waiting. Soon the whole platoon was there in the small gully at the edge of the clearing.

"Is everyone ready?" Jake asked as he looked into the faces of the troopers. He could see the fear in the eyes of the new men and knew that the veterans felt it, but had learned to hide their emotions. All nodded. "Then let's go, straight across, and don't stop till we get to the trees, where we'll reform."

The platoon spread out along the gully and waited for the signal. Jake was next to Durgovits and after a short pause told the lieutenant to get the men going. They all jumped to their feet and started across the clearing at a run. Not a shot was fired at the twenty-five men as they dashed across the opening and reformed a line on the other side. They had now successfully positioned themselves on the enemy's left flank and a little behind their first line of defense.

"All right, now let's go get those guns!" Jake yelled to the platoon, and the men stood and started through the woods in a long, spread out line perpendicular to the Boche defensive position, shooting at everything that moved. Jake was on the far right deep into the trees. Because of the shrubbery, he fell somewhat behind the rest of the men. He worked his way through some thick underbrush and when he broke through he saw a German machine gun crew take aim on the men of the platoon. Before they could squeeze the trigger of their gun, Jake shot his Springfield from the hip and dispatched all four men.

The Germans were caught totally off guard and the advance began. It wasn't long before the southern portion of the wood was in American hands. The rest of the company moved easily across the clearing and soon they were penetrating ever deeper into the stand of trees.

During the middle of the afternoon the enemy launched a counterattack and held up the 167th's progress for a while. The Germans attacked with overwhelming numbers and dislodged several companies, forcing them back towards the clearing.

Jake's company, still on the far right, started an attack on the Boche left flank. Thompson went into the fray like a wild banshee, running and yelling for all he was worth. When he was out of ammunition, he threw down his rifle and picked up a Stokes mortar he found nearby, and without the aid of a stand or firm platform started lobbing shells point-blank into the German advance. Even though he was shot two times by the Boche, he kept up the barrage until the Germans started withdrawing. He single-handedly stopped their counterattack and finally forced them into retreat, before he fell dead with the mortar still cradled in his arms.

Jake witnessed Thompson's action and rushed to his side when the fight had ended. The sergeant was dead when he got there. Jake bit his lip to hold back the tears he felt well up in his eyes. He took the mortar from Thompson's hands and laid him on his back. He jammed the bayonet on his own rifle into the ground next to Thompson and placed the sergeant's helmet on the butt of the stock.

Lieutenant Caldwell was soon at Jake's side. "I never witnessed heroics like that before, he deserves a medal."

"He'll get one, but we just lost the best damned soldier this army has ever seen," Jake said as he turned away and started to organize his company and check on his other casualties.

The fighting slowed late in the day and even though the Rainbow had made great strides, they still did not possess the Cote. This wouldn't happen until two days later, following savage hand-to-hand combat. At the end of the sixteenth of October, the strong points of the Kremhilde Stellung were in the hands of the American Army. The back of the German resistance had been broken and the Argonne offensive could continue forward.

The fighting was not over by a long shot, as German resistance remained strong although they continued to fall back in an orderly fashion.

When the Rainbow was ordered to take the line and relieve the First Division on Saturday, October 12, they began moving that very afternoon. As a part of this order, the 149th Field Artillery Regiment traveled nineteen kilometers in sixteen hours. They passed through Cheppy and Varennes before the individual batteries began dropping out of the line of march to take up their positions south of Fleville, along the Aire River. Battery F was the first to pull into their designated site, laid out for them by Sergeant Baker and Lieutenant Allen some hours before. The remaining batteries of the regiment continued on until all of them dropped out in turn, each about a kilometer apart to establish their own position in the valley. This valley was scattered with small wooded areas and none of the batteries put up their camouflage netting, hoping that the stands of trees would cover them well enough to prevent their detection from the prying eyes of enemy observation aircraft.

It had rained all night and the weather was turning cold. The road was jammed with troops, vehicles of all types, and artillery. No one had slept in nearly thirty-six hours, and all were drawing on the limited reserve strength left in their tired bodies. Whenever a halt was encountered the men would drop into some nearby ditch and try to sleep in the light drizzle, only to be awakened within minutes as the line got underway. The drivers would fall asleep on their mounts only to be prodded from their slumber as the traffic started forward once again.

Tom stayed behind with Paul's remains until the burial detail came along to bury him. It wasn't until Monday that he returned to the guns. Pat and Hank filled in and performed his duties until he could pull himself together.

Everyone was so tired that it was an effort just to move. Fortunately the battery wasn't called upon to fire on Monday and most tried to rest as best they could under the conditions. The food, what there was of it, continued to be inadequate and terrible, and the men's hunger only added to their weariness.

Starting at 4:00 in the morning on the fourteenth, the 149th Field Artillery, as well as all of the other batteries taking part in the assault, began firing their guns at the German defenders atop the Cote de Chatillon and Kremheilde Position. They continued their uninterrupted fire for twelve straight hours, then at 10:00 p.m. they resumed the shelling. Before the day was through, Battery F alone sent forth a grand total of 2723 rounds.

The Rainbow's infantry started their attack on the slopes of the Cote exactly one hour after the artillery barrage began. The 168th Infantry quickly seized Tuillers Farm and Hill 288 before starting their move on the southwest slope. All during the remainder of the day the repeated attempts at charging the well-entrenched Germans were turned back by the stiff defense put up by the Boche from the Kremhilde line.

Late in the morning a German Platz observation plane flew high over the artillery entrenchment of the 149th, and it wasn't long before a barrage of enemy shells rained all around D Battery. This was followed by another volley landing in and around F battery. One shell exploded near the second section, wounding six men. Five were quickly carried off to the field hospital. None of the injuries suffered were considered life threatening, and three of the men returned to the battery within the week. In the meantime, Lieutenant Allen put in a desperate call for more cannoneers to be held in reserve at the rear horse line for just such a contingency.

The guns fell under periodic fire from the enemy throughout the rest of the day, but only one shell landed close enough to be considered a threat and it did little damage.

The cannoneers were too occupied firing their own guns to seek shelter. Ammunition was their utmost concern and as the gunners of the third piece rammed home their last shell the caissons finally galloped up to the position. The traffic on the roads during this offensive was so bad that the trip for ammunition took much longer than anticipated. Shells were taken directly from the caissons, prepared, and pushed into the guns to maintain an uninterrupted rate of fire. One caisson after another arrived at the guns to discharge their deadly loads and the two drivers assisted in the unloading while the gunners continued their fire.

The next day saw a diminished rate of fire for the regiment. The infantry's progress was slow and soon the lines stabilized along the river valley to the south.

Early in the afternoon, during this lull in the fighting, Pat accompanied Jack Bayless on a short trip into Fleville in search of food and tobacco. There they found numerous dead Boche and doughboys lying in the streets. The battle had been a terrific one, costly to both sides in terms of the human sacrifices. The retreating Germans had destroyed the bridge across the Aire River, and as Pat and Jack entered town the American engineers were putting the finishing touches on a temporary span that would be used for all vehicular and foot traffic.

Little food or tobacco could be found, so the two stood in line at a Salvation Army hut waiting for a cup of hot chocolate and some candy. As they were in line, Pat read a newspaper he found on one of the chairs outside the hut.

"Hey, Jack, this article says that there's a peace council in progress, and it's written by my Uncle Clint. You remember Clint Phelps when he came to camp a few months back?"

"Yeah, I remember him. Is that a *Chicago Globe*?"

Pat took a quick look at the masthead, "Nah, it must be a syndicated article. This is the *Stars and Stripes*. Hmm, I don't see anything in here by my brother, though. Small world, isn't it?"

Just as they received their hot chocolate, German mortar fire fell on the town. Jack and Pat ran for the bomb shelter down the street, spilling the chocolate all over themselves as they ran for their lives. "They almost got us that time," Jack exclaimed, "and I spilled every last drop before I even got a taste. Crap!" he yelled out to nobody in particular.

"Well you can have some of mine, I only spilled half of it."

"I'm goin' back to the position where it's safe," Jack said after he took a sip.

"Yeah, I'm with you."

The regiment stayed put in the valley for the next ten days, suffering under a tremendous barrage of shells poured in on them by the Boche. They were lucky in that they didn't suffer any more casualties or serious damage to their equipment. The morale sunk during this time, buoyed only a little when word came that the infantry had finally taken the Cote de Chatillon and the Kremhielde Position on the sixteenth.

On Thursday the seventeenth, the first and third guns were sent to the rear for new barrels. On the next Sunday after the first and third guns were finished and returned to the position, the second and fourth pieces were sent for new barrels. It was found that all of the gun tubes were so badly pitted that a premature explosion, which would possibly destroy the gun and probably the crew, was just around the corner.

Pat had accompanied the guns to the rear on both occasions and was happy to get to a quiet area. Tom and Hank stayed at the positions performing the required maintenance on the remaining two cannon. This was part of a plan Hank had thought of in order to give him time alone with Tom. Hank felt that because of his own great loss, he might be able to help Tom overcome his grief over the loss of Paul.

The battery wasn't able to engage in heavy artillery duels until the twenty-first, when the second and fourth guns were returned. During the interim they were subjected to heavy shelling, and because of the inclement weather the Germans used gas, as the rain kept it from circulating any distance. This was frustrating to the cannoneers, because they were unable to retaliate in strength.

Early in the morning of the seventeenth the Boche sent over nine rolling kitchens, or elevated trains, as the crews liked to call them. These were heavy-caliber shells that made the loud rumbling noise for which they were named. Huge fragments fell all around the position. One of these large shells hit a nearby farmhouse, sending timbers, stones and fragments hundreds of feet in the sky. Craters created by these large shells were large enough to hide an entire battery. Enemy artillery was a constant problem and if it weren't for so many duds, the damage and casualty rate would have been much higher.

On one occasion, Sergeant Martyn who was trying to sleep in his pup tent when a shell ripped through the canvas covering and fell within inches of the slumbering soldier. It stripped the blanket that had draped him and buried it deep in the ground under the deadly shell. If it hadn't been a dud, no one would have known of the incident. When he scrambled to his feet and was free of the tent he was as white as a ghost, stuttering unintelligible sounds. For five minutes he shook like a leaf before regaining his usual stoic manner.

The war continued at a somewhat reduced pace for the 149th through the twenty-fifth. The horses and mules were in a sorry state from the lack of sufficient forage. They were so starved that they tried to eat the bark off of the trees, the harnesses, and even the spokes of the wheels. There weren't enough carriages or trucks to fetch hay, because all vehicles were needed to haul ammunition. During a lull in the fighting on the twenty-fifth, Sargent Baker located some hay in a former German storage depot in Fleville and detailed two carriages to haul as much as they could to the horse lines.

All during this time there was a great deal of aerial activity, and no less than three planes fell from the sky near the position of F Battery, two American and one Boche. The infantry did not think much of the American pilots and held them somewhat in disdain. At the same time they secretly admired the heroics of the Boche airmen, who were willing to take greater risks, even though these enemy airmen were raining bullets and bombs down on their own heads. On several occasions during this period, the enemy planes dropped leaflets over the Americans urging them not to die for France but rather surrender to the Germans and be well treated and fed.

Shortly after lunch on the twenty-sixth, the limbers and caissons left the horse line went to the guns in order to move them to a new position north, beyond Fleville. The roads were crowded with Allied artillery, all moving north, and it wasn't until 5:00 that evening that the guns were finally limbered up and positioned in the line of march.

At sunset, just as F Battery entered Fleville, German planes pounced upon the column of artillery moving through the town. With guns blazing, the Boche planes strafed the column unmercifully. The MPs stuck to their jobs and kept the traffic moving as well as they could.

Just in front of F Battery's lead wagon, upon which Pat and Hank were riding, was a caisson of the 150th Field Artillery. Pat had jumped down to the ground, ready to run to a nearby ditch just in case a plane dove on them. He kept his head swiveling, looking for enemy planes. As he looked to his left for the hundredth time, he saw one plane diving at the line and immediately yelled for the others to duck as he dove for cover, with Hank and the driver close behind.

The Boche pilot had the caisson in front of them in his sights and began his fire before the hapless crew could jump free of the carriage. Three horses were killed and two drivers were wounded.

"That was close, way too close," Hank said over and over as he climbed back aboard and their wagon skirted around the disabled caisson and continued on through town. Somehow Battery F managed to get through Fleville without suffering damage or casualties.

Soon the strafing ceased as the twilight was slipping into total dankness. The traffic was still heavy and movement was slow. Though the battery only traveled four kilometers, they did not arrive until well after 10:30 p.m. Once the guns were unlimbered and the caissons unloaded the cannoneers fell victim to an hour-long shelling. One stack of ammunition was hit and set off quite a fireworks display. During the shelling the men hugged the ground under whatever shelter they could find. They all pitched in and dug extra deep flop trenches when the bombardment stopped. All were beginning to believe that enemy artillery fire was heavier than what they'd suffered during the Champagne offensive back in July.

Early the next morning the Germans shelled the position again; a mixed assortment of high explosives and gas. At one point a gas shell landed next to the number one gun and before the men could get their masks on some had taken a large dose. Jack Bayless, Jason Newcum and Dan Dreyer were suffering. Pat, who was about twenty meters away, ran to their aid, holding his breath as long as he could as he helped the men get their masks on. When he was through helping them, he put his on, but only after he took a few gulps of the stuff himself. The three gunners were sent to the hospital, but Pat stayed, though it was four or five days before he could talk above a whisper.

From the twenty-seventh to the end of the month the entire regiment was heavily shelled at various intervals. The regiment's guns were also active returning the German fire. Aerial activity was increasing. On the thirtieth, an American balloon was brought down by a Boche aviator who quickly escaped from a pursuing SPAD into a cloud.

Finally, on the thirty-first, the regiment was put on alert for a large offensive set to start at 0500 hours the next morning. This was to be the big push into the city of Sedan.

Ike was learning all too quickly that he really didn't want to be in command of the squadron. He wished things were the way they were when Captain Worthem was in command, but no one had heard a thing about Worthem. However, Ike had a feeling that all was well with him.

There seemed to be an endless stream of papers that needed to be reviewed and signed. There always were way too many casualties that required reports, as well as the letters that needed to be written to the victim's families.

On top of all of this he still felt it necessary to fly as much as before. He wasn't going to let his boys go off on a mission by themselves as his predecessor had. These men needed the experienced guidance that only he, Frank, and a few others had to offer.

The worst part of the new situation was that he had precious little time to correspond with Agnes. He had explained his predicament to her, but not being in touch on a daily basis, even by letter, was a loss. He knew she understood but still it was difficult.

During the early part of his tenure as commander, albeit temporary, Ike made some major changes in the command structure and in the personnel involved in running the squadron. He purposely tried to put more responsibility on the shoulders of his staff and on the individual flight leaders. Captain Mendel had screwed up the chain of command and limited the individual initiative of all his people. Ike soon reversed that situation and called upon all to get involved and make decisions on their own.

He insisted that his flight leaders train the new pilots thoroughly in aerial tactics before sending them out against the enemy. The combat training the new pilots had received in the states and elsewhere was woefully inadequate; which, in the past, had led to a high loss rate.

"I will support your decisions," he told his flight leaders, "for it is better to make a decision on your own than to make none at all, but you must get involved in teaching the newcomers about the tactics we use in this sector!" He also relayed the same type of message to his mission support staff and to his ground maintenance crews. He felt that not only would this take a great deal of weight off of his shoulders, but also it would create a more efficient organization dedicated to winning the war in the air.

The Kicking Mule Squadron had moved from Toul to a forward field just south of Montfaucon on the twenty-fifth of September, the day that Ike had gone to Paris to get his new plane. As soon as the offensive began on the twenty-sixth, they were busy hammering away at the German supply lines north of the front. Their missions were directed primarily towards ground targets, which were repeatedly bombed and strafed. The 94th Aero Squadron joined in with them but spent more time at altitude engaging enemy aircraft as they provided the air cover for the ground attack squadrons.

Every day the Germans were out in force fighting with an intensity that belied the rumor that the war would end soon. The 95th was on the attack, flying two or three sorties during the daylight hours in support of the ground troops. It was during one of these excursions across the front that Ike downed his tenth confirmed kill, just thirteen days after taking command of the 95th.

On this particular occasion he had become separated from the flight on their way back to the aerodrome from a raid against German ground emplacements on the Cote de Chatillon. As he was cruising along at 500 meters he nearly ran head-on into a Boche balloon that had been obscured by clouds and the general low visibility. Before turning away he fired a full five-second burst of both guns into the nose of the gasbag. As he kicked hard right rudder and banked nearly to the vertical with aileron to avoid running into it, it exploded in a ball of fire and smoke and fell like a rock out of the sky. Ike thought he saw the observer take to his parachute, but he was too busy dodging debris and ground fire to confirm the fact. This made him a double ace, nowhere near the number of kills that the leading French and English aces had accumulated, but not too shabby for his being in combat for just over six months.

Unlike St. Mihiel, the movement of the Allied forces through the Argonne had been slow and arduous. Casualties had been heavy on both sides, in the air as well as on the ground. Even though there were numerous rumors of the war ending soon, the intensity of the fighting had not abated, not in the least. In fact, the air war had intensified, as both sides were learning the importance of using this lethal tool effectively in both offensive and defensive operations.

The 95th was losing its share of planes and pilots. Many of these losses were to ground fire, but a substantial number were lost to enemy aircraft. Even though their primary mission was ground support, they had frequent encounters with enemy aircraft, and the twenty-fifth had been a particularly bad day for the squadron—two planes had been lost to German fighters, one killing the pilot in the resulting crash.

So it was in the early morning of October 26 that Ike, Frank Linki, and Bill Summers flew a short patrol north across the line in search of the other pilot who had been in one of those planes shot down the day before by a Boche Albatross. This pilot's wingman had loitered a short while over the crash site and saw the man escape a nearby German patrol. As the Americans were advancing on this sector, Ike hoped that they could find the downed airman and indicate which way to head for safety. It was a long shot, but Frank and Bill insisted that they try. Against his better judgment, Ike agreed to go along.

Ike flew high cover as the other two intrepid airmen flew an ever-increasing outward circular search pattern with a maximum radius of five miles around the crash sight. Both planes drew occasional light ground fire from a few German patrols located in the area, but not enough to drive them away from their quest. After nearly forty minutes of searching, Frank located the pilot and frantically signaled Bill to join him. Bill swooped down over the lone figure standing in the open near a wheat field. Apparently he'd been hiding in hedgerow at the edge of a medium-sized wood.

On his second pass, Bill tossed a note tied to a rock that had a long streamer attached. The young pilot limped to the note and after a frantic search found it. He read the detailed instructions, acknowledged it with a wave, and the SPADs flew off.

Ike had witnessed the proceedings and lost some altitude in order to join Bill and Frank as they climbed away from their mission. The three joined up at 500 meters and turned south on their way home.

Up to this time Bill had managed only one kill and was always anxious to increase his score of enemy planes. This day was no different. As the three were headed towards their home field, Bill spied a single observation aircraft proceeding towards the line. He quickly left the formation and climbed to 1000 meters, above the lone Boche, and positioned himself behind his would-be target. There was no sun, as the sky was overcast at 1500 meters.

Since he had been flying to the rear of the flight, Ike did not immediately see Bill leave the formation, but soon noticed that he was gone. He caught a glimpse of Bill climbing away. He signaled Frank and began a 180-degree climbing turn to the right in order to follow Bill. Bill's eagerness to add to his score caused him to throw caution to the wind, and he immediately bore in on the target. He began firing at the victim too far out, and Ike could see his tracers curve away from the enemy.

Three Fokker D.VIIs dropped from near the cloud base and fell in behind Bill. Both Frank and Ike saw the D.VIIs at about the same time, but they were too far away to go in and protect Bill. Both men firewalled the throttle of their SPADs as they raced to his rescue.

"Look over your shoulder, look over your shoulder!" Ike kept saying aloud.

Bill was intent on the target. The enemy gunner in the rear seat saw the SPAD coming at him and held his fire until Bill was within 100 meters. Ike could see some of the tracer's spark off of the SPADs engine before Bill swooped below the German craft. Bill then went into an immediate climb and fired a long burst into the belly of the enemy. The plane shuddered and burst into flames. Bill brought his plane to level cruise before doing a victory roll through the plume of smoke, then dove, following his victim to the ground. He was jumped by the flight D.VIIs, whose lead ship sported a brilliant blue paint.

As Ike and Frank had been late in joining the fray, the German pilots had not seen the SPADs that immediately fell in behind their Fokkers.

Bill had been totally unaware of the presence of the three enemy planes until he was under attack. It wasn't long before he knew he was in a desperate situation. He immediately entered into a diving right turn, trying to outrun his advisory. The enemy pilot was battlewise and had anticipated the maneuver, and was immediately on his tail firing into the SPAD.

Ike instinctively went to Bill's assistance as Frank jumped in to cut off the other two Fokkers. Ike dove his plane and made a beeline for the enemy on Bill's tail. The SPAD soon indicated 140 mph, well above the "never exceed speed". The engine screamed in his ears as the wings and tail surfaces groaned under the stress. The fabric on the upper wing surface vibrated as if it were being hammered with a thousand ball bearings.

Ike could see smoke come from the engine compartment of Bill's ship.

"There's that son of a bitch again. I hope I'm not too late," Ike said to himself as he fell in behind the brilliant blue plane. The anger he felt against the enemy when he first recognized this particular Boche pilot soon left him and he became focused on the job at hand. He flew the plane as if it were part of his very being, moving the controls as if they were an extension of his own hands. He coolly anticipated the German's moves and soon he was about 70 or 80 meters from the Fokker. As he bore in on the target he pulled the trigger on the guns and held it. He could see pieces of fabric and wood fly off of the tail surfaces and the right aileron as his bullets found the target.

The pilot of the D.VII was as surprised at finding another SPAD on his tail, as Bill had been to find the Fokker on his. The German pilot turned to look in disbelief at the SPAD following him. Ike continued the engagement and briefly thought of last spring when this very same pilot had nearly shot him out of the sky in a surprise attack.

The damage Ike did to the Boche was enough to degrade the performance and thus make him an easy target. The roll rate of the D.VII had slowed considerably, as had the rudder and elevator control. Immediately, Ike closed in for the kill. He was soon within fifty meters of the blue Fokker. The Boche pilot was not going to give up without a fight. He rolled left, dove a short distance to gain speed, and immediately started a steep climb towards the safety of the clouds some 1000 meters above. Ike moved in behind him, pushed the throttle full forward, and pulled the stick back. When the German was in his sights, he again pulled the trigger on his guns and held it for a full five to ten seconds. Just as the plane started to pull away in the climb, it exploded in a ball of fire. Ike saw bits of debris flying past his wings and then it was gone.

He turned and looked at the falling wreck for a brief second, then began searching the sky for Bill and Frank. He soon located Frank near the base of the clouds, where he had inflicted heavy damage on one of the Fokkers. This plane, along with the other D.VII, turned and ran for the safety of the their home field, as they saw that their leader was no more.

Afterward Ike climbed 500 meters to join Frank in the futile search for their comrade. They flew until their fuel was nearly exhausted before heading back to the aerodrome.

Upon landing, they learned that Bill had not returned. Neither Frank nor Ike had seen him go down. "We were too busy saving our own butts," Frank stated emphatically to the debriefing officer.

During the ensuing days, Bill was listed only as missing as Frank combed the area looking for telltale signs of his plane. Ike, when time permitted, called all of the front line units hoping that Bill would show up.

By the evening of October 31, Ike had no alternative but to list Bill Summers as missing in action and presumed dead. This was hard for Ike, as Bill had been around since the spring and was considered a veteran. Besides, Bill had been a close friend to both Frank and him.

The heavy hand on his shoulder awakened Pat with a start. He heard a faraway voice announce, "Up and at 'em. The barrage starts in an hour."

Pat shook his head as if to get the cobwebs out. It was dark as pitch and he couldn't see a thing. He didn't even know where he was. He'd just had this very real dream that he was at the university and had his final exam in chemistry, and couldn't remember a thing. He felt this great fear of failing and didn't want to get out of bed.

Slowly it began to dawn on him that he wasn't in Champaign, but somewhere in France and the challenge that he faced was not a final exam, but the very real struggle for life itself.

He got to his knees and shook Hank, who was snoring peacefully next to him under the awning of the pup tent. They all had been so tired the night before that they had fallen asleep with their clothes on, but that was normal. He tried to think of the last time he'd had a change of uniform. Hank stirred a little and mumbled something about being awake, so Pat stood up out in front of the tent, stretched, then began to grope his way through the darkened woods to the cook stove, hoping to find some hot food and maybe a decent cup of coffee. But there hadn't been anything edible for over a week. The last of the oatmeal had been thrown out two days earlier when it became alive with maggots. This thought made him shiver as he felt his way along the path to the rolling kitchen.

Along the way he remembered that today was the start of the big push, their target being the city of Sedan still some 40 kilometers to the north of the line. He'd felt let down the day before when the Rainbow's infantry was relieved from front line duty by the Second Division and placed in reserve, but the artillery had to stay on the line to help with the bombardment. "The lucky infantry can sit this one out!" he said to himself. Then he changed his mind—he knew what they had been through. He only had to dodge the shells, while those poor bastards were dodging bullets, mortars, shells, and worst of all, machine guns.

H Hour had been set at 0530 hours this very morning, November 1. All of the batteries of the 149th were awakened early as the preparatory fire was set to commence at H hour minus 120 minutes, or 3:30 a.m.

Pat joined the other men of the firing detail as they gathered around the stove for breakfast. No one had much to say other than that today marked the one-year anniversary of their landing in France. As they were talking in subdued voices, a small-caliber shell landed in their midst. At the moment of impact, Dan Dreyer stepped in front of Pat, shielding him from the blast. The shrapnel inflicted a deep gash in Dreyer's right thigh. Pat heard a groan from Dan as he fell to the ground, where he writhed in pain. Lieutenant Allen was on the scene at once. He pulled Dan's belt from around his waist and cinched it tight around the leg as a tourniquet to stop the bleeding.

"Littler, go get a medic and tell them we need to send Dreyer here down to the field hospital."

"Yes, sir!" Pat yelled as he turned and ran to the first aid station about 100 meters to the south. It was indeed a miracle that no one else suffered any injuries, as there were several other men standing near Dan at the time of the blast. As Pat ran, the thought foremost in his mind was that if Dan hadn't of stepped in front of him when he had, he would be the one on the ground waiting to be transported. It wasn't long before Dan had been treated and placed on an ambulance headed to the rear for the field hospital.

Soon after this incident, the cannoneers went to their guns as the 149th Field Artillery prepared to begin the barrage. As the men were readying the guns, the battery was subjected to a short enemy shelling. Some of the incoming were gas. Hank and two others had taken a deep whiff of the stuff and were having difficulty breathing. They were sent to the rear echelon to try and regain their normal breathing in the somewhat fresher air.

Once the battery began firing, their sustained rate was 100 rounds per gun per hour. The American and French cannon pounded the German defenders to the north with the heaviest concentration of artillery used by the Allies since the beginning of the war.

At H hour minus ten minutes, the batteries started the barrage that would accompany the infantry on their attack on the Boche positions. The third piece of each battery began firing only smoke shells and continued doing so for the next five hours of the barrage, to help conceal the infantry as they moved across the open ground.

As the infantry continued their forward movement against the well-entrenched enemy, the range of the guns was increased between 100 and 250 meters every six or seven minutes. The cannoneers had a good picture of the rapid progress the infantry was making by the ever-increasing ranges at which they were firing. That day a new record was set for the number of rounds fired in any one day since their war service began.

From the very start of the barrage, the sound of the Allied artillery had been painfully loud and the flashes of the guns lit up the dark, foggy sky as if sunrise had decided to come early. The roar of the guns was constant. All in the firing battery and even those a little to the rear had stuffed cotton in their ears to help reduce the crashing sound of the cannon as they sent forth their deadly missiles into the enemy lines. For Pat, the thunder of the ordnance was all he heard.

In the rear and not long after the doughboys started forward with their attack, Boche prisoners were being moved back from the front in large numbers. Those not otherwise engaged in firing guns conversed with some of these men, those that could speak English. It was from these prisoners that the battery members began to learn of the magnitude of the offensive.

Those at echelon found that most of the prisoners seemed happy to be out of the fighting and that for them the war was over. The members of the battery were able to acquire numerous souvenirs, including a German shepherd that had taken some shrapnel in his right foreleg. It fell upon Hank, the veterinary student, to remove the offending metal and to bind Fritz's wound. This earned him the dog's undying allegiance. Fritz then followed him wherever he went and soon he became the battery mascot, accompanying them on all of their marches.

As news of the success of the offensive filtered back to the battery, the men became more and more hopeful that the war would soon end.

Shortly after the battle had begun, the incoming shells had ceased. Apparently the Germans stopped firing their artillery in order to move it northward in the general retreat. The Allies, as few Boche planes ventured out, owned even the skies. The German air service also had to retire their aircraft to the north.

As the dinner hour approached, those not manning the guns were lounging near the rolling kitchen when a lone shell exploded near the aiming stake of the first piece. The men jumped up and ran for the nearest cover. It was soon presumed that one doughboy had pulled the lanyard of an abandoned German canon to see if it were loaded, which it apparently was, and more unfortunately pointed towards the American lines.

Following their meager dinner, orders were received placing the Rainbow's artillery into reserve status, as all of the day's objectives had been achieved or surpassed, thus relieving them from the front line position they had held at the beginning of the day. This meant a night of uninterrupted sleep for the first time in a very long time.

All during the second day of the offensive there was a constant drizzle, but to the Rainbow, anything was better than being under continuous shellfire. The rumor mill put out the news that both Austria and Turkey had surrendered unconditionally. Finally, at 4:30 p.m. the next day, amid the ongoing drizzle, orders were received to continue the advance. Within an hour the battery was harnessed and hitched and positioned in the line of march. All of the men were required to carry their own equipment, as the condition of the horses was so frightful that Lieutenant Allen had ordered all nonessential gear and especially souvenirs, be left behind.

The hike lasted all night and the road was a sea of mud, at times surpassing ankle depth. Finally, at 8:30 a.m., after an 18-kilometer march, they arrived at Thenorgues. The men as well as the animals were totally spent, and following a warm meal all tried to sleep. This was soon interrupted and they were on the road again by 2:30 that afternoon. By 5:30 they passed through Bar, an abandoned Boche aerodrome, before arriving in Harricourt, some six kilometers north of their starting point. Here the artillerymen were put up in some former German barracks.

Pat, Jack and Hank were selected to stand guard duty for the first shift, and their mood was not pleasant, as none of them had had any sleep during the preceding thirty or so hours. A lone German Gotha bomber flew over the town and dropped its load before turning north. No one seemed to care, as they were all too exhausted to seek shelter. Fortunately, the blasts were not close enough to inflict any damage or cause any casualties in the nearby Allied units.

The condition of the 149th, particularly the animals, had reached a critical state, and at a late night commander's meeting, it was decided to reorganize the regiment into four batteries—E Battery was combined with the First Battalion and B Battery with the Second. With that completed during the very early morning hours, all units of the 149th were harnessed and hitched and on the march by 7:00 a.m. The rain had turned the thoroughfare into a quagmire, and it was especially bad where the Germans had blown up a bridge and long stretch of the road north of Brieulles-sur-Bar, forcing the vehicles to navigate a broad swamp. The engineers were in the process of constructing a new road over the area using materials found in the vicinity. This new road consisted primarily of logs and stones and wasn't much of an improvement.

All of the carriages became stuck at least a couple of times, sometimes even more often. Finally, after hiking eleven kilometers, the batteries went into position south of Les Petites Armoises at 3:00 p.m. The rain continued to fall as the men unloaded the ammunition. When these chores were completed, the pup tents were set up and the blankets spread out on the soggy ground.

Late that evening orders were received placing the 42nd back into the line relieving the American 78th Division. The rumor mill had it that the Rainbow was to assume a lead position in the final drive on Sedan.

The night was cold and wet, only adding to the misery of the time. And with very little sleep, particularly during the past two days, all of the cannoneers were on edge. Before dawn on Wednesday, the battery was awakened and ordered to be on the road by 7:30. Amidst vehement protests, the ammunition was loaded back on the caissons as the call to harness and hitch echoed throughout the camp.

The route continued to be miserable, for the Boche had blown up all the bridges and the ground was thoroughly waterlogged.

As the artillery moved northward they came upon more and more dead horses, Germans and doughboys. The Boche had not given up without a fight and they were continuing a strong rear guard action.

As Battery F continued the march, many of the men noticed that all of the dead horses displayed very similar wounds; the meat on the hindquarters had been cut away. A short time later the limbers overtook a lone cook wagon driven by an Algerian. Jack Bayless asked this strange little fellow, who could barely speak English, for something to eat, and the man quickly presented him a gooey handful of rice and meat, which Jack thankfully took and began to eat.

Pat, who was next to Jack, took one whiff of the mixture and declined the meal. He had an idea of where the meat had come from. "Jack," he said, "did you know that horse meat is a delicacy in Algeria?"

"What?" Jack asked in disbelief as he wiped his face with his sleeve. "You mean I'm eating horse meat?"

"Exactly. From all of those dead horses we just passed on the road."

Jack tried to control himself as best he could. He threw what remained on the ground and quickly wiped his hands on his trousers as he struggled to keep down what he'd already consumed. Some of the others went ahead and ate the mixture, as their hunger was too great to pass up anything edible.

The battery pulled into the small village of Neuville-a-Maire. Here they were greeted with a joyous celebration, as the locals had been living under the Germans for the past four years, up until that very morning when the Boche had evacuated to the north. The citizens told stories of the occupation and the work they were forced to do to help the German war effort. The Boche had even confiscated food supplies sent to them by the Belgian relief commission. Their gratitude to the Americans for their liberation almost made the battery's labors seem worthy of the effort.

After enjoying a short rest and placing the horses in local stables filled with hay that had been gathered by the enemy, the firing echelon was ordered to a position on the north edge of town and told to dig in. This order was greeted with howls of protest from extremely tired men. While the men worked, the horses and mules ate as if there were no tomorrow.

The guns were cared for, a warm dinner was served and eaten, and the men settled down for long rest in dry barns. But at midnight, new orders came down for them to be underway. Hardly had they closed their eyes when they were rudely awakened and ordered to harness and hitch. The explosive profanity and curses of the men probably awakened the whole town.

The tired men of Battery F continued the march northward, many still half asleep. The night was wet and the darkness nearly total. A short distance north of la Neuville they forded a narrow stream, the Rau de Terron. The road dropped off abruptly into the stream and those not paying close attention soon found themselves waist deep in the icy cold water. Pat was one of them and suddenly he was wide-awake. Tom and Hank, who had escaped the dropoff and crossed on a nearby footbridge, roared with laughter at those who had fallen into the stream. The event brought on the first laughter the battery personnel had enjoyed in a very long time. The grossly profane remarks by those who had taken the plunge only added to the glee of those who had escaped the freezing water.

Shortly after crossing the Rau de Terron they passed through Chemery, and once through the town they halted for breakfast. As they were trying to digest a couple of slices of bacon and bread washed down with a lukewarm cup of weak coffee, a detachment of the 1st Division infantry trudged by. The major in charge asked Corporal Bayless what artillery unit he was with that had come so far and in advance of his infantry.

"This is the 149th of the 42nd Division," was the proud reply.

"You oughta be applauded, as our artillery is still way back behind us. The condition of the road and bridges makes it even difficult for our troops to move forward, let alone the carriages. So good luck to you men." The major spurred his horse and galloped on ahead.

When the short breakfast was over, the battery continued northward. By this time the fog was lifting and the men could see that their column was on the upward side of a rise in the road. The first carriages topped the hill and started downward for the town of Cheherry just one to two kilometers away. As the third and fourth vehicles crested the hill, German shells began whistling overhead, landing a short distance from the road on the right. The next volley landed to the left. The drivers goaded their nags to a gallop as they raced to the seeming protection of the town. All of those afoot broke into a run, diving for the ditches whenever they heard the whistling of the incoming shells. The carriages were driven into town, where Sergeant Baker ordered them to disburse along side streets near the small houses located at the edge of town. The men ducked behind and into anything that looked sturdy enough to withstand the shelling as they awaited the return of the captain, who had gone on ahead to find a firing position. The doughboys that had preceded the artillery into Cheherry, loudly criticized the cannoneers for bringing the deadly fire down on their heads.

Pat, Hank, Tom, and some others sought refuge in a ditch behind a potholed wall on the south end of town. The enemy fire, which could be seen all up and down the valley, went silent for a short while and when they resumed, the heaviest concentration seemed to be on Cheherry and the battery. This only enraged the doughboys even more, and they cursed the artillery for their plight.

The battery was helpless unless moved. The captain had been caught out in the open when the bombardment began and he ran to the carriages, dodging the incoming shells. Without accurate information as to the whereabouts of the American troops, who were attacking the Germans to the north of town, the artillery could not be used for fear of killing their own men.

The captain ordered the carriages pulled out of the town and into a field on the right behind a hedgerow of trees that lined the north end.

At about the same time the carriages arrived in the field, a company of French Pouluis also took cover there. Shells were raining down everywhere. The drivers, along with Captain Case and Lieutenant Allen, unhitched the horses and led them to a wood about two kilometers to the south. A great number of the incoming shells were gas, however, and the captain and Pappy were unable to put their masks on, as they needed to shout instructions. Lieutenant Allen was gassed pretty badly, but continued saving the men and horses.

Once the first and second sections had unhitched the teams and the horses were sent off to safety, the cannoneers sought shelter from the shells. There seemed to be no escape from the terrible barrage—if the shells didn't blow the men to bits then they would be badly gassed. There seemed to be no escape from death. Between shell bursts there was a mad dash from one ditch or shell hole for another, one that might offer greater protection. As soon as a cannoneer would prepare to jump into a hole, it would disappear in a cloud of smoke, fire, and flying debris. Many of the doughboys from the First Division were killed or wounded by the shellfire. Jason Newcum suffered a wound in the left shoulder and was attended to by Sergeant Martyn who helped him to the basement of a small nearby cottage. Once in the cellar, they were confronted by officers from the First Division who felt that this location was not to be used as an aid station and demanded that the sergeant leave. Which he did, but not until after he told these gentlemen exactly what he thought of them and particularly of their ancestry. The sergeant half carried and half dragged the wounded trooper to a nearby ditch and remained there until the bombardment ended, which was nearly forty-five minutes later.

Jack Bayless and Paul Stuart sought refuge in a brick outhouse near the edge of town. No sooner had they entered than the door was blown off with a nearby blast. They quickly exited the shelter and headed for a deep shell hole. As they dashed along the path, another shell landed squarely on the building blowing it to kingdom come. The concussion of the blast threw them head over heels into their destination, leaving them badly shaken and covered with debris but miraculously unhurt.

Pat, Hank and Tom dived into a ditch near the hedgerow and found that they were sharing it with numerous French soldiers. They soon agreed that safety was in the trees where the horses had been taken.

They waited until one particularly heavy volley let up, then jumped up and ran thirty meters to a ditch just south of the hedgerow, where they dived headfirst into its safe confines. Tom peeked over the top just as a heavy concentration of shells enveloped their previous location. "Those poor frogs really caught hell with that last volley," he yelled to his companions.

The others looked back and saw the carnage as Pat whistled and said, "We almost bought it ourselves. Let's get the hell out of here!"

They jumped up and continued their trek south towards the trees. It took nearly ten minutes between dodging shells and trying to locate the animals before finding safety.

When the shelling abated, the battery members gathered under the protection of the trees. No one had been killed. Two suffered superficial injuries and only one, Jason Newcum, was sent to the field hospital, indeed a true miracle. By 5:00 in the afternoon the shelling ended altogether, as the infantry had forced the German guns to withdraw.

The captain ordered the men to return to Cheherry to retrieve the carriages and an inventory found that seven horses had been wounded and three killed. The rolling kitchen was shot full of holes, but was still usable. They hitched up what they could and left one man to guard the three carriages that had to be left behind due to the lack of animals. The column turned around and headed back the way that they'd come and shortly before sunset went into position on the north slope of a hill located near the Connage-Bulson road.

The captain sent six drivers and sufficient horses back for the three carriages left behind and ordered the gunners to dig in their guns in preparation for a barrage mission the battery had received at sunset.

The final news of the day was received right after the meal—the 42nd Division's infantry had reached the outskirts of Sedan, though the city was still held by the Germans.

The next day, November 8, the battery was underway soon after sunup. The cannoneers were in a foul mood, for after all of their work, the guns hadn't been fired once. Still they had to arise early to prepare for the march. The captain ordered that the men take only bare essentials and everything else be left where it lay.

The animals had given their all and with their numbers dwindling the loads were lightened considerably. Soon after starting their march the battery encountered a hill that initially looked like little more than a rise in the road that disappeared into the fog, but it soon became a major undertaking. Not more than halfway up the incline the first hitch stalled. Sergeant Baker ordered more horses to help pull it on up the hill. This didn't work, as the animals were nearly played out. It was up to the men to pull the twenty-eight carriages to the crest of the hill. The men were divided into two groups, and with the aid of prolongs and sheer muscle power; they pulled the vehicles to the top. Men tugged at ropes tied to the carriages and others pushed the carriages and the horses till the job was finished some four hours later.

By the time that the battery gathered at the top of the hill the fog had lifted. From their vantage point they could see the small town of Bulson some two kilometers away. The town was being shelled by the Germans, who must have seen elements of the artillery regiment, for it wasn't long before they started pouring fire onto the road they were on. Battery D was just in front of Battery F and started their dash into Bulson. When the lead carriage of D Battery reached a point just beyond halfway, one of their caissons received a direct hit, blowing it off of the road. The horses ran away before becoming entangled in the rubble of some of the buildings on the edge of town. A shell exploded under the horses of the next carriage in line, killing all four animals as well as the driver and wounding three others riding in the rig. The other carriages made the town safely and fortunately found covered protection.

Captain Case had timed the volley of shells and determined that he could let one carriage at a time go after each shell burst. It took awhile but all arrived safely. The last to go was the rolling kitchen driven by the Greek born cook, Henry Pontious. He got confused about the timing and took off too late, and was dodging shells all of the way into town, Cursing loudly in Greek and English at every blast that rained havoc on the road he was traversing. He, too, arrived safely, but the kitchen had many more holes in it.

Finally, shortly after midnight, the guns went into position just north of Bulson and within range of Sedan. It was also announced that the Rainbow's infantry had reached the furthest point into the enemy's defense of any Allied unit.

During the morning of November 9, orders were received to hold their position. This was a relief to the men in F Battery, as they were near total exhaustion. The guns were used to answer any incoming fire, but the day remained relatively quiet.

November 10 turned out to be a cold, damp day. When the men arose, the ground was covered with a heavy frost and their blankets were as stiff as boards, as were their shoes and socks, all of which had to be thawed over the campfire.

Another relatively quiet day was enjoyed. There were some incoming high explosive shells, but a little to the west of the line. Some of the incoming shells were fired from the formidable siege guns that the Germans had situated to the west of Sedan. These shells shook the ground and sent up huge geysers of earth.

Late in the afternoon a small task force of American troops marched to the position flying a US flag. This was odd since the flag was seldom flown so near the front. The commander of this small detachment informed the captain that a truce would be signed at 11:00 in the morning and then they moved on with their message to the next battery. Soon after they left the area Captain Case announced the news to the men and it was greeted with a few sarcastic hurrahs and little enthusiasm. These rumors had been all too numerous over the past few weeks to be taken seriously.

It was indeed good news when the commander of G Company of the 167th Infantry Regiment learned that they weren't taking part in the assault planned for the morning of November 1. Jake felt he'd had enough of this dodging death each time he went across the line out into no-man's-land. It was time for someone else to take the chances his men had been taking for nearly a year now.

His men. The thought hit him like a ton of bricks. These men in his company were nearly as green as those new divisions just in from the States. This was the result of the high number of casualties the regiment had suffered during the numerous battles they'd been through. Nearly seventy percent of his troopers had arrived in France since the middle of July. Their advantage, though, was in the number of battle hardened veterans that still remained and the lessons they could teach these new men about survival.

The fact remained that all of the men in the company were his responsibility, whether they'd been there a week or a year. They were his men and he was doing what he could to keep them alive.

The regiment, though in reserve, was still marching northward just behind the attacking divisions. They were never very far away from the sound of battle. The thunder of artillery was a constant din in their ears, day and night. They even fell victim to occasional artillery bombardments.

The first five days of November found the 167th moving ever closer to Sedan as the battle zone continued to maneuver rapidly to the north. Finally, on the evening of November 5, the Rainbow was ordered to take the front line position that, up until this time, had been occupied by the 78th Division.

"The Rainbow has received the honor of assuming a lead role in the taking of Sedan," the major said during a late night company commander's call. "We, along with the First and 77th Divisions, will have first crack at entering the city."

"Some honor!" Jake said somewhat sarcastically to the major after the meeting.

"Jake, wait a minute. I want to talk to you after the others leave."

Jake hung back, saying little to the others until the major was ready.

When they were finally alone five minutes later, Major Davidson turned to Jake. "Are you all right? I'm concerned about you."

"Oh, Major, I'm fine, you know my sense of humor. I'm doing just great."

"Well, if everything isn't straight up here," the major said, tapping his temple, "then I can get someone to take your place. You're like the son I never had. You do your job better than anyone else in my command and I need you on the line, but if you're not up to it let me know."

"Sir, there's nothing wrong. I may be sarcastic, but I'm looking forward to getting back into action."

"That's my boy. Remember, I've said this before, you're just one step from glory. If we take the city of Sedan the war will end that very day. The German cause will have been thwarted and they cannot win. And there's no question about us taking the city within the week. We have been given the go-ahead signal to advance along the line of least resistance, crossing the path of other divisions if necessary. The Rainbow wants the honor of entering Sedan first, and we'll do it. When we succeed, you'll bask in the glory of being an American hero. If you don't make it, then you'll bask in the glory of God. How can you lose?"

"Well, sir, put that way, I guess I'd better make it into Sedan. I'm not ready to meet my maker yet."

"That's the spirit, Jake. God be with you."

In the cold early mist of November 6, the division continued its northward march. The Rainbow was situated on the far left of the line, the 77th occupied the center, and the First had started on the right, back on November 1. But by the sixth of the month, the First Division had moved to the left, cutting in front of the battle weary 77th Division. The Rainbow continued in a straight line towards the objective. They spent the night just north of Chemery, for in the morning their relentless forward movement would take them into Chehery.

The Germans had become masters of fighting rear guard actions. As the main body of troops continued their retreat, strategically placed machine guns were located in the towns and on north throughout the valley. Boche artillery, further to the north, was set to bombard the advancing American troops.

From the crest of the hill, Jake's company was directly in front of Chehery just two kilometers down the slope. At 0800 hours on the seventh, the Division began their attack on the valley. Jake's objective was to take Chehery and clear it of the enemy. As his troopers started down the hill towards the village, the return fire from the Boche was light and the men moved confidently forward. Jake admired the sight as he saw the glint of the doughboys' bayonets all up and down the valley, reflecting the sun that was trying to peek through the broken clouds. It was an inspiring sight to view the bravery of his men as they walked rapidly towards the town. When they were less than a kilo away the enemy machine guns opened up and some of his troopers fell on his right and some on his left. Still he continued forward and soon broke into a run, yelling to the men to hit the ditch that ran along the south edge of town.

He didn't know how he made it, but he and three others were there, taking cover in the mud of the soggy ravine. It wasn't long before the other platoons had joined them. The machine gun fire continued to rake the top, keeping the men below the parapet. The German artillery fire intensified, bringing a terrible storm of shells on their heads.

Jake, with his new first sergeant, Irv Bliss, wiggled to the top of the lip of the ditch and, with field glasses in hand, scanned the town for the machine guns. "There are three of them, Sarge. I've got them all spotted," he told the man at his side. "Go get Lieutenants Caldwell and Durgovits." Without a word the sergeant was gone as Jake continued scanning for the German guns. Soon the two platoon leaders were at his side.

"Okay, Sam, you take that one on the left, see it in that building? Durgo, you take the one on the right, got it?" Both men nodded. "I'll take the center and each of us will take three good men." Jake took a quick look at his watch as he compared it with the others. "We'll begin the attack in five minutes, got it?"

"Yes sir!"

"Irv, get two good men and bring them here while I keep watch."

The minutes passed slowly, and at the agreed upon time, all three teams were in place and ready to start forward. Jake stared at his watch— it seemed to take forever for the second hand to complete the last circuit.

"Please God, do with me what you will, but keep the men safe from harm," he prayed under his breath as the second hand finally reached the twelve.

Jake and the three men jumped to their feet and began their rush to the building that held the middle gun some twenty meters away. When the guns opened up, the four hit the dirt under the tall stalks of grass. Before disappearing in the grass, Jake saw that both of the other teams were advancing. "Spread out, ten feet apart!" Jake yelled to the men. "You, on the left, start to run then hit the dirt. Next, on the right and I'll go third, then you, Sarge." The others nodded and Jake yelled, "Go!"

The attack was underway. None of the men were hit. Jake was the first to the building. He stood with his back to the wall some five feet west of the window. He took one of his grenades in his left hand and pulled the pin as he inched his way towards the window. A foot from the opening, he released the triggering mechanism, held it a second, and tossed it through the window before diving to his stomach against the wall to the south. Within seconds there was the explosion and the victory was won.

Sergeant Bliss jumped to his feet and ran around to the front of the building and through the door to find two dead Germans at the gun. He leaned out the window and yelled, "It's secure sir."

Jake stood and saw an explosion coming from the machine gun nest that was attacked by Sam's team. From the right, Durgo was running towards him. "We're clear, captain," he yelled.

When Jake turned around he heard some rifle fire from the left and Sam Caldwell soon waved the okay to him. Jake next motioned for the men taking refuge in the ditch to begin their entry into town. He walked to the end of the building and turned the corner to proceed forward in front of the others. He suddenly felt a tremendous thump on his chest followed by a searing pain before everything went black.

Late in the evening, Major Davidson heard the news that Jake had been killed. He showed no emotion to the bearer of this news and responded that Lieutenant Caldwell should assume command of G Company. "Immediately," he told the messenger. He turned and went to his tent that had been set up on a field north of Chehery. He sat heavily on his cot for a few moments with his head in his hands, then went to his knees with his elbows on the cot and quietly prayed for Jake and for all of the other men that had been lost this day. "Lord, where do all of these brave young men come from? Thank you, Father, for without their courage and resourcefulness we could never win this war. Take Jake into your arms and commend him for a job well done. Amen."

There had been few days off since Ike took command of the squadron. Occasionally the rain, clouds and low visibility kept the pilots on the ground, but this downtime went all too quickly. Of late, Ike and the other pilots found themselves flying in weather that just a few short months before would have kept them grounded. However the Allies were pushing hard to end the war, which called for an ever-increasing support role for the Air Service, thus forcing flights into lower and lower weather minimums.

The rumors of an armistice were becoming more prevalent during the last week of October and on into early November. It was the topic that dominated most conversations around the squadron's mess. Confirmation that these rumors were closer to fact came on October 31, when the newspaper headlines declared that Turkey had surrendered, and then on November 3, when Austria surrendered unconditionally. Was it really true? Was there to be an end to all of this madness?

On their days off the pilots would undertake rigorous games of baseball, football, and other contact sports while those less interested in athletic endeavors would party all day and eventually drink themselves into a drunken lassitude. It was a way of hiding from their fears and forgetting those fellow pilots that had been lost.

Ike and Frank were the only original members of the squadron left, and it would be anyone's guess as to how long it would be before one of them or both would succumb to an enemy's guns. Some of the more fatalistic crewmen had even placed bets on the first one of the two to be brought down.

Ike buried himself in his work so this thought never weighed heavily on him. He didn't allow his mind to dwell on the matter, as he had a wedding to look forward to. If he didn't take control of his thoughts, he knew he could become very depressed. Frank, on the other hand, would join in on the sporting events as well as the partying whenever he had time off.

With the November 1 attack, when the American Army began their strike north in order to take the city of Sedan, the 95th Aero Squadron was out in front of the troops striking at the retreating German columns and also at their artillery located further north.

At this time in the war and even though the Boche possessed a superb fighter in the Fokker D.VII, the German Air Service was unable to utilize its full potential, as they were rapidly running out of fuel and ammunition. Their squadrons or Jagdgeschwaders continued to rise to meet the Allied air forces on a daily basis, but in a more limited way. They found that by concentrating their air arm over a small sector of the front they were able to achieve local superiority, but they could no longer dominate the skies over the entire front as they had all during the summer months. This situation was all right in Ike's view, as it meant that he would deal with far fewer losses.

The squadron flew in support of the ground troops on the first of November, but was then grounded due to inclement weather for the next two days. During this time Ike was able to send off two long letters to Agnes and to complete all of his paperwork for the squadron.

On the fourth and fifth, they flew a ground support sortie each morning and in the afternoon flew escort missions for American bombers.

The morning of the sixth they were back in the air attacking the retreating Germans at the very outskirts of Sedan. The ground fire was intense that day and two of the squadron's SPADs were shot down. One pilot was captured and the other died in the smoking ruins of his plane. In the afternoon the rains fell in torrents, keeping the planes on the ground once again. There had been few encounters with Boche aircraft because, it was later learned that their Jagdgeschwaders were being employed against the English forces to the northwest.

On the morning of the seventh, the squadron was called upon to provide support for the American 42nd Division attacking the town of Chehery and the valley to the northeast. Fifteen minutes prior to the time the troops were to begin their attack, Ike, with his flight of eight aircraft dove from a height of five hundred meters onto the town, strafing and bombing German positions and troops. They found the Boche columns moving north, leaving the town as rapidly as possible. The flight made two passes on the retreating troops before turning away toward the south. As Ike gained altitude from his last run he flew directly over the town, and as he passed by the south end he saw some doughboys attacking that end of town as they charged the buildings from a ditch that ran along the south edge of the village.

As they approached their home base, the rains began to fall again, mixed with fog, bringing the visibility down to less than two miles and producing a ragged ceiling of 100 meters. After completing his landing roll, Ike taxied his craft to parking. As he began his shutdown routine, Frank pulled up beside Ike, cut his engine, and clambered out of the cockpit. The two friends greeted one another before heading back to the debriefing room.

"Looks like you got some ground fire," Frank said as he noted some large holes in the fabric just behind the cockpit of Ike's plane.

"Yeah, they were throwing a lot of lead our way. Did you take any hits?"

"I don't think so. Did we lose any planes?"

Ike shook his head. "I took a quick count and it looks as if they all came back. That sure makes me feel good. It doesn't look as if we'll go up again, so a good day."

On the tenth, the Americans were ordered to stay on the ground. The orders stated that an armistice was going to be signed the next day. Ike kept his fingers crossed and hoped that this was not just another rumor. He spent most of the day in his office, not doing work, but trying to place a long-distance telephone call to Agnes in Paris. The call did not go through for various military reasons, but early in the morning of the eleventh, shortly after receiving confirmation that the armistice would take affect at 1100 hours that very morning, his aide knocked on his door to tell him that Agnes was on the line.

"Agnes, have you heard the news?" Ike shouted into the mouthpiece before he even had the earpiece to his head.

"Yes, the war will be over."

"It's great. I'll do no more wartime flying. Will you marry me?"

"Oh, Ike, of course, I love you so much."

"I love you, too. We can get married on the first of December."

"Oh, that would be wonderful. What about your parents?"

"It's strange. My mother received a letter from Mr. Phelps and somehow he changed her whole outlook. I just received a letter from her and she and my father, who's home, gave us their blessing. Clint must be some writer. Isn't it great?" Static had begun to make most of their words almost unintelligible. "I'll see you in Paris next weekend," Ike said.

"Did you say next weekend?"

"Yes."

And the phone line went dead.

The Final Day

The loud knocking on his door woke Roy with a start. As he struggled out of bed he tried to look at his watch, but it was too dark to see it. He stumbled to the door, tripping over the one chair the hotel room had. Again came the incessant knock on the door.

"Who's there?" Roy called out as he reached the lock and twisted the knob to unlatch it.

"It's Clint, Roy. Open the door."

"Oh, Clint, what's going on?" Roy said as he swung the door open.

"Get your clothes on, we're going to the front. I have a car waiting."

"To the front? Is the armistice signed? What time is it, anyway?"

"It's 4:00 a.m. The armistice will be signed soon, early this morning, and will go into effect at 11:00 a.m. I've talked with Colonel Hinkle and he has invited us to join him at the front to view the proceedings."

Roy and Clint had been staying in the old fortress city of Verdun. Both had come in anticipation of covering the war's end for their papers. For various reasons each wanted to be in the American sector, so they had elected to leave Paris the day before, the tenth of November, and come to Verdun.

"Let me wash up and shave and I'll be right with you," Roy said excitedly. "Have a seat on the bed."

"Not much time, my boy, so please hurry. We have a twenty-five-mile drive to Mouzay to pick up the colonel and then another few miles to the overlook of the lines."

It wasn't long before the two of them were in the vehicle and Clint was driving like a maniac towards their destination. The road was in pretty sad shape and Clint was forced to slow down due to the ruts and potholes.

"This is the way the colonel said to come. Most of the supply vehicles use the road to the west."

Not many words were exchanged during the first hour of the trip as Clint concentrated on the road and Roy tried to sleep in the right front seat. They encountered quite a number of military vehicles headed towards the front, and these also impeded their progress. Roy soon found that sleep was out of the question, so they talked of home and of their future plans.

At exactly 9:00 a.m. they arrived at Mouzay and found Colonel Hinkle waiting. Without stopping the engine, the colonel climbed into the rear seat and began giving directions to the position he had in mind. Their destination was an artillery observation post that afforded them an unlimited view of the valley below, where the two armies still faced one another.

"I thought this a great place to view history in the making," Colonel Hinkle said after they parked the car and climbed to a grassy knoll that overlooked the front.

"I still hear some artillery," Roy said after they sat down. "Is the armistice going to take affect and hold?"

"Yes, the Germans have literally run out of gas and they know it. They have no alternatives. The guns that are firing are probably from the diehards on both sides. But in less than an hour all will grow still."

"I appreciate your wanting to view this with a couple of newsmen," Clint said.

"Well, you fellows are friends and you are here to objectively record this occasion for posterity. I am here to look at this as a moment in history. If I stood with my fellow officers, I think it would be viewed more out of emotion than for the true historic event it really is."

The three men sat and said little for the next forty-five minutes. At the end of that time Clint pulled out his pocket watch, for the tenth time, and started counting down the last minute. At exactly 11:00 a.m., when the chime on the watch began to toll the hour, they heard one last gun report way to the north and then all went silent. Each man held his breath for fear the roar of the cannon would resume. At eight seconds past the hour there was another explosion, followed by a lasting stillness not experienced in that place for nearly five years.

Next they saw men in the valley emerge from their hiding places and cautiously stand. On each side of the front these men looked at one another in the shock that they did not need to seek cover from the enemy. Slowly, and as if on cue, men from both sides cautiously advanced towards their previous enemy and soon they met in what had been no-man's-land, where many threw their hats in the air and greeted their former enemies as long lost friends.

The three onlookers took it all in, in silence, each with tears in his eyes.

"Words cannot describe this moment in my life," the professor almost whispered.

The other two remained silent, and the only sound they heard for the next half hour were the cheers and the yelling of the joyous, former combatants as they celebrated the end of the Great War.

The three spectators sat spellbound for a time before Clint said, "I have some champagne here." He opened his briefcase and produced a bottle and three glasses. He quickly poured the wine and gave a glass to each of the other two men, returned the stopper to the carafe, then raised his glass.

"To a peace that will last a thousand years!" Clint said.

"Hear, hear," the others responded as each lifted his own glass to his lips.

The final word made it to the front just before daybreak. The rumor was now a fact—the war was going to end in the morning at 11:00 a.m. There was going to be a truce. They had heard rumors all week, but this time it was official, as it had come from divisional headquarters.

You could feel the excitement all about. Finally, this madness would end. With the excitement there was great tension and apprehension. No one wanted to die now. Who would be the last victim of this bloody war? For the first time since arriving at the front, all soldiers saw a light at the end of the tunnel. Home was finally a reality, not just doom and destruction.

The cannons of war were still firing; they sounded like distant thunder.

"Why do they keep firing? They must know that it will all end soon," Hank said.

"I don't know, it's all a little scary," Pat answered.

"We're this close to the end and I don't want to die. Hey, I'm looking forward to going home and sleeping for a year. Interspersing that with huge steaks three times a day."

Pat laughed. "Boy, that sounds great to me. I think I'd put the steaks first, though, followed by a featherbed with a mattress about two feet thick."

"You know, Pat, I've been thinking, that old artillery observation bunker about 200 yards up yonder hasn't been hit for the past few days and all the shells that have been incoming today have fallen to the east of us. You know, I think I'll sneak up there, go to the lowest level, and sleep until eleven. They sure can't get me there without a direct hit. C'mon with me, no one will miss us. I'm sure there won't be any more work to be done on the guns."

"Naw, you go ahead. I'm gonna stay here with the others. I'll cover for you if old Ramrod Baker comes a-looking."

"It's your funeral. Come on, Fritzee, let's go," Hank called to his dog. "Come and get me if things get sticky."

"Yeah, get a good rest. I'll see ya later this morning."

Corporal Adolph Krause had been a walking hellion ever since he awoke at 5:00 a.m. "To think the high command was going to concede victory to the Allies at 11:00 this very morning." All these years of bloody fighting and for what? Defeat? Corporal Krause had been in the army too long to just give up. He'd been in on the invasion of Belgium; he'd been with the army when they were in sight of Paris. He had served for a year on the Eastern Front. He had been at the spearhead of the great Ludendorf offensive in March of 1918. He was not going to quit and run like a dog with its tail between its legs. Not Adolph. He had to do something to let the Allies know they were up against a real soldier. There were just 15 minutes left in this war and he was going to make them count. As commander of the 305mm Skoda howitzer gun crew he would send off the last heavy shell into the Allied trenches. He quickly called his crew together and forced them to load the 846 lb. shell into the breech of the gun. Those under his command protested his actions, but did it anyway, so once the big gun was loaded Adolph sent the gun crew away. "You yellow liveried sots, you don't deserve to wear the uniform of a German soldier, get out of here."

These men were strange to him, all young boys barely 15 or 16 with a few old men sprinkled in. These were not the proud and strong men he had entered France with. Those were real soldiers, strong and courageous, but they were all gone now and all that was left were these sniveling cowards.

He checked his watch, there was only 15 seconds left before the war would end. He knew that the big gun had been last aimed at the American lines. He also knew that when last fired, yesterday, the shells had zeroed in, in a devastating barrage. The weather conditions were quite different from the day before as there was a strong wind out of the west, but that didn't matter to Adolph now.

He grabbed the firing lanyard and counted off the remaining seconds.

At precisely the eleventh hour of the eleventh day of the eleventh month of 1918 he pulled the lanyard. With a thunderous report the huge projectile left the muzzle of the long barrel and penetrated the heavy cloud cover before rising into the morning sunlight.

As the projectile reached the apogee of its arc it was traveling at the slowest speed it would travel until impact. At 3000 meters it nosed over slightly and began its return to earth. Picking up speed as it continued its downward trajectory. As the speed increased so did the eerie sound it made as it sped through the air. The breeze from the west moved the flight path ever so slightly to the east with each passing second.

Pat and the other cannoneers whiled away the morning hours in idle chatter, most speculating on what would happen to the division once the war was over. There was the very disconcerting rumor, from a reliable source, that they would become part of the Army of Occupation and eventually march into Germany. The prospect of a quick return to the States was not very good.

The morning hours slipped by very slowly and the men became more restless as the magic hour of 11:00 a.m. approached. Slowly the sound of battle diminished and after 10:00 there were only a few shots fired. Many speculated that this was the result of premature celebrations.

Pat checked his watch at least every five minutes in the closing hour, and at 10:45 he gazed at it almost continuously. By this time there were few sounds as the men waited anxiously for the official start of the armistice.

At 10:59 two men started counting the seconds. Jack Bayless gazed at his watch and began counting one, two, three… up until the eleventh hour. At that moment all was still except for the loud report of one gun to the north. Everyone held his breath.

At the sixth second past 11:00, all heard the eerie sound of the large incoming shell. Someone yelled, "Hit the dirt!" just before the tremendous explosion shook the earth.

Everyone hesitated, afraid that the shell was a precursor to a larger bombardment. But nothing followed except silence. Slowly the men began to stir.

The unmistakable voice of Sergeant Baker could be heard. "Is everybody all right?"

No one spoke, silently getting to their feet.

"Is everyone accounted for?" Again there was no reply.

"Where did it hit?" Jack asked.

"Up on the hill over to the east!" came the reply.

Pat looked to where Jacob Neely was pointing and felt a cold chill go up and down his spine. "Hank," he called loudly. "Hank, where are you?" There was no reply.

"Has anyone seen Hank?" he called as loud as he could.

"I saw him head up to that old bunker hours ago." Someone down the cannon line yelled.

Pat felt fear grip at his heart and started running for the bunker up on the rise to the east. "Hank, Hank, where are you, buddy?" he screamed as he ran. Immediately some of the others began following him, running for all they were worth towards the old bunker.

Pat felt as if he were moving in slow motion as he ran as hard as he could towards the hill. His legs felt like lead weights by the time he started up the incline. The others were still some yards behind.

When he got to the top, where the bunker had been, there was nothing but a huge crater fifteen yards across and five yards deep. There was nothing but rocks and dirt; the structure that had once stood there had been vaporized. Pat felt sick to his stomach and quickly sunk to his knees. By this time the others had caught up with him and stood at the edge of the gaping hole in the ground.

Tom quickly called and whistled for the dog, "Fritz. Here Fritz, come on, boy."

There was no response.

Pat sat a long time on the ground, he didn't know how long. He conjured up scenarios that Hank had left the bunker and would show up any moment. As he became more encouraged by these thoughts, he started to get up. On his hands and knees, ready to push himself up, he felt a piece of metal under his fingers. He gripped it between his thumb and forefinger and slowly got to his feet. Standing, he looked at the disk, and his eyes welled with tears. It was Hank's dog tag, unmistakably imprinted with his name and serial number. The war was over, but its last shot had taken his best friend.

At last Hank was with his wife and baby.

Epilogue

After the signing of the armistice, The Rainbow Division held their positions for four days. On the fifth day or November 16, the 149th received orders to harness and hitch and begin moving in a northeasterly direction. The men of Battery F hoped that their trek through France would take them to a port city and onto a ship headed for the States. This was not to be, for after two days of travel they turned in a northerly direction towards the city of Luxemburg and then on into Germany as part of the US occupation of that country. They arrived at Rech, Germany situated in the Ahr Valley on the 15th of December and stayed there through April 6, 1919.

Finally after five grueling months of occupation duty they were allowed to return home. They set sail on April 16 and arrived in New York on the 25th. From there the 149th went by train to Chicago where on May, 8 they marched down Michigan Avenue on a long delayed victory parade. As soon as they marched through the parade route, they went to Dearborn station and boarded another train that carried them to Camp Grant, about a hundred miles west of Chicago. Here the guardsmen were mustered out of the service after serving 22 months in Hell.

Pat returned to his home in Champaign where he enrolled in school at the University of Illinois and completed his Bachelor of Science degree before going to the Chicago campus to earn his Doctor of Dental Science degree. He married in 1925.

At the completion of hostilities Ike went to Paris where he was reunited with Agnes and they were married on Christmas Day, 1918 in St. Nazaire. Shortly thereafter they were on board a ship that took them to New York. Ike continued in the Army Air Service and became a career officer.

Clint Phelps returned home to Illinois during the summer of 1919 after covering the signing of the Treaty of Versailles on June 28, 1919. He was tired of the carnage of war and resigned his post with the Chicago Globe before returning to the *Champaign Daily Herald*. There he lived out his life as editor-in-chief. Clint retired in 1939 and lived to 1944.

Roy Littler resigned his post with the *Stars and Stripes* in early 1919 and returned to New York where he was a reporter for the *New York Times*. He died in 1929.

In the fall of 1919, Professor Hinkle resumed his duties as professor of history at the U of I, from which he retired in 1932 to write about the events of the Great War.

Within fourteen days of the Armistice, on November 25, Josiah Wortham was released from a German prisoner of war camp located near the German, Belgium border. His injuries suffered during his controlled crash were minor and, after spending a little over a week in a Parisian hospital, he was released and shipped back to the states. From there he was discharged from the service and returned to his law practice in Michigan. He remained in the Army reserve and was activated back into the Army Air Corps in 1940. He was killed while flying a combat mission over Germany in late 1944.

It was a typical June day in central Illinois. The temperature had been in the high eighties and the humidity, as is common for that time of year, was disproportionately high.

At the end of his workday, the man closed his office and went up the stairs to his home. You see he was a dentist who maintained his office in the half basement of his house.

The living room, dinning room and kitchen were on the main floor, above the basement and the bedrooms were on the second floor above the living area.

His practice had plenty of patients; however, few of these people had any money and much of his work was done on the old-fashioned barter system. Farmers paid with food and others with maybe their services, if indeed they had any to offer. He was a kind and caring man and took on many patients with the prospect of not receiving one cent for his services. The year was 1937, America had not fully recovered from The Great Depression, and very few people had jobs.

He felt tired and was worried about paying all of the bills, but he tried to put that aside as he walked into the kitchen and sat at the table. His wife was cooking dinner and his youngest son, a two year old, was playing with some blocks on the floor while the five year old was drawing with crayons at the table.

The father opened the evening newspaper and read a few of the headline stories to his wife as she continued with the dinner. The big news of the day concerned the missing aviatrix, Amelia Earhart, who was overdue for a landing and refueling. At the time she was known to be somewhere over the Pacific on the final leg of her around the world flight. They both briefly discussed their concern and then he set the paper down to admire a picture the older son had drawn of their pet dog.

There had been clouds building all that afternoon. Finally by dinnertime they developed into giant thunderstorms that had reached their maturity, and it started to sprinkle. It began slowly at first, and then it came down ever harder with each tick of the clock. The breeze quickly built up and soon those sprinkles turned to a heavy rain driven by gale force winds that slapped loudly against the side of the house.

Madge looked out of the window positioned over the kitchen sink and said to her husband, "Pat, why don't you go up and shut the bedroom windows and when you get back we'll have dinner?"

"Sure thing," he responded and without another word left the room and started up the stairs.

Five minutes passed, then ten. Madge couldn't imagine what was taking so long so she turned to the older son and asked him to go get his father.

The boy dutifully went to the stairs, and she could her the thump of his bare feet on the wooden steps.

Not long after, she heard those same bare feet descend and the boy returned to the kitchen where his mother was putting the final touches on dinner.

"Mommy," the boy said, "Daddy's asleep on the bed, and I couldn't wake him. Is something wrong?"

Yes, there was something wrong. That man, age 39, was dead. He died of a massive heart attack brought on by stress and the lingering effects of the gas attacks suffered during *The Great War*.

The end can come quickly, like a thief in the night. Have you prepared to meet your God? Through our faith commitment to Jesus Christ, we can assure ourselves of life everlasting. We can come to know the Father, but we must come to know Him in this life if we are to attain eternal life.

www.ingramcontent.com/pod-product-compliance
Lightning Source LLC
Chambersburg PA
CBHW060300100726
47907CB00002B/224